5

DEATH OF A TYRANT

DEATH OF A TYRANT

Christopher Nicole

This first world edition published in Great Britain 1997 by
SEVERN HOUSE PUBLISHERS LTD of
9–15 High Street, Sutton, Surrey SM1 1DF.
First published in the USA 1997 by
SEVERN HOUSE PUBLISHERS INC., of
595 Madison Avenue, New York, NY 10022.

British Library Cataloguing in Publication Data

Nicole, Christopher, 1930-
      Death of a Tyrant
      1.   Stalin, I. (Iosif), 1879-1953 – Fiction
      2.   Soviet Union – History – 1925-1953 - Fiction
      3.   Biographical Fiction
      1. Title
      823.9'14 [F]

      ISBN 0-7278-5210-8

Typeset by Palimpsest Book Production Limited,
Polmont, Stirlingshire, Scotland.
Printed and bound in Great Britain by
Hartnolls Ltd, Bodmin, Cornwall.

Ruffians, pitiless as proud,
Heav'n awards the vengeance due;
Empire is on us bestow'd,
Shame and ruin wait for you.
                    William Cowper

THE BOLUGAYEVSKI FAMILY

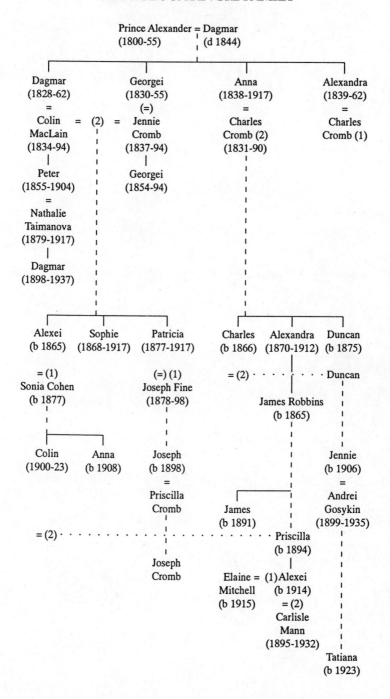

CONTENTS

Prologue

Big Ben chimed the hour, it seemed immediately above his head, as Halstead entered the room. "Always punctual," Lawrence said. "Seat."

Halstead sat down, carefully, knees together. He was a careful man. He dressed with careful exactitude, in unremarkable suits, and his face was a study in anonymity. Lawrence sometimes felt even the moustache was anonymous. His one eccentricity might be thought the red carnation in his buttonhole. But in London in 1946 a great many businessmen wore carnations in their buttonholes. "Pretty good shots, those." Lawrence gave him several large photographs.

Halstead studied the mushroom-shaped cloud. "Not something to be underneath."

"They make the United States the greatest force in history. Oh, we shall have one of our own, soon enough. But we're on the same side. So they say. Uncle Joe is no doubt feeling something of an inferiority complex at this moment."

"Has he nothing on at all?"

"He has quite a lot on, but so far it's been low priority, in Russia. Now the shooting has stopped, they can think about other things. Our information is that without help they could be ten years away from the Bomb. With help, well . . . could be two or less."

Halstead nodded. "And they're obtaining help."

"They are certainly working on it. In the States, mainly, but also here. Now the Yanks, and us, are monitoring the situation, but we need to know just how much they have, and how much they need. It won't be easy, but with your special contacts inside the Soviet Union . . ."

Halstead nodded. "I'll need cover. And time."

"Just tell us what you want. But time . . . that's in short supply. I need to have it on record that you volunteer."

Halstead smiled. "I volunteer, Mr Lawrence."

"Will you work alone?"

Halstead shook his head. "It's too big for that. I have someone in mind. Someone who worked for me during the war. Is there anything else?"

"You have carte blanche." Lawrence waited. He had known Halstead for many years, and sure enough, Halstead took the carnation from his buttonhole, looked at it, then crumpled it between his fingers and dropped it into the waste basket.

Lawrence smiled. "Then I shall wish you good fortune."

Part One

The Trap

Treason doth never prosper: what's the reason?
For if it prosper, none dare call it treason.

Sir John Harington.

Chapter One

The Spring

The underground gymnasium was redolent of sweat and resin, anxious humanity and eager endeavour. There were three men in the room, one wearing uniform, the other two singlets and shorts; they all snapped to attention as the door opened. The man who entered also wore uniform. He was tall, well built, and utterly bald. His features were large, and bland; pince-nez sat on his nose. His eyes were permanently opaque.

He acknowledged the men with a nod, advanced to the table which was the only furniture in the room, apart from the vaulting horse against the far wall, the rings hanging from the ceiling. On the table there was an automatic pistol. But the newcomer ignored this in favour of watching the woman running round and round the room. She was, he knew, twenty-three years old. She was tall, and strongly built. As she also wore only a singlet and shorts, and these were wet with sweat, her figure was displayed for him to appreciate. She had heavy breasts, bobbing beneath the thin material, tight buttocks and thighs, long, powerful legs. Her hair was as black as her eyes; tied in a ponytail which reached the centre of her back, it flopped up and down as she ran. Her features were quite beautiful.

And for all her youth, she was a veteran of the Great Patriotic War, a woman who had killed, time and again. Killing was in her blood. She was a treasure. The question was, whose treasure would she turn out to be?

5

The woman had not stopped running when the man had entered, nor did she stop now. Round and round the gymnasium she went, bare feet leaving damp imprints on the polished floor, sweat scattering out of her hair. The man waited until she came abreast of the table for the fourth time since his entry, then he said, loudly, "Now, Tatiana!" Instantly the woman stopped, turned towards him, and snatched the pistol from the table before turning away from him again. Behind her, on the far wall, a target in the shape of a man had appeared. With only the slightest hesitation to take aim, and for all her gasping breath and twitching muscles, she squeezed the trigger four times. The noise reverberated in the confined space.

Slowly the woman lowered the pistol, standing still as the two uniformed men went forward. "They all go deaf, eventually," the instructor commented. "Even I shall go deaf, eventually, Comrade Beria." Laverenty Beria ignored the complaint, stood in front of the target. It had been pierced by all four of the bullets. "This would have been the first," the instructor said, indicating the hole on the right arm. "Lacking accuracy, although effective in disarming. But the second struck here . . ." He touched the target's groin. "That would have incapacitated him. And the third and fourth . . ." He touched the target's chest and his forehead. "Gosykinya is about the best we have, Comrade Commissar. She is a true daughter of her father."

Beria glanced at him, and he gulped. "I meant as regards skill, Comrade Commissar. Not politics." Tatiana Gosykinya's father had been executed during the Great Purges of the previous ten years. Beria walked back towards the table, and the woman, still motionless, save for her heaving chest. "You work her very hard, Comrade Commissar," the instructor ventured. "I assume there is a reason?"

Beria gave him another glance, and he gave another gulp. It did not pay to be too inquisitive about anything that went on inside the Lubyanka Prison . . . or anything that emanated from it. "The best," Beria remarked, "must be the best, at everything." He nodded to Tatiana Gosykinya. "Shower."

Tatiana placed the pistol on the table, and left the gymnasium.

Beria followed, as she knew he would. The changing room was unisex, but there was no one else there at the moment. She stripped off her soaked clothing, let it lie on the floor; an attendant would remove it later. As she stepped into the shower stall she heard the door close. Thus she did not draw the curtain. She knew he had come to watch her bathe. But she also knew that he would not touch her, however much he liked to look at her. The hot water bounced off her skin, and she sighed with relief, and soaped, slowly and sensuously. She had released the pony tail on her way in, and when she had finished with her body she shampooed her hair, again slowly and luxuriously.

"Smerdov says you are the best," Beria remarked, leaning against the wall.

"At killing? I was that, Comrade Commissar, before I joined the KGB."

"Killing Germans with machine-guns and grenades is not the same thing as killing a specific target, at a specific time and place, with a single weapon," he pointed out.

Tatiana stepped from the shower stall into a puddle of water. She wrapped her hair in a towel, and began drying her body. "I look forward to it, Comrade," she said, softly. "Will it be soon?"

"It will be when I am ready. You may go home now. Take three days off. I am leaving Moscow for three days." Beria's great moon-face split into a cold smile. "Enjoy yourself."

Tatiana wore the uniform of an officer in the Red Army, save that as she was not on active service she used a skirt and khaki stockings instead of trousers. That she was not actually a serving officer in the Red Army was apparent to no one; members of the KGB did not wear any special insignia. Thus enlisted men she passed on the street saluted her; civilians, men and women, gazed at her with admiration. With her looks, and her carriage, and her uniform, she exemplified all that was noble in the Soviet Union. Tatiana, who actually did have a sense of humour, could not help but reflect that these people would probably still admire her even if they knew she was a trained assassin: they were conditioned to admire whatever measures the State deemed necessary for their well-being.

The doorman at the block of flats known as the Government Building saluted, and she climbed the stairs to her mother's apartment. "I've put the kettle on," Jennie Ligachevna called as she opened the door. Although the Government Building was a showpiece of Soviet architecture, it was still jerry-built, and she had heard her daughter's footsteps on the stairs. Now she bustled into the small living room, drying her hands on a towel.

The two women made a strong contrast. Both were tall, true Bolugayevskas, even if that name was long buried in Russia. But Jennie, now approaching forty, had put on weight since the end of the Great Patriotic War; even her always big features seemed to have grown, while her once magnificent auburn hair was streaked with gray. It would have been difficult for any outsider to pick her as Tatiana's mother, for Tatiana took after her father, the dead agent Andrei Gosykin, with her more delicate features and her raven hair. "What did you do today?" Jennie asked, chattily.

"Train." Tatiana took off her cap and sat down. "That is all I ever do, train."

"You will get an assignment eventually," Jennie said, and poured tea.

Tatiana wondered just how much her mother knew about the workings of the state within the state that was the KGB? She did know that Mother had been married to Father for a dozen years before she found out that *he* was a government assassin. And she had only found out then when the time had come for him to be executed. Tatiana had been twelve then, and she had been just as shocked as had Jennie. That traumatic incident in her youth had fashioned her entire life. That her beloved father should have turned out to be an enemy of the state that had employed him had been the shock, not the sudden knowledge that he had killed for a living. She had never doubted the truth of what she had been told, because it had been Uncle Josef himself who had told her, and she worshipped the ground on which Uncle Josef walked. She knew there were all manner of rumours about the thousands, perhaps millions, of people who had died during the thirties when Uncle Josef had been restructuring the nation. But she had no doubt it had all been necessary.

And it was Uncle Josef's determination and leadership that had defeated the Germans in the War. No one could argue with that. Thus if she was directed to kill for him, she would do so without hesitation, as she had during the War. Unlike her father, she would never be a traitor to the Motherland.

"Will you be going out, later?" Jennie asked, a trifle wistfully. She and her daughter had so little in common she valued their rare moments together,

"I am meeting Gregory," Tatiana explained.

Jennie snorted. "I do not see what you find in him. He is younger than you."

"We were comrades," Tatiana said simply. "We are still comrades. He is all I have left, from the war."

The Ilyushin transport drooped low as it came down from the mountains. In front of it the Caspian Sea glimmered in the noonday sun, while beneath it, as it turned into the wind, lay the delta of the Volga, a mass of rivers, streams and marshes emanating from the mighty flow that was the greatest river in European Russia. At the head of the delta lay the city of Astrakhan.

The airport was some distance north-west of the city itself, and Lavrenty Beria released his seat belt with a sigh of contentment as the Ilyushin touched down. Although from the outside the aircraft looked like an ordinary transport of the Red Army, inside it was luxuriously fitted out as a travelling home for the Commander of the KGB, as he pursued his duties of ruling Russia with an iron hand in the name of his master, Josef Stalin. But he came to Astrakhan more often than anywhere else; he had a dacha here, from whence he could go fishing as he chose. That it was a place seldom visited by other members of the Politburo suited him very well. He considered it an ideal base for a man who had a personal empire in mind; in past centuries, Astrakhan had been the capital of the Golden Horde, that fearsome offshoot of the Mongol legions of Genghis Khan, which had for so many years dominated Russia. Now it was possible to call it the Venice of Asia, for it was built on several islands, and was a mass of bridges and shallow waterways. It actually was a seaport of some importance, although because the northern Caspian had become so shallow in recent years, deep-draft vessels had to approach via a dredged canal.

The Commissar was greeted by his representative in Astrakhan Province, Georgei Polkov. "Did you have a good flight, Comrade?" Polkov asked politely.

"Yes, thank you. Is all well here?"

Polkov shrugged. "The water level continues to drop. In another hundred years, Comrade Commissar, we will be able to walk on this sea."

"In another hundred years, Comrade Polkov, we will be dead," Beria pointed out. He seated himself in the back of the black limousine for the drive. "I was thinking of another matter."

Polkov was one of his most trusted aides, a man who knew that should the Commissar ever fall, he would fall with him. Therefore he had been trusted with the most important secret in Lavrenty Beria's life. "The lady is well, Comrade," Polkov assured him.

Beria glanced at him. Polkov was an obedient, unimaginative man, small in both body and spirit, with a long nose and shifty eyes. But all human beings were curious. "Do you speak with her?" Beria asked.

"It is necessary, from time to time," Polkov conceded. "She keeps very much to herself."

"And how do you address her?" Beria asked.

"By her name, Comrade. Sonia Cohen, is it not?"

Beria wondered what Polkov would say if he knew the truth, that the woman who resided at the Commissar's dacha, and had done so since the end of the War, carefully guarded – and who Polkov obviously supposed was nothing more than the Commissar's mistress, regardless of her age – was actually the erstwhile Princess Bolugayevska? More important, she was also the erstwhile mistress of Leon Trotsky, a man she had, oddly, Beria thought, loved. And waited to avenge? That was what she claimed. And that was what he wanted of her.

The dacha was situated outside the town, to the north-east, on the banks of one of the rivulets which flowed into the sea, here only a mile away. There was enough movement in the water to limit the mosquitoes, and in any event the house was screened. The car pulled to a halt at the foot of the front steps, and a waiting manservant opened the door for the Commissar. Beria went up the steps, and the front door was opened for him by another servant. He did not speak to any of them, but walked straight through the house and up the stairs. At the top a woman servant gave a quick curtsey. Beria turned left on the landing, and opened the first door. This was a separate apartment, within the building. It consisted of a living room, a bedroom, and a bathroom. Meals were sent up from the kitchen on the lower floor. As prison cells went, with its views out over the delta and the sea, it was luxurious. But there were bars on the windows. It *was* a prison cell.

Sonia Bolugayevska stood by the window, looking out. She had obviously heard him arrive. Now she turned to face him. Lavrenty Beria was always surprised when he first saw this woman after an absence. He knew that she was all but seventy years old, yet she stood as straight and as tall as a girl a third of that age, as Tatiana Bolugayevska, her step-grandniece. The pair had never met, so far as he knew, but Sonia had been beside Tatiana's grandmother, Patricia Bolugayevska-Cromb, when she had died. Violently. Sonia Bolugayevska had been close, innocently, to so many people when they had died, violently.

He also knew that in the days when she had been the wife of Prince Alexei Bolugayevski, and therefore Princess of Bolugayen, in that heady time just before the First World War, she had been about the most omnipotent woman in Russia, after the empress and the grand duchesses. Her omnipotence had rested on the love of her husband, and when Prince Alexei had realised that the military and political advancement he wanted, and had reckoned was his due as the premier non-royal prince in Russia, would never be forthcoming as long as he was married to a Jewess, her power and prestige had come to an abrupt end with her divorce. Yet Beria still could discern traces of that age-old arrogance, in her look, her manner, even the way she stood. And why not? She was alive, where Prince Alexei and all of her detractors were now dead.

She had survived by embracing the Revolution. Literally. She

11

had fallen into the clutches, and then the arms, of perhaps the greatest revolutionary of them all, Leon Trotsky. Now he too was dead, struck down at her side. And still she had survived. And now she had fallen into his arms. A woman to be nurtured. A woman to be used, when the time came, to complete his ambition. A woman everyone else in the world thought was dead herself, executed by his own KGB! "I had not expected you today," she said, her voice soft. "Is it time?"

"Are you that impatient?" He went to the sideboard, where a bottle of champagne had hastily been placed in an ice bucket. He uncorked it, loudly, and poured. It might please him to live like one of those princes he and his followers had so rudely overthrown, but he understood none of the niceties of civilised living, and that the champagne had not been sufficiently cooled did not bother him in the least. Nor did he offer her a glass.

"I am that curious," she said, and sat down, her hands folded on her lap.

"He is very concerned, about this bomb business." Beria sat down himself, opposite her.

Sonia frowned. "There has been an attempt on his life?"

"No, no." Beria waved his hand, impatiently. "*The* Bomb."

"I'm afraid I do not understand you," Sonia said.

Of course, he kept her locked away, with no access to newspapers or the radio. "Japan surrendered, year before last, because the Americans have manufactured a bomb of incredibly destructive power. Two of them were dropped, and the Japanese, even the Japanese, realised they had no chance. So they surrendered. I will confess we did not take this seriously enough at the time. All we knew was that it was a big bomb. The implications only became apparent later. It is an elemental force. It does not merely knock things down and kill people. It obliterates them. It generates the kind of heat we are told is found only at the earth's core. It would be quite impossible to wage war against any nation that possesses such a bomb."

"A portent of the future," she murmured.

"Oh, indeed. The problem is that the West has such a bomb, and we do not. This is exercising his mind, greatly. Perhaps the strain will do the job for us. Perhaps you will not be necessary."

"I should hate to think that, having been kept a prisoner by you for four years now, I should suddenly become redundant."

Beria gave one of his cold smiles. "You will never be redundant, Comrade Bolugayevska. I shall find a use for you. But for the time being, we practice patience. He is sixty-nine years old. That is old, when one has led as stressful a life as Josef. I think the moment of decision is rushing at us. As long as we are ready, we have nothing to fear. There is no saying what might touch off a crisis that would be too much for him."

They rolled and wrestled together, naked bodies glistening with passionate sweat. "I love you, Tatiana Andreievna," Gregory Asimov whispered. "Oh, how I love you."

Tatiana playfully bit his ear, and as he had just climaxed, rolled off of him and lay on her back, taking deep breaths. He rose on his elbow beside her. Still in his early twenties, he looked much younger. Gregory Asimov had always had a baby face. Sometimes, when he had been shooting or knifing an enemy, in the Pripet, he had looked about to burst into tears. But he never had. "Will you not say you love me?" he asked.

Tatiana's face grew serious. Lies and deceit were part of her business, as a KGB officer. She refused to practice either in her private life. "I value you, Gregory Ivanovich," she said. "I value you as an old comrade in arms, as a present comrade in arms, as a friend, and . . ." she smiled. "Most of all, as a lover. No one has ever satisfied me as you do. That is more important than love, which is transient. I will *value* you for the rest of our lives."

Gregory kissed her. "Then I will hope that we will grow old together, dearest Tattie."

"This is rather good," Josef Cromb said. "There is a lot of blah de blah, then we come to: 'Another of the guests was the erstwhile Princess Bolugayevska, now Mrs Joseph Cromb, and her husband. The Princess, dare we say it, is now fifty-three years old, and yet no one can deny that, despite the exhausting adventures that have composed her life, her reputation as the most beautiful woman in Europe, or perhaps the world, remains unquestioned.'" He looked at his wife over the top of the fashion magazine.

Priscilla Bolugayevska-Cromb was sitting up in bed, her breakfast tray on her lap. "Me," she said. "Always me. You have led a much more adventurous life than I, Joseph." But she smiled as she spoke. When Priscilla Bolugayevska-Cromb smiled electric lights were liable to dim. As she well knew. With her still golden hair, which she continued to wear long because Russian princesses – even ex-Russian princesses – never cut their hair, and with her features, which had clearly been chiselled by some immortal sculptor, not to mention her still flawless figure, she felt that the journalist had written nothing but the truth.

As for the events of her life, from marrying her own uncle, the then Prince of Bolugayen, as a teenage girl before the First World War, to surviving the Red Revolution and all the horrors that it had inspired – for her more than almost anyone else – through a life of high society and financial crises that had involved the suicide of her second husband, she had indeed adventured, until she had at last been able to settle in domestic bliss with the only man she had ever loved. And even Joseph she had had to go to China to rescue from the clutches of the KGB. Now she stretched out her hand to touch his cheek. "We have adventured together, my love."

Joseph kissed her fingers. In this spring of 1947 they had now been partners and lovers for twenty-eight years – long before they had been able to marry – and he still adored her. Well, Priscilla Cromb was the sort of woman men did adore. But he knew her worth, her tremendous courage and determination – and, when necessary, ruthlessness – which far transcended her physical attributes. Just as he knew that she had adventured, and experienced, and endured, to a far greater extent than was even suspected by the media. Joseph was actually four years younger than his wife, although he looked a great deal older; his hair was grey and there were lines of suffering etched on his face. He put those down to the twelve years he had spent in the Gulag Archipeligo as a prisoner of Josef Stalin's horrific

14

government, more than anything he had experienced in two world wars.

But even that was behind him now. He and Priscilla had not even entered the twilight of their years. There was so much still to do, still to experience, even if he hoped and prayed there would be no more brushes with death and destruction. He folded the magazine. "Anyway, it's nice still to be famous. Now I must rush. I have a meeting with the bankers in an hour. Sure you do not wish to come?"

"Absolutely." If the family money was all Priscilla's, she was perfectly content to let her husband have the management of it. "Just be sure to be back for lunch."

He kissed her lips, and hurried off. Priscilla picked up the house phone. "Send Mottram up, please."

The Savoy was one of the few truly civilised hotels left in the world, Priscilla considered, because it provided accommodation for one's personal maids. She had had several personal maids in her life; one of them, the Tatar woman Grishka, had died for her. She did not anticipate Pamela Mottram, the very epitome of British correctitude, would ever have to go that far. "What a nice day, madam." Mottram bustled into the room. "Will madam take her bath now?"

"Thank you, Mottram." Joseph had left the magazine, and she glanced at the report of the duchess's ball before discarding it and picking up *The Times*. Mottram bustled happily in the bathroom, filling the huge tub, but reappearing as the phone rang. "I will take it," Priscilla said.

"Mrs Cromb?" asked the girl at reception. "I have a visitor for you."

Priscilla looked at her gold Omega. It was half-past nine, and she supposed there were people out and about. But . . . "Give me his name."

There was a moment's silence, then the girl was back. "He says his name is Morgan, madam. He says you do not know him, but you knew his father."

Priscilla stared at the phone in consternation. Harold Morgan's

15

son? But Harold Morgan hadn't had a son. "Send him up," she said, and replaced the phone. Mottram's eyebrows were waggling. "My dressing gown, Mottram," Priscilla said.

Mottram produced the garment. "Your bath will grow cold, madam."

"Then you will have to draw another." Priscilla got out of bed, allowed herself to be encased in her dressing gown over her satin nightdress, sat before her mirror to have her hair brushed. She wished she had had the time at least to clean her teeth, as of course she had, merely by telling this man to wait . . . but if he was a relic from her past . . . There was a knock on the door. "Let the gentleman in, Mottram," Priscilla said, and moved to sit in the chair beside the bed. She poured herself another cup of coffee, amazed to discover that her hand was shaking.

Mottram was opening the door to the suite's sitting room. A moment later she appeared in the doorway. "A Mr Morgan, madam."

"I am coming." Priscilla drank the coffee, looked at herself in the mirror once again, then went into the sitting room. The young man stood in front of the window, looking down at the Thames. Now he turned. He was of medium height, stockily built. Like his father. His hair was black, his features chiselled. Like his father. He was conservatively dressed, and held his flat cap in front of him. As his father had used to do. "Mr Morgan?" she asked.

"Andrew Morgan, your highness."

Priscilla smiled. It was a long time since anyone outside of her own family had called her by her erstwhile title. At the same time, there was a complete absence of any trace of a Welsh accent. She advanced into the room. "You find me in dishabille, Mr Morgan. Did the receptionist say I knew your father?"

"My father was in the employ of your family, your highness. He died in that employ."

Priscilla sat down, gestured him to a chair on the far side of the room. "Tell me when and how that happened?"

Andrew Morgan sat down. "He attempted to defend you, and your family, your highness, when your estate of Bolugayen outside

Poltava was overrun by the Bolsheviks in 1917. He did not survive the attack."

"My God," Priscilla said. "You'll forgive me, Mr Morgan, but I did not know your father had any children. I did not know he was married. He was employed by my father and mother-in-law as a butler. For some twenty years before 1917. He was never married, to my knowledge."

Andrew Morgan looked suitably embarrassed. "That is quite true, your highness. However, my father, ah . . . had an acquaintance. An English lady."

"Who is your mother."

"Was, your highness. She has recently died."

"Oh. I am most terribly sorry. But I do not quite understand . . ."

"When your mother-in-law, the late Countess Bolugayevska, determined to return to Russia to see if she could bring out her stepmother and the rest of your family . . ."

"Which included myself," Priscilla said softly.

"Indeed, your highness. The Countess Patricia intended to bring you all to safety. However, because of the war she was forced to travel across the Atlantic, and then America, and then the Pacific, and then the whole of Russia, to reach Bolugayen. Naturally, in these circumstances, she could not make such a journey alone."

"I know. She brought Morgan and her maid with her."

"Yes, your highness. But immediately before leaving, she gave my father two days off, to put his affairs in order, and he, ah . . . visited my mother. They had been acquainted before, for some time. I was born in the spring of 1918."

"Good Lord!" Priscilla exclamined. "You mean you never saw your father?"

"I did not know who my father was, your highness," Andrew Morgan said. "My mother always gave me to understand that he was her husband, and that he was killed in the Great War. It was not until she was on her deathbed, three months ago, that she told me the truth."

"There is nothing in what she told you that you need be ashamed of, Mr Morgan. Your father did die in the Great War. He died like a hero. He was one of the bravest men I ever knew."

17

"Thank you, your highness. Will you tell me of it? I know the memory must be painful for you," he hurried on, as he saw the shadow cross her face. "But I would beg you to understand . . . I only learned of him, as I have said, three months ago. I was, well, astounded, I suppose, to know that I had been born out of wedlock, and indeed, remained, if you will pardon me, your highness, a bastard. I felt extreme resentment against the man who had done this to me. Then I knew I had to find out more about him. But I had very little idea how to set about it. I did trace his birth certificate, but of course there is no death certificate. My mother had told me that he was employed by the exiled Bolugayevski family, but she knew nothing of where they were now. I discovered that you lived in the States, but I had no means of getting there – I have very little money. And then, this morning, I read that you were in London."

"Pardon me," Priscilla said. "But do you make a habit of reading society magazines?"

He flushed. "Yes, your highness. Always seeking some kind of information about you or any Bolugayevski. Never before have I had any success. Then I knew I just had to speak with you, and see what you could tell me."

"Of course." Priscilla leaned across to touch his hand. "I quite understand. Your father, as you say, accompanied the Countess Patricia to Bolugayen. They reached us in the summer of 1917. By then Kerensky had been in power for about six months, and Russia was officially a Socialist state, but there was very little evidence of it down in Bolugayen. We were far removed from the centres of strife and power. Thus I am afraid we did not respond to the Countess's wish for us all to leave immediately and accompany her to England. The journey sounded horrendous, and Bolugayen was our home. No decision had been taken before that fateful day when a company of deserting soldiers reached us. The first we knew of it was when . . ." Priscilla paused, as terrible memory came flooding back. "When they came across the Countess out riding, and murdered her. They tore her to pieces, Mr Morgan." Morgan swallowed. "With her was the previous Princess of Bolugayen, Sonia Bolugayevska." Priscilla gave a wry smile.

"She had sought shelter with me, her successor as Prince Alexei's wife. We had become friends. The Princess Sonia escaped the mob and reached the house. When we heard what had happened, we realised immediately that we would have to defend ourselves. Mr Morgan was an old soldier . . . you knew he had been a soldier in his youth?"

Andrew Morgan nodded. "My father served with the Twenty-Fourth of Foot, the South Wales Borderers. He was at Rorke's Drift."

"That is absolutely right. So I placed him in charge of the defence of Bolugayen House. It was a forlorn hope. We had only a couple of men, and about a dozen women. We all expected to die. Your father was killed in the first attack. He was defending the front doors when they collapsed, and he was shot."

"But you did not die, your highness?"

Priscilla's head came up, her cheeks tinged with pink. "No, Mr Morgan. I did not die. I watched your father die, and I watched my grandmother die. But with some other women, including the Princess Sonia, I was taken by the Reds." Her lips twisted. "We were reserved for what is popularly known as a fate worse than death."

"I do apologise . . ."

"It happened, Mr Morgan. If I may say so, in view of what took place after the house was captured, your father was one of the most fortunate of us: his death was instantaneous. And I repeat, he died like a soldier, facing the foe." Andrew Morgan sat in silence, but Priscilla guessed it was less out of a sense of grief for a father he had never known than embarrassment at having forced her to recall those memories. "Please do not blame yourself," she said. "You had to find out, I know. As for me, well, as you have reminded me, I survived. Even rape can become only a memory with the passage of sufficient time. And at least I had the satisfaction of seeing my tormentors hanged, when my husband retook the village." Andrew's head came up. "Do you think it is unbecoming, in a woman, to wish to see people hanged?"

"Of course not," he protested. "They deserved it. Your highness, I have applied for a visa, to visit Russia."

19

Priscilla frowned. "Whatever for?"

"I am a journalist, by profession. Not very successful, I'm afraid. I would also like to write a book. Again, my attempts have not been very successful. But that was before I had ever heard of my father. Now . . . I would like to write of his life. I wish to visit this place Bolugayen. To see my father's grave. Have you any objection to my doing that?"

"Of course I do not. But I do not think you will be able to find your father's grave, Mr Morgan. Bolugayen House was burned to the ground, by the Reds, with all the dead still inside it."

"Then that is his grave, is it not?"

"It was. But so far as I know, the land was then made into a collective farm."

"Is there no trace at all of the house?"

"I cannot say. I have never been back."

"Well, I shall go there," he declared.

Priscilla could not help smiling at his youthful enthusiasm. Although he had to be about thirty. "Are you sure that is wise?"

"Why should it not be?"

"Well . . . the Reds are not the most friendly people on earth."

It was his turn to frown. "Aren't they our allies? We just won the war together."

"I'm not sure how important that is, to the Russians, at this moment. At least, to the Russians who run Russia. They're a very suspicious people. Their leader is quite paranoid."

"You mean Premier Stalin?"

"Yes."

"Have you ever met him?"

"Oh, yes," Priscilla said. "I spent some weeks as his 'guest', once upon a time."

The young man did not pick up the nuance. "Then . . . perhaps you could help me. A letter of introduction . . ."

"To Josef Stalin? From me?" Priscilla gave a tinkle of laughter. "I do assure you, Mr Morgan, that would not help you in the least, except perhaps into a gulag."

"A gulag?"

"A Russian political prison, Mr Morgan. That is not somewhere

20

you should ever wish to be." She considered. "I could give you a letter of introduction to my sister-in-law."

"You have a Russian sister-in-law?"

"She is actually English. Or American. She is something of a cosmopolitan. But she lives in Moscow, yes. The important thing is that she is the Countess Patricia's daughter."

"Oh, that would be splendid, your highness. Would you?"

Priscilla studied him while she considered. She had no doubt that Joseph's sister Jennie Ligachevna – Ligachev happened to be the name of Jennie's last husband, although she might well have married again since his death in the Great Patriotic War – had betrayed her in 1942, which had led to her imprisonment. Just as she knew Joseph himself felt that Jennie's late husband had tried to murder him. But those had all been orders from above, as it were. And despite it all, she also knew Jennie to be an essentially simple, gregarious soul – they had become quite friends again once the intrigue was over. And of one thing she was quite sure: Jennie worshipped the memory of her mother. Here was the son of her mother's most devoted servant, seeking only what glories could be discovered in the past. Jennie would have to respond to that. Especially as he was such a charming young man. "It will be my pleasure, Mr Morgan," she said.

"Did I do right?" she asked Joseph, at lunch.

"I suppose no harm can come of it. It might lead to regaining some contact with her." Joseph was wearing that haunted expression which overtook him every time they discussed his sister. Priscilla knew he had attempted several times to reopen communication with her since the end of the War, and that she had not answered any of his letters.

Joseph's problem was guilt. He blamed his own prolonged absence from England when he had gone off to fight for the White Armies of General Denikin – and, incidentally, first met and fell in love with the Princess Priscilla – for the fact that Jennie had returned to Russia at all, in the 1920s, eloping with Andrei Gosykin, an agent of the NKVD, as the Russian secret police had then been known. Priscilla knew there was nothing

21

he could have done about it, save lock her up, and that had not been practical in laissez-faire England. Jennie was a true daughter of Patricia Bolugayevska, a wildly romantic spirit who had been at heart more of an anarchist than a revolutionary. Jennie had sobered up over the years of experience in Soviet Russia, but even if she had to know a great deal about the awful crimes that had been committed in those years – both her husbands had been heavily involved in carrying out Stalin's directives – she remained devoted to that terrible man. While as for that gorgon of a daughter of hers . . . Priscilla had never met Tatiana Gosykinya, but her son Alexei had fought beside the Heroine of the Soviet Union during the Hitler War. Alexei had described her as a killing machine, who had used her beauty not less than her ability with gun and grenade to lure men, and women, to their deaths. But Priscilla had more than a suspicion he had almost fallen under her spell himself, although he would never even talk about it, much less admit anything that might have happened in the Pripet Marshes during those desperate days when the hand of Hitler had lain heavy across European Russia. Yet the country, and its people, not less than its history, and the part she had played in it, continued to stir her blood. How she wished she could be accompanying that handsome young man on his odyssey!

"My dear Jennie. How good it is to see you. It has been too long." Josef Stalin beamed, as was his habit when he wished to charm. Now he stood before his desk in the Kremlin, drawing Jennie Gosykinya into his arms for an embrace.

Stalin was now sixty-nine years old, but superficially he looked as healthy as ever in his life. The hair was iron-grey, as was the moustache, but they had been grey for some years. The eyes were occasionally opaque, but this was surely because the great man was lost in thought, while the occasional slowness to respond to a question or a remark could be put down to the same cause. He still ruled the most servile nation on earth. That it was not at that moment the most powerful nation on earth was known only to himself and a few close associates. Certainly not to Jennie.

Their relationship was a peculiar mixture of utter intimacy

22

and cautious regard. Stalin, as Lenin's eventual successor, had inherited Jennie's first husband, the man with whom she had so romantically eloped from England as a sixteen-year-old, as his own private assassin. As such, he had welcomed Jennie almost as a daughter, had always, indeed, treated *her* daughter Tatiana as a grandchild. But the requirements of the state had led him to have Gosykin executed in the great purges of the thirties. Jennie did not bear him a grudge for that, he knew; she had been utterly horrified when she had learned Gosykin's true character and occupation, the more so as her Uncle Joe had been able to prove to her that Gosykin had only married her on orders from Lenin, in order to bring at least one member of the famous Bolugayevskis back to Russia, for propaganda purposes. She had endured all a woman's fury that she could have been so used, and been made a mother, by such a despicable lout.

The truly surprising thing was that she loved her daughter, Gosykin's child. Just as she remained totally committed to the Soviet Union, as run by Josef Stalin. Of course she was unaware of many of his more devious or vicious machinations. But she, and her daughter, remained two of his favourite people. They were links with the past he had played so big a part in destroying, but which he secretly envied. He thought he would have made a splendid prince, in the old days. Well, now he was a splendid monarch, even if that word no longer had any place in the Russian vocabulary. "You have something on your mind," he suggested, gently.

"I have had a letter, from Joseph. Well, it is from Priscilla, really. But Joseph has added a note."

Stalin's face remained impassive, shielded as it was by his huge moustache. But his brain was seething. He was a man who over the years had succeeded in achieving everything he had set his heart on. Now he was regarded as virtually a god by his people. No man could want more than that. But he had never succeeded in taking the Princess Bolugayevska to his bed. He knew now that even to consider doing that had been the folly of an old man. But the woman haunted him. When he had first met her, more than ten years ago now, he had lied to her and betrayed her, only to discover that she had resources of courage and determination far beyond those which he had ever expected to find in any woman, or perhaps in any man.

Thus when she had slipped back into his clutches during the Great Patriotic War he had been unable to resist the temptation to seize her, hold her, have her. Well, he had seized her, and he had held her. But he had never had her. He, Josef Stalin, the Man of Steel, had been impaled upon those china-blue eyes, so utterly cold, at least when returning *his* stare. She had been utterly in his power. He had dreamed of what he would do to her, and perhaps with her, from the obscene to the romantic. And he had done absolutely nothing. He had opened his hands, and like the fabulously beautiful butterfly that she was, she had fluttered her wings and flown away.

He did not think he would be so foolish another time. Another time, he would simply crush her to death, before she had the opportunity to captivate, and then do whatever he wished to her corpse. But he had never dreamed there could ever be another time. Now he frowned at Jennie. "She is not proposing to return to Russia?" That would be fortune indeed.

"No, no." Jennie had no idea what had happened to Priscilla on her previous visit, but she did know it had been a traumatic experience; she could not conceive of any circumstances in which her sister-in-law would ever set foot in Russia again. "It is to do with a man named Morgan, who wishes to visit us."

"You will have to explain," Stalin said, still with the utmost gentleness.

"This man's father worked for my father and mother," Jennie said. "I remember Harold Morgan very well. He left England in 1917 to accompany Mother back to Russia, when she came to take the family out. Well, as you know, she was murdered, and Morgan himself died trying to defend Bolugayen House. Now this man, who says he is Morgan's son, wishes to visit his father's grave. And Priscilla has written to say she has given me his address, and that anything I can do to help him will be much appreciated."

Stalin smoothed his moustache. "You say this man *says* he is Morgan's son. Is there some doubt about this?"

"Well . . . as I say, I remember Morgan just before Mother left

England. He was Father's servant, had been for some years. He was a bachelor. I mean . . ." Jennie flushed. She might have eloped as a girl, but over the years she had become the most orthodoxly moral of women. "Well, it's possible, I suppose."

"But improbable, you think, having knowledge of this fellow."

"Well . . . yes, I do think Priscilla is being taken for a ride. And then, well, Harold Morgan doesn't have a grave, as I understand it. He was burned with Bolugayen House. And that later became a collective. There can't possibly be a trace of him anywhere. All of the family, save for Priscilla and Sonia and Alexei and Anna, were burned with the House. Now they are all dead as well. Except for Priscilla."

"Except, as you say, for Priscilla," Stalin agreed. "A devious woman, who has ever dreamed of avenging herself for the destruction of her family and her home. And her wealth, of course."

"Oh? Do you really think so, Josef? I mean, as the last Cromb, save for her son Alexei, she is a very wealthy woman in her own right."

"There are degrees of wealth, and power," Stalin said severely. "When Priscilla was twenty years old, she had both, in total abundance. Then it was all torn away from her, in conditions of extreme pain and grief, and humiliation. Hell hath no fury like a woman humiliated, eh?"

Jennie was not going to argue with the mis-quotation. She thought he might well be right. "So . . . you would like me to write and tell her I shall be unable to receive this man Morgan?"

"Of course you must not do that," Stalin said. "Priscilla is your sister-in-law. Whatever devious machinations she may be up to, I think you must assist her in so far as it is possible. No, no, write back and say you will be pleased to welcome this Morgan, and give him all the assistance possible. That way we may find out what he is really after. And Priscilla, to be sure."

"Well, if you're sure it will be all right."

Stalin handed her back the letter. "I am sure it will be all right."

He kissed her fingers, and she left the office. He waited until the door was closed, then pressed the switch on his intercom. "I wish to see Comrade Beria," he said.

Chapter Two

The Trigger

"What is the news from Larionov?" Stalin asked, having gestured his Interior Minister to a seat in front of his desk.

Beria took off his pince-nez to polish them. "Nothing recent. I know he is working on the project. But obtaining such information will obviously be very difficult. It is a matter of persuading certain people to betray their country."

"Or *forcing* them to betray their country," Stalin suggested.

"That is always a possibility. But persuasion is a better bet. More people yearn after money they do not have and cannot believe they will ever have, than are sufficiently interested in deviant sex to allow themselves to be blackmailed. And it is often a surprisingly small amount of money."

"Meanwhile," Stalin said. "Our own program goes slowly."

"We will just have to sit it out," Beria said, polishing away. "We will get the atomic secrets in time. Meanwhile, we keep our noses clean and stay close friends with the West, eh?"

"That would be the biggest mistake we could make," Stalin remarked. Beria replaced the pince-nez on his nose. "There are three reasons why it would be a mistake," Stalin said.

Beria waited, while his employer commenced filling his pipe. Beria was as aware as anyone that this meant the mighty brain was working overtime. "The first is that should we, how shall I put it, change our accepted behaviour, the West would become suspicious. They would know we were waiting for something to turn the tide of events in our favour, and it would not require too much thought on their part to deduce what that something would be. The second is that this new man, Truman, is a different kettle of fish to Roosevelt. Roosevelt was an aristocrat, and had all the arrogance of an aristocrat. He believed he could handle me. He has said so in his writings. He believed he could do so better than that other aristocrat, Churchill. Because Churchill has been around longer, and has hated us for that much longer. He has said *this* in his writings. Truman is not an aristocrat. He comes from a small town and has had his ups and downs, including a bankruptcy, I am informed. He will have a suspicious, careful nature. And when we met at Potsdam I did not like him. Nor do I think he liked me." Beria shifted in his chair, uneasily. "But the third factor is the important one," Stalin said. "America, not even Truman, will ever use the Bomb, in the present circumstances. He is still feeling the guilt of Hiroshima and Nagasaki, is too aware of the weight of public opinion. While America herself feels the weight of world opinion. That is the big problem all democracies have to face. Their leaders have always to look to the next election. Their people always seek to justify their very existence by being loved and respected. We can only benefit from such weaknesses. No, no, Lavrenty Pavlovich, we shall press ahead with our plans to communise as much of Europe as is possible, *before* we obtain the secrets of the Bomb. Secure in their power, the Americans will attempt to contain us with rhetoric rather than force."

"As you say, Josef Vissarionovich," Beria conceded. Having read detailed accounts of what had happened in Japan, and seen the photographs, he fervently hoped the Party Leader was correct in his assumption.

"We must also forward our plans to get them out of Berlin. It will be difficult to transform all of Germany into a Communist state while we have the Americans and the British and the French in the very heart of the country."

Beria swallowed. "That will be a very dangerous procedure, Josef Vissarionovich. Suppose they refuse to go?"

"I think they will go, if we exert enough pressure. Right up to the brink of war, Lavrenty Pavlovich. The democracies will not fight another war, while the memory of the last one is so fresh. Their people will not let them. And as I have said, having the Bomb is a positive disadvantage to them. Their people will say, and are saying, why do you fear anything the Soviet Union can do? The Soviet Union can never attack us, while we have the Bomb. That is *our* strength." Beria was back to polishing his pince-nez. "Once *we* have the Bomb, of course," Stalin went on. "Things will be different. The Americans will cease to treat us as a nuisance which can always, at the end of the day, be contained, and have to treat us as an equal."

"A nuclear war is unthinkable," Beria ventured. "It would destroy us as much as them."

"True. But always remember they have more to be destroyed, in terms of wealth and what they call civilisation. However, it must be our business to use the time we have as successfully as possible. Thus we must keep the West guessing as to how far we have progressed towards obtaining a Bomb of our own for as long as possible. This is why I have sent for you. The West is very interested in our progress. Especially the British are very interested. The British, as I am sure you appreciate, Lavrenty Pavlovich, are basically a far more aggressive people than the Americans, if only because they are less diverse, racially. They are also jealously anxious to preserve their position as a world power, even if they must know that has gone forever. But they will try, and they are undoubtedly in cahoots with the Americans. There can also be no doubt that they possess the best secret service in the world, simply because it has been around the longest. This is what I wish to discuss with you. Have you ever heard of a man called Halstead?"

"He is a spy. Or was a spy," Beria said. "We have a file on him from when he was here in 1942."

"Some say he was the best spy there ever was. Certainly when it came to obtaining information. Why do you say was?"

"Well, nothing has been heard of him since just before the invasion of Normandy. It is supposed he was caught and executed by the Nazis."

"Then what do you make of this?"

Stalin picked up the sheet of paper from his desk and held it out. Beria took it suspiciously, and studied it even more suspiciously. Then he raised his head. "Where did you get this, Josef Vissarionovich?"

Stalin had got his pipe alight, and now he puffed contentedly. "From one of my private sources in England."

Beria breathed heavily. He was the chief of Russian security. It was humiliating, and it was downright dangerous, for his boss to possess sources of information to which he did not have access. Why, he might even have such sources inside Russia! In Astrakhan, for instance. Stalin was smiling at his Commissar's obvious discomfort. "You will see that my informant says that Halstead is not only alive and well but has been observed entering the building on Curzon Street in London that is known to contain the headquarters of the British Secret Intelligent Services. This can only mean that he has been brought out of retirement."

"Why was I not informed of this, immediately?" Beria demanded.

"I am afraid simply because I did not take it very seriously," Stalin confessed. "One interview, between a retired secret agent and his erstwhile masters, well . . . it was something to be considered, but not necessarily to require immediate action."

"And now you would like action taken," Beria remarked. "Well, as you have this secret source of information in England, I am sure you also have this man's address. Disposing of him will not be difficult."

"Disposing of him in England might not be difficult, but it would be a mistake," Stalin said. "No matter what he is presently pretending to be, what he *is*, or was, is certainly known to British Intelligence, and if he were suddenly to fall under a bus they would certainly suspect he was pushed. As only we would have been interested in doing the pushing, it would reveal that we are onto their activities. Specifically, Halstead's activities. This would put them on their guard. No, no, it is not necessary to play our hand that openly. Halstead is on his way to Russia. Once he is here, well, we will be able to handle it as we wish."

Beria smoothed his bald head. "Your source has also informed you of this?" He simply had to find out who this source was, and get rid of *him*, certainly.

"No, no," Stalin said. "I have other sources. I have just, for instance, received a visit from Jennie Ligachevna." Beria controlled his features with an effort. He did not like Jennie Ligachevna, much as he enjoyed watching her daughter train . . . and bathe afterwards. "Jennie brought me a letter," Stalin went on. "Which puzzled her. It was from the so-called Dowager Princess of Bolugayen."

Now Beria frowned. He was the only man in Russia who knew the true relationship between Stalin and Priscilla Bolugayevska-Cromb. "The Princess has written to her sister-in-law," Stalin went on, "requesting her to give what assistance she can to a man called Morgan. This man claims to be the son of the Countess Patricia Bolugayevska-Cromb's manservant, who died with her during the disturbances on Bolugayen in 1917. You know of this, Lavrenty Pavlovich?"

"It is on file, Josef Vissarionovich," Beria said, cautiously. The matter of the Bolugayevski family was dangerous ground, and not only because of the Dowager Princess's activities. The Countess Patricia, in the days when she had been an anarchist and a Communist herself, had been exiled to Siberia, with Lenin, and had later fought on the barricades, so it was said, beside Stalin himself. But she had been murdered by Red forces. He had never been sure how Stalin stood in connection with that, or indeed how he stood now.

"Yes," Stalin said. "Well, this is another example of that arrogance with which the British feel they can treat the rest of the world. They assume that anyone who is not British is necessarily a halfwit. As for that cursed family . . . this is open war."

"Ah . . . I am not sure I understand your meaning, Josef," Beria ventured.

"Well, obviously, this man is the spy."

Beria raised his eyebrows.

"Have you ever heard of a man going looking for his father's grave, thirty years after that father's death? Even if there were a grave, which there isn't, as must be known, certainly to the Princess. She was there when it all happened."

Beria stroked his chin. "The name Morgan suggests that this man is Welsh," he remarked. "The Welsh are a very romantic people. It is possible that he is telling the truth."

"Bah! It is all very obvious to me," Stalin said. "The Princess, and that scoundrel of a husband of hers, are working with the British Government. I have a suspicion they have always been working with the British Government. Thus it is clear that they are assisting the British Secret Service in getting their man Halstead into Russia, in the most plausible of all guises."

Beria frowned. "You think Morgan is Halstead?"

"I have no doubt of it."

Beria knew that his employer suffered, increasingly often, from an advanced case of paranoia which sometimes amounted to madness. He also knew that Stalin hated the Bolugayevski-Crombs, and Priscilla Bolugayevska-Cromb in particular, more than anyone else in the world – and Stalin hated a lot of people. But this was really stretching the limits of even a diseased imagination. However, Stalin *was* his employer, and it was his business to keep the ogre happy, until he could destroy him. "So, you would like this man Morgan taken care of the moment he enters Russia."

"No, no," Stalin said, somewhat impatiently. "Not Morgan, or Halstead, or whoever he really is. I think he is a fish we can play for a while. Is he not coming to visit Jennie? And does not Jennie have a daughter who works for you? He will not know this. I think you should let Tatiana develop a . . . what do the Americans call it? A crush on him. She will take him around, show him everything he wishes to see. She will even accompany him down to Bolugayen, if that is where he wants to go. She will find out everything about this man, Lavrenty Pavlovich. I am told she can make men forget all their troubles. And all their responsibilities."

Beria drew a deep breath. He knew, of course, that Tatiana Gosykinya, having spent the entire War behind the German lines fighting with the partisans, had lost her virginity at a very early age. But he also knew that since the Great Patriotic War had ended she appeared to have lost her interest in sex; well, everyone can

31

have too much of a good thing. But he had intended that when her interest returned, he would be the beneficiary. Of course, he could command it, whenever he chose; she was his servant. But she, and her mother, were also two of Stalin's favourite people; he would have preferred a relationship between Tatiana and himself to be something mutual. Now, to have her seduce this English spy . . . What made it worse was the possibility, the certainty as far as he was concerned, that this man was *not* the spy Stalin's paranoia had immediately supposed. In which case she would be entirely wasting her time, and that splendid body.

Stalin was watching him. "You do not like this idea? Is it not time Tatiana was usefully employed? One cannot train forever."

Beria licked his lips. "I think it is an excellent concept, Josef Vissarionovich. Tatiana will certainly find out everything about this man, and very quickly."

"I have no doubt of it. And while she is attending to him, you will be attending to the more serious matter."

Beria raised his head.

"It is time for our final reckoning with the Bolugayevski-Crombs, Lavrenty Pavlovich. I have had this in mind, for some time. As you know, I had arranged for it during the War. Those plans went wrong, and in the euphoria of victory, well, they got away. I might even have been inclined to allow them to exist, so long as they no longer attempted to interfere in our affairs. However, now that they are working for the British Government . . ."

"With respect, Josef, but you do not know that."

"It is as plain as the nose on your face, Lavrenty. They are a danger to the state. They have always been a danger to the state. The evidence is plain. They live in America, but presently they are in England. While they are in England, Halstead is summoned to the British Secret Service headquarters. The next day, Halstead appears at Priscilla Bolugayevska-Cromb's hotel, for his final briefing, no doubt."

"This is assuming Halstead and Morgan are the same man," Beria murmured.

"Of course they are the same man. Now I wish them destroyed.

And at the top of the list . . ." he pointed. "I wish the Princess, here in Russia, to answer for her crimes against Soviet Russia."

"She will never come to Russia. Again."

"I agree with you. She will have to be brought."

Beria took off his pince-nez, looked at them, then put them back on his nose. He was very tempted to remind his chief that he had had Priscilla Bolugayevska-Cromb, sitting right where he was, on at least two previous occasions, and had done nothing more than talk. And then his desire for revenge could have been accomplished with no repercussions. But perhaps, then, he had not yet felt the desire for revenge. "You have, I am sure, people capable of accomplishing this task," Stalin said.

"Oh, indeed. But . . . if the Princess were to disappear, no one would be in any doubt what had happened to her. While when she reappeared, here in Russia . . ."

"She is not going to reappear, here in Russia," Stalin said. "She is never going to reappear again. As for her disappearance in America, or in England, where she happens to be right now, well, it will cause a sensation. But nothing more than that. As I have said, we possess at this moment more freedom of action than we are likely to in a couple of years time. One pseudo princess, however beautiful, however famous, is not something the Americans will go to war about."

Beria inclined his head. "And her husband? And her son?"

"The son is a nothing. The husband . . . after what he has written about us . . . I issued the order for his death a dozen years ago, and was betrayed. I issue it again, now."

Lavrenty Beria had a distinct feeling that he had been in collision with a bus, as he returned to Lyubyanka Square. But while he fully intended to step into Stalin's shoes the moment that was possible – and equally fully intended to make it possible sooner rather than later – he knew that until the vital moment arrived he must be the most faithful of servants. However difficult, or almost impossible, the task set him. He sent for Kagan, told him what he wanted done.

Kagan was a short, heavy man of Tatar origin. He was about the most deadly agent Beria employed, if only because he possessed tunnel vision, and would let nothing deflect him from his allotted task. But he also had a cool and quick brain. "Can you do it?" Beria inquired.

"Of course, Comrade. But not by snapping my fingers."

"Tell me what you wish and you shall have it."

"In the first place, Comrade, while the Princess and her husband are presently in England, this is clearly a visit; they will be back in America before we can organise anything."

"If the Premier is correct, and they are linked with the British Secret Service, they may well remain in England for some time."

Kagan's eyes were hooded. "Do you believe the Premier is correct, Comrade? With the greatest possible respect." Beria sighed. But walls, even his walls, had ears. Kagan took his silence as agreement. "Therefore, while I shall investigate the situation in England, I will also prepare plans to remove the Princess from her home in America. Boston."

"Will that not be greatly more difficult?"

"Not at all. Possibly even easier. We need an infiltrator."

"The Princess, and her husband, will be totally suspicious of anyone from Russia who attempts to contact them."

"I am sure that is so, Comrade. However, the Princess's son, and his wife, both fought with the Partisans during the Great Patriotic War, did they not?"

Beria stroked his chin. "They belonged to a highly successful group," Kagan went on, "which operated out of the Pripet Marshes. The group came into being almost the day war was declared, and was still there when we finally reached them again, in 1944. A great deal of comradeship must have sprung up amongst them for them to survive at all. In addition, a member of that group, the commander, in fact, was a Bolugayevska herself, by descent. If this woman were to appear in the States, seeking perhaps asylum, there is no doubt the family would take her in. And then . . ."

"That is not possible," Beria said. "Are you not aware that Tatiana Gosykinya works for us? For me?"

"I was aware of that, Comrade. Surely that would make her

employment in this matter easier, as she is not in a position to refuse."

"She is reserved for other duties," Beria said. "In any event, there is no way any of her American cousins would believe that Tatiana would wish to defect, or if she did, that she would not contact them before leaving Russia, through her mother. The whole concept is too fraught with inconsistencies and possible dangers. But the idea is a sound one. Yes. An old comrade, turning up in Boston, and seeking the help of the people with whom he fought to become established . . ."

"You know others in the group, Comrade?"

"Oh, indeed. I think I know the very man."

"Well, Comrade? Are you not pleased to have an assignment at last?" Beria asked.

"I am very pleased, Comrade Commissar," Tatiana said. She sat before his desk, upright in the straight chair. She might have been an applicant for a secretarial position. Equally, she might never have bathed in front of him. Was she totally devoid of feeling?

"Tell me what it is you have to do."

"I meet this man Morgan, I befriend him in the name of my mother, I show him whatever it is he wishes to see, I discover what is the real purpose behind his visit to Russia. I report to you." Her voice was utterly toneless.

"You will remember that your mother knows nothing of his true purpose."

"I understand."

Beria knew Tatiana did not altogether like her mother, however much she might respect her – *as* her mother. "You will receive assistance, of course," he said. "This man is a devoted and cunning enemy agent. Whatever happens, he must be destroyed."

"I understand that," Tatiana said. "Whether or not he is carrying incriminating evidence, such evidence will be planted upon him. And to obtain what the state requires, I shall seduce him."

Still not the slightest suggestion of emotional involvement. She was either a spymaster's dream, or a lurking disaster – for someone. "Does this prospect disturb you?"

At last she looked directly into his eyes. "No, Comrade Commissar. Not if it is for the good of Mother Russia."

How trim she was in her uniform. How delicious was the white flesh beneath it, as he well knew. How much did he long to touch her, stroke her, command her to do his every sexual bidding . . . but she was too close to Stalin, through that demented mother of hers. It was a pleasurable thought that when the monster fell, at his hands, both Jennie Gosykinya and her daughter would be at his mercy. Jennie was worth nothing more than a bullet in the base of the skull. But this gorgeous creature would be all his. She was worth waiting for. And meanwhile . . . "You understand that you will not wear uniform for this assignment."

"I understand, Comrade Commissar."

"I have procured some proper clothes for you," Beria said. "In those boxes." Tatiana turned her head. She might be a glacier, emotionally, but she was also a woman. A pile of boxes had to interest her, especially when they were secured by ribbons and carried the GUM label. "Open them," Beria invited.

Tatiana hesitated only a moment, then got up and untied the ribbon round the first box. She lifted off the lid with both hands, and then with both hands took out the frock inside the box. She gave a little gasp. Beria estimated she had never owned anything made of taffeta before. "Do you like it?"

The bodice was red, the flared skirt black. "It is . . . decadent."

"This man is used to decadent women. Go on."

Tatiana hesitated, then laid the dress across his desk, opened the next box, lifted the brassiere in total disbelief. "Have you never worn one of those?"

Tatiana shook her head. She was staring at the lace panties in the bottom of the box. "What about the American woman, Mitchell, who served with you in the Pripet? Did she wear those?"

Tatiana gave a grim smile. "The Pripet was not the place for wearing lace, Comrade Commissar."

"Try them on," Beria invited.

Tatiana glanced at him, then at the door. He knew she was less

36

concerned with someone coming in while she was changing, than with someone seeing her wearing such clothes.

"I am waiting," Beria said, his entire being consumed with desire. Tatiana unbuttoned her tunic and laid it on the chair. Then she stepped out of her skirt. "Ah," Beria said. "Stockings. That box." Tatiana opened the box, took out the silk stockings and the suspender belt with a growing expression of disbelief. "I believe the belt goes on under the panties," Beria explained.

Tatiana glanced at him, then slid down her drawers. As he always did when he saw those magnificent buttocks, that frothing pubic hair, Beria had a quick attack of indigestion. "Sit down to do it," he said, surprised at how even his voice was. "You must be careful not to ladder the stockings." Tatiana fastened the belt round her waist, then sat down, facing him, and slowly and carefully slid the stockings up her legs, clipped them into place. "Make sure your seams are straight," Beria said. "That is very important."

"You know a great deal about women's habits, Comrade Commissar," Tatiana remarked, as she checked her seams.

"I know a great deal about women," Beria pointed out.

She thought he was optimistic, as she put on the panties and with some difficulty fitted the brassiere. "This is a little tight."

"It can be let out as required. Now the dress." Tatiana put on the dress, faced him. "You are superb," he said.

"Why, Comrade Commissar, it is very nice of you to say so." He had never actually paid her a compliment before.

"You will turn this fellow's head so far he will be looking behind him. But you must be subtle. You must play him like a fish."

I must be subtle, Tatiana thought. Wearing clothes like these? But . . . "I will play him like a fish, Comrade Commissar," she agreed. "How will the meeting take place?"

"I have arranged a suitable situation for you, Tatiana," Beria said.

Andrew Morgan knew western Europe well, from his experiences during the War. He even knew Berlin fairly well. But when the train pulled out of the station and across the Polish frontier he was breaking new ground. He found it exciting. By then he had already encountered the East German border guards, had had all his papers perused and passed from hand to hand; apparently the idea of someone travelling to Russia to visit his father's grave was incomprehensible to them.

The excitement had begun with his meeting with the Dowager Princess It was incredible that his father should have worked for so glorious a creature. Should have died for her, in fact. Should have been intimately involved with that whole remarkable family, now so reduced in numbers. But it was equally incredible that the Princess should have so willingly agreed to help him. He had not expected that. The whole idea had only been a nebulous one until he had read that article in the glossy. Even then he had half intended only to use it as an excuse to meet the woman. But her enthusiasm no less than her beauty had turned a dream into a determination. Because she wished to see him again, when he returned.

And before then, she had given him an introduction to the Russian half of the family. That was hardly less credible, that he would actually be meeting the Countess Patricia's daughter. The Countess had been Father's actual employer. He should certainly have something to write about after that. He lunched, as he had the two previous days, in the dining car. The menu was printed in Russian, Polish, German and French, and he had learned just enough Russian to know what he was getting, much to the amusement of the waiter. Again, as he usually did, he read some of his guide book during the meal, and was surprised when, as he stirred his coffee, someone sat opposite him; the train was not that crowded. "I hope you don't mind," the stranger said, in English. "But I couldn't help seeing that you were reading an English language guidebook. My name is John Smith." He was a nondescript looking man, quite well dressed, but with a face so featureless it would be difficult to remember any of it. It was a face to go with the over-common name.

"Andrew Morgan." He shook hands.

"It is unusual to meet another Englishman going to Russia," Smith remarked. "Business?"

"Only in a manner of speaking. I'm researching a book."

"Is that a fact. You want to be careful just what you research. The Soviets like to keep their secrets."

"I don't intend to tread on any corns. Have you been on board all the way from the Hook?" He found it strange that he hadn't seen him before.

"No. I joined last night, in Berlin." Smith grinned. "Had rather a heavy night, with my associates, so I've only just got out of bed."

"And you're going to Russia on business?"

"That's right. Typewriters. They're in short supply in Russia. I suppose you know all about typewriters, being a writer?"

"I have one," Morgan conceded.

"What make?"

"A Remington."

"Oh, good lord. Old hat, if you don't mind my saying so. What you need is a PinPointer."

"Never heard of it," Andrew confessed.

"I have a demonstration model in my compartment. Would you like to see it?"

Andrew considered. He didn't really want to get too close to this man, or any man, for that matter; he knew there was a lot of clandestine movement of both people and material in and out of the Soviet Union, and it was his business to keep his nose absolutely clean until he had got what he had come for. And even more, afterwards. But he didn't want to offend this fellow. "If you wish to show it to me," he agreed. "However, I must warn you that I am not in the market." He grinned. "I haven't the money."

"But you will have, when you have written this story," Smith said. "Whatever it is."

Smith enthusiastically demonstrated the workings of his machine, which had several new features, some of them quite interesting. It was late afternoon before Andrew managed to escape him, and obtain a cup of tea from the guard, who as always was sitting next to his samovar at the door to the carriage. "When do we reach the border?" he asked.

"Tonight," the guard said. "Late. Do not worry, they will disturb you as little as possible."

But they will still disturb me, Andrew thought, and returned to his compartment and his book. He was determined to keep his mind in limbo until he actually reached Moscow. To his surprise, and relief, John Smith did not appear at dinner. Maybe his hangover had returned. Andrew ate well, drank the invariable carafe of vodka that was placed on his table, and retired to bed. He was asleep in minutes; the movement of the train added to the vodka in his system was soporific. But when the light was switched on he was awake instantly, his mind quite clear.

There were three people in the compartment, which meant that it was very crowded. The conductor and the frontier guard were normal; the conductor held Andrew's passport, and the guard was comparing the photo with Andrew's face, and nodding, reassuringly. It was the third person who took Andrew's attention. This was a young woman, he put her in her middle twenties, no older, and who was, in her own fashion, quite as beautiful as Priscilla Bolugayevska-Cromb. In fact, it was almost possible to detect a certain resemblance between the two.

But that was impossible. In any event, this girl was dark, where the Princess had been utterly fair. She wore no hat, and her hair was the colour of midnight, straight and very long, descending past her shoulders to her waist. The features were flawless; they might have been carved in marble by a master sculptor. And the rest of her . . . she wore no uniform, but a loose blouse and a pair of pants, which also seemed loose-fitting. But he didn't doubt what lay beneath was as perfect as the face and the hair. She had been studying his ticket. Now she raised her head. "This is not correct," she said, to his amazement, in perfect English.

"Eh?" He hated to sound dim, but she had taken him by surprise.

"This ticket is from London to Brest-Litovsk. You must leave the train here."

"But that is ridiculous. I am booked through to Moscow."

The girl gazed at him. One eyebrow twitched. "You wish to go to Moscow?"

"Yes. I have business there." Andrew looked at the conductor. "Tell this lady I am going to Moscow," he said in Russian.

"That is what he said, Comrade," the conductor explained.

To Andrew's relief, the guard handed the passport back to the conductor, saluted, and left the compartment. He felt it would be more possible to carry on a reasonable conversation without the presence of a sub-machine-gun. "Then the ticket needs to be changed," the woman said. "You will come with me, please."

"Come with you?" At any other time it would have been a pleasure. "Where?"

"To the ticket office in the station." She might have been speaking to a small child.

"You mean . . . leave the train?"

The woman gave a brief smile. "The train will be here for more than an hour. The tracks must be changed, you see, from the European broad gauge to the Russian narrow gauge. The train will be put on a turntable to do this, then it will return here. But we must hurry."

"Oh. Right-ho." When I get back to London, he thought, I am going to strangle that ticketing clerk. On the other hand . . . "Just give me a minute to get dressed."

"There is no time. Come now."

"Ah. You see . . ." All she could see was his pyjama jacket. Now he slightly moved the covers to reveal a naked thigh. "I must get dressed. Or I'll be arrested for indecent exposure."

The woman regarded his thigh. "Put on a a pair of pants," she recommended, and stepped into the corridor.

Andrew looked at the conductor, who shrugged, and also left. The woman was just outside, and the door remained open. Andrew rolled out of the bunk, grabbed his pants and pulled them on, thrust his feet into his slippers, straightened, and found the woman standing in the doorway, looking at him. How long had she been doing that? The idea was quite a turn on. "Come," she said.

He pulled on his dressing gown and followed her. There were quite a few people in the corridor, who regarded him with varying degrees of surprise. Once again, to his utter relief, Smith was not to be seen, the door of his compartment firmly shut. Obviously there was nothing the matter with *his* ticket.

The spring air was far colder than he had anticipated; it cut through his robe like a knife. But when he followed the woman across the platform and into the station itself, it was as warm as toast. The station interior, however, was also packed with people. They showed only the slightest interest in a man who had clearly just been dragged from his bed, but to his dismay he saw that the line in front of the one ticket window was at least forty people deep. They waited patiently, and moved very slowly – it required only the simplest arithmetic to deduce that it would be over an hour before he reached the window. He had reckoned without his escort. The young woman marched forward, announcing, "Intourist. Intourist. Step aside." And everyone stepped aside.

Feeling acutely embarrassed, Andrew found himself standing before the window, while his ticket was suitably altered. He hadn't actually had an opportunity to examine the ticket since being told it was incorrect, as the woman had kept it in her possession. He was sure he had checked it before leaving London, and found nothing wrong with it. Now too he could not see what was being done to it, save that a piece of paper was being pasted across his destination. "There we are," the woman said, reverting to Russian. "Now there will be no more problems, eh?"

"Thank you very much," Andrew said. "You are an Intourist guide?"

"I work for Intourist, yes," she said.

"I should like to know your name."

"My name is not relevant to you, Mr Morgan. Come." She led him back into the body of the hall. Here there were several benches, all full. "Make space there," she commanded, and an elderly couple got up and joined those standing. "You sit here."

"I can stand," he protested.

"No, no. Of course you must sit. You are a guest in our country."

Andrew sat down. "Will you stay with me?"

She smiled. "I have things to do. The train will soon be here.

But remember, it will only stop for a few minutes. As soon as it comes, you must get in."

"I'll remember. And thanks again."

She gave another smile, and disappeared into the throng, leaving him more embarrassed than ever, and not a little nervous; these were the people who had been forced to step aside to let him be served. But there was no hostility in any of the glances directed at him, only curiosity. Well, he thought, quite an eventful day. He could not remember having been so immediately turned on by any woman. Not even the Princess. Of course, the Princess had not been accessible. Not only was she old enough to be his mother, but she lived up there in the sky, where he was firmly rooted to the earth.

But so, he estimated, was this girl. Not that she had shown the slightest interest in him; she had refused even to give him her name. Equally, he was not likely ever to see her again in his life. But she was excellent material for a few dreams. He became so absorbed in thinking about her that he nodded off, awoke with a start as all around him there was a gigantic rustle. People were moving towards the door. Andrew leapt to his feet and joined them. Now there was no idea of a queue; it was push and shove to get into the open air and gain the train, standing at the platform and hissing and puffing, while the various conductors waved their flags and shouted, "Hurry up!"

Andrew looked left and right. He had been so besotted with his charming companion he had forgotten to make a note of exactly where the first-class carriage was located, and at the moment he certainly couldn't see anything that looked like it. And the train was starting to move: he was about to be abandoned on a freezing platform in Brest-Litovsk, with no clothes, no money, no passport, and a ticket for a train that had long departed.

Desperately he ran forward, grasped the first door that came to hand, wrenched it open, and tumbled into the train, landing on his hands and knees. The door slammed behind him. "You left it late, Comrade," a man said.

Andrew got to his feet, looked at a man and a woman, both

quite young, and four children, not one over ten. "I apologise for coming in like this," he said.

"It is better not to miss the train," the man said. "You are going to Moscow? We are going to Moscow." He was proud of that.

"Yes," Andrew said. "I am going to Moscow. Now I must get to my compartment."

"You are welcome to share ours," the man said.

Andrew looked around himself, and gulped. There was nothing in the compartment save for four bunks, two upper and two lower, one on each side. The bunks consisted of bare boards, with not a mattress in sight, there was no washbasin, no let-down table . . . he licked his lips. "You are very generous," he said. "But I have a compartment. A few carriages along. I must return there."

"You cannot change carriages, Comrade," the woman said.

"I am not changing carriages," Andrew explained. "I am returning to my compartment. Good morning to you." He opened the door and stepped into the corridor; they made no further effort to stop him. He was sure the first-class carriage was nearer the front of the train, and so turned to his left.

He passed a succession of compartments, each as crowded and uncomfortable as the one he had just left, reached the end of the corridor, looked through the glass of the door to the sign, 'Second-Class', on the next door. But this door was locked. On the other hand, there was a conductor, seated in the corridor by his samovar, just as in first-class, reading a newspaper. Andrew banged on the glass, and again.

The man raised his head, frowned at him, and resumed reading his paper. Andrew banged again. This time the man glared at him, then got up and unlocked the door. "What do you want, Comrade?"

"To return to my compartment, Comrade. It is in first-class."

"You are in third-class," the conductor pointed out.

"But my compartment is in first," Andrew explained, resisting the desire to shout. "I had to leave the train at Brest, and when I got back on, it was into the wrong carriage. Now I wish to return to my own compartment. Here is my ticket. First-class."

"You cannot leave third-class," the conductor said, ignoring the ticket. "No one can leave third-class."

Andrew felt like hitting him. "I cannot stay here, all the way to Moscow!" he shouted.

The conductor shrugged and turned away, closing the door. Andrew stared at it, and him, in impotent fury. He just could not contemplate the next forty-eight hours. He wasn't even sure he could survive them.

He banged on the glass again, but the man ignored him. Then he looked past the conductor, along the corridor . . . and saw the Intourist agent coming towards him.

"I saw you on the platform," Tatiana said, as she escorted Andrew the length of the second-class carriage. "I knew you had got into the wrong carriage."

"So you came to my rescue," Andrew said. "May I say that I have never seen a more beautiful sight? But I would have said that anyway."

He was feeling quite light-headed with relief, but she did not take offence. Instead she smiled. "It is very kind of you to say so." They reached the end of the corridor, and encountered another locked door. But a word from Tatiana and it was opened for them, the conductor, *his* conductor, Andrew thought, touching his cap to them. "He wishes your ticket," Tatiana said.

"There you are," Andrew said. "All correct now, eh?"

The conductor nodded. "You know where your compartment is, now," Tatiana said.

"But . . . won't you at least have a cup of tea with me? The night's all but gone anyway."

Tatiana appeared to consider, then nodded. "All right. As I suppose I was partly responsible for your predicament. Two cups, Ivan," she said.

Andrew held the door for her. "I didn't even know you were on the train," he said.

"It is my business to be everywhere I am needed," Tatiana said, enigmatically. She sat on the bunk.

"It's a little untidy, I'm afraid." Andrew sat beside her. "It was all rather sudden."

"I have apologised," she pointed out.

Ivan arrived with the tea, and left. Andrew closed the door again. Tatiana made no comment. "Perhaps you'll now at least tell me your name?" he suggested.

"My name is Tatiana Gosykinya," she said, watching him carefully.

"Tatiana! What a splendid name. Very Russian."

"Thank you." She sipped her tea from the long glass cup contained in a pewter mug. "Is this your first visit to Russia?"

"Yes. I'm a journalist."

Tatiana frowned. "You have not come to write bad things about us, I hope?"

"No, no," Andrew protested. "I'm actually researching the death of my father. He was killed here, in Russia, you see, in 1917. Ah . . ." he realised he might be getting himself into deep water: this girl was an employee of the Soviet Government and was therefore presumably a loyal Communist.

"In the First Great War?" Tatiana was sympathetic. "It was a good time to die. But a better time to live." Andrew gave a sigh of relief. She was not going to probe into exactly how his father had died, or for whom he had been fighting. "And you are going to Moscow? Is that where your father died, in Moscow?"

"No, he died in the south. I am going to Moscow because . . ." more deep water. "I have a letter of introduction to someone there who knew my father."

"All those years ago," Tatiana said thoughtfully. "Tell me of this person. I may know him."

"It's actually a her. Her name is . . ." Andrew opened his notebook, and couldn't believe what he was seeing. The name had sounded familiar when she had said it, but what with everything else that had happened tonight it hadn't registered, but the entry for Jennie Ligachevna contained the note, née Gosykinya, née Cromb. "My God!"

"We do not use such expressions in Russia," Tatiana said. "Is there something wrong?"

"This woman . . . she once had the same name as you."

Tatiana looked suitably amazed. "And you say she knew your father? How odd. What is this woman's first name?"

"Jennifer. She's actually English, but she married a Russian."

"Jennifer Gosykinya is my mother," Tatiana said. "Is that not the strangest coincidence in the world, Mr Morgan."

"Yes," he said. "It is." But he wasn't interested in coincidences at that moment; could it possibly be that he was going to be able to see more of this gorgeous creature? "Well, I think in all the circumstances, that you should call me Andrew."

"And you will call me Tatiana," she said. "And I think, in all the circumstances, that I should give you a proper Russian greeting." She held his shoulders, and kissed him on the lips.

"You will be coming, Alex?" Elaine Bolugayevski demanded of her husband. "They will be most disappointed if you are not there."

"If it's humanly possibly, darling," Alexei Bolugayevski said into the phone. "Believe me."

"I shall be expecting you," Elaine said, and hung up.

Dr Bolugayevski grinned at his staff sister. "Women never understand that there may be more important things in life than their agenda. And my wife was once a doctor herself, you know."

"Is it urgent?" the sister inquired.

"Well, in a manner of speaking. My parents are returning from England, on the *Queen Mary*. They land tomorrow, in New York. And naturally they expect me to be there to meet them. Parents also have their own agendas. I happen to be on duty tomorrow."

"I'm sure we can arrange a switch for you, doctor," the sister said.

Elaine packed an overnight bag, her somewhat long, solemn face taut with concentration; her experiences in the War had left her a somewhat tense person. Amazingly, they had not affected her health, or her femininity. Her figure remained good; she had always been slender, with her height, a trifle willowy. Now she had filled out a little. Perhaps the most amazing thing of all was that her life in the Pripet, even her mishandling by the SS when she had been captured, had left her with no permanent injuries, not even a permanent scar – that was visible, at any rate.

She packed a bag for Alex as well. She entirely understood his problems. But she also knew he would wish to meet his parents, if, as he had said, it was humanly possible. They were that kind of family. Into which she had so strangely been drawn. Actually, the decision to become a Bolugayevski, or Bolugayevska, as she would be known in Russia, had been entirely hers: she had fallen in love with Alex almost the moment they had met, when they had both been internees at Boston General. She could still remember her excitement when he had first taken her home to meet his mother, the fabulous Princess Priscilla. But she did not think their relationship would have developed had it not been for the War.

When the Russians, fighting desperately for survival against the Nazi menace, had appealed for help, they had needed, apart from the necessary materiel with which to wage war, the assistance of trained doctors, to release their own medical people for service at the front. Alex had of course volunteered: he might be an exile from his motherland, but he was still the last Prince of Bolugayen. Elaine had volunteered too. It was more than a desire to be with Alex; it had also been a desire to help that huge country she had always found fascinating. She had little understood where her careless pseudo-patriotism was going to lead her, or she might have hesitated. Her war had come to fruition in the depths of the Pripet Marshes, fighting with the partisans, with people like Tatiana Gosykinya and her half-brother Feodor Ligachev, engaged in the bloodiest and most savage of conflicts, where quarter had neither been given nor expected.

But Alex had been there too, and although he had from time to time revealed the innate savagery of his own Russian background, their love had grown. And survived. And now she was his wife. She still needed to pinch herself from time to time to make herself understand it had really happened. That she would be standing on the quayside tomorrow when the *Queen Mary* docked, that she would be hugged and kissed by the most beautiful woman in the world, that she would address her as Mom. That was the most unbelievable thing of all.

She no longer practised as a doctor. That was the one regret she had. Her other regret, that she was not a mother, would be history in another six months. But the wife of the Prince of Bolugayen did not work for a living. Why, it could be asked, did the Prince work for a living? Alex, or at least his mother, held a large number of shares in the Cromb Shipping Line operated by Priscilla's brother. They were wealthy people in their own right. But Alex felt the need to serve, someone, all the time. He was a prince.

The doorbell jangled as she closed the second suitcase. Elaine looked at her watch. But it couldn't possibly be Alex yet; she didn't even know if he was driving down with her or would catch a late train. Mary the maid appeared in the bedroom doorway. "Someone to see you, Mrs Bolugayevski." Elaine raised her eyebrows. "A man," Mary explained. "Foreign type. I showed him into the den."

"I hope he's not pinching the television set." Elaine fluffed out her dark hair, which she wore long and straight because that was how a Russian princess always wore her hair when not making a public appearance, checked to make sure her lipstick wasn't smudged, and went down the stairs. The den was beyond the drawing room, but she could see the man, standing at the French windows leading into the garden, looking out. He had his back to her, but . . . Elaine frowned, and hurried forward. The man turned. "Good Lord!" she commented.

The man smiled. "I was hoping you'd remember me, Princess. We fought together, in the Pripet."

Chapter Three

The Bullet

"Gregory!" Elaine cried, and before she could stop herself was embraced. When she had first met Gregory Asimov, only five years previously, he had been a seventeen-year-old boy; he hardly looked older now, his face revealing the same eager innocence she remembered, even if, like hers, his body had filled out. But even at seventeen he had been a veteran of war and destruction, and she had fought beside him for more than two years. And as one of the doctors with the partisan group, she had tended to his various ailments as well, from frostbite to diarrhoea. Nor could she deny that he had been a dedicated and brilliant soldier – even if he had also been a savage one. But then, they had all been savages during the War: it had been necessary to be savage to survive.

He was also about the only member of the group who had never made a pass at her. But that was because he had always been hopelessly in love with Natasha Renkova, the lovely girl who had been tortured to death by the SS. After Natasha's death he had transferred his love to their commander, Alexei's cousin, Tatiana Gosykinya. Now, to see him here, in Boston . . . "I have come at a bad time," Gregory said.

"No, no," she protested. "It's just such a surprise. And where did you learn to speak English so well?"

"I have been studying. To come to America."

"Whatever for?"

"I wish to emigrate."

"You? Good lord, where are my manners. Would you like something to drink? A cup of coffee . . ."

"Do you have vodka?"

"Ah . . . yes." She went to the bar, poured two fingers, glanced at him. "I don't suppose you wish anything with it?"

"With it?"

"Absolutely." She poured two more fingers, handed him the glass, took one finger for herself and filled the glass with tonic. "Well . . . it's great to see you again. And looking so well." Her memory was of a handsome boy in a tattered uniform, never lacking a tommy-gun, and with a sprouting, untidy beard and moustache. Now she was looking at a man, handsome, certainly, clean-shaven, and very well dressed in a three-piece suit. It was difficult to envisage the tommy-gun.

"As are you, Dr Mitchell. Oh, yes, it is good to meet old comrades. And so you married Prince Alexei." Odd, she thought: Gregory, a dedicated Communist, at least during the War, had never before referred to Alexei as a prince. But he was clearly anxious to make a good impression.

"Yes, I did. We had always intended to, you know. Only the War got in the way."

"And now you live in this beautiful house, in this beautiful city, in this beautiful country . . ."

That was a bit too thick. "You say you have come here, to emigrate? I didn't know you could do that. I mean, out of Russia . . . well . . ." she hesitated, embarrassed.

"I am a war hero," Gregory explained. "I was decorated by Premier Stalin himself. So they have allowed me to do this."

Elaine frowned. "And the US Immigration people have just let you in?"

"No. They have given me a three months visitors' visa. But I mean to stay."

"I wouldn't recommend doing anything illegal," Elaine said.

"I would not do that. But if I can get a job . . ."

"You'd need a work permit. And if you're on a visitor's visa, you wouldn't get one."

"I need a permit for any job?"

51

"I'm afraid so. I mean, there are people who employ illegal immigrants around the house . . ." she gazed at him. "I'm afraid my husband and I are not inclined to do that. Anyway," she hurried on, "we have nothing to offer you. I mean . . . what exactly can you do?" Apart from being able to kill people, very efficiently.

"I garden," Gregory said. "I am good with the flowers, eh?"

"Ah! Unfortunately, we don't really have much of a garden. Just what you see out the back."

"But perhaps you have friends who have gardens."

"Well . . ." Elaine observed that he had drained his glass, and refilled it. How on earth was she going to get rid of him?

"Does your mother-in-law not have a garden?" Gregory asked.

"Well, yes, she does."

"I should very much like to meet the Princess," Gregory said reverently. "I have heard so much about her. From Tatiana. You remember Tatiana?"

"Of course I do."

"She spoke of her, often. Of her charm, and her beauty."

Elaine frowned as she tried to remember if Tatiana had ever actually met Priscilla. Priscilla had been in Moscow during the War, but Tatiana had spent the entire War in the Pripet. But . . . Priscilla had also been in Moscow in 1935, looking for Joseph. She could have met Tatiana then . . . Tatiana would have been a girl of twelve. But she would remember her glamorous aunt who was also her cousin. "Would she not like to have a Russian gardener?" Gregory asked.

The trouble was, Elaine knew that Priscilla would indeed like to have a Russian gardener. Priscilla, even more than her son, believed in cultivating every possible link with Russia, confident as she was that one day Stalin would fall, and with him the whole Communist regime . . . at which time all things might be possible. Even the reclamation of the family estates of Bolugayen. It was an impossible dream, of course. But it might amuse Priscilla to meet this man, especially as he was an old comrade-in-arms of both her son and her daughter-in-law. Certainly Priscilla would know how to get rid of him, if she chose to do so. But the decision could not possibly be hers. "My husband will be here in a little while,"

52

she said. "I know he would like to meet you again. And he will know if we can help you or not." She bit the bullet. "Why do you not wait for him, and in the meanwhile, have another vodka."

Tatiana looked at her watch. "Soon we will be in Moscow," she said. "I must get dressed." She gave a surprisingly girlish giggle, which Andrew had found one of the most attractive things about her. "I must be back in my own compartment, when we arrive." She sat up, but her giggle was only *one* of the most attractive things about her. Andrew put his arms round her waist to bring her back down on to him, then slipped his hands up to caress her heavy breasts.

He was still not sure that he was not dreaming this, that he had not been dreaming since that midnight stop in Brest-Litovsk, more than twenty-four hours ago. He had thought that a nightmare, then. But out of it had come possession of this superbly strong and mature body, so willing, eager to yield to him, to accomodate his every desire.

The last twenty-four hours had passed in a sexual daze. They had left the compartment together twice, for lunch and dinner, and from time to time Ivan the conductor had brought them tea. Andrew had been embarrassed by that, afraid that she might be getting into trouble. But Tatiana and Ivan appeared to be old friends, which made sense if she regularly travelled this train as an Intourist guide. Certainly *she* had not been embarrassed, or concerned by the conductor's intrusions. If she had dressed herself to leave the compartment when necessary, she had undressed herself again with a hungry enthusiasm the minute she had returned. She had overwhelmed him with her body, surprisingly white where her hair and eyes were dark. But he gathered the average Russian worker did not have much time for lying in the sun, even were the sun readily available, most of the year. For the rest he could only glory in the magnificence of that hair, matched by the curling coating of her groin, by the deliciously large breasts, by the strong legs and supple thighs between which he was sucked time and again.

And even more, by the aura of her. He wondered if he should not have been shocked by what she had to tell him of her experiences

53

during the War. She had been only eighteen when the Germans had rolled across the frontier. She had been on that frontier, in summer camp in that June of 1941, with her companions of the Communist Youth. She had been captured and raped, time and again, while many of her friends had been shot for being Jews. She had escaped, into the Pripet Marshes, and spent the rest of the War there, living a hand-to-mouth, sexually casual existence . . . and killing Germans, often with a self-confessed savagery he found hard to accept. But if only a tenth of what she claimed was true, she had certainly killed a lot of Germans. And yet she could lie in his arms with the enthusiastic naivity of a girl first experiencing life, and love. "Did you never love, amongst the partisans?" he asked.

For a moment her face was rigid. "I loved," she said. "One. But he died."

"Oh. I'm sorry."

"It was a long time ago."

"How did it feel, to leave the army, after such experiences, and become a tourist guide?"

Tatiana shrugged. "It is necessary to work. Did you not fight in the War?"

"Yes. But I was a journalist before the War, so when it ended I merely went back to what I had been doing before."

She kissed him. "I could not go back to being a schoolgirl. Or a virgin. Some things are irrevocable." She seemed to have abandoned the idea of returning to her own compartment, for the moment. "Tell me about the Princess Bolugayevska."

"What about her?" Andrew asked, lazily, stroking her body.

"She is my cousin, you know. As well as my aunt."

"How can the same woman be your cousin and your aunt?"

"We have a very tangled family history. Did she not tell you of it?"

"Not a lot."

"Well, you see, her husband is my mother's half-brother. So she is my aunt. But her mother and my mother were cousins. So she is also my cousin."

"And you're all really Anglo-American, and not Russian at all."

54

"I am Russian," Tatiana said, almost fiercely. "My father was a Russian. My mother is a Russian citizen."

"I'm sorry. I didn't mean to offend."

"How could you, offend me?"

Andrew found that a little enigmatic. Did she mean because they were lovers? Or because he was not of sufficient importance in her life ever to cause offence? "You were going to tell me about the Princess," she said. "Is she as beautiful as they say?"

"Have you never met her? She told me that she had been to Russia several times. She even lived her once, did she not?"

"That was before I was born. She came again, during the War, but I was in the Pripet. I should like to meet her. Tell me of her beauty."

"In her own way, she is very beautiful, yes. I prefer you."

"You are nice to me," she said. "Now I really must go. Do not worry, I will see you at my mother's apartment. I will arrange a vacation for myself, and then I will be able to show you everything you wish to see."

"I have an idea that I have seen everything I really want to see, right here in this compartment."

She kissed him. "You are a lecherous man who thinks only of sex. You are here to work. I will help you do that work." She got out of the bunk, pulled on her clothes. "I have enjoyed myself," she said, and closed the door behind her.

Another enigmatic statement, Andrew thought. Yet she seemed very anxious to see him again, and had virtually promised to spend the entire duration of his stay in Russia in his company. That was such an alluring prospect he was not the least inclined to start wondering if she really loved him or was just interested in a new face, a new body, a new technique. He was determined that by the end of his visit, she *would* love him. He would take her back to England with him. That would be a coup. Not an easy accomplishment, but if her mother was really an intimate of Stalin's . . . of course, the mother would have to be charmed into agreeing first. He didn't doubt he could do that.

He got dressed himself, stood at the window to look at the Moscow suburbs drifting by. There were a group of women working beside the track. Women navvies? But they looked up and laughed and clapped their hands at the train. The door opened. "You are packed, yes?" Ivan asked.

Andrew turned in surprise; Ivan had shown not the slightest desire to assist him when he had boarded the train. "All packed, yes."

"I will take your bags," Ivan volunteered.

Feeling extraordinarily conspicuous, Andrew followed the conductor along the corridor, which was now filling with people preparing to disembark. But Ivan cleared a way with a series of sharp, barked commands. Andrew almost bumped into Smith. "I never realised you were such an important fellow," the typewriter salesman remarked. He looked quite put out.

"Neither did I," Andrew agreed, with an embarrassed grin. But then he was on the platform, and Ivan was even helping him through the barrier. Tatiana was not to be seen. "Does Comrade Gosykinya travel with you regularly?" Andrew asked.

"She is a Heroine of the Soviet Union," Ivan replied.

That was apparently all that he was required to know.

"What do you reckon?" Elaine asked, as they took the freeway south.

Alexei was driving. If their years in the Pripet had left her with the odd streak of grey in her dark hair, they did not seem to have affected Alex at all, physically. Of course he was blond, and it was less easy to discern grey or silver amidst the gold. But his features had not hardened as much as they might have done; he remained a big, handsome man, with the bold Bolugayevski features and the broad Bolugayevski shoulders. They did not often discuss those years, although they had fought, and eaten, and slept, and done everything else, shoulder to shoulder. There were too many memories neither of them wanted to return. But Gregory . . . "Seeing him again sure takes you back," Alex said.

One of the memories Elaine did not wish to return was that like Gregory, Alex had also fallen under the sexual spell of their commander, who had also been his cousin. It had been a brief surrender, and then he had returned to her. But had that only been because Tatiana had used him as an object, rather than considered him as a human being? Tatiana had used everyone like that. Even Gregory. Even herself! Elaine had only been happy to have Alex back. She did not think she was actually jealous of Tatiana. It is difficult to be jealous of a monster, however beautifully wrapped. But . . . she didn't think she would have wept if she had been told that Tatiana had not survived the War. But she had. Like Gregory, she had been decorated by Stalin himself as a Heroine of the Soviet Union. Elaine wondered what she was doing, now that she was no longer required, or presumably allowed, to spend her time killing people? Life must have become a bit of a bore. But there had been no communication with the Russian half of the family since their return to the States. "Do you think Mom will be interested?" she ventured.

"Oh, Mom will be interested," Alexei said. "No doubt about that. What interests *me* is why Gregory has turned up."

"You don't believe he *is* meaning to emigrate?"

"Gregory? Can you think of a more dedicated and loyal Communist amongst all the people we served with? Except Tattie herself."

"Circumstances change. He may have become fed up with the system."

"It's possible."

"But you think there's another reason? Do you think he's a spy?"

"I very much doubt it. He's not bright enough to be a spy. He was a schoolboy at the start of the War, got cut off in the Pripet, wound up serving under Tattie. He's a professional soldier. A professional killer, if you like."

Elaine took a quick breath. "You're not supposing . . ."

"No, I'm not," Alexei said. "There'd be no point."

"I was thinking of Joe. He escaped from the gulags before the War, he wrote all those articles condemning the Soviet system . . ."

"And he went back to Russia in 1942, at the Soviet's invitation, and stayed there for the rest of the War. If they'd meant to bump him off, they could have done it then, and no questions asked: he spent enough time at the front."

"And was wounded at the front. In Stalingrad. Has he ever talked to you about that? He was shot in the back, in a battle," Elaine said. "Can you imagine Joe ever turning his back on an enemy?"

Alexei stared at the road unwinding in front of them.

"Andrew Morgan!" Jennie Ligachevna said. "You look just like your father!"

And you look just like every photograph I have been able to unearth of the Bolugayevskas, Andrew thought. Except of course, for Priscilla and Tatiana. The Princess was clearly a member of the family, but in her the big, bold, handsome features had been chiselled, thanks to her American blood, into that peculiarly breathtaking beauty which set her apart from other women. Similarly, Tatiana's features had been tempered by her father, the classic Bolugayevski looks seeming to be slightly encapsulated, which had made her the more attractive. Jennie was simply an extremely handsome middle-aged woman, her auburn hair almost entirely grey, her body, which must once have been big and strong and compelling, sunk into overweight rolls of flesh, not enhanced by the shapeless dress she was wearing.

But she seemed pleased to see him. She held his hands and drew him into the apartment, which he took in with a quick, practised glance. It looked surprisingly affluent, for a widow whose daughter worked as an Intourist guide. But then, both this woman's husbands had been senior Party officials, and she was supposed to be on intimate terms with Stalin himself. "This is my friend, Galina Schermetska."

Andrew had been so absorbed by the Bolugayevska woman that he had not noticed the other. Galina Schermetska was a solidly built, dark woman, perhaps a few years older than Jennie. Her somewhat heavy face was a strange mixture of peace and sorrow.

"Galina has the flat above," Jennifer explained. "Our daughters fought together in the Pripet, during the Great Patriotic War."

"Mine died in the marshes," Galina Schermetska said, squeezing his hand.

"I'm most terribly sorry . . ."

"I have another," Galina said.

"And now we are widows together, sharing our old ages," Jennifer said.

How the hell was he going to get out of this emotional impasse? "I have a letter from Mrs Cromb," he ventured.

"The Princess, you mean. It seems strange to hear her called Mrs Cromb." Jennie took the envelope, laid it on the table. "She wrote me a few weeks ago, saying that you were coming, and that I must help you in any way possible. Have you an hotel?"

"I am at the Berlin."

"Oh, yes. You will be comfortable there. And you wish to go down to Bolugayen? There is nothing left, you know, of the old home."

"I would still like to see it, Mrs Ligachevna. It's where my father died."

"I know," Jennie said, sympathetically. "Dear old Morgan."

"Did you know him well?"

"Oh, yes. He was my father's valet, butler and general factotum. As my father wasn't very well, from time to time, I suppose your father was just about in loco parentis to me, a lot of the time, when I was a girl. Of course, Mother was there then, too, but . . . Mother was so often doing other things."

"Would you talk to me of those days?" Andrew ventured.

"If you do not think it would bore you. But where are my manners? Here we are, standing in the middle of the room . . . sit down, Andrew. You do not mind if I call you Andrew?"

"I should be flattered."

"And you must call me Jennie. Now, vodka! Would you like some vodka?"

"Thank you very much."

Jennie poured three liberal portions. "Here is to old comrades!"

They drank, then Jennifer cocked her head. "My daughter is home."

The footsteps were clearly audible beyond the thin door. Andrew stood up as it opened, and Tatiana stepped inside. He gaped at her. She had discarded the utilitarian pants and blouse of the train and was wearing a western-style taffeta dress with a flowered pattern, very fashionable in its flared, ankle-length skirt. While on those ankles . . . he was certain he was looking at silk stockings. He had not supposed there could be a more beautiful sight in the world than Tatiana Gosykinya naked in bed. But Tatiana Gosykinya dressed like a woman and smiling was a pretty close second.

From the stifled comment beside him, he gathered that Galina was as surprised by this apparition from a fashion magazine as himself.

"Tatiana!" Jennie said. "This is Mr Andrew Morgan, the gentleman I spoke of, who has come to Russia looking for traces of his poor dead father. Our family servant."

"It is a pleasure to meet you, Comrade," Tatiana said.

Joseph and Priscilla listened to what Alexei and Elaine had to say on the drive back home to Boston. "I suppose you think it's pretty far-fetched," Alexei said, defensively.

"Nothing that happens inside Russia, or that comes out of it, can be far-fetched," Joseph said. "But it is always governed by a kind of logic, however insane the logic might be to our way of thinking. I agree with you, that this man Asimov certainly has not come to America to emigrate: he wouldn't have a hope in hell of doing that anyway, with his history. How he ever got a visitor's visa is beyond me; someone must have falsified his background. But I don't altogether agree that he cannot be a spy, simply because you remember him as a common, if somewhat bloodthirsty, soldier. The war in Europe ended more than two years ago. We know he was decorated by Stalin at the same time Tatiana was. It is quite possible that in the interim he has been given some concentrated training. I am not presuming that he would be any good rushing around with a mini-camera photographing secret documents. But there are a hundred and one ways of spying, of acting as your country's agent. Stirring up labour problems is one, and we have some of those already."

"Then you think we should report him to the FBI?" Elaine asked.

They all looked at Priscilla, who had up to now taken no part in the conversation. "I would like to meet him," Priscilla said. "I think you are all being a little paranoid. We are agreed that to suppose he has come here to harm Joe is just not logical, even by Russian logic. Now you say that he has come to stir up labour trouble. To do that he has to become a blue-collar worker, and join a union, illegally. He says he wants to be a gardener. Is there a gardener's union?"

"Well . . ." Joseph scratched his head.

"But he is certainly an enemy," Priscilla went on. "I would like to meet him. I always like to look my enemies in the face. After that, we can decide what to do with him."

"And you don't think meeting him might be dangerous?" Elaine asked. "This man is a trained killer, Mom. Alexei and I have seen him at work."

"Just as he saw you at work," Priscilla pointed out. Elaine flushed. She had never told her mother-in-law all the things they had had to do in the Marshes, fighting for survival. Or all the things that had been done to them, her in particular, when she had been taken prisoner by the SS. But she had an idea Priscilla, who had undergone a fair amount of physical suffering in her own life, could guess. "Anyway," Priscilla went on. "What harm can it do? You have filled us in about this man. You will bring him to meet me. Joseph has a gun. You'll carry it, Joe. I assume you own a gun, Alexei? You will carry it. And I also have a gun," Priscilla said. "Which I shall carry. What about you, Elaine?"

"Guns are not really my scene," Elaine said. "I still think it would be best to turn the whole thing over to the cops."

"We are Bolugayevskis," Priscilla reminded her. "We wash our own dirty linen, in private. I am quite excited at the prospect of meeting this old comrade of yours." Alexei and Elaine exchanged glances. They knew Priscilla was excited, because she craved excitement. After the life she had led, the idea of gently slipping into a boring old age terrified her. But as with everything in their family, she was the boss.

"Well?" Beria asked.

Tatiana stood to attention before his desk. "As yet he has

revealed nothing more than what he pretends to be, a journalist looking for the remains of his father."

"He will reveal more when you start travelling. Are you enjoying his company?"

"Very much. He is very . . . refined."

"And I am sure he is enjoying *your* company."

"I think he is, Comrade Commissar."

"But you will not, I hope, forget that he is an enemy of the Motherland," Beria said. "Are you looking forward to interrogating him?"

Tatiana's nostrils flared as she inhaled. "Am I to do that, too?"

"Would you not like to? I think that would be rather amusing. The ultimate in psychological destruction. First you make him fall in love with you, then you gratify his every desire regarding you, and then you destroy him, physically. After which, or perhaps at the same time, you destroy him mentally. I shall look forward to seeing you do that." Tatiana's tongue showed between her teeth, for just a moment, and was then withdrawn. "I can tell that you find it an attractive prospect," Beria said. "But you will remember that you just string him along until I say so. I am going down to Astrakhan for a few days. When are you leaving for Bolugayen?"

"Tomorrow."

"Good. You can report to me on what you have discovered when I return."

Tatiana hesitated. "May I ask a question, Comrade Commissar? Is there news of Comrade Asimov?" Beria raised his eyebrows. Tatiana flushed. "I know it is incorrect to inquire after fellow agents, Comrade Commissar. But Comrade Asimov has not been seen for some time . . ."

"What do you know of him?"

"He fought beneath me in the Pripet."

"Ah," Beria said. So she does have a lover, he thought. Well, well. "No, Comrade Gosykinya, I have no news of him. He is on an important mission, overseas. I will inform you when he returns."

*   *   *

Sonia Bolugayevska walked in the marshes of the delta, picking wild flowers. She was allowed this liberty, because it was not actually liberty: she was accompanied by two armed guards. They kept their distances, one to either side, and did not interfere with her in any way. They knew she could not escape them, and they were prepared to terminate her walk the moment any outside party appeared, if that should ever happen. But she could pretend she was free, and enjoy the warm sunshine, and even allow herself to be happy. Because, as she understood, this was as much freedom as she had ever been allowed, by Fate.

Being born a Jew in Tsarist Russia meant that you were born unfree. One was not a slave, but one was surrounded by so many rules and restrictions, so many imminent catastrophes, that one might as well have lived within a barbed-wire fence. Being arrested for sedition, being charged with treason, had seemed an almost inevitable consequence of her situation. Being tortured by the Okhrana into saying things that were not true but which had to be said at least to alleviate the pain had been equally inevitable, looked at in the light of cold logic. That she had survived, and had not forgotten how to smile and even how to laugh, had been because her companion in distress had been the Countess Patricia Bolugayevska, the ultimate patrician.

Sonia had never been certain in her mind, for all the mental and physical intimacy the two of them had been forced to share for so long, whether Patricia had become involved in the plot against the Tsar because she genuinely believed in the Revolution, because she had not had any clear idea of where her political dabbling was taking her, or because she had simply become bored with the meaningless life of an effete aristocrat! But Sonia was certain that she was alive today because of Patricia. The Tsar, poor, weak, wife-dominated man, had not been able to bring himself to execute the daughter of one of the oldest of Russian princely families. And if he could not execute her, then in all justice he could not execute her accomplice either. Thus Siberia, and a long lesson in how to hate. But how to love, also. Certainly for Patricia and her Jewish lover.

But no freedom. When they had escaped from Irkutsk, with

Vladimir Ulianov, who would later call himself Lenin, and his wife Krupskaya, it had been in search of freedom or death. They had found neither. How much more free could a woman be, it had seemed, than to be swept off her tortured, blistered feet by the dashing, handsome, Prince Alexei of Bolugayen? Sonia had no doubt that in the first instance Alexei had cared for her simply because he was also caring for his sister. But he had fallen in love with her. Princess of Bolugayen! But that too had been a prison, of position and privilege, that had been ended so abruptly when the Jewish lawyer, Mordka Bogrov, had shot and fatally wounded the then prime minister, Peter Stolypin. That act of senseless vengeance – struck for what, she had often wondered? – had launched one of the greatest pogroms in Russian history. As Princess of Bolugayen, she had been immune from the catastrophe that had overtaken so many of her people. But she had very rapidly discovered that it was no longer possible for her to remain Princess of Bolugayen. At the time she had even considered her divorce as a release. But she had merely plunged into another prison, that of the professional revolutionary, of eternal midnight trysts and sudden, frightening doorbells.

Out of which had come the imprisonment of being Trotsky's mistress. She knew now that she had never loved Trotsky. She could have. The power of his personality was all-pervading, and all protecting, up to a point. But even as she had succumbed to his undoubted charms she had been repelled by his savage intensity, his ruthless determination to take the party to success, sparing neither man, woman nor child on the way. Living with Trotsky had been as brutal a prison as she had ever known. But she had never attempted to flee him. He had fled her, unintentionally, lying dead at her feet after the assassin Mercador had attacked him with her own icepick. Then, for a few months, she had actually been free. For the first time in her life. Perhaps it had been too strange for her. She had sought to regain contact with her family by marriage, with the woman who had replaced her as Mistress of Bolugayen, and who had, in such strange, such terrible circumstances, become her friend. As she had anticipated, she had been welcomed by the Bolugayevski-Crombs. Thus she had been unable to resist the temptation to return to Russia with Priscilla, assuming she had been under the aegis of that all-embracing personality. But there had been no aegis, and thus she had again been plunged into prison. And from this prison there would be no escape.

She knew that she had been condemned to death by Stalin personally. She knew that as far as the dictator was concerned, that sentence had been carried out. She had disappeared from the face of the earth. Only half-a-dozen people knew that she was still alive. Equally she knew that her captor intended her to die, when she could do so most usefully – for him. He reckoned that her reappearance, on a carefully calculated occasion, might just tip the ageing megalomanic who held the lives of all Russians in his hand over the edge.

Not that she supposed Beria intended to leave it merely to her reappearance. Her new master had intended that his coup should be sprung some years before. He had supposed that Stalin could not survive the savage losses and defeats being inflicted upon the Russian armies by the Nazis. He had been mistaken. Stalin's stature amongst the Russian people, and indeed on the world stage, had risen to unprecedented heights, as the Germans had first been held, and then repelled, and then defeated. But Beria was a patient man. Stalin was old and ill. Beria still waited, and watched, and planned.

The odd thing was that she bore him no hatred, any longer. She did not even fear him, or what he intended, which involved her fate. Her husband was dead. Her lover was dead. Her children were dead. Only vengeance was left to her. That she would die when Stalin died left her perfectly content. And for the time being, in her latest prison, she lived in as much comfort as ever before in her life. She only wished it would happen, soon.

"We must return, Comrade," called one of her guards. Sonia gathered her flowers into her basket, straightened, and walked back along the path. The guard moved closer. "Comrade Beria has come," he explained. "We saw the plane, some time ago."

Sonia had not noticed the plane. Presumably it was their business to notice such things. She was pleasantly excited. Whenever Beria came to Astrakhan, it promised something.

What an odd thing, to feel that an event which guaranteed her death should be exciting.

By the time they reached the garden, Beria was standing on the veranda. He wore the clothes of a country gentleman, which always looked incongruous on his huge, sloping-shouldered frame, and the sun was reflecting from his pince-nez. "Sonia!" he called. "You are looking well."

"Thank you, Comrade Commissar," she said, as she laid down her basket and took off her hat. "And so are you."

"And are you feeling well? Strong?"

Sonia caught her breath. "I am perfectly strong, Lavrenty Pavlovich."

"Good. I have a present for you. A surprise."

He gestured at the door into the house, and Sonia went through it, frowning. Her frown deepened as she gazed at the woman who stood at the back of the room. The woman was considerably younger than herself, she estimated, although her hair was entirely white – where once it had been golden? Her figure too, was emaciated; her clothes, poor and ill-fitting in any event, hung from her shoulders as if she were a scarecrow. But she was still tall, and once that figure would have been as voluptuous as any of her relations. But . . . Sonia looked at Beria.

Who was grinning, his great moon-face split in half by the two rows of big teeth. "Aren't you pleased? After all of these years?"

Sonia took a deep breath, and stepped forward. "Anna?" she asked. It was more than thirty years since she had last seen her daughter – Anna had then been not quite ten years old. They had been separated by the exigencies of the Revolution, and she had supposed Anna dead, murdered by Tatiana Gosykinya's father, Lenin's hit man, when he had also murdered Anna's brother – and *her* son – in Paris in 1923. Beria had told her Anna had actually survived that, and become a fervent Nazi, married to a German officer and even a friend of Hitler, her origins hidden beneath her golden hair and the Aryan features she had inherited from her princely, and mainly English, father;

the fact that she was the daughter of the erstwhile Prince of Bolugayen had apparently precluded any investigation into her background.

"Oh, they found her out in the end," Beria said. "And put her in one of those camps of theirs. But we got to her before they got around to eliminating her. Then she went to a displaced persons camp in Russia. It was there I tracked her down. Are you not pleased?"

Sonia's head was spinning. Could this creature really be her daughter? Yet she knew she was. But after so long, and so much, could they ever be mother and daughter again? Did they have the time, while she was under sentence of death. "Can she not speak?" she asked.

Anna Bolugayevska glanced at Beria, and received a quick nod. She licked her lips. "I can speak, Mother."

Sonia held out her arms, and Anna again looked at Beria who nodded, and the woman came forward to be embraced.

Sonia could feel the bones on her back beneath her fingers.

"Mother and daughter. What a happy sight," Beria said. "She needs care, and resuscitation. Ask for anything you wish for her, and you shall have it."

Anna would have stepped back, but Sonia continued to hold her close, while looking at Beria over her shoulder. Her mouth framed the word, why?

Beria continued to smile. "I knew you would be pleased," he said again.

"They're here." Joseph had been standing at the window, looking through the drapes. He was nervous. He knew Priscilla was a law unto herself, but in her determination to pursue her own agenda he sometimes felt that she defied logic.

"Then come and sit down," Priscilla said. "Not here . . ." She was on the settee. "Over there." The chair she indicated was on the other side of the room.

Joseph obeyed, sat down, adjusted his jacket; his revolver was in his side pocket. "I feel a complete fool," he said.

Priscilla gave him one of her bright smiles. "Hopefully we will

67

all have been wrong about him," she said. But she slipped her hand beneath the cushion beside her, just to make sure her own small automatic pistol was ready for use; Joseph knew that she was having the time of her life.

Rollo the butler appeared at the door. Rollo had been in Priscilla's employ for more than ten years, and allowed nothing to disturb the even tenor of either his face or his voice. "Prince Alexei and Mrs Bolugayevska are here, your highness," he said. He always addressed Priscilla by her Russian title. "With a . . ." he hesitated. "Gentleman." Rollo would need only a glance to have established that Gregory Asimov was not a gentleman.

"Show them in, please, Rollo," Priscilla said. "And you may pour the champagne."

Rollo gave his usual stiff bow, and opened wide the double doors to the drawing room. Elaine came in first, followed by Gregory, with Alexei bringing up the rear. Priscilla and Joseph both stood up, and moved forward. Elaine held her mother-in-law's hands. "Mother," she said formally. "How good to see you." They had actually seen each other yesterday.

"My dear." Priscilla drew her forward for an embrace.

"Mother!" Alexei was also embraced, while Gregory waited behind them, looking embarrassed. "This is Gregory Asimov," Alexei said.

"Your old comrade-in-arms from the Pripet," Priscilla said. "It is very good to see you, Mr Asimov. I have heard so much about you."

She extended her hand, and Gregory clicked his heels as he bowed and brushed her knuckles with his lips. Elaine and Alexei exchanged glances. The last thing they would have expected of the Gregory they had known in the Marshes was that he would kiss a woman's hand. "As I have heard so much about you, your excellency," Gregory said.

Priscilla smiled at him. "This is my husband, Joseph Cromb."

Gregory bowed again. "It is my great privilege, sir."

Joseph shook hands. Rollo appeared with the tray of champagne glasses. "What shall we drink to?" Priscilla asked.

"Ah . . . why not old comrades?" Gregory asked, smiling at Elaine.

"Oh, indeed, old comrades," Priscilla said. They drank.

"The memories we share," Gregory said.

"We are doing our best to forget them," Alexei said.

"I do not blame you, Alexei. And here in America you are privileged to do so. In Russia, things are very bad."

"Tell us about them," Priscilla invited, gesturing him to sit beside her on the settee.

"Is that why you wished to leave?" Joseph asked.

"A man must hope to make a better life for himself, your excellency. And when one looks around oneself, at the splendour in which it is possible to live, here in America . . . that man who served the drinks . . . ?"

"He is our butler," Priscilla explained.

"And he looks after all of this for you?"

"Oh, good lord, no. We have six other servants." Priscilla looked embarrassed. "But you do not have servants, in Russia?"

"Would that we had, your excellency. Seven servants! Here, all the time, serving you!"

Elaine frowned. His adulation was going over the top. But Priscilla, needless to say, was basking in it. "They are not here all the time," she said. "Two are on their afternoon off. This is a very democratic country. But do you know how many servants I employed, in Bolugayen?"

"Hundreds, I am sure," Gregory said. "So, seven servants." He grinned. "But no gardener."

"I'm afraid we do have a gardener," Priscilla said.

"Ah. Then you mean there is no job." He did not look particularly upset.

"I'm afraid not, at this moment. With us," Priscilla said. "However . . ." she paused, at the sound of fresh tyres on the gravel drive.

"Are you expecting other guests, Mother?" Alexei asked.

"No, I am not."

Elaine stood at the window. "It's that car I saw following us on the way here," she said. "I think they're FBI agents."

"Oh, dear," Priscilla said. "I hope there isn't going to be any unpleasantness." She looked at Gregory from beneath arched eyebrows.

Gregory grinned. "No unpleasantness, Princess," he promised. And moved with startling speed, hurling his champagne glass at Alexei, and in the same movement drawing a pistol from inside his coat.

Chapter Four

The Wound

The flying glass struck Alexei on the side of his head; he had turned away to look at the window. He staggered and sat down. In the same instant Gregory had drawn a pistol from inside his jacket. This he now levelled as Joseph reached for his own gun, only to go tumbling over a chair and hit the floor with a crash as Gregory's bullet slammed into him.

Elaine screamed, and instinctively reacted to her years of warfare in the Pripet by dropping to the floor. Priscilla gasped and sat down, thrusting her hand beneath the pillow in search of her pistol, and Gregory hit her on the side of the head with his free hand. She gave a little shriek and fell right out of the settee to sprawl on the floor. Gregory reached down, twined his fingers in her bodice, and jerked her to her feet: she gaped at him in consternation, like everyone else utterly taken aback by the power and ruthlessness of his sudden action.

From the front hall there came a crash, followed by a shout from Rollo, and then another sharp crack. "Help me!" Priscilla shouted at her son, as Gregory dragged her towards the door.

Alexei shook his head uncertainly as he sat up. His cheek was cut where the glass had shattered, and his collar was soaked with a mixture of champagne and blood. He reached for his hip pocket, and Gregory shot him. Alexei half turned and slumped over the chair again. "Alex!" Elaine shrieked, rising to her knees and throwing both arms round her husband.

"Bastard!" Priscilla shouted, trying to pull herself free, and failing, scraping her nails down Gregory's face, drawing blood. Gregory threw her away from him with tremendous violence. She staggered across the room and crashed into an ornamental table, falling with it to the floor.

The drawing-room doors opened to admit three men. "Hurry," Gregory said, in Russian. "There are servants."

Two of the men grasped Priscilla's arms and lifted her from the floor. Another held a wet cloth to her face, and the room became filled with the odour of chloroform. Priscilla subsided into their arms.

Alexei moaned, and tried to move, and then slumped again.

"You've killed him!" Elaine screamed. "You filthy bastard!" Her eyes widened as Gregory levelled his gun. For a moment they stared at each other, as his finger tightened on the trigger. Then he suddenly stepped forward and struck her across the head. Instantly unconscious, she collapsed in a heap on the floor. One of the other men levelled his pistol at her inert body. "No," Gregory said. The Russian raised his eyebrows. "She was a good comrade," Gregory said.

"Who will be able to identify you."

"Who will never see me again," Gregory said. "Let us get out of here."

Rollo's dead body lay in the doorway. There was so sign of any of the other servants, who remained totally unaware that anything untoward had happened in the front of the house. It was simply a matter of carrying Priscilla's body to the car. Priscilla was a slender, light woman; Gregory lifted her with one arm round her waist, her head resting on her shoulder. The other men got into the car, which had waited with its engine running. They pulled out of the drive and onto the freeway, drove for a quarter of a mile, and pulled off again. Down a quiet lane another car was waiting for them, a man behind the wheel. They left the original car and got into the new one, Priscilla bundled between them, her clothes dishevelled, her hair drifting down in golden wisps over her face; even beneath the hair the bruise on the side of her head where Gregory had struck her was clearly visible. Gregory sat at one end of the seat; the woman was stretched across the laps of the three men in the back. "She is very beautiful," one of the men said. Priscilla's back rested on his knee.

"Once she was the most beautiful woman in Russia," the other man pointed out. Priscilla's legs were on his lap. One of her shoes had come off and been left at the house. Now he took off the other to stroke her stockinged instep.

"I would say she is still the most beautiful woman in Russia," said the man in the middle.

Gregory said nothing, but he gently brushed some of the hair from Priscilla's face. Her breathing was less heavy now; soon she would be waking up. "What is to happen to her?" asked the man at her legs.

"I think she is to be executed," Gregory said.

"But we were told not to kill her, to deliver her alive and unharmed. That must mean she is to be interrogated, first."

"Yes," Gregory said, watching Priscilla's eyebrows flutter.

"She needs some more chloroform," the man in the middle said. Gregory soaked the cloth again, and held it over Priscilla's face. She sighed, and went back into a deep sleep.

"If she is going to be interrogated," the man with her legs said, "then she will soon cease to be beautiful. And as we have her here, comrades . . ." he pushed Priscilla's skirt up to her knees, and then slipped his hand beneath it.

"Yes," said the man in the middle, resting his hand on Priscilla's breast.

"No," Gregory snapped. They both looked at him in surprise. "She is not to be assaulted," Gregory said.

"You have orders about this?" asked the man in the middle, still holding Priscilla's breast.

"I have orders that she is to be delivered to Comrade Beria, unharmed," Gregory said.

"Playing with her a little will not harm her," the man with Priscilla's legs pointed out. He grinned. "Especially as she is unconscious. I have never seen a naked princess."

"Comrade Beria will know if she has been molested," Gregory

insisted. The other two men exchanged glances. But neither was prepared to get on the wrong side of Comrade Beria.

The car was slowing, where yet another car waited for them on a quiet street. This was a limousine. They stopped alongside it, and transferred Priscilla, laying her on the middle seat. Another man waited, sitting in the very back of the limo. "Did it go well?" he asked. He was short and squat and heavily built. His name was Shatrav, and like Gregory, he had served under Tatiana Gosykinya in the Pripet. But he was much older than either Gregory or his erstwhile commander, a professional soldier who had been one of many who had fled the Germans at the beginning of the War and been brought back to their duty by the commissars. He was not a man who had ever loved, or even liked, anyone. His only emotion was hate. Even of his comrades.

The Russians had all got into the limo, and it was moving away, leaving the getaway car parked beside the road.

"All went well," Gregory said.

"The others are all dead?"

"Ah . . . so far as we know."

"He is lying," said the man who had held Priscilla's legs. "He did not kill the young woman."

"Why did you not do that, Comrade Asimov?" asked Shatrav.

"He said because she was an old comrade, from the Pripet," said the man who had held Priscilla's breast.

"That was foolish of you," Shatrav said. "She will be able to identify you. Did she see any of you others?"

"Only for a few seconds."

"You must remember Dr Mitchell, Shatrav," Gregory said. "She was a good comrade. Did she not take that bullet out of your body, in the Pripet. I did not like having to kill her husband. But she . . . she has never harmed anybody. She is a doctor. She cared for us, in the Pripet."

"And you have become soft, since the Pripet," Shatrav said. "Softness can lead to serious consequences." He drew an automatic pistol from inside his jacket.

Gregory sat up straight. "Are you mad, comrade? I was given this mission by Comrade Kagan himself."

Shatrav gave a thin smile. "So was I, comrade." He squeezed the trigger, twice.

Memory was a haze of pain and confusion. Elaine couldn't be sure what was real and what was her tortured imagination. She sat up, violently, and screamed as there was hasty movement all around her. But then she was being gently eased back to lie down. On a bed. She blinked at the faces and the white uniforms. A hospital bed! She was wearing a hospital bedgown. "You're going to be all right, Mrs Bolugayevski," the sister said. "But you need to rest."

"Am I hurt?" Elaine asked.

"There's a nasty bruise. But you're all shaken up."

"How . . ." Elaine turned her head to and fro. "I need the police."

"They're waiting to speak with you, whenever you feel up to it."

"Now," Elaine said. "I want to speak with them, now."

The sister considered. Then nodded. "Okay. If you really feel all right." She nodded to one of the nurses.

Elaine caught her arm, as memory started to flood back. "My husband!"

"He's in surgery, Mrs Bolugayevski."

"But . . . surgery! You mean he's not dead?" Her last memory of Alexei was of him slumped across the chair, totally inert.

"He's badly hurt."

"Will he be all right?"

"We think so, Mrs Bolugayevski."

Elaine clutched her stomach as she thought she felt movement. "Am I going to lose my baby?"

"Your baby's fine, Mrs Bolugayevski. Here's Lieutenant di Salvo."

The detective was short and slight and dark. "How do you feel, Mrs Bolugayevski?"

"How do I look?"

He grinned. "Like a woman who's taken a beating." He pulled up a chair, sat beside the bed.

"What happened?"

"Some thugs broke into your mother-in-law's house, shot the place up, and snatched Mrs Cromb."

"Joseph . . . my father-in-law . . ."

Di Salvo sighed. "I'm afraid he's badly wounded, Mrs Bolugayevski. It's touch and go."

"Oh, my God!" Joseph had always seemed indestructible.

"And your husband is having a bullet taken from his gut now. They say he'll be all right. Your butler is dead. Now you . . . they only whacked you across the head. You came to long enough to call for help, get the rest of your mother-in-law's servants in from the back of the house. Then you passed out again. So here we are."

Elaine licked her lips, as full memory returned. Gregory! And she had introduced him into Priscilla's house. With such terrible consequences! "Gregory!" she muttered.

"Come again?"

"Priscilla," she said. "My mother-in-law. What's happened to her?"

"I would say she's been snatched, like I said. We haven't had a demand, yet, but it's early days. Mrs Cromb was a pretty wealthy woman, right?"

"Well . . . I suppose so. But . . . not so wealthy to be worth several lives."

"Mrs Bolugayevski, there are people who will kill for a dime. Now let me ask you a question that's been bothering me. These people bust into your mother-in-law's house. They shoot her butler, they shoot her husband, they shoot her son. But they don't shoot you. You reckon they were gentlemen in disguise?"

His sarcasm rankled. "They didn't shoot me, Lieutenant, because they weren't ordinary kidnappers."

"You'd better explain that."

"They were Russian agents. Their leader was a man my husband and I had known in Russia during the War. That's why he didn't shoot me. We had been comrades in arms. We had fought shoulder to shoulder against the Nazis. He just couldn't do it."

"But he could shoot your husband."

Elaine drove her hands into her hair, and winced. "God, I don't know. That's the only explanation I can think of."

76

"Russian agents," Di Salvo said, sceptically.

"Didn't you know we're a family of Russian emigres? My husband's family, anyway."

"Lady, you got any idea how many families of Russian emigres there are living in this country today? I never heard of any of them being attacked by Russian agents. Russian agents!" He got up. "We'll talk again later. Maybe by then we'll have had a demand."

"There isn't going to *be* a demand," Elaine shouted, and winced again. "Listen, Lieutenant." Di Salvo had reached the door, but he checked, and turned. "Your idea is that the Princess has been kidnapped," Elaine said. "Right? You say she was kidnapped for ransom. Right? Now you tell me who's going to pay this ransom? She's the one with the money. What are they going to do, make her write them a cheque?" Di Salvo frowned. "There is only one person in the world, other than Priscilla herself," Elaine went on, "who has access to her money. Her husband, Joseph. So they shoot him and leave him for dead? Does that make any logical sense to you?"

Di Salva scratched his head. Then his expression brightened. "Her brother is President of Cromb Shipping Lines. Now he *is* loaded. And she is his only sister."

"Jim Cromb also has a wife and three children," Elaine snapped. "Wouldn't it have made more sense to snatch one of them, if it's his money they're after?"

"We'll talk later," Di Salvo decided again, clearly needing to think about the situation. "After we've had the ransom note."

"God!" Elaine shouted, nearly mad with desperation.

The door opened, and sister looked in to make sure she was all right. But with sister there was another man, who also had detective written all over him. He began whispering to Di Salvo, whose eyebrows went up and down like yoyos. "You okay, Mrs Bolugayevski?" sister asked.

"I'm fine. How is my husband doing?"

"He's going to be all right. The operation was successful."

"Thank God! Now, if I could just make this moron listen to me . . ."

Di Salvo had returned to stand beside the bed. "What do you

know?" he asked. "The guys have found a body. So what's new? This guy, they reckon, was shot twice and then thrown from a moving vehicle. They've also found the first two getaway automobiles used by the kidnappers, and this body is in the general direction those cars were heading. Could be nothing, could be support for your idea of what happened, Mrs Bolugayevski. So any time you reckon you can come down and have a look at this stiff, see if you recognise him, it might be a help."

"How do you feel?" the woman asked. Priscilla had actually been awake for some time. But she had lain still, trying to come to terms with her situation. And her feelings. She felt so sick she thought she might be about to vomit. She also had a frightful headache, and she wasn't sure where her arms and legs were. As for where *she* was . . . there was movement and noise all around her. She was either on an aircraft or on a ship. She rather thought it was a ship, because the sound of the engines was remote. But then, she might have gone a little deaf.

When she had woken up she had been in a box. At first she had thought it was a coffin, had for the first time in her eventful life actually known terror. She had faced death on more than one occasion, but the thought of being buried alive . . . Then she had realised she was in a truck, and that she was being transported, somewhere. The air was relatively clean inside the box, so there had to be some ventilation, but when she attempted to move she couldn't; like her mouth, her arms and legs were taped together, at ankle and knee and thigh – under her dress – and wrist and elbow and shoulder, and then her entire body had been taped, again at ankle and thigh, round her waist and breasts and even forehead, to various projections inside the trunk itself. It was impossible for her to move anything save her fingers, toes and eyelashes.

And her head had been opening and shutting with a succession of blows, which almost made the other discomforts, the awareness that she must have been manhandled in every possible way, seem irrelevant. The muzzy feeling might have been caused by that, but as there was also some soreness in her right arm she reckoned she had been injected with some drug which had kept her unconscious for a good while, while she could still taste the chloroform that had first been used to subdue her. The claustrophobic feeling of being so enclosed and so helpless had all but overwhelmed her.

But she was alive, and whoever had snatched her from her home was interested in keeping her alive, that was obvious. Priscilla had been in sufficient traumatic situations in her life to be able to cope with this one. She had to be patient, and wait, and watch, and silently suffer . . . until she could act. She had spent her time trying to remember. And experienced a growing sense of horror. A man called Gregory Asimov!

Asimov had been brought into her house by Alexei and Elaine. He had pretended that he was looking for work . . . then he had suddenly attacked them. She had been warned to expect that might happen, and she and Joseph had been armed, but the suddenness and ferocity of the attack had taken them by surprise, and Joseph . . . Joseph had been shot! He might be dead! And Alexei! She didn't know what had happened to Alexei; Asimov had hit her when she had tried to defend Joseph. Asimov!

The true horror of the situation rose up in a cloud around her mind. Joseph! The only man she had ever truly loved. The man she had travelled half round the world to rescue and restore to health.

Desperately she had tugged against the tapes before collapsing in exhaustion. Meanwhile, movement. She had been unloaded from the vehicle in which she had been travelling, and then loaded again, into whichever vehicle she now was. She had heard various muted sounds, men talking, speaking English, then others, speaking Russian. They were very efficiently removing her from the world. For their own purposes. But Asimov had been Russian. She had been kidnapped by the secret police. By Stalin!

That was the thought that had made her feel physically sick. She had been Stalin's prisoner once before, and had survived. Because he had been unable to have sex with her! She had actually supposed she was going to be executed after his humiliation. Instead he had expelled her from Russia. But now . . . why should he want her back again, now? He could hardly have regained his sexual

79

potency! Did anyone know what really went on inside the mind of a mad dictator?

Just as few people believed the truth of what went on behind the closed doors of his secret prisons. Joseph had known. Now she was going to find out. But at last the lid had been raised. Blessed light, and more air. And the tape had been taken from her mouth, leaving her feeling that she had been slapped, hard. Yet it was such a relief. Not that she cared for the face looking at her. It was as hard as granite, and although it was smiling, it was a cold smile. "I asked you a question, Princess."

"I feel like shit," Priscilla muttered. She had every intention of meeting them on their own ground until they tore the tongue from her mouth.

The woman snapped her fingers, and two other women loomed over the trunk. They pulled the tapes away from her arms and legs, throwing up her dress to tear the tape away from her thighs, ripping her stockings as they did so. As she was utterly in their power, that did not seem important besides the other things they might soon be tearing. "Can you sit up?" a man asked.

Slowly and painfully Priscilla pushed and pulled herself into a sitting position. She scraped hair from her face and looked around her. She was definitely in the cabin of a ship. Which had not yet put to sea. Therefore all things were possible. "Please do not get any stupid ideas about screaming," the man advised. "This cabin is sound-proofed. It is a special cabin, reserved for the use of me and my people."

Priscilla tried to lick her lips and found that she could not. The man smiled at her, almost sympathetically. "You must be very dry. Valya, water, and then brandy."

A glass of water was held to her lips. Priscilla drank greedily. Then there was a glass of brandy. She shook her head, but the glass remained in front of her, and the man leaned forward. "Drink it," he said. "Or we will make you. You must learn to obey us."

Priscilla drank the brandy; she didn't want to encourage them to touch her more than they had to. As if anything she did would stop them touching her, when and where they chose! "Good," the man said. "I like women who behave themselves. My name is Kagan, Princess." He waited, as if supposing she might have heard of him. But she hadn't.

"Do you think you can get away with this?" she asked in a low voice. "You will never be allowed to leave the country."

"But we are leaving now," Kagan said. "Listen." Priscilla listened to the wail of a siren, even as the noise beneath her feet began to grow in intensity. "Long before the police get around to thinking about which ships or planes might have left the country with you on board," Kagan went on, "we shall be beyond the twelve-mile limit."

"They'll still come after you," Priscilla said.

"You think so? I do not think they will. For one thing, this is not a Russian ship. It happens to belong to a country, and a shipping line, which is sympathetic to us, certainly, but the United States coastguard would have to be very sure you were on board before they would dare risk stopping us at sea in international waters. And additionally, you see, you are not important enough to anyone in America even to create an international incident."

Priscilla glared at him. "If I am not important enough, why have I been kidnapped?"

"Because you are important to us. The Americans do not know who you really are. To them you are merely an effete aristocrat who persists in dabbling in matters that should no longer concern her. Do you know . . ." he grinned. "I imagine there will be members of the State Department who will be happy to see the back of you, considering the chaos you have caused over the past forty years. Get out of that box."

Priscilla glanced right and left at the women standing to either side of her. She presumed they were waiting to assist her if she hesitated. She grasped the sides of the trunk and pushed herself up, stepped out. Her legs were trembling in any event – her shoes had come off or been taken off – and as she attempted to stand the ship moved away from the dock to the accompaniment of whistles and changes in pitch from the propellers. Priscilla gave a little gasp as she fell, but she was caught by Kagan, who sat her on the bunk beside him. "You will get used to the motion," he assured her.

Priscilla panted. "Why am I important to you?" she asked. "What am I supposed to have done?"

"Now that I cannot say. You are important to my superiors. That is all that matters."

He signalled his assistants, and another glass of brandy was produced. This Priscilla drank without hesitation. Perhaps it would end the nightmare. "Will you tell me what has happened to my husband?"

"Your husband is dead." Priscilla gasped, and nearly choked. "He was shot by Gregory Asimov. You remember Asimov?"

Priscilla stared at him, trying to get her thoughts together. Joseph was dead, dead, dead. Her Joseph. Murdered by that thug . . . who was in the employ of this thug. But there was so much else. "My son?"

"Prince Bolugayevski is also dead," Kagan said.

Her entire family! Gone.

"Asimov shot him too," Kagan said. "But for some reason he did not kill your son's wife. That was very remiss of him. Who would have supposed that Asimov might have a soft spot for a woman, merely because they had once fought side-by-side? No doubt they slept side-by-side as well. But that is no excuse for dereliction of duty. Valya, I think the Princess could do with some more brandy."

What am I to do? Priscilla wondered. I should be dead myself. What have I got to live for if Joseph and Alexei are both dead? But of course, she was going to die anyway. When they were finished with her. She drank the third goblet of brandy. Perhaps she could stay in a stupefied alcoholic state until the gun muzzle was placed on the nape of her neck. But that had to be a dream.

"Obviously this news is upsetting to you," Kagan suggested. He seemed to have a perverted sense of humour. "But if it is any consolation to you, Asimov is now also dead. He was executed by his commanding officer. For dereliction of duty."

"And human life is that cheap, to you," Priscilla muttered.

Kagan shrugged. "Life is cheap, everywhere. There is too much of it." He grinned at her. "Except where it needs to be preserved, for a special purpose. As are you. Now listen to me, Princess. This voyage will take us ten days, to Leningrad. For that time you will remain in this cabin. I'm afraid I have no change of clothing for you, but through there is a bathroom, and you may wash your clothes as you wish. Or you may take them off. I shall not mind. I might even enjoy that. What I really wish you to understand is this. As I have said, you will remain in this cabin. I am sorry about the lack of opportunity for exercise, but it is only for ten days. I am sure there will be ample opportunities for exercise when we reach Russia, and if you really do feel the lack of it, you can practice running on the spot, or something like that. However, I should tell you that two of my girls will be in here with you for every minute of the voyage, and therefore you must behave yourself, and not attempt to resist us or make yourself a nuisance. If you behave yourself, you will be well fed and given as much to drink as you wish. If you make a nuisance of yourself, you will be punished. Do you understand me?"

Priscilla continued to gaze at him. I am the Dowager Princess of Bolugayen, she thought. Time was I had a hundred servants waiting on my every wish. Those days were gone, she knew, but she was still a millionairess. She spent her time moving from her various luxury homes to various luxury hotels. She had a maid to lay out her clothes and brush her golden hair. And she had several wardrobes full of clothes scattered around the world. Could she really be reduced to some kind of slave, possessing but a single dress, threatened with physical violence? She supposed that she had done some things during her life that might not be approved by everyone, but she had surely never committed such a crime as to deserve this. Unless being the Princess of Bolugayen was so considered a crime by these people. But that was the one certain fact that she must never let herself forget. No matter what happened, these people had once been her serfs. She must die making them remember that.

The ship was trembling now, as it gathered speed, and rolling slightly in the swell. The three glasses of brandy added to the movement which caused Priscilla to stagger, and she might have fallen had the woman Valya not caught her arm. Kagan patted the space beside him. "Come and sit down, your highness, and let us get to know one another better."

Before Priscilla could attempt to resist, Valya had pushed her onto the bunk beside her commander. Kagan put an arm round her shoulders. "You see," he said. "I am the one who is going to be here most of the time. This will be your berth, and I will sleep over there." He pointed to the other bunk. "I should think that in ten days of such intimacy, you and I will be very old friends by the time we reach Leningrad." He rested his other hand on her thigh, began sliding the dress up from her knee. "I think you should take this off now, or it might get crushed." Priscilla threw her resolutions out of the window, and spat in his face.

"So there, you see," Tatiana said. "There is really nothing to see. At least from up here." She had parked the hired car at the top of a rise, looking down into the valley beneath. Andrew was still in a state of continuing amazement. Travelling with an Intourist courier had quite altered his concept of what Russia might be like. Tatiana, it appeared, had but to whisper in someone's ear, and whatever she wanted had immediately been forthcoming.

They had travelled south from Moscow to Poltava in a first-class compartment, and in Poltava there had been this hired car waiting for them. Andrew had not been aware that it was possible to hire a car in Russia. Or that Tatiana could drive a car as well as she did everything else.

And in addition to those magical properties, she remained the most fervent, uninhibited, exhausting lover he had ever known. If all Russian women were like Tatiana in bed, he thought he had discovered the answer to the conundrum that puzzled so many Western observers: how the Russians had so meekly and for so long put up with tyrannical overlords, whether Tsarist or Communist – all they ever really wanted to do was get home to bed! His persistent euphoria at being in her company had aroused considerable feelings of guilt. He had not, he felt, paid sufficient attention to the country through which he was passing, and which was the vital background to his book.

In fact, the country had been in the main as boring as the

people, and while he had made copious notes of the various pieces of information Tatiana had offered him, when she was talking of Russia she was as boring as anyone. Even Poltava had been boring, and, being a student of Russian history, he had been anticipating seeing the site of the famous battle, probably the most important battlefield in all Russia, not excluding Stalingrad. Here on the banks of the Vorksla, in 1707, Charles XII of Sweden, probably the greatest *fighting* general the world had ever known, and Peter the Great, the Tsar who had created modern Russia, had come face to face.

Not for the first time. For the preceding ten years Charles had dominated Eastern Europe, so feared by his enemies that he had captured cities by walking up to their gates and tapping the wood with his cane, so much a natural genius at the art of warfare that he had repeatedly destroyed armies five and six times the size of his own. At Narva in 1700, with 8,000 men, he had put 40,000 Russians to flight, and at the head of the running Russians had been their Tsar. Outside Poltava, seven years later, the odds had been smaller, 20,000 Swedes against 60,000 Russians, and no sooner had the Swedish assault begun than Peter's staff had with difficulty restrained their master from again fleeing the field. Had Charles gained another of his habitual victories, Russia would have relapsed back into barbarism, unable to become a threat to the rest of Europe, much less the rest of the world, for another several hundred years.

But at Poltava, Charles had been wounded, the Swedish onslaught had for the first time in history faltered, Peter had recovered his nerve, and it was the Swedish army that had been destroyed. Charles had escaped the field, and continued his berserking ways for another eleven years. That was neither here nor there. The power of Sweden had been broken – forever, as it turned out – and the power of Russia had been launched, on its way not only to the conquest of half Asia, but into the centre of European affairs, for the next three centuries. And now into the centre of the world.

But there had been more traumatic events in this neighbourhood since then. "Can we go closer?" he asked.

"Of course." Tatiana engaged gear, and the automobile moved down the hillside. To their left now was the village of the cooperative; a single tractor droned in the field, groups of women followed it, sewing the corn.

"Is there only one tractor?" Morgan asked.

Tatiana raised her eyebrows. "It is only one cooperative. We do not have tractors to spare. It is only a few thousand acres, you know." Morgan made no reply, as the car bumped its way over the uneven surface to the foot of the hill. "My father created this," Tatiana said, dreamily. Morgan turned his head, sharply. "Of course, to persuade the kulaks . . . you know this term?"

Morgan was also well read in as much recent Russian history as he had been able to unearth. "It was the word used for wealthy peasants," he suggested.

"The kulaks were fat cats who grew rich while those around them grew poor," Tatiana said vehemently. "As I say, it was necessary to persuade them to hand over their ill-gotten wealth and join the cooperatives. This cost a few lives."

"I have heard the figure put as high as ten million," Morgan murmured.

Tatiana glanced at him. "Well . . . their families had to be disposed of as well."

"Is that how you look at it?"

"My father did what was necessary."

And was shot for it, Morgan thought. But he didn't say it. It was certainly not part of his plan to quarrel with this gorgeous creature, whatever her antecedents. It was at least part of her antecedents that had drawn him to this spot.

The car was stopping before a field of very green grass, in some contrast to the corn that was sprouting all around them. "Don't tell me this is hallowed ground," he said.

"Not in the sense you speak of," Tatiana said. "But it has been preserved as being historically important. You must know that the Bolugayevskis were the premier princely family in all Russia, short of royalty."

"This was your family," Morgan ventured.

"Yes," Tatiana agreed, unselfconsciously. "My grandmother's

brother, and her parents. Well, this was where the family was finally destroyed."

"But not entirely. You are here. And you have cousins in America, have you not?"

"They were destroyed as a princely force," Tatiana said. She got out of the car, and Morgan followed her to the edge of the grass. "The gates would have been about here. This is where my grandmother was crucified."

"You can speak of it, as calmly as that?"

Tatiana shrugged. "She was an enemy of the State." She led the way across the grass. "The drive curved, towards the house." Morgan could see that the grass was discoloured in a vast swathe. "And then, the house." Here the discoloration was more extreme, in a vast square. "It was a big house," Tatiana said. "There are no houses like it in Russia any more, except for the museums. The Red forces broke down the front door and took the house by storm." She walked a few feet further, on to the deep discoloration. "There were steps, of course. Say about here. I believe your father was defending the front doors, when they were forced. So, he would have been standing about here. This is where he would have died."

"Do you know what happened to his body?"

"I think it was left where it lay. When the Red soldiers broke in, they were after the women." She made a moue. "And destruction, to be sure. They were not interested in dead bodies. When they had had the women, they killed those they did not wish to keep, and took the others to the village. Those included both the princesses. You say you have met the Princess Priscilla." Morgan nodded. "And she is still beautiful? After living as a sexual slave for a year? That is remarkable. Anyway, after they took the women, they burned the house, with all the bodies still inside. I do not think they moved any of them."

"So my father's bones could be exactly underneath where you are standing."

"Perhaps. But it is unlikely. When it was decided to turn Bolugayen into a collective, while the decision was taken then not to sow on the site of the house, the area was still bulldozed and turned over, to a depth of several feet, in order to plant the grass. I imagine what bones are down there are no more than splinters, now. If you dug them up, you would have no means of knowing whether they belonged to your father." She glanced at him. "Does this distress you?"

Morgan shook his head. "My father's bones have long mouldered into dust. They would have done so even had he been buried with full military honours and a huge stone erected over his grave. This grass is as good a monument as any."

Tatiana linked her arm through his. "But nonetheless, you are sad. Let us go back to the hotel in Poltava, have a good dinner, get drunk on vodka, and then make wild, passionate love all night. Would you like that?"

"Yes, I would." He held her hand. "Do you really love me, Tatiana?"

A shadow crossed her face. "You are a man with whom it is easy to fall in love."

"Well, then . . . I have really seen all there is to see, have I not? I should be returning to England. Will you come with me?"

"To England?"

"I mean, as my wife. I would obtain British nationality for you. You would be the mother of my children." A woman who could speak of people being 'disposed of', as if they were sacks of garbage. But that was her upbringing, he was certain. He would wean her away from such attitudes. "And we would be very happy."

The shadow, which had faded, returned. "You make it sound very attractive. But I cannot do that."

"Why not?"

"Well . . . my mother, for one thing."

"We could take her with us. For Heaven's sake, she is English, herself."

"Mother would never leave Russia. This is her home. As it is my home." She kissed him. "Do not let us think of the future, tonight, my Andrew. We are going to make love." She led him back to the waiting car. "And then," she said, as she started the engine. "We will think of something to do, tomorrow. I know what we shall do.

88

Did you know that there is an atomic research plant, not far from Poltava?" She glanced at him. "You know about this atom."

"You mean the Bomb? I know about it. Everyone knows about it. But I did not know you were trying to make one, in Russia."

She giggled as she turned the car to drive back up the hill. "Do you not think we should? If America has the Bomb, should not Russia have it also?"

"I hadn't really considered that. Yes, I suppose you're right. It would be a great temptation to ride roughshod over the rest of the world if you were the only country with such power."

"So, you see, we need to make a bomb of our own," Tatiana said. "Thus there is a great deal of research going on, and as I say, one of these research centres is not far from here. Would you like to visit it?"

"You mean, we can? In America, and in England, such establishments are top secret."

"Oh, this is top secret too. But I have a cousin who works there. He would be able to get us inside for a visit. I know this." She gave him another glance. "Would you like to do this?"

"Why . . . yes. I think it might be interesting."

"Ah!" Tatiana commented.

The nights were so bright, in Moscow, in the spring. Soon it would hardly be dark at all. This made surreptitious movement very difficult, Smith considered.

He had had to wait until nearly midnight before he had ventured from his hotel, and that was risky. There were not many people about, in Moscow, at midnight; the Muscovites believed in the good life, in so far as they could – if there was not sufficient good food, and if there were no consumer goods available, there were unlimited supplies of vodka, and they did not need state permission to play music and dance. They danced, and drank themselves insensible, every night. But they did these things early. The hotel restaurant was packed every afternoon, from four until about seven. Then everyone went home. Or was carried home. And Moscow settled for the night. Thus people who were abroad a few hours later were necessarily suspicious; there was a large black market in Moscow, as well as considerable organised crime. But Smith was an expert, and he had gained this apartment block without being stopped by a single policeman.

He opened the door, sidled into the hall, closed the door behind him, waited. These apartment buildings had paper-thin walls, and any movement was likely to disturb a light sleeper. But there was no sound. He climbed the stairs, slowly and carefully; a creaking floorboard could be equally disastrous. But by sticking against the bannister, he made his way up three floors without a sound. Then he could lean against the door as he drew his knuckles across the panel, once, twice, three times.

One of them, he knew, was always awake, and in the front room; the apartment only had two rooms. Thus within seconds he heard movement, and then the latch was drawn. Smith could see the gleam of the automatic pistol even in the darkness. "I sell typewriters," he whispered.

The gun muzzle ceased to be aimed at his chest, and the door swung in. The man stepped aside to allow him to enter, and then closed the door again. In the darkness Smith could not see him very well, but he knew who he was. "We expected you before this," the man said.

"Getting about isn't easy," Smith said. "When I saw Antonina I gave her a query."

"It has been answered." The man switched on a night light, above the desk, sat down, riffled through some papers. He was a surprisingly young man. This always disturbed Smith, the youth of the people with whom he had to deal. But perhaps only the young were prepared to take such risks. The man selected a sheet of paper. "It reads: 'Andrew Morgan is journalist. Has links with Bolugayevski family. Visit probably Bolugayevski business.'" The man raised his head. "Is that good for you?"

"It pays to be careful," Smith said. "Now, I need to send a message."

"Do you realise how dangerous it is, every time we send a message?" the man asked.

"This is a dangerous business," Smith said. "And are you not well paid?"

"If we can ever get to the money," the man grumbled. "Give me your message."

Smith handed him a sheet of paper, and he frowned at it. "They will understand this?"

"It is in code," Smith said. "They will decipher it."

"Very well. I will bid you goodnight, Comrade."

"When will it go?"

"As soon as we are sure it is safe. Within twenty-four hours."

Smith knew he would have to be satisfied with that. "Then I will bid you goodnight."

The man nodded in assent. Clearly he wanted to see the back of him. But as Smith turned to the door, the landing outside creaked. He looked back at the man. His face was the picture of dismay, as he drew his revolver. "Kill yourself," he said.

Smith stared at him in consternation; he had been in this business for some years, but he had never been faced with such a stark proposition. There was a crash, and the door thudded open, almost ripped from its hinges before the impact of the two burly shoulders hurled against it.

There was an explosion. Smith had turned to the door, now he looked back at the man, this time in horror. He had placed the muzzle of the revolver in his mouth and squeezed the trigger; his head had disintegrated into blood and brains and shattered bone as he fell from the chair. The inner door opened and a woman stood there. She was younger than her husband, her light brown hair tousled and untidy, her eyes heavy with sleep, but widening in horror at what she saw. She was a pretty woman, with a full, plump figure. But there was no beauty it her face at that moment. Smith turned back again, looked into two gun muzzles.

Morgan rolled, luxuriously, as he awoke. The woman was still in his arms, as she had been in his arms most of the night, warm and sexual. Then what had awakened him?

It had been a tap on the door. Now it came again, and this time it awoke Tatiana. "Tell him to go away," Andrew suggested, looking at his watch. "It is only six."

"It may be important." She switched on the light, rolled out of bed, pulled on her dressing gown. She went to the door, unlocked it. Andrew listened to a mumbled conversation. "It is a telephone call, for me," Tatiana said. "I will not be long." There was no telephone in the room.

Andrew sat up. "Who on earth would be ringing you at this hour?"

"Probably my mother," she said, and left the room.

Andrew scratched his head. If Jennie Ligachevna had started worrying about her daughter's habits at this odd time . . . he lay back with a sigh. He did not suppose he had ever spent a happier fortnight. When he remembered with what apprehensions he had begun his project – it had been a great adventure but he had anticipated nothing but obstruction and difficulty, even from Jennie herself, and despite the Princess Priscilla's letter. Instead he had met with nothing but cooperation and friendship . . . and love. The most remarkable love he could ever have envisaged. He inhaled her scent as he rolled over, waiting for her return. He heard the door open, and rolled onto his back again. Tatiana closed the door behind herself, went to the wardrobe, and took out her clothes. "Going some place?" he asked, lazily.

"We must leave."

"At this hour?"

"Yes." She was dressing herself rapidly. Andrew frowned. This was quite unlike her. Her day had always begun with a bath and a leisurely cup of tea. "Get dressed," she said.

"Surely we have time for a bath?"

"There is no time," Tatiana said. "If you do not get dressed, you will regret it."

Andrew threw back the covers. "I don't understand. What's happened? Was that your mother? Is there something wrong?"

"Yes," she said. "Will you please get dressed." Andrew went to the bathroom, checked as he heard the door open again. He turned, gazed at two men who had suddenly appeared there. He didn't like the look of them. "I asked you to get dressed," Tatiana said. "Give him time," she told the men.

"There is no time, Comrade Gosykinya," one of the men replied.

"He is not armed," Tatiana said, as the men came into the room.

"That makes it easier for us," the first man said, seizing Andrew by the shoulder and half throwing him across the room.

Andrew, taken entirely by surprise, landed on his hands and knees. His reaction was entirely outrage and anger, that he should have been so treated, and in front of his mistress. He made to get up, fists doubled, and was struck a paralysing blow in the back which stretched him on the floor. Only half conscious, he looked at Tatiana's boots. "I am most terribly sorry about this," Tatiana said, and kicked him in the ribs.

Part Two

The Pit

He that diggeth a pit shall fall into it.

Ecclesiastes x. 8.

Chapter Five

The Question

Andrew Morgan stared at Tatiana in total consternation. "Is this some kind of a joke?" he asked.

"Get dressed," Tatiana said again. "Or my men will take you out of here, naked."

Andrew licked his lips; he had never seen her looking like this, her face like flint, and her eyes too. She meant what she was saying. He pulled on his clothes, trying to ignore the pain where he had been kicked, watched by the three people. "Am I allowed to ask what this is about?" he ventured.

"You are being arrested for espionage against the Soviet Union," Tatiana said.

"Espionage? What espionage? You have been with me every moment of my time in Russia, just about, Tattie. You know I am guilty of nothing except loving you." Had he made an impression? Had her face softened at all? Before he could decide that, one of the men stepped forward and hit him in the stomach. Andrew gasped, and fell to his knees. Then the man kicked him, again in the stomach. Andrew struck the floor with a crash, his brain and his nerves paralysed by the sudden tremendous pain. He saw boots beside his head, and tried to tense himself for the next kick, then realised these boots belonged to Tatiana. Did that make any difference, he wondered? She had already kicked him once.

"You will address me only in reply to a question," Tatiana explained. "Or my men will beat you again. Now get up." Slowly, painfully, Andrew pulled himself to his feet, staggering to and fro. But the pain was receding. "To save you a question," Tatiana said. "I am an officer in the Komitet Gosudarstvennoy Bezopasnosti. Do you know what that means?"

"The KGB," he muttered.

"It is the Committee of State Security," Tatiana said. She jerked her head, and the men came forward to handcuff Andrew's hands behind his back.

"Will I see you again?" Andrew asked. He still could not believe this was happening. The man who had hit him before hit him again, and he sank to his knees in agony.

"Yes," Tatiana said. "You will see me again."

Andrew was dragged to his feet and thrust through the doorway. Unlike what would have obtained in a British hotel, as there must have been considerable noise coming from his room, every door remained tight shut, and not a soul was to be seen. He was thrown down the stairs, arrived at the foot in a cloud of pain and disorientation. There was no one in Reception, either. He had read that the KGB was a state within a state, and had not believed it. But it seemed that they could bring an entire hotel to a standstill whenever they chose. An entire society, for when he was thrust out into the street it too was deserted, save for a policeman at each end, keeping traffic away.

And he had contrived to fall in love with a member of this horrendous organisation! Almost from the moment of their first meeting, a little warning light had been flashing at the back of his brain, telling him that no man could ever be so fortunate as to meet a beautiful girl on a train and have her, apparently, fall head over heels in love with him. Moreover a girl who just happened to be the daughter of the woman he was going to see, and equally happened to be able to open any door and unlock any secret for his benefit . . . Subconsciously he had known that had to be impossible. Yet he had fallen for it, and her, hook, line and sinker. And now must pay for it. In what way?

His only hope lay in the continuing belief that no woman could act *that* convincingly. Unless she was a monster. He twisted his head. Tatiana was walking immediately behind him. Her face was impassive. Perhaps she *was* a monster.

A car was waiting, into which he was thrust, one of the two men following, while the other got in the other side. Tatiana sat in the front beside the driver. "Please do not attempt to do anything stupid," Tatiana said. "Or my people will beat you."

Andrew attempted to swallow, and found that his mouth was absolutely dry. He had served as a soldier through the recent war, and had in fact been wounded on two occasions, although both times slightly. He was no stranger to death and destruction, and physical pain. Yet he knew this experience was going to be outside anything he had known, or had ever suspected could happen to him. Was he afraid? He supposed he was. But at the moment he was more disappointed, crushed, he supposed would be more accurate, that what he had been coming to regard as the love of his life should have been built upon such a disastrous deceit.

They drove out of the town to the airport, where a plane was waiting for them. Andrew was pushed on board and strapped into his seat. Tatiana sat opposite him. "I would like you to know that I am sorry," she said, when they were airborne.

"Sorry!"

She shrugged. "I was given a job of work to do. You were a soldier. You have always obeyed orders, have you not?"

"You mean it was *all* play acting?"

Tatiana made a moue. "I enjoy having sex."

"I asked you to marry me."

"That was very kind of you. But it was not relevant."

Andrew gazed at her. "So, what are you going to do to me, now?"

Tatiana sighed. "I am going to destroy you."

Andrew caught his breath. "Just like that?"

"It is my job."

"To destroy people. Even someone with whom you have, dare I say it, shared something of value?"

"I have never done this before," Tatiana confessed. "It will be a new experience for me."

"But you will do it."

"Oh, yes. It is my job."

"And you will enjoy it."

Tatiana shrugged. "I think, very probably, that I shall."

She got up and went forward to sit with the pilot. Andrew was so obviously shattered it was frightening. But she was herself trembling. As she had confessed, it was a new experience for her. Would she really enjoy it? The terrible aspect of the situation was that she probably would. Running through her system there was a streak of vicious sadism, inherited from her father, she supposed, but brought to fruition in the Great Patriotic War, when she had held so many lives in the palm of her hand, and ended so many of them. Her induction into the KGB at the end of the War had but intensified those feelings. She sometimes supposed that she was like some prehistoric goddess, whose maw needed to be fed every so often.

So, her couple of weeks as Andrew Morgan's mistress had been in the nature of a holiday. But she had always known how it would end. Perhaps that had heightened the intense enjoyment of it. But that too would heighten the intense enjoyment of watching his disintegration, mental to begin with, and then physical. Beria had assured her there would be no necessity to worry about him being presented in a court of law for trial. She found her entire body becoming alive at the thought of it.

But she did not want to look at him again until it was time to commence. She did not leave the flight deck until the plane had landed, and Morgan had been removed. Then she too went to Lyubyanka, but in a different car.

"Tatiana!" Beria smiled at her. "You are, as always, a sight for sore eyes. Have you enjoyed your vacation?"

"Is that what it was, Comrade Commissar?"

"I would say so. Where is the subject?"

"Downstairs."

"What have you done to him?"

"I have done nothing to him, yet, Comrade Commissar. I am awaiting your instructions. What is it you wish to know from him?"

"We have arrested a member of the spy organisation. Actually, we have arrested two of them; the third committed suicide. It is your task to make all three of them confess to their activities, and more important, give us names and addresses of the others in their organisation."

"You are assuming that Morgan is linked to these other two."

"Of course he is linked to them, Tatiana. One of the men arrested is the one you reported on the train, meeting with Morgan, and indeed, taking him back to his compartment."

"Smith," Tatiana said.

"That is what he is calling himself, certainly. I would assume that is an alias."

"And the third person? Is he too, English?"

"She, is Russian. She and her husband were operating a message service for the English. It was her husband who blew his brains out when he realised the game was up. She did not have that resolution. I should think she is the weakest link in the chain. Have you ever interrogated a woman, before?"

"Only Atya Schulenskaya as part of my training."

"Did you enjoy it?" Tatiana licked her lips. She made Beria think of a tigress, awaiting her next meal. "Then you will enjoy this one even more," he said. "She is a pretty little thing. There is one thing I wish you to bear in mind. Amuse yourself as much as you like with Morgan, but I do not wish him to die. Do you understand this?"

I do not wish him to die, either, Tatiana thought. "But the others . . ."

"Oh, do what you like with them; they will not be seen again. Just get the answers. Morgan I want kept alive and in reasonably good health. There is someone who will soon be in Russia, with whom I wish to confront him. You understand?"

"I understand, Comrade Commissar."

Tatiana found that she was trembling, with a mixture of anticipation and apprehension. The apprehension was of herself. As she had reminded Beria, she had been trained, both to interrogate and to resist interrogation, or at least to appreciate that resisting interrogation was impossible. She had been exposed to total darkness and continuous light, to more food than she could eat and to starvation, to endless sleepless nights as she had been forcibly kept awake . . . just as she had been strapped to the bars and suffered the most painful and humiliating of physical torture. But up till this moment in her life, it had all been play-acting, whether experienced or delivered. One can stand almost anything, if one knows there is an end in sight, and even more if one also knows that the person who is inflicting the torment is actually a friend, with whom one will share a jug of vodka when the training session is completed.

When one is forced to accept that the pain is going to go on and on and on, until one dies or surrenders absolutely, the situation is far more difficult. And when one is told that the torture must go on and on and on, inflicted by oneself . . . she simply had no idea how she was going to react to that. What she would feel like afterwards. She was afraid of that.

But she was going to do her duty, and already her mind was being controlled by the sadistic sensuality of that duty. She took the elevator down into the basement, where the huge KGB building spread itself beneath Lyubyanka Square itself, and where there existed a hell those who had never been here could scarcely imagine.

The guard on the door of the cell block was today a woman, who was an old and intimate friend; as Tatiana had told Beria, they had trained together, had thus shared pain and ecstacy together – and had often carried the ecstacy beyond the training rooms: both were creatures of insatiable appetites, when in the mood, and as Atya was several years older than Tatiana, at that time she had been the leader in their relationship, although Tatiana, by virtue of her War experiences and triumphs – Atya had spent the War in Moscow and never actually fired a shot in anger – had always been the senior in rank. But their careers had bifurcated, catastrophically; just as they were completing their training, Atya had had a horrendous accident, falling from a tram and being run over. The doctors had saved her life, but left her with one leg permanently shorter than the other. The KGB had retained her services, in view of the amount of time and money spent on her training, but as she could no longer be considered for field work had relegated her to the duties of gaoler for the damned as it was called, guardian of those destined for torture and death at the hands of their inquisitors. Atya was entirely suited for the task, as since her accident she seemed to have conceived a hatred for the entire human race, with, Tatiana thought, the exception of herself. Isolated by her injury, Atya actually craved affection and love, and Tatiana was prepared to give her that, when she had the time – making love with a cripple was a new experience. And Atya was a still pretty woman. She was short and slender, with straight yellow hair which hung about her ears and a pert face. One had to know her very well to understand the dark forces that roamed behind those blue eyes, the desire to revenge herself upon the whole human race. To be at the mercy of this woman would make the devil himself seem an angel – and everyone down here was at her mercy, when she was on duty.

But she was as nothing compared with herself, Tatiana reflected. Only no one suspected that, either, save for those, like Atya, who had actually come face to face with her manic sensuality. "Eighteen, Nineteen, and Twenty-seven," Atya said, looking at the paper Tatiana gave her.

"Show me," Tatiana invited.

Atya limped in front of her down the corridors. Each door was shut and locked, the peepholes closed. "It is a resting time," she remarked, jocularly.

"Have the prisoners seen each other?" Tatiana asked.

"Well, Eighteen and Nineteen were arrested together, Comrade Captain. But they were immediately separated. They have not seen each other since." She paused before Number Eighteen.

"Just the window," Tatiana said.

Atya slid the panel back, and Tatiana looked in. The woman was smaller than she had expected, and younger, too. Seen from the peephole, she appeared as a mass of pale brown hair, which shrouded her naked shoulders and back; she crouched on the bare floor, turned away from the door, huddled into herself. She was an attractive prospect. "Has she been searched?" Tatiana asked.

"Oh, yes, Comrade Captain. I searched her myself," Atya said, with considerable satisfaction.

"But you found nothing."

Atya chuckled. "I found a great deal, Comrade Captain. I made her squeal. But there was nothing of importance."

"Bring her to the interrogation room," Tatiana said.

Atya reached for the keys at her belt, from which there also hung several pairs of handcuffs. Tatiana stood back, and Atya unlocked the door, allowing it to swing wide. The young woman's head turned, sharply, her mouth sagging open. She had a pretty face, the features small, in keeping with the rest of her, but clipped and attractive. Even the distortion of fear could not make them ugly. "Up, Antonina," the guard said. "The Captain wishes a word."

The woman Antonina licked her lips, then slowly got to her feet. There were marks on the pale skin, red blotches here and there; Tatiana presumed they had happened when Atya had been 'searching' her. She even retained some modesty, attempted to close her hands in front of her pubes, but Atya seized her arms and pulled them behind her back, clipped the handcuffs onto her wrists. "She is all yours, Comrade Captain."

All mine, Tatiana thought, and realised that she had descended into as deep a pit as those Nazi interrogators who had, almost literally, torn one of her best friends to pieces. 'Do what you like,' Beria had said. 'They will never be seen again.' But whatever she did to this girl, certainly in front of Atya, had to be in the line of duty. "Bring her," Tatiana said.

Atya jerked her head, and Antonina stumbled out of the cell, looked left and right, as if expecting an execution squad to be waiting for her. "Number Nineteen," Atya said.

Tatiana stepped forward, opened the panel, looked in. She was disappointed. The man Smith, if that was his name, was sandy-haired and uninteresting. His thighs were thick, his penis too long, even in repose. She supposed some women might find that attractive. "Did you search him as well?" she asked.

"Oh, yes, Comrade Captain."

"And did he squeal?"

"He thought he was enjoying it, until I hit him in the balls."

"Well, bring him too."

This time Atya raised her eyebrows. Having received the same basic training, she knew that there were three methods of interrogating, or to be realistic, torturing members of the same group, or people suspected of the same crime. The one most recommended by the experts was separatism. You tortured one at a time, out of sight or hearing of the others, and let them sweat with anxiety over what might be happening to their comrade, or more important, what he or she might be confessing. The second most efficacious method, so it was said, was to question the suspect out of sight and almost out of hearing of his associates. But close enough so that they could hear him, or her, scream in agony. This could terrify certain people into confessing whatever was required without having to lay a finger on them. The third method was that apparently chosen by the KGB captain, to interrogate one suspect in front of the other. This was a promising thesis, both because one could learn a lot from watching the expressions and reactions of the one *not* being interrogated, especially with regard to any information that might be elicited, and because the sight of a companion-in-arms being systematically destroyed before one's eyes could often break one down before a single electrode was attached.

But it had also been proved, by experiment, that where two agents were both experienced and determined, they could actually encourage one another to hold out by being able to look at each other, and even speak to each other. Of course, Atya doubted the woman Antonina was either very experienced or very determined . . . but the men both looked hardened cases. However, she was here to obey orders. She glanced at Antonina, who was trembling from head to foot. "I will look after her," Tatiana said. Atya shrugged and unlocked the cell door.

Tatiana looked at Antonina, who licked her lips. "Please don't hurt me, Comrade Captain," she whispered. "I will tell you anything you wish to know."

Tatiana drove her fingers into Antonina's hair, closing them on the scalp. Antonina's trembling increased to a long shudder. "Of course you will tell me everything I wish to know, Antonina," Tatiana said. "But it can do no harm to jog your memory a little." Antonina gasped.

From inside the cell there was a flurry of movement, and another gasp. The man who called himself Smith had made an attempt to resist Atya, who was hardly half his size, and Atya had kicked him in the groin. Now he knelt, bent double, panting with pain. He could no longer resist when Atya pulled his hands behind his back and handcuffed them.

"Number Twenty-eight?" she asked, as she pushed Smith out of the cell.

"We will secure these first," Tatiana said.

The two prisoners were marched along the corridor to the inter-rogation room. Here there were four men waiting. Two were the habitual denizens of this pit of hell, but there was also a doctor in attendance, and a male secretary, seated at a table in the corner, notebook already open. The prisoners looked around themselves at the bars and the whips, the chains and the magnetoes. They looked at each other, for the first time since leaving their cells. Then Antonina opened her mouth and began to scream, a wailing, high-pitched sound which reminded Tatiana of an air-raid siren.

Atya swung her hand and hit Antonina in the stomach. The wail became a moaning gasp, and Antonina fell to her knees. "Speak when you are spoken to," Atya recommended, and grinned. "You will have sufficient opportunities."

"Prepare them," Tatiana said. "I will fetch Number Twenty-Eight." She held out her hand, and Atya hesitated; these keys were her most precious possession, because they represented her power. But this woman possessed a power far greater than that of the keys. She unclipped them from her belt and held them out. She also unclipped one of the remaining handcuffs, but Tatiana shook her head. "I shall not need that." Atya shrugged. She thought it might be amusing if the captain had overestimated her strength and ability, and Number Twenty-Eight got the better of her. But of course, the captain had a revolver hanging from her belt.

Tatiana returned along the various corridors to Number Twenty-Eight. She stood outside the door for some minutes, drawing deep breaths to get her emotions under control, then unlocked the door. There were red blotches on Andrew Morgan's body as well, but she reckoned those might have been inflicted when he was being brought in. Certainly he was fully alert. His head jerked as the door opened, and now he stood up, facing her. "Is it time?" he asked, his voiced controlled.

"That is up to you," she said. "Come with me." He looked her up and down, then past her into the empty corridor. "I know you are an ex-soldier, Andrew," she said. "But do believe me when I say that I can break you in two before you could even touch me. Equally, I have but to give a single shout and there will be guards in here. I am afraid they would beat you up if I summoned them. So please do be sensible."

"You mean you wish me to walk like a lamb to my slaughter."

"It need not come to that. Walk in front of me."

"Like this? Can I not even have a pair of pants."

"No."

"All part of the drill, eh?"

She stepped back, and he walked past her into the corridor. "Turn right," she commanded.

He did so, and they went towards the interrogation room. "I don't suppose you'd care to tell me just why I have been arrested? Just why I am being treated like this?" he asked over his shoulder.

"I am hoping you will tell me that," Tatiana said.

The door was opened for them and they stepped into the Interrogation Room. Andrew stopped so suddenly she nearly bumped into him. But she did not blame him for checking. In front of him, in the centre of the room, the man Smith was strapped to an iron frame. His wrists were secured above his head, his ankles to each leg of the frame, and his waist to the frame itself by a leather strap. An alligator clip had aleady been taped to his penis, and another thrust into his anus and also taped into place, the wires leading away to the waiting control box.

Opposite him, the woman Antonina was strapped to another

frame. She was similarly secured, but with her face to the frame, so that her back was exposed. But her frame had been arranged so that she faced Smith. Smith's face was reasonably composed; Antonina's was a mask of terror.

The door closed behind Tatiana and Andrew, and she stepped past him, looking from his face to that of the other two. Antonina's never changed. Smith frowned. "Jesus!" he commented.

"You know this man?" Tatiana asked. Smith licked his lips. "You?" Tatiana asked Andrew.

"We met on the train," Andrew said. "But you must know that. You were on the train."

"You met by arrangement?"

"Good God, no. He said he was a typewriter salesman. He showed me a typewriter. But I wasn't interested."

Tatiana turned back to Smith. "Is what he said true?" Smith licked his lips again. Tatiana knew he was trying to work out how this could be used to his best advantage. "What about the woman?" she asked Andrew.

"I have never seen her before in my life," Andrew said.

And he was telling the truth, about them both, Tatiana was certain. "What was found in the apartment?" she asked the secretary.

"Nothing of importance, Comrade Captain."

Antonina opened her mouth, and Smith gave a quick shake of his head. Well, well, Tatiana thought. Something *was* found, but it has not been provided. That decision had to be Beria's. But he was the boss, and she had her work to do. "You," she said. "Antonina, have you ever seen this man before?"

Antonina's eyes flickered, and she looked at Smith, again seeking guidance. But she had not looked at Andrew. Tatiana realised she had a problem. Andrew was quite innocent, she was certain. But to tell Beria that might be fatal. Beria had said he wanted Andrew alive, for confrontation with some other agent he had apparently managed to capture. But that was on the assumption Andrew was involved. If he was *not* involved, Beria might order him to be shot out of hand; it was certain that he could never be released, after the way he had been treated. The only way she could

108

be certain of keeping him alive was to act, and to treat him, as if she was certain of his guilt. And to prove it in front of these people, who were quite capable of reporting to Beria behind her back – perhaps even Atya. However painful that might be for Andrew. "Secure him," she told the guards. "Position number one."

Andrew's head turned, sharply, but before he could react they had pulled his arms behind his back and handcuffed him to one of the uprights. He stared at her, opened his mouth as if he would have spoken, and then closed it again. She was glad of that.

She stepped up to Antonina, again twined her fingers in her hair, gave it a slight tug. She ran her hands over Antonina's body, cupping her breasts, caressing her buttocks, squeezing her pubes. "All this beauty," she whispered into Antonina's ear. "Don't you wish to have this beauty, still, when you leave here?" Antonina panted. "So tell me now," Tatiana said softly. "Who are these men, really."

Antonina sucked air into her lungs. "I know that man as Smith. He was a friend of my husband's. He came to see us, and my husband sent messages for him."

"What kind of messages?"

"I don't know. They never showed them to me."

"Then to whom were these messages sent?"

"I don't know." Antonina began to weep.

Tatiana continued to stroke her breasts and buttocks, giving her belly gentle squeezes as it inflated with each breath. "What about the other man?"

"I don't know him. I have never seen him before."

"I do not believe you, Antonina. If you don't tell me the truth, I am going to hurt you, very badly."

"I don't *know* him," Antonia said. "I don't know him," she shouted.

Tatiana released her. "Six strokes."

The cane was so thin as almost to be made of wire; in fact, it had a length of wire passed through its centre so that while it might splinter, it would not snap. Atya held it in front of Antonina's face, and grinned at her. "Now you may speak, my little one." Antonina gasped, and her whole body sagged. Then she threw back her head

109

and uttered a tremendous shriek. "And I have not even touched her, yet," Atya complained.

"Tatiana," Andrew said. "You cannot do this."

The guard standing beside him hit him in the stomach. Andrew retched, and his body, held against the pillar only by the handcuffs, doubled forward. "Speak when you are asked a question," the guard told him.

"We were couriers, nothing more," Antonina gasped. "We received messages, and we passed them on. Paul . . . my husband . . . travelled. Oh, God, Paul. Now he is dead."

Tatiana nodded, and Atya slashed the cane across Antonina's buttocks, creating an immediate huge weal. Antonina's body stiffened, and she screamed again. "Couriers," she shrieked. "We knew nothing. We took and received messages."

Tatiana nodded again, and Atya delivered her next blow, with perfect aim and precision, creating another deep red weal an inch above the first, neatly bisecting the tight buttocks. Again Antonina's howl of agony reverberated through the chamber. Slowly Andrew straightened, still gasping for breath. "You will only kill her," Smith said. "She is telling the truth."

Atya glanced at Tatiana, received another nod, and struck again. This time Antonina's body arched against the frame so violently it trembled. But she could no longer utter a sound. Her mouth sagged open, and her head fell back. "Silly little bitch has fainted," Atya grumbled.

"Then revive her."

Tatiana went forward, stood beside Antonina, drove her fingers again into the girl's hair to raise her head. Antonina's eyes drooped open, and her lips puckered. "Do not scream," Tatiana said. "Speak to me. You carried messages. From Smith?" Antonina gasped, and Atya poured a mug of water onto her face. Antonina gasped again. "From Smith?" Tatiana asked again.

"Tell her," Smith begged.

Antonina's mouth closed. She was gaining courage. But not enough. Tatiana nodded, and Atya struck her a fourth time. Now the cane was splintering, little pieces of bamboo flaking off to stick to the tortured flesh, exposing the wire beneath. "The next one will make you bleed," Tatiana warned her. "You received messages from Smith?"

"Yes," Antonina gasped. "Oh, God, yes."

"And who else?"

"I do not know their names."

"You know Smith's name, Antonina."

"My husband told me his name," Antonina sobbed. "He did not tell me all of their names."

"But he told you some. List them. You . . ." Tatiana nodded to the male secretary, who had remained seated at the table. "Take these down."

"I . . . I cannot remember," Antonia said.

Atya struck her again. Antonina had regained sufficient breath to scream, an even more unearthly sound than before. Blood trickled down her buttocks to gather in a pool between her feet. "The next one may well expose a bone," Tatiana told her. "I wish all the names you can remember."

Antonina began to speak. The secretary wrote diligently, occasionally bending forward to listen more closely as her voice dwindled. Antonina listed eight names, of which seven were Russian. Tatiana began by watching Smith's reactions to his partner's disclosures, but soon became more interested in the names themselves. Especially the eighth. The Russians would easily be found and identified, but . . . "Moonlight?" she asked. "Would you say that again?"

"Moonlight," Antonina whispered.

"Give her something to drink," Tatiana commanded. Atya poured a glass of vodka, held it to Antonina's lips, and the girl drank greedily. The vodka would, of course, increase her thirst in a matter of seconds. "Is that all you know him as?" Tatiana asked.

"Yes," Antonina said. "I swear it."

Atya raised the cane, but Tatiana shook her head. "You have met this man?"

"He came to the apartment, once. I did not speak with him. Paul spoke with him. He was only a shadow to me."

Tatiana had no doubt she was again telling the truth, as when she had disclaimed any knowledge of Andrew. How amusing it would be if Andrew in fact turned out to be Moonlight. But also, how tragic. She turned to Smith. "Tell me about Moonlight."

"He is a name, nothing more," Smith said.

"Antonina has just established that he is more than a name," Tatiana pointed out.

"I meant, to me. I have never met him."

"I do not believe you, Comrade. Will you not tell me about this man? If you do not, I must hurt you, very badly."

Smith licked his lips. "I do not know him."

Tatiana stood beside him, went into her stroking routine. Andrew, gazing at her, could not believe that she had done those things to *him*. He had lain in the arms of a tigress, and supposed it was love. "You have ten seconds, Comrade," Tatiana whispered. "Then we are going to make you wish you were a eunuch. His name."

"I do not know his name," Smith said stubbornly. There were great beads of sweat on his forehead.

Tatiana stepped away from him and snapped her fingers, and one of the male guards depressed a button on his control box. It was almost possible to hear the electricity crackling through the wires in the split second before Smith screamed, a howl of the most utter agony as his body arched away from the steel frame. The force of the charge even erected his penis, for a moment, before he collapsed, hanging from his wrists, legs still jerking against the bars. "Are you trying to kill him?" Tatiana snapped.

"I am sorry, Comrade Captain," the guard said. "I must have pressed too hard."

Tatiana pulled on a pair of thin rubber gloves to hold Smith's chin, just in case there was still some electricity about. She lifted Smith's head, looked at the blue lips. The eyes were open, but bloodshot and sightless. She snapped her fingers again, and Atya handed her a mirror. Tatiana held the glass in front of Smith's nostrils, frowned. "Cut his wrist," she commanded.

The guard stepped up to Smith, a knife in his hand. He made a small incision in Smith's left wrist, opening the vein. Only a drop of blood came out. "That was very stupid," Tatiana said.

"There is the other one," Atya suggested.

Andrew stared at her. This cannot be happening, he thought. I cannot be standing here, tied to this pillar, watching a man killed by sheer carelessness, and a woman being systematically destroyed as a human being: what had just happened to Antonina must scar her mind for life, even if the scars on her flesh eventually faded – although even that was doubtful. And now it was to be his turn, because Tatiana was looking at him. "Get rid of this one," she said.

The guards released Smith, and he slumped into their arms. They carried him from the room, but returned very quickly; presumably they had dumped him in an empty cell. Supposing there was such a thing as an empty cell in this hell. Andrew realised that he was thinking, urgently, desperately, rubbish to stop himself from facing the reality of what was about to happen to him.

Tatiana stepped up to him. "Tell me about this Moonlight," she said.

"I know no one named Moonlight," he said, relieved that his voice was not actually trembling. "That is the truth. You have to believe me."

Of course I believe you, Tatiana thought. But I must still torture you, for the benefit of these others. "And I know that you do," she said. "Comrade Doctor." The doctor stepped forward, apprehensively. "You examined the man Smith?" Tatiana inquired. The doctor licked his lips. "And you noticed nothing wrong with his heart?"

"It is difficult, with a cursory examination, Comrade Captain. The heartbeat was irregular, but I put that down to fear. The charge was simply too strong."

"Well, examine this man."

"I have already done so, when he was brought in, Comrade Commissar. He is very fit."

"Do it again, now," Tatiana commanded.

The doctor obeyed, using his stethescope with great deliberation, while Tatiana waited, staring at Andrew. Who stared back. I loved you, he thought. I would have loved you forever. Perhaps he would still love her forever. Even after she had reduced him to

113

a gibbering wreck. "He is absolutely fit, Comrade Captain," the doctor pronounced.

Tatiana snapped her fingers, and the electrical clips they had taken from Smith's body were brought to her. She attached them herself. "This is your last chance," she said.

"You know I have nothing to tell you," he said. "My God, you know that, Tatiana."

Tatiana moved to the box, took the control herself. "We do not want any other accidents to happen," she said.

"There's a gentleman to see you, ma'am," Mottram said. "He said to give you his card."

Elaine took the piece of pasteboard. "The State Department! Oh, thank God! We're getting somewhere at last."

"Do you really think so, Ma'am?" Mottram had been the most affected of all the servants by Priscilla's kidnapping. She seemed to take it as a personal affront that she had not been present when Gregory Asimov had made his move, if not to protect her mistress, at least to go with her.

"You bet, Pamela." Elaine had never been able to get into the habit of calling a ladies' maid by her surname. "Show Mr . . ." she peered at the card, "Eldridge in."

Mr Eldrige was very tall and very thin. With his hatchet-face he made Elaine think of a vulture. Even his smile as he shook hands was vulture-like. "Good of you to see me, Mrs Bolugayevski," he said, pronouncing each syllable with great care. "May I ask how your menfolk are?"

"My husband is doing well, Mr Eldridge, thank you. My father-in-law . . . not so good."

"But he's going to live?"

"They think so. As to whether he'll ever walk again . . ."

"That's bad luck."

"Please sit down," Elaine invited. "Would you like something to drink? Tea? Coffee?" Mottram was still hovering.

"A glass of water would be very nice, thank you."

"A glass of water." Elaine looked at Mottram, who nodded, and left the room.

"Shocking affair," Eldridge commented.

"Have you news of my mother-in-law? Have the Russians admitted kidnapping her?"

"We're putting out feelers."

"Feelers?!"

"These are early days, Mrs Bolugayevski. As I say, we're putting out feelers, but there's nothing yet."

"Then . . ." she bit her lip.

"Why am I here? Well, I'll tell you." He accepted the glass of water Mottram had brought in on a silver tray. "There are some loose ends the Department feels should be cleared up. Mrs Cromb is a Russian, right?"

"Wrong. She's an American citizen, born and bred."

"But at one time she called herself the Princess of Bolugayen. That's in Russia, right?"

"At one time, Mr Eldridge, she *was* the Princess of Bolugayen. She married the Prince."

"Who was also her cousin."

"He was her uncle," Elaine snapped, beginning to lose her temper. "He was from the Russian half of the family."

"Right. And after he died, she married another Russian. Mr Cromb is Russian, right?"

"He was born there. He is now an American citizen."

"Right. Now both he, and Mrs Cromb, and you and your husband come to think of it, were in Russia during the War, and fought with them. Right?"

"Yes, Mr Eldridge. They were our allies, then, you may remember."

"I sure do. But things have changed, although not, you might say, the Bolugayevski-Crombs."

Elaine's head came up. "Just what do you mean by that?"

"I mean, Mrs Bolugayevski, that we know your mother-in-law has maintained close contact with her Russian sister-in-law, Jennifer Ligachevna."

"I'm afraid that is news to me."

"You telling me you didn't know that Mrs Cromb sent an agent of hers . . ." he took out a notebook to check the name, "called

Andrew Morgan, to Russia a couple of months ago, specifically on a visit to Mrs Ligachevna?"

"I have no idea what you are talking about."

"Well, then, let's talk about something else. Would you deny that Mrs Cromb has regularly, over the past couple of years, entertained Russian emigres, or so-called emigres, at this house?"

"Of course she has. My mother-in-law has an abiding interest in Russia, and sympathy with those who, like herself, were forced into exile by the Revolution. To many of these people she is still the Princess of Bolugayen. They call here, leave their cards, so it is natural that they should receive invitations to the appropriate soirée. My mother-in-law is very fond of entertaining."

"Right. So you agree that Mrs Cromb kept in touch with a lot of emigres. Some of whom may not have been emigres. Like this fellow Asimov, whose body you identified."

"Mrs Cromb had never met Asimov. He was an old comrade of my husband's and myself during the War. We introduced him to Mr and Mrs Cromb."

"An old comrade," Eldridge said thoughtfully. "How do you know Mrs Cromb had never met Asimov?"

"Well . . . she hadn't. She would have said so, if she had. Anyway, it was not possible for them to have met."

"Right. Not possible for them to have met. But he was a pal of yours. Right. Okay, Mrs Bolugayevski. Thanks for your time and the water. We'll be in touch."

He stood up, and Elaine stood up also. "I would like to know just what you intend to do about Mrs Cromb's disappearance."

"Well, like I said, we're putting out feelers. If we get a positive response, we'll let you know."

"But you think I am lying to you."

"Oh, no, no, Mrs Bolugayevski. I think you're telling the truth, as you see it. I just don't think you know all the facts. But you see, it isn't part of our business to get egg all over our face."

At last the penny dropped. Elaine was aghast. "You think Mrs Cromb engineered this whole thing, and has voluntarily returned to Russia?"

"Isn't that a possibility?"

116

"That is the most absurd, and obscene, suggestion I have ever heard," Elaine snapped. "You seem to be forgetting that the Russians intended to kill both Mrs Cromb's husband and her son. It is pure fortune that they did not."

"Yeah. Well, wheels within wheels, eh? Russian agents do some mighty queer things, by our standards, when they're ordered to do it."

"Russian agents? My God . . ."

"You going to deny that Mrs Cromb has been quite pally with Premier Stalin from time to time in her life?" Elaine opened her mouth and then closed it again. She did know that Priscilla had been a prisoner of the KGB for a while during the War. Priscilla had always refused to speak of it, Elaine had supposed because the experience had simply been unspeakable. But she did not *know* that. She did know that there had been no signs of any physical mistreatment on Priscilla's body. Eldridge had observed her confusion. "Like I said, we'll be in touch, Mrs Bolugayevski." He left the room.

Chapter Six

The Victim

Atya climbed the stairs to her apartment, slowly. When out of uniform she looked what she actually was, a crippled Muscovite woman, who was not in the best of condition. Going up stairs always made her puff. But she was happy, now. The days, weeks, months, after her accident were nothing but a nightmare. At the time the nightmare had been unbearable. It had all but driven her to suicide.

From the bottom of that pit she had been rescued, to became a gaoler for the KGB. She knew that Tatiana Gosykinya, her only living Russian friend, had been largely responsible for that. Atya had no illusions about Tatiana. Beneath that glowingly lovely exterior there lurked the mind and soul, and instincts, of a totally amoral and evil woman. But there was also a strong thread of loyalty, both to her superiors, and to her friends. Atya flattered herself that Tatiana herself did not have very many friends. The boy Asimov, she knew of, and was not jealous. Tattie was omnivorous in her sexual appetites. But then, was not she also omnivorous? Once she had not been sure of that. Now she knew, and was happy. Even Tatiana was no longer important. Not since *he* had come back into her life.

Atya had once been a beautiful woman. The world of men, and women, had been her oyster in the morally easy attitudes of the Communist Youth. But she had still dreamed of things outside her immediate knowledge, of places and people who would be sophisticated, knowledgeable, attractive. His appearance, early in the Great Patriotic War, had been as unexpected as it had been unforeseeable. He had been a member of the British Mission which had come, along with the Americans, to see how Russia could be helped to resist the Germans. They, especially the Communist girls, hard at work filling sandbags and anticipating rape by the Germans when Moscow fell, had been warned not to fraternise with the foreigners. But how could one fail to fraternise with a man who looked like a film star of that period – complete with little moustache – and acted like one too . . . and who had fallen head over heels in love with her. Or so he said. Atya had believed him, even if she had very rapidly deduced that he was not a member of the British Mission at all, but an agent for British Intelligence. She had considered informing on him to her superiors, and decided against it. His love had become important to her, and their relationship could not harm the State. Even the questions he asked, for she was already employed by what had then been the MGB, in a menial capacity, could not really harm the State, and it had given her a sense of importance to be able to tell him about the inner workings of that already mighty organisation.

Then he had gone, back to England, in 1943. They had shared an emotional farewell. She had not expected ever to see him again, but a year ago he had returned, reappearing in her life like some long-forgotten dream. She had been embarrassed, terrified – surely his erstwhile love would turn to disgust, as she had seen in so many eyes since her accident. Instead he had appeared to love her more than ever. He had not even been shocked when she had told him she was now a fully-fledged member of the KGB, which was stretching the bow a bit, as she was after all only a gaoler. She had been overwhelmed, fallen into his arms with all the desperation of a woman whose life had passed her by, save for this one man. So, now he was totally clandestine, entering and leaving Russia by a secret route, taking on the identity of a Siberian official, thus he was now quite as much in her power as she was in his; betrayal – which included desertion – would be a mutual catastrophe. She knew he had come back seeking information rather than her, but she was content with that. She could keep him happy while betraying none of her country's secrets – only those of the darkest cells in the Lyubyanka.

He was waiting for her in the privacy of her tiny apartment; she had given him a key. As even a subsidiary member of the KGB she was allowed space to herself. Equally, as a member of the KGB her comings and goings, and those of any friends she might entertain, were not subject to scrutiny. Not many people knew exactly what Atya Schulenskaya did, but all knew where she worked, and for that reason feared her. He greeted her with a kiss. "I am just making tea."

"You are a darling." She took off her coat, hung it on a hook.

He handed her a cup. "I hope you have had an enjoyable couple of days?"

Atya sat down, and smiled. "They would interest you, I am sure."

He sat beside her. "Tell me."

"Is that all you wish of me, that I should tell you things?" However true it was, she appreciated *some* romance.

"Of course it is not. But I think someone I know might be involved."

"A man called Morgan?"

Halstead frowned. "Morgan?"

"You do not know this man?"

"I have never heard of him."

"He has been arrested for spying, for Great Britain."

"Good heavens."

"So were his two accomplices. A man called Smith, another Englishman, and a woman called Constantina Kuslova. She is Russian." She studied his expression. "You know of these people?"

"They have been interrogated?"

"Of course." She smiled. "I was present."

"What did they confess?"

"Nothing. The man Smith was accidentally electrocuted before he could say anything. The woman had a mental breakdown."

"And Morgan?"

"He refused to give any information. You should have heard him shriek with pain. But he said nothing." Halstead slowly allowed his breath to escape. "These were your people, eh?" Atya asked.

"I knew of them," Halstead said, cautiously.

"Then you also know of the Princess," Atya suggested. Halstead put down his teacup. "The Princess Bolugayevska," Atya explained. "She is a famous enemy agent. She has been arrested too. She was arrested in America and is being brought to Russia."

"The Princess Bolugayevska," Halstead said, thoughtfully. "You think she is connected to Smith and the woman Kuslova and Morgan?"

Atya shrugged. "When she gets here, we will surely find out, Comrade Johnny."

Priscilla stood at the porthole to watch the islands go by as the ship made its way up the strait to the harbour. She found it incredible that she should have lived for several years in this country, and revisited it twice, and yet never before had she been to Leningrad, not even when it had been known as St Petersburg, and then Petrograd. Despite herself, she was excited, for the first time in ten days. Throughout all of that period she had only been able to think, Joseph is dead! Alex is dead! My family is destroyed, save for the babe in Elaine's womb, who I shall never see, and who will undoubtedly be brought up as an American boy, not a Russian prince. Then, had she had the means, she would have cut her own throat.

But one can feel total despair for only so long, and she was a woman who had always responded to challenges. Now, at the prospect of this final challenge, the adrenolin was again flowing. She was fully dressed, and had been since dawn, for the first time since leaving Boston. Shatrav had not liked her to be fully dressed. He preferred her naked, or at best in her underclothes. Yet he had never actually touched her, not even when, that first day, she had spat in his face; he had merely looked. And looked and looked and looked.

Of course he had been obeying orders. Wherever she was going to be delivered, and to whatever fate, she was not to be harmed, in any way, before then. Not even to be touched. And as they had

121

shared the cabin with one of her women gaolers, always, he had not even been able to risk doing something which might not be readily apparent to his masters. However much he so clearly wanted to. Yet it is of course possible to be raped by eyes, when they are ever present, ever watching, seeking every movement, every breath. But Priscilla took a simple pride in the fact that where a great number of women might have gone out of their minds with such on-going humiliation, she was able to take it in her stride, as it were. She had survived too much not to believe in survival, once one had the patience and the fortitude. As a girl she had shivered in a lifeboat from the *Titanic*, knowing that her mother was dead, awaiting death for herself, or rescue, with patient determination. As hardly more than a girl she had refused to beg or scream when those vicious animals who had called themselves Bolsheviks had been tearing the clothes from her body, while all around her had again lain death and destruction. As a woman she had accepted Stalin's version of the gulag without a single whimper. So this promised to be her last adventure. Well, then, let it be. She could still enjoy new sights, new smells, new sensations, while she could still see, and feel.

Shatrav stood at her shoulder. "On that island," he said, "is the fortress of St Peter and St Paul. Where the tsars are buried." He chuckled. "Some of them. Nowadays it is used as a prison."

"Is that where I am going?" she asked.

"No, no, Princess." For just a moment his hands closed on her buttocks. "You are going to Moscow. To Lyubyanka. The ultimate prison."

"And then?" Priscilla found that she was holding her breath.

"I have no idea, Princess. But I imagine . . ." he drew his forefinger across her throat.

"You are such scintillating company," Priscilla remarked.

"You are not afraid of this?"

"Why should I be? Better men than you have tried to kill me. And . . ." she nearly said, "I will be going to join my husband and my son," but thought better of it. A lout like Shatrav would hardly understand such sentiments. "Will I have time to look at Leningrad?"

"You will have no time at all to look at Leningrad," he told her. "It is time to get back into your box."

Guards and officials stood to attention. Most of them were very nervous. It was only on rare occasions that Premier Stalin visited the Lyubyanka. Commissar Beria was like a dog with two tails, as he fussed around his master, and showed him into his private office.

Stalin looked around himself with an almost ingenuous air. "What is the news from America?" he asked.

"What you read in the newspaper, Josef Vissarionovich. The media consensus is that the Princess was kidnapped for ransom, but as nothing more has been heard of her, the assumption is that the kidnap went wrong and she died."

"That is the media consensus," Stalin remarked. "What do your people in Washington say?"

"Nothing but rumours. Oh, there is a school of thought that we had something to do with her disappearance, and as you know, they have made official inquiries into Asimov's background. But as they can prove nothing, they are saying nothing."

"And her family?"

"Her husband and son went into hospital for emergency surgery and have not been heard of since. I think they are both dead. Her brother is distraught, but he is a businessman, not a man of action. Her daughter-in-law is also distraught, and may well remain so. It seems that she is pregnant. I consider the whole situation as closed. In our favour."

"And the Princess?"

"Awaits your pleasure, Josef Vissarionovich."

Stalin glanced at him. His Commissar for Internal Affairs was the only person in Russia who understood the true relationship between the Princess and himself. To everyone else, that he had arrested the Princess, kept her in custody for more than a year, and then released her, was merely evidence of the Premier's omnipotent power, fairness of mind, and generosity: the Princess had been suspected of spying, had been taken into custody and interrogated over a lengthy period by the Premier himself, and then, as he had been unable to prove her guilt, he had let her go again. Even those who understood that in Soviet Russia, once arrested, a man or a woman was very unlikely ever to be seen again unless it was considered appropriate to produce them for a show trial, took comfort in the fact that even Stalin could from time to time be generous. Only Beria knew better. "She has not been harmed?"

"I'm afraid she received a bang on the head from that young madman Asimov, when she was being arrested," Beria said. "But the bruise has faded now, and since then, not a hair on her head has been touched." He grinned. "Or even on her body."

"Show me."

Beria took his master down by his private elevator and ushered him into a small room, an observation chamber which looked down into a specific cell. The window was fairly large, but it was one-way glass and set high in the wall of the cell beneath; even if the inmate was prepared to stare at it all the time, there would be no way of telling when he, or she, was being overlooked. Priscilla sat on a straight chair in the centre of the room. It was the only piece of furniture, and she sat absolutely straight. She was facing the window, but she was not looking up. She was naked, her pale skin unblemished, her golden hair brushed in a straight mat past her shoulders. Stalin caught his breath. He had not remembered how beautiful she was, how perfect her figure remained; there was only the slightest sag to her heavy breasts, and her hips were as slender as a girl's. Her legs were flawless; even her toes were uncrushed, from her refusal to wear ill-fitting shoes, however fashionable. There was a small scar on the right side of her abdomen, where she had had her appendix removed some years before. But this only enhanced the beauty of the rest of her.

Beria had been watching his master's expression. "Do you wish her brought to you?" he asked, softly.

Although he knew they were alone in the room, Stalin looked over his shoulder, almost guiltily. "Why is she naked?" he asked.

Beria shrugged. "Routine. She is a prisoner, awaiting interrogation." He grinned. "She thinks she is waiting to be shot."

"Who undressed her?"

124

"My women."

"But you were there?"

Beria shook his head. "I have not yet let her see me."

"You merely watched." Stalin's tone was contemptuous, but he was also angry, Beria could tell. Silly old man, he thought. He is jealous of me for looking at the woman who defied him and reduced him to half a man.

"She is a prisoner, awaiting interrogation," he said again. "It is my duty to study such people."

Stalin turned back to the window, staring at Priscilla for several seconds. Beria waited. He dared not remind his master of what had happened the last time he had summoned that woman to his bed, nor did he dare suggest that this time things might be different. Stalin drew a long breath. All men have weaknesses, but men who rise to the very top of the tree, certainly in gangster-politics, are those who have learned, if not to eradicate their weaknesses, certainly to control them. He wanted Priscilla Bolugayevska-Cromb more than he had ever wanted any woman in his life. But that desire, and her presence, was a weakness. To which he had once succumbed. It could not be allowed to happen again. "Photograph her," he said. "I wish a complete set of prints. Every angle, every movement, every expression. You will enjoy that, Lavrenty Pavlovich."

Beria's collection of erotica was well known.

"And then?" Beria asked.

"Send the file to me, and destroy the negatives."

"Of course," Beria said, smoothly. "And then?"

"Dispose of her. Quickly and without pain."

Beria inclined his head.

Stalin returned to Beria's office, sat down. He was clearly under considerable emotional stress. Beria hastily poured him a glass of his favourite Madzhari, a light Georgian wine. Stalin drank, deeply, and sighed again. Beria knew that when he considered what he had just commanded, he would probably have a fit of rage. Every time he had a fit of rage, the increase in blood pressure meant that his life was shortened. "There was that other matter," he said.

Stalin drank some more wine, and Beria hastily refilled the glass. "Your report said there had been arrests."

"Indeed. Including the man Morgan. Tatiana did that, as you commanded."

"She is a good girl," Stalin said, thoughtfully. "She will go far."

"You find nothing sinister in the copy of that message I gave you, that the man Morgan is in Russia on Bolugayevski business?"

"What does Tatiana say about that?"

"She has said nothing, because I have not shown it to her."

Stalin studied him for some seconds. "Well," he said, "I do not think Tatiana would even admit to having Bolugayevski blood, much less be involved with the family machinations. Has this Morgan confessed to his real identity and purpose?"

"He is proving a very tough and resilient man. He breaks down entirely under interrogation, yet he will admit to nothing. Sometimes I wonder if he has anything to confess. But of course it is more likely that he is merely a well-trained agent. The matter is in Tatiana's hands. She will break him eventually. She can be a demon when aroused. However . . ." he paused.

"Yes?"

"If he confesses to being a Bolugayevski agent in Tatiana's presence . . . I think we should clean this matter up as soon as possible. If, as you deduced, Josef Vissarionovich, the Princess is working with the British Government, and played her part in bringing Morgan to Russia, a confrontation may well give us the truth." Or are you interested in the truth? he wondered. Do you merely wish the Princess destroyed, so that no one else can ever have her, but whose memory you will always possess in her photographs, her beauty never fading?

"You may use her for that purpose," Stalin said. "For whatever you may learn. But she is not to be tortured, and she is to be executed as soon as she has served her purpose."

"I understand this," Beria said, understanding that his master merely did not wish any other man, or woman, ever to get their hands on her.

Stalin stood up. "Let me know when it is done."

"Of course. But before you go, will you not congratulate our people for their success?"

Stalin frowned at him. "What people?"

"Tatiana, certainly, for the way in which she snared Morgan. And Shatrav, for the way in which he kidnapped the Princess."

"Do I know this Shatrav?"

"You decorated him, once, for his work in the War. He served under Tatiana."

"And he kidnapped the Princess? Then he knows she is alive."

"He is absolutely trustworthy," Beria assured him.

"He had her in his power, for ten days," Stalin said.

"That is true. But he never laid a finger on her."

"Is he a eunuch? Or a homosexual?"

"He is certainly not a eunuch. But he was acting under orders, from me. He does not disobey orders. Anyway, the Princess was in the care of my women."

"Nonetheless . . . it were best he was eliminated, as soon as it is convenient. Certainly I do not wish to see him."

"As you wish, Josef Vissarionovich. And Tatiana?"

"I will consider Tatiana later. Now I must return to the Kremlin."

Beria escorted him out, then returned upstairs and sent for Tatiana and Shatrav. "Premier Stalin wishes you both congratulated," he told them, as they stood to attention before his desk, wearing uniform. "You, Shatrav, for carrying out the kidnapping so successfully. I am sorry about Comrade Asimov. That was unfortunate. And you, Tatiana, for the way you have handled the man Morgan. Now this matter must be cleared up. Tatiana, I will discuss this with you now. Shatrav, you are dismissed."

Shatrav saluted and turned to go. Tatiana remained standing to attention before the desk. "With respect, Comrade Commissar," she said. "But what did you mean about Comrade Asimov?"

"Sadly, Tatiana, Comrade Asimov did not return from his mission. He died on duty. None of us can ask for a more noble end than that."

Tatiana turned, to look at Shatrav. Who in turn looked at Beria. Who gave a quick nod. "Comrade Asimov was shot, by me, Tatiana," Shatrav said. "He was guilty of disobeying orders, in that he did not eliminate the woman Elaine Bolugayevska, when he shot the rest of the family."

Tatiana swallowed. "You shot your old comrade?"

"It was my duty to do so," Shatrav said.

Tatiana looked at Beria.

"You were very fond of that boy, were you not?" Beria asked.

"He was like a brother to me," Tatiana said. And he was my lover, she thought.

"Well, he disobeyed orders, and suffered for it. You know the rules, Tatiana. And so did he." He pointed. "I will not have any grudges in my department. Tell Shatrav that you understand he did his duty, Tatiana."

Tatiana stared at Shatrav, and Shatrav swallowed. "I understand that you did your duty, Comrade Captain," Tatiana said in a low voice. Shatrav did not look reassured.

"There," Beria said jovially. "The matter is now closed. Dismissed, Shatrav." Shatrav left the room. "Now," Beria said to Tatiana. "There are certain things I wish done with, and about the Princess. She is the only member of that accursed family left alive. I mean, the princely part of the family, of course. I put you in charge of her, Tatiana. I am sure she has things to tell us which will be very useful. There is also a requirement. But . . ." he held up his finger. "I do not want any visible marks."

Tatiana's smile was cold.

Tatiana opened the door of the observation cell. Priscilla still sat there, although she was becoming restless. Now her head jerked as the young woman entered. Tatiana bowed. "Your highness."

Priscilla frowned. She knew what the uniform of a Russian officer looked like. But she also knew that they would play a succession of games with her until they obtained whatever it was they wanted. Or grew tired of her and shot her. "How long am I to remain here?" she asked. "Like this."

"That depends," Tatiana said.

128

"I wish to go to the toilet," Priscilla said, wondering if it was possible she had met this woman before; there was something very familiar about her.

"Well, then," Tatiana said, "come with me."

Priscilla stood up, hesitated. "Like this?"

"They all say that," Tatiana remarked. "Yes, your highness, like that. No inmate of the Lyubyanka is allowed to have any secrets, from us. Are you ashamed of your body? It is a magnificent body, for a woman of your age."

"Thank you for those kind words," Priscilla said. But the woman was right. She had nothing to be ashamed of, and she had been sufficiently humiliated during the last fortnight for it not to matter any more. Yet she had to take a deep breath to step through the door which Tatiana was holding for her. However, there was no one in the corridor, and no one in the toilets either, although it was disturbing that Tatiana watched her throughout.

"My name is Tatiana Gosykinya," Tatiana said.

Priscilla's head, and body, came upright. "Jennie's child?"

"That is so."

"But . . . my God, my dear girl!" She held open her arms, and after a brief hesitation, Tatiana stepped forward to be embraced. The poor fool thinks I am her saviour, she thought, with considerable satisfaction. Her whole being was so consumed with anger at Gregory's death that she would willingly have torn this aunt apart with red hot pincers. But Beria had said she must not be marked.

"And now you are a member of the KGB?" Priscilla asked. "Then perhaps you will be able to explain all this to me."

Tatiana gave her a last hug, and released her. "I don't think I can do that," she said.

"You fought with my son and his wife, in the War," Priscilla said, refusing to be put down.

Tatiana smiled. "It would be more correct to say that they fought with me, your highness. I was their commander."

"I know. And you became a Heroine of the Soviet Union."

"So tell me," Tatiana said. "How are Prince Alexei and Dr Mitchell."

129

"They're . . ." for a moment, so overwhelming had been the relief at finding a relative in this hell, Priscilla had forgotten reality. "They're dead," she said. "Shot by your people." Her voice seethed with anger and outrage.

"You saw this?" Tatiana asked.

"I . . ." Priscilla bit her lip. "I was hit on the head, by the young thug who was their leader."

"Who is now also dead."

Priscilla frowned. "I don't remember that. After being hit . . . the next thing I remember is being in a trunk, on the ship."

"Did you see Gregory Asimov shot?"

"I told you, I was unconscious. Was this man a friend of yours?"

"He was my lover," Tatiana said.

Priscilla opened her mouth, and then bit her lip instead.

"Come." Tatiana opened the door.

"Where are you taking me?"

"It is not good to ask questions," Tatiana said. "As it happens, I am going to have you photographed."

"Oh. Yes." Standard criminal procedure, she supposed. Only she wasn't a criminal. She stepped into the corridor. It was empty. She turned. "Tatiana . . . you are my niece. By marriage. But we are also cousins. Do you understand this?"

"I have been told this," Tatiana said.

"Well . . ." Priscilla licked her lips. She was not used to asking people for help. "If you were to help me, for the sake of our blood, of our family . . ." she paused; Tatiana's expression remained cold. "I am terribly sorry about your man," Priscilla said. "I honestly didn't know what was happening. And I am sure whoever shot him did so in self-defence. I have lost more than you, Tatiana. A lover can be replaced. But not a husband and a son. Not at my age." She drew a deep breath. "Will you help me?"

"I am going to make you suffer," Tatiana said.

"For this man's death?"

"That. And for being what you are."

Priscilla stared at her. "Have I at least the right to ask to see my sister-in-law? Your mother?"

130

"No," Tatiana said.

I must never beg again, Priscilla told herself. She had never begged Stalin, the last time she had been in his hands. To beg now was a greater humiliation. But was she actually in Stalin's hands? And what did she have to live for, if everyone she loved was dead? Saving only revenge, and this time she did not think that was going to be practical. Thus, she told herself, I must not scream, or even wince. I must close my mind to these people. I must suffer and then die with dignity, as a Russian princess.

She had anticipated some physical violence; Joseph had told her some of his experiences, from floggings to electric currents racing through his body and seeming to tear it apart. She did not wish to have to endure any of those things. She wanted to address this so handsome cousin of hers in reasonable terms. Tell me what you want me to say, she wanted to say, and I will say it. But that was a form of begging.

What made it more difficult was that she was subjected to nothing such as she had anticipated. Instead she was, as Tatiana had said, photographed. It began in a most conventional manner, even if she had found it difficult to sit still, naked, at a desk in a room suddenly full of people, men as well as women. But she had sat still, and they had photographed her face, full and side. She had expected to be fingerprinted, but apparently they were not interested in that. Instead, Tatiana said, "Now you run."

Priscilla looked at her in astonishment. "Run where?"

"Round and round the room," Tatiana said. Priscilla looked at the eager faces, then down at herself. "You will look lovely when you are running," Tatiana explained.

Priscilla begun to run. As jogging was not a hobby of hers, within seconds she was panting and sweat was rolling out of her hair and down her cheeks and neck. And they continued to photograph her, moving close for shots of her panting face, her flowing hair, her heaving breasts, her straining thighs and buttocks and legs, and of course, her sweat. She ran until she collapsed on her hands and knees, and then two of the men picked her up and placed her face to on a steel frame, shaped like an X, so that her arms and legs were spread, her ankles and wrists secured, and a leather belt passed round her waist to hold her body rigid. Once again she anticipated instant agony, at least a whipping, and once again no one laid a finger on her, but she heard the clicking of the camera lenses.

When they had taken some dozen shots of her, she was released, but only to be placed on the frame again, this time facing the room, and the grinning faces. This was harder to bear, but it was only for another photographic session. Then Tatiana nodded, and Priscilla was released again. She was still exhausted and panting from her exertions as well as the combination of humiliation and apprehension – she refused to admit fear – and could do nothing more than sink to the floor. She anticipated being plucked up again but instead she heard the door open, and a moment later she looked at naked feet. And heard a gasp. "Princess? My God! But . . ."

Priscilla raised her head, gazed at Morgan. And was equally taken aback. Like her he was naked, but his body had most certainly been marked. He had lost weight, and he trembled constantly. "Mr Morgan?" she muttered.

Tatiana stood beside Morgan. "You admit you know each other?"

"He is the son of one of my servants." As she only had one pair of hands, Priscilla folded them over her pubes. Being naked in front of Morgan was an embarrassment she no longer felt with these goons.

"I know that is true," Tatiana said. "What I wish to know is why you sent him to Russia."

"I did not send him to Russia," Priscilla protested. "He wished to come, to research a book on his father. Why do you not ask him this?"

"I have done so, and he says the same thing. But we know you are lying." She glanced at Morgan, who continued to stare at the Princess.

His head jerked as he seemed to recover himself. "What have you done to her?"

"We have done nothing to her, yet," Tatiana said. "But you know that I can destroy her, as I destroyed the woman Antonina.

I showed you Antonina yesterday morning. She is a gibbering wreck. Would you like to see your princess reduced to a gibbering wreck?"

"You cannot *do* that," Andrew protested. "She is your own flesh and blood."

"Sometimes they are the most interesting," Tatiana said. "Atya! The Princess is all hot and sweaty from her exercise. I think she should have a bath."

Atya grinned, and summoned two of her aides. The men grasped Priscilla's arms and lifted her up. Another aide was filling the bathtub against the far wall. Priscilla did not resist them; she had no idea what was going to happen. Andrew took a step forward. Tatiana moved with him. "Well?" she asked.

He glanced at her, then at Priscilla again. Tatiana nodded. One of the guards swept Priscilla's feet from the floor, and the two men held her over the now nearly full tub for a moment. Then they slowly lowered her into the water. Priscilla gave a gasp, initially of consternation, which became a strangled scream as she was totally immersed, even her head being forced beneath the water. "That comes straight from our refrigerating plant," Tatiana explained. "It is about two degrees above freezing."

"Aaaagh!" Priscilla gasped as her head was dragged up, the guard's fingers twined in her hair. Then her face was forced under again.

"Stop it!" Andrew shouted. "You're killing her!"

Priscilla's head was brought up again, but now she was past speech. "When she dies depends on the strength of her heart," Tatiana said. "But it is true that few people survive more than ten minutes in the bath." She glanced at her watch. "The Princess has only endured two, so far." She nodded, and the man began to push Priscilla's head down again.

"Wait!" Andrew shouted. "Wait. I will confess. Take her out of the bath, and I will confess."

Tatiana moved her hand, and the men held Priscilla clear of the water, which dripped from her hair and her body. She shivered constantly. Water even dribbled from her mouth, which sagged open, and her breath rasped as she cleared her nostrils. "If you do not tell me what I wish to know," Tatiana said. "They will put her under again. And again."

"Just tell me what you wish to know," Morgan panted.

Tatiana motioned one of her aides to take down what was said. "Your codename is Moonlight."

"Yes."

"You are an agent for the British Government."

"Yes."

"You were sent here to investigate our nuclear programme?"

"Yes."

"This woman is the agent for the British Government who employed you."

Morgan hesitated. Tatiana stood very close to him. "If you answer as I wish, she will not die. You have my word," she said softly. "Answer loudly."

"Yes," Morgan said.

"Well," Tatiana said, "that is very satisfactory. Wrap her up and warm her up," she told Atya. Priscilla, still unable to speak or to stop her teeth chattering, was bundled into a warm robe. "Do you know," Tatiana remarked to Andrew, "I have flogged you, tortured you with electricity, starved you, and you would confess nothing. Now you have confessed everything, just to save the life of that woman. And I once thought that you loved *me*."

"Excellent," Beria said, sitting at his desk and sifting through the photographs, eyes gleaming. "Where are the negatives?" Tatiana held out the envelope. "There are no other prints?" Beria asked.

"No, Comrade Commissar. Are they for your collection?" Tatiana asked, with apparent innocence.

Beria looked up. "That is no business of yours, Tatiana. Now tell me, is the Princess well?"

"She is recovering. She has suffered no permanent damage. Do you wish her disposed of?"

Beria appeared to hesitate. "Not at this time," he said. "It may be possible to get more information out of her. But that she remains alive must be known to just you and me."

"That will be difficult, Comrade Commissar."

134

"If it was a simple job I would give it to someone else, Tatiana. You will remove the Princess from the Lyubyanka, secretly, and then follow my instructions. She will be delivered to a specific gulag, as a number, nothing more, and she will remain there . . . until I choose to send for her again. Do you understand this?"

"Yes," Tatiana said. "I still think it is a risk. If her identity ever became known . . ."

"There would be nothing anyone could do about it. We have a signed confession from her agent as to what she really is."

"With respect, Comrade Commissar, but that confession is a lie." Beria's head came up. "The man Morgan is not a British agent," Tatiana said. "He is nothing more than he claims, a hack journalist who wished to write a book about his father."

"How do you know this?"

"It is my business to interrogate people, and to know when they are telling the truth."

Beria leaned back in his chair. "Who else knows this?"

Tatiana shrugged. "I do not think anyone knows this, in Russia. You told me to get a confession, and I have done that. It was really very simple. Too simple. But the confession is there, and my assistants heard him make it. Of course, if inquiries were to be made in England, the British Secret Service would know that we have the wrong man . . ."

"Are you saying that the man we want is still at large?"

"I am saying that Morgan is not the man we want, Comrade Commissar. As to who that is, well . . . it is possible it was the man calling himself Smith. But due to that fool Radnarski he died before I could properly interrogate him."

Beria pointed with his pencil. "As commander of the interrogation squad, you are ultimately responsible for what happened."

"I understand this, Comrade Commissar."

"Ha! I will have to consider the matter. Anyway, this Morgan has served his purpose. Dispose of him."

Tatiana drew a deep breath. "I would like Morgan kept alive."

"*You* would like. You have just said there is no information to be got from him."

135

"Nevertheless, Comrade Commissar, I would like him to live. He can go to a gulag, like the Princess."

"So, you think you can demand a private prisoner, eh? What is it? A big prick?"

"I obeyed orders, Comrade Commissar. I sucked him in, seduced him, on the understanding that he was an enemy agent. Now I know that he was not. I do not think he deserves to die."

"And you believe he would rather exist in a gulag than be dead?"

"If he exists in a gulag, however unhappily, he would be alive, Comrade."

Beria waved his hand and turned back to the photographs. "Well, the answer is no. Shoot him. Or if you cannot do it yourself, have someone else do it. That is an order. Dismissed."

Tatiana never moved, and after a few moments Beria raised his head. "Does Premier Stalin know that the Princess is being sent to a gulag, Comrade Commissar?" Tatiana asked, her face the picture of innocence. Beria stared at her, but she remained looking straight ahead. "It is just that my mother and I have been invited to tea in the Kremlin tomorrow afternoon. I should not like to say the wrong thing."

Beria took off his pince-nez and polished the glass. "Do you think that you, a chit of a girl, can blackmail the Commissar for Internal Security?"

"I am merely asking for direction from my superior officer," Tatiana pointed out. "Who I desire only to serve, and certainly who I have no wish to make trouble for. Am I to mention those photographs to the Premier, or . . ." she had a sudden flash of insight. "Will he already have them, as a perpetual memory to a woman he now supposes to be dead?"

"You understand, Tatiana," Beria said, "that one day you may be dead yourself."

Tatiana's lips twitched. "But *you* will not kill me, Comrade Commissar. Not while Premier Stalin lives."

"As you say," Beria agreed. "Very well. Have your Englishman. As Premier Stalin has also commanded that he be executed, we will share a secret, you and I. Will that not be enjoyable?"

"I am sure it will be, Comrade Commissar."

"Yes," Beria said. "But I think, as we are to be partners in secrets, we should become partners in everything. Do you not agree, Tatiana? I have admired you for a long time, Tatiana Andreievna. That I have never touched you is because you are Jennie Ligachevna's daughter, and virtually Premier Stalin's god-daughter, if we any longer have such things. But now I feel I need no longer restrain myself. Do you not agree?"

Tatiana licked her lips. "I agree, Comrade Commissar. If you command me to do so."

"I do command you, Tatiana. I would like you to visit my apartment tonight. You will use the secret entrance; I will give you the combination. We have much to discuss. And celebrate. We shall have a party." Tatiana bowed her head.

Tatiana strode through the corridors beneath Lubyanka Square. She felt angry, vicious. More angry and vicious than ever before in her life, even when she had been told of Gregory's execution. There had been periods of white hot fury, during the War. But these had been immediately expiated. When, as an eighteen-year-old, she had been captured and raped, again and again by the Germans, she had hated all mankind. But she had escaped, and in the process had killed the two men most responsible for her mistreatment. When her half-brother, and first lover, Feodor Ligachev, had drowned in the Pripet Marshes, again she had known nothing but fury . . . but there had been a whole army on which she could wreak her vengeance, and she had done so with consummate ability and success.

When the War had ended, she had supposed such extremes of emotion were behind her. She was well aware of her beauty, the hold she exerted on men, and even women, by her sheer presence. But she had resolved that there would be no more involvement, no more personal feelings in her life. Not even to her profit; she needed no profit. Even when she had been informed that it had been Beria's personal wish that the ex-guerilla commander should be incorporated in the KGB, and that the quick way to promotion was to give herself to the Commissar, she had not been interested.

137

Actually, she had been repelled by the great moonface and his reputedly obscene desires. And she had known, however much he hinted, and however often he had clearly enjoyed watching her train and then afterwards, watching her bathe, he would never dare take her by force because of her links with Premier Stalin. But she had been unable totally to suppress the instincts of her own nature. She and Gregory Asimov had adventured together to the ultimate degree, lain shoulder to shoulder as they had slain the enemy, and come close to being slain by them, eaten and slept and bathed together. During the War, she had not been interested in a boy. And he, while his heroine-worship had been plain to see, had realised that she was beyond his reach and had sought the comfort of Natasha Renkova's arms. After Natasha had been taken by the SS and tortured to death, he had been distraught, and she had comforted him. But still as a younger brother.

Only the end of the War, and their joint recruitment into the KGB, had finally brought them together, sexually. And although she would never have admitted it to anyone, much less Gregory himself, she had fallen in love with him. The thought that he was dead, shot down by his old comrade-in-arms Shatrav . . . Now she wanted only vengeance. During the War they had called her the Ice Maiden. Now she again wanted to be that demonic figure. But she could not touch Shatrav. At the moment!

And again she had been betrayed by her own instincts. She refused to admit that she could have fallen in love with Andrew Morgan. She had entered upon the task of seducing him and destroying him with all the eager venom of her training and personality. That he had been a charming, thoughtful, indeed, *nice* man, had meant nothing to her in the context of her job. That he was also totally innocent should equally have meant nothing to her; it was part of the Russian system, as created by her Uncle Joe, that if to preserve the State it was necessary a hundred innocents be eliminated in order that one guilty person might also be removed, that was for the good of the State. Perhaps it was this stroke of weakness, surfacing for the first time in her life, causing her to reject that monstrous concept, that was most distressing. But equally distressing was where it had led her. She had sought to raise herself to Beria's level, or bring him down to hers, by the simple means of using what her brains had told her. And she had stepped into a trap. Last night had been the most terrible of her life. When the German officers had been holding her down and thrusting their filthy members between her legs, she had never doubted that she would destroy them, even if she died doing so.

So perhaps she could now destroy Lavrenty Beria, and herself at the same time: were she to go to Uncle Joe . . . but there was the point. She could no longer be sure of Uncle Joe. Not even Mother could be sure of Uncle Joe. That he could be terrible was well known. But always in the past he had kept in reserve at least an aspect of kindness, certainly to her mother and herself, almost of love, at times. Now, the way he looked at them when they had tea together reminded her of a huge lizard, waiting to snake out its tongue and seize and swallow its prey, just as the way he would drift off into an almost somnolent reverie, sometimes scarce appearing to breathe, made her wonder if he was not about to die. That was the most important point. The Premier was getting older every day. The War had taken more out of him than anyone not in his innermost circle suspected. And when he died, what then? There were several aspirants for the all-powerful position. There was Georgy Malenkov, chubby and apparently good-humoured, but petulant and unsure of himself. There was Nikita Kruschev, even more chubby and apparently good-humoured; but Kruschev, who had been a party boss in the Ukraine before and during the Great Patriotic War, had proved himself to be as ruthless as any other member of the Politburo, without, like Malenkov, suggesting that he possessed the single-minded ferocity of Stalin.

And then there was Lavrenty Beria, who already controlled the immense apparatus that in turn controlled Russia. Beria was Stalin's obvious successor. He was already making plans for that succession. Thus he had to be accommodated, in everything he wished. There was a horrifying thought. Especially when one had been literally sucked into his embrace, forced to submit to his questing fingers, forced to use one's lips on every nook and cranny of that white, moon-like body, so like his face and head

– and to do all of this in the company of others, also worshipping at the shrine of the future Master of Russia. Horrifying indeed.

She could do nothing about it. He was omnipotent, and would become more so. She could only suffer those obscene embraces and rise with him. The alternative was to perish. And in the meantime, be as vicious as was her master.

"Atya," she said kindly. "How is your leg today?" She knew Atya's leg ached when it rained.

Atya was taken entirely by surprise. Tatiana had never inquired after her health before, since her return to duty. "It hurts, Comrade Captain. But my shift ends this afternoon. I shall be able to rest it." She could hardly wait to get home; she had so much to tell her man.

"You will have to extend your shift," Tatiana told her. "By several days. I need you, for special service. Do not worry, you may extend your leave period when you have completed your task. And there will be a bonus. Will you not like that?"

Atya was still gathering her thoughts. "Of course, Comrade Captain. I am to remain on duty here?"

"You will accompany me on a mission," Tatiana told her.

Despite her concern at having her arrangements disrupted, Atya swelled with pride; she had never been taken, or sent, on a mission before. "We are to deliver the two prisoners," Tatiana told her. "We shall enjoy doing that, eh?"

"Oh, yes, Comrade Commissar." Atya's brain was working overtime. "They are to be executed?" But that would hardly require several days.

"No," Tatiana said. "They are to be delivered to the archipeligo."

"Ah," Atya said. Yes, she thought, several days. And Johnnie was expecting her, tonight. There would be no way of letting him know why she was delayed, or that she was being delayed at all – that would be too risky. Would he wait for her? For a while, certainly. But if it was too long a while he would have to assume that she had been found out and arrested, and that therefore his own life was in danger. Then . . . she did not know what he might do. She would have to risk it. "With respect, Comrade Captain,"

140

she said. "I would like permission to return to my home. I shall be very quick."

"Why is this necessary?"

Atya flushed. "My cat, Comrade Captain. He is very old, and very precious to me. Normally he is fed by my neighbour when I am on duty. But as I am expected back this afternoon, he will no longer be fed, unless I can make another arrangement."

She waited, trying to keep her face immobile, as the Captain studied her. Then Tatiana smiled. "We cannot possibly put your dear old cat at risk, Atya. Of course you may go home. Give me your keys." Atya unclipped the bunch of keys from her belt. "Be sure to return here by six," Tatiana said. "We will leave as soon as it is dark."

"I will be here, Comrade Captain," Atya said. "And thank you."

Tatiana watched her limp up the steps. She thought it odd, and potentially dangerous, that neither she nor anyone else, certainly not Beria, had ever given any thought to the possibility that people like Atya might have lives of their own, outside the confines of the Lyubyanka. An elderly cat, indeed. She picked up the phone on Atya's desk. "Captain Budenski. Captain? Captain Gosykinya here. The woman Atya Schulenskaya is just leaving the premises. I wish her followed, clandestinely, and a report made on where she goes and who she meets. This report must be delivered to me, personally."

"It shall be, Comrade Captain."

Tatiana replaced the phone, picked up the valise that had been packed for her, and went down into the cells. She went to where Priscilla was confined, unlocked the door. The Princess sat on the bare floor, leaning against the wall, turned away from the door and its peephole. She only half stirred as the door opened. Tatiana closed it behind her. "Well, Aunt Priscilla," she said. "How are we today?" The plate of food was untouched, although the water and the vodka had been drunk. "You must eat," Tatiana remonstrated. "You must keep up your strength. You will need it. If you will not eat, voluntarily, you will have to be force fed. I am sure you will not like that."

Now at last Priscilla turned her head. "You mean I am not to be executed?"

Tatiana chuckled. "Now, whatever gave you that idea, Aunt Priscilla." She placed her valise in the corner, knelt beside the older woman, stroked the silky golden hair. "You are going somewhere you will be safe. I am taking you there myself. And do you know what is going to happen to you when you reach your destination?" She ran her hand across Priscilla's shoulders and down her back. "Your guards will rape you, time and again." She pulled Priscilla's arms apart and caressed her breasts. "Then they will flog you, time and again." She stroked Priscilla's hips and buttocks. "Then they will cut off your hair. This hair too." She slid her hand over Priscilla's thighs and between her legs. "Then they will send you into a barracks with other women. These will almost certainly rape you again, time and again. Will you not enjoy all of that, dearest aunt?"

Priscilla had made no attempt to resist her. Now she looked into her eyes, and Tatiana suddenly felt, almost for the first time in her life, a small spasm of fear. Those grey eyes had looked upon so many people, perhaps just like that, and those people were all dead. But, she reminded herself, people who went to gulags very seldom came back. She stood up. "There are clothes in that valise. Put them on. Be dressed by the time I come back. Or I will beat you myself."

"And the man?" Priscilla asked. "Morgan?"

"I am going to visit him now," Tatiana said.

Chapter Seven

The Quest

"She's going to be a looker, just like her mother," Alex said.

Elaine looked down at the tiny scrap of humanity cradled in her arm. This should have been the most joyous occasion of her life. Instead, she could only think: just like her grandmother. "Nothing?" she asked.

Alex's shoulders sagged, and then squared again. Elaine knew that even after several months he had not yet fully recovered from the effects of the two bullets slashing into his body; he had not yet been able to resume his practice. But he could move, and he would improve, they had been promised. He was more fortunate than his stepfather. Joseph might have survived the assassination attempt, just, but it was not anticipated he would ever walk again.

"I'm afraid they've closed the case," Alex said. "There is simply no trace. They reckon it was a kidnapping that went wrong, that Mom fought them until she died, and they were left with a corpse on their hands which had to be disposed of."

"But . . . Asimov's body . . ."

"Had two bullet holes in it, remember? That would figure if Mom managed to get hold of a gun."

"So they disposed of her body, but left his lying by the roadside?"

"The FBI figure maybe they panicked. They've checked Asimov out with the Soviets. Gregory Asimov opted out right after the War, emigrated without permission, and disappeared. Had he

143

been slightly more important it would have been hailed as a defection. He clearly entered this country illegally. The Russians have even been apologetic, that one of their nationals should have been engaged in kidnapping one of our citizens. They say he must have got in with the mob when he arrived here."

"And you believe that?"

"Of course I don't, Elaine. But the fact is that Mom has disappeared without trace and has been gone over six months now. We just have to face facts."

"You think she's dead."

Alex hunched his shoulders. "Yes, dearest. I don't want to, but there comes a time when you have to face facts. She's dead, and we shall probably never find out where she's buried."

The baby began to cry, as Elaine's muscles tensed. A nurse hurried in, and she willingly handed over the child. She had never less wanted to be inhibited by the responsibilities of motherhood. "Okay, so the FBI have closed the case. What about the State Department?"

"I told you," Alex said patiently. "They've checked with the Soviets, and been given a full account of Gregory's background. It's all there, the Pripet, war hero . . . then a job as a schoolmaster or something . . ."

Elaine snorted. "What was he supposed to teach? The art of blowing up trains?"

"I don't know. But the fact is, there is no reason for the State Department to take it any further, even supposing they could. Anyway, they don't want to create any additional tensions with this Berlin thing coming to the boil."

"Are we going to go to war over that?"

"Of course we aren't. But we aren't going to abandon Berlin either. We're going to keep it supplied by air."

"And when the Russians shoot down our aircraft?"

"That'll be another matter. But the State Department doesn't think it'll come to that. They reckon it's all a big bluff. But you'll see they don't want any additional crises cropping up."

Elaine refrained from telling him that this particular crisis had actually cropped up long before the Russians had cut off access to Berlin, and the State Department had refused to create a fuss about it then. Except make those absurd allusions – she had never told Alexei about that, as she had not wanted to excite him while he had been in a critical condition. "What does Joe say?"

"Oh, you know Joe," Alex said. "He lives in the past, recalling all the great deeds he, and Mother, accomplished."

"So he still believes she's alive."

"Elaine, Joe, bless his dear heart, sometimes still believes the Tsar is ruling in Russia."

As soon as she was settled in at home, Elaine took Alexandra along to visit Joseph, who was still in hospital, although well enough to sit in the grounds in his wheelchair on good days. "The last of the Bolugayevskas," Joseph said. "At least, in the direct line. Priscilla will love her."

Elaine sat on the bench beside him, pushed the pram to and fro. "You know she's alive, don't you, Joe."

"Well, of course she's alive, Elaine. People like Priscilla don't die before their time. And hers isn't yet, by a long shot."

Elaine studied the lined, wrinkled face. Joseph looked a lot older than his age. He always had, because of the life he had led, especially those twelve years in Stalin's prisons, but he had aged even more since his narrow escape from death – and the disappearance of the woman he loved more than life itself. "Then where do you think she is?"

A shadow passed across his face. "Stalin has her." Then he smiled. "But I am going to get her back. The moment I get out of this chair."

Elaine bit her lip. And then forced a smile. "Would you like to tell me how you intend to do that? I want to help. So does Alex, even if he won't admit it."

"Well, the first thing to do is find out where she is being held."

"How? How do we do that?"

"We collect every scrap of evidence we can. Everything we know or can find out, and we make every logical deduction possible. As for instance, Stalin held Priscilla prisoner once before, during the War. He held her a prisoner in the Kremlin. And then just let her go."

"Was she ill-treated?"

"No, she wasn't. It was a sexual matter."

"You can just say that?"

Joseph shrugged. "Your mother-in-law has been through many worse sexual experiences than that. As it happened, Stalin was impotent. Even with Priscilla."

"And you both got out. Wouldn't that have had some propaganda value?"

"Perhaps. But we had mutually agreed to, how shall I put it, call a truce between the Bolugayevskis and the Bolsheviks. We didn't want them coming after us as they went after Trotsky. So that was how it was left, and we kept our part of the bargain. Then suddenly, several years later, Stalin up and snatches her again."

"Maybe he regained his potency. I'm sorry, Joe, I didn't mean to be flippant. But there has to be a reason."

"Of course. And I'll tell you what it is. A man called Andrew Morgan."

"I'm not with you."

"Let me tell you about it," Joseph said, and did so.

"How come you never told us about that before?" Elaine asked.

"It didn't seem all that important, at the time. To Priscilla, of course, it was just too exciting for words."

"I still don't see what connection a romantic Welshman setting off to find his father's grave can have with Mom being kidnapped."

"The connection is obvious, Elaine. That fellow wasn't looking for his father's grave at all. He was a British spy, using your mother's well-known desire to be involved to get himself not only into Russia, but into the heart of the Kremlin. Priscilla gave him a letter of introduction to my sister, who's a bosom buddy of Stalin's."

"I met your sister during the War," Elaine said, thoughtfully. "She seemed a very nice person."

"She is. But she's also a dyed-in-the-wool Red. Some people are," he added, ingenuously.

"And you think the Reds found out that Mom helped this Morgan get into Russia?"

"Well, as she wrote to Jennie, they would certainly have known about it."

"And then, when they learned Morgan was a spy . . . but that means he must have been arrested."

"Not necessarily. The Russians are very good at fishing, playing their catch until they're ready to scoop him up. Or her."

"So they snatched Mom. But why? So she gave a British spy an entrée. That doesn't mean she's a spy herself."

"You don't understand how the Russian mind works," Joseph explained. "They're paranoid. And additionally, they still regard Priscilla as one of theirs. She may have been born over here, but she's a Bolugayevska by descent, by marriage, and by inclination."

"You mean she's been in their hands for eight months now, being treated as a spy? My God! She could've been shot."

"Priscilla is alive," Joseph said, fiercely. "I know it. And as soon as I get out of this goddamed chair I am going to go find her." The baby began to cry.

"As I said, much as I love the dear old soul," Alex said, "you have to admit that sometimes he's half round the bend. Can't blame him, really. Quite apart from being crippled for life . . ."

"He refuses to admit that."

"You read the report from his doctors. So he doesn't accept it. Just as he doesn't accept that Mom is dead."

"Listen," Elaine said. "If the State Department won't help, we could at least see if *we* can turn up something. We could write your aunt. Or Tatiana. For God's sake, we fought with her in the War, And she had something going for you, remember?"

"That's something I'd rather forget," Alex said.

"It happened, Alex. And now we need her help. If you won't do it, then I will. There's the man Morgan, too. I think we should get in touch with him."

"Just how to do you propose to do that?"

147

"Well . . . advertise. He asked for Mom's help, once. Surely we're now entitled to ask for his?"

Alex looked sceptical. The trouble with Alex, Elaine reckoned, was although he was a super guy, a marvellous lover and a tremendous man of action when pointed in the right direction and told to go for it, he was also a Russian, and that meant he was a fatalist. That led him to accept that his mother, who had courted death and disaster on so many occasions, had finally met with the end many would have said she so richly deserved. Elaine was an American, and couldn't accept that point of view. She also had much in mind, and on her conscience, that *she* had really brought about this entire situation. If she had just said to Gregory when he had appeared at her house, "Nice to see you again, to see you nice. Now goodbye," this situation would never have arisen. Or would it? If everything she had read, and indeed knew, about the Russians was correct, once they set out to get somebody they generally did just that.

What a time to be a mother, unable to move a muscle while she had Baby Alexandra to care for. But if she couldn't go to Moscow, she could still write letters.

Lawrence had never seen Halstead so agitated. He entered the office with his hat still on his head, took it off, and threw it onto an adjacent chair. He was not wearing a buttonhole. And he had shaved off his moustache, some time ago, Lawrence reckoned. "Welcome back," he murmured.

Halstead placed a file on the desk. "It's all there. Russia will test an A-Bomb within a matter of weeks. I'm afraid my mission was not a success."

"On the contrary," Lawrence murmured, opening the file but doing no more than glance at the first page. "We knew it was going to happen. And as nearly all their worthwhile information came out of the States, our hands are entirely clean."

"It's very nice of you to say so," Halstead said. "I don't like failing. I also don't like losing good operatives with no end result."

"Quite," Lawrence said, sympathetically. "How many did you lose?"

"Just the three. But Crabtree was one of the very best. He went under the name of Smith. Not very original, but the Russians don't really go for originality. The Kuslovs were a sad case. They only wanted a little extra money."

"You say only three." Lawrence picked up a note from his desk. "What about Morgan?"

"Morgan was an innocent bystander," Halstead said. "How he got involved, I have no idea. I think the Russians realised that, too. They didn't execute him, but packed him off to a gulag."

"Have you any idea which one?"

"Yes. Number Seventeen. Not a nice place. But then, none of them are."

"And you say he was an innocent bystander. Then what of the Princess Bolugayevska?"

"Now, that I cannot say. My information is that there was, is, some kind of personal vendetta between the Princess and the Kremlin."

"Is?"

"She too has not been executed, to my knowledge. But she's in Gulag Number One. Now that is serious business. No one has ever come out of Gulag Number One. Someone must dislike her very much."

"I am not going to ask the source of all your information, James," Lawrence said. "That is your business. However, have you never had the slightest suggestion that Morgan was *not* an innocent bystander?"

Halstead's frown was back. "No. Why?"

"You are aware that he and the Princess Bolugayevska were in cahoots?"

"In what way?"

"She sent him to Russia."

"You know this?"

Lawrence had a file of his own. This he now handed across the desk. "These letters and advertisements have been appearing in English newspapers for the past year."

Halstead studied them with his usual care. "This young woman being?"

149

"The Princess's daughter-in-law."

"Who wants to find out what has happened to her mother-in-law. With respect, Mr Lawrence, I don't find anything sinister in that. Okay, so they do tie Morgan to the Princess, but I don't see what it has to do with us."

"You are obviously not aware that the Princess Bolugayevska's sister-in-law, an Englishwoman named Jennifer Ligachevna, is a rabid Bolshevik, who lives in Moscow, and is a member of the Kremlin's inner set. That includes Uncle Joe himself."

"Tangled," Halstead admitted.

"More than you think. The Princess did not go to Russia of her own free will. She was, as our American cousins would have it, snatched from her home in Boston. The matter was hushed up, because no one wanted a crisis at that time. Well, we've had a few crises since, with that Berlin impasse. That's behind us now. Now there are other things afoot. As for example, one of the reasons the Americans, and ourselves, are not too bothered about the Russians having an A-Bomb is that we are working on something much bigger and more destructive. This one is based on the hydrogen atom, and as I say, makes the Atom Bomb look like a hand grenade. That'll leave them with some more catching up to do. Obviously we would all like to know just how much."

"So it's back to square one." Halstead sighed.

"I have no right to ask you to go back on such a dangerous mission . . ." Lawrence hesitated.

"It goes with the job," Halstead said. "And I have become quite fond of my number one over there, even if she is a thug."

"She?" It was Lawrence's turn to raise an eyebrow.

"One takes them where one finds them," Halstead pointed out. "However, I still don't see where this Bolshevik princess comes into it."

"I will have it explained to you. I just wanted to put you in the picture." He pressed his intercom. "Show Mr Eldridge in, will you, Polly. Eldridge, by the way, has no idea what you really do, Halstead. Nor should he."

Jonathan Eldridge was a tall, thin man with a hatchet face. He had State Department written all over him before he opened his mouth. When he did, he spoke with a slow drawl.

"This is Mr Halstead," Lawrence introduced. "He works for our Russian department, and has some sources of information over there. We feel he may be able to help you. Us."

Eldridge shook hands. "Pleased to meet you, Halstead." He looked at Lawrence.

"Oh, please sit down," Lawrence said. "And just to put your mind at rest, Halstead has Class A clearance. I've put him into the general picture."

"What we would like, Halstead," Eldridge said, "is to discover where Mrs Bolugayevska-Cromb is being held."

"And?"

"You can leave the rest to us."

"I can tell you now where she is being held, Mr Eldridge. But if you are thinking of either getting at her or getting her out, I would forget it. She's in a top security prison, situated in a Kazakhstan desert."

"Right. Would you take offence if I asked you to verify that information?"

"I think I am entitled to ask why, as it could be risky."

"Well, as you have Class A clearance, I guess I'll tell you," Eldridge said. "I need to fill you in on this so-called Princess Bolugayevska. She was born in the States, to American parents, but her mother was half-Russian, and that half was Bolugayevska. This Priscilla ups and marries her cousin, Alexei Bolugayevski, the then Prince of Bolugayen, a guy twenty-nine years older than her, and thus becomes Princess of Bolugayen. Then comes the Revolution, and she has to flee, with her lover, a guy called Joseph Cromb, who, would you believe it, is also a cousin. This dame sure believes in keeping her favours close to home. Now these people are aristocrats. People hated by the Reds, so they say. But it is a fact that Joseph Cromb's mother, who was a Countess Bolugayevska, was a Red herself, and the family remained very involved with what was happening in Russia. Joseph Cromb's sister married a Red agent, a hired killer for Lenin and Stalin. Joseph Cromb himself disappeared into Russia for several years in the twenties and thirties . . ."

"I've read some of his articles," Halstead remarked. "But he was imprisoned by the Reds and treated quite savagely."

"That's what *he* says, Halstead. The fact is that he got out. Not too many people do that, unless the Reds want them to."

"And the articles?"

"So who paid any attention to a few articles? Except the State Department, who assumed they were genuine. Because they wanted to, at that time. And in that time, guess who also returns to Russia, and is fêted? The Princess Bolugayevska. You think the Reds would have sent her to join her boyfriend, if there was anything genuine about the set-up. Then they both returned to Russia during the War. Okay, so Joseph Cromb was sent by the State Department as an assistant to Hopkins. He was the obvious man, fluent Russian speaker, Russian himself by birth, what more could we ask? And his wife goes too. Heck, their kid even fought with the partisans. But again, that was when we wanted to be friends. Things have kind of changed since then. One of our senators, a guy named McCarthy, is investigating the infiltration of the State Department by Reds, and it's beginning to look like our entire society has been so infiltrated. Now here are a few facts I would like you to consider. Over the last few years we have had some success with rooting out the atomic spies, so they say. The Rosenbergs, Chambers, Hiss . . ."

Lawrence raised a finger; he was an exact man. "Hiss was never convicted of betraying atomic secrets. Only perjury."

Eldridge shrugged. "Same thing, in my book. Anyway, those are the names everyone knows. They weren't all, or even a fraction, of the agents involved. Now, you tell me why, as soon as it gets real hot, and as soon as Senator McCarthy starts looking for Reds under the bed, the Princess Bolugayevska ups and flees to Russia."

"Our information is that she was kidnapped by the KGB," Halstead said.

"Poppycock, if you'll excuse the expression. The Reds were looking after their own."

"They shot and nearly killed both her husband and her son. And one of their own people was also killed."

"So there's a mystery. It'll all come out in due course. Although we do know that all Russian agents are prepared to sacrifice their own families if required to do so by their bosses. And the fact is, the Princess did a bunk. Now, before all this happened, she sent an agent of hers into Russia. An Englishman named Morgan, Right?"

"I think Mr Morgan would prefer to be known as a Welsh-man."

"Same difference."

"Our information is that Morgan was a totally innocent bystander who went to Russia to research a book and asked the Princess for letters of introduction."

"He asked an old-style Tsarist aristocrat, as she claims to be, for letters of introduction to Communists? And the moment he gets to Russia he sets up house with the Princess's Red cousin, Tatiana Gosykinya. Now there is a toughie."

"Mr Eldridge, Morgan was arrested by the KGB and savagely tortured, by this same Tatiana Gosykinya. So was the Princess Bolugayevska."

"You believe that? You were there?"

Halstead frowned. Atya had been there. Or so she claimed. "They were heard screaming," he said, half to himself.

"Big deal. If I started hollering now, don't you think your secretary would think you guys were knocking me about?"

"So, Mr Eldridge, your theory is that the Princess Bolugayevska is, and has been for some time, a Red agent, that she has betrayed atomic secrets, that she sacrificed her husband and her son to escape America when she felt she was about to be found out, and that she is now living on caviar and champagne somewhere inside Russia. Am I right so far?"

"You got it."

"What possible connection can she have had with any atomic secrets?"

Eldridge gave a thin smile. "We're hoping she's gonna tell us that, when we get her back."

"And that's what you want us to do?"

"Hell, no, this is our baby. All we want you guys to do is pinpoint her for us. We'll do the rest."

Halstead rubbed his nose. "You don't think it might be a good idea just to let things lie? She can't harm you any more, now that she's in Russia, even if she is a spy."

"We reckon she can put the finger on every Red agent in the States," Eldridge said. "According to the lists McCarthy has given us, most of the people who attended her soirées in Boston were Reds. Or at least Pinks. Come along, guys, all we're looking for is a little cooperation."

"Mr Halstead will give you all the cooperation you require, Mr Eldridge," Lawrence promised.

"Right. Well, we look forward to hearing from you, some time soon." He shook hands, did not appear to notice Halstead's slight hesitation.

Halstead waited until the door had closed, then he remarked, "That man is as mad as a March Hare."

"I agree that he is drawing a very long bow." Lawrence sat down again. "The Americans are going through one of their periods of hysteria. I'm afraid this happens from time to time. Down to ten years ago it didn't matter all that much, although their hysterics in 1929 wrecked the world economy. But then they were playing no political part of any significance. Now they are the most powerful nation the world has ever seen, well, us lesser mortals need to go along with their moods. The fact is, James, while I do not know this chap McCarthy, and have no idea whether he is a genuine investigatory politician or a publicity-seeking demagogue, there have been some disquieting aspects of American government over the past few years. I'm not talking about the atomic secrets right now. But Roosevelt certainly felt that he was the only Western statesman who could handle Stalin and the Reds. To do this, he needed around him men who *knew* Stalin and the Reds, spoke their language, literally and metaphorically. A lot of these people obtained posts in the State Department, or worked for them at some time or other. Joseph Cromb is a case in point. Some of them rose quite high. I am not saying that all of these people were Comnmunist sympathisers. But it seems certain that some of them were. Now, we became aware of these goings-on as early as anyone, and we even tried to warn Roosevelt of the possible risks. He wouldn't be warned. Truman of course has no illusions about the Reds, so I suppose it was inevitable that some kind of backlash had to follow. The point I'm making is that while there seems to be one hell of a lot of smoke, there could actually be a little fire down below. I'm sure you'll agree that the possibility of some high-ranking American official with access to God knows what secrets being a card-carrying Communist is just too horrifying to contemplate. And now we're coming up to a moment of crunch. I told you the Yanks are developing something really big, based on the hydrogen atom, and we are told that one bomb made on this system will deliver a payload a hundred times more devastating than the atomic bomb dropped on Hiroshima. That one atom bomb laid a big city flat, and is supposed to have killed more than fifty thousand people outright, with God alone knows how many dead since from radiation sickness. Multiply that by a hundred and see if you can sleep nights. You can understand that the idea of the Reds getting hold of *that* formula is causing a few ulcers. If the Princess Bolugayevska is the mastermind behind the Red system in the States, then you can understand that the State Department would like to talk with her, desperately."

"And if I told you that I am perfectly sure the Princess is entirely innocent of any crime other than hating the Reds more than your friend McCarthy?"

"That would be a great pity. It does not alter what we are being asked to do by our allies."

Halstead put his hand up to his left lapel, as if he would have plucked out his buttonhole and thrown it away, realised he wasn't wearing one, and left the office.

"Jimmy!" Atya positively squealed, and then hurled herself across the room at her lover. "I did not expect you back. Not so soon, anyway. Is it not terribly dangerous?"

Halstead kissed her several times. "Not more so than usual."

"But, with your people arrested . . ."

"More than a year ago. The fuss has died down. Are you not pleased to see me?"

"Oh, Jimmy . . ." she squirmed against him. "I thought I'd never see you again."

"Presents." He indicated the box on the table.

Atya tore it open, pulled out the silk stockings. She could only wear them when off duty, or questions would be asked, but she still loved to feel the silk against her skin. "Oh, Jimmy!"

"I can't stay very long," Halstead said, "I need information."

"Information. Always information. Sometimes I think you come to me only for information."

"Strip off and I'll prove you wrong," Halstead said. When she was satisfied, he lay on his back and smoked a cigarette. "Tell me about the Princess Bolugayevska," he said.

Atya also smoked. "What about her?"

"You said she had been placed in Gulag Number One. That you were with Captain Gosykinya when she was transferred there from the Lyublyanka."

"I went with her. And the man, Morgan. We took him to Gulag Number Seventeen."

"That was last year. Is the Princess still there?"

"People do not leave Gulag Number One, Johnny. They also do not stay there very long, above the ground. I would suppose the Princess is dead by now."

"Can you find out for me?"

Atya rose on her elbow. "Why is this woman so important?"

"Just take my word for it that she is. There must be lists about, in the Lyubyanka, as to who is where, who is dead, who is still alive."

"It would be very dangerous for me to attempt to see any of the lists. I am a gaoler, not a clerk. My business is in the cells, not the offices and filing cabinets. Anyway, it would do no good. The Princess was top secret. Her identity is known to very few people. She is, or was, Prisoner Number Seven Hundred and Six. Nothing more. I should not think she is on any list."

156

"You are telling me she is only the seven hundred and sixth prisoner to be sent to Gulag Number One?"

Atya grinned. "Of course not. She is *Special Prisoner* Number Seven Hundred and Six. Those are the ones for whom there can be no identity. They have been condemned to death, but the State has decided to keep them alive for the time being, just in case they may be useful."

Halstead stroked his chin, thoughtfully. "I still need to find out if she is alive, and if she is still in Gulag Number One."

"Men," Atya grumbled.

Lawrence slid the sheet of paper across his desk, and Eldridge picked it up. He had waited a year for this report, and now he was suspicious. "You trust this guy, Halstead?" he asked.

"Halstead is just about our most reliable source of news inside Russia," Lawrence said.

"And he says the Princess Bolugayevska is still inside this Gulag Number One. I find that hard to credit."

"If she were, as you suspect, a Russian agent, I would agree with you. Although even Russian agents fall out with their masters, from time to time. However, if she were *not* a Russian agent, but someone suspected by them of being a Western agent, or merely a maverick aristocrat who has spent her life causing trouble for the Soviets, it entirely makes sense that she should be locked up for life in the most unpleasant circumstances. I feel very sorry for her."

"You do, huh? Well, how about another scenario: that she is just what we think she is, and that she has been honourably retired by the Soviets?"

"Into a gulag?" Lawrence asked incredulously. "That has to be absurd."

"You reckon? Do you, does anyone, know what really goes on in those so-called prisons? There aren't too many people about who have been in, and come out."

"Joseph Cromb did it."

"Joseph Cromb *says* he did it. But even if they are prisons, where safer could a retired agent be? I can see her now, in

157

some private apartment, living on that champagne and caviar you were talking about . . . but she's not going to get away with it. No, sir."

Lawrence's stare was even more incredulous. "You're going to try to get her out? With respect, Mr Eldridge, that has got to be madness."

"So it'll be tough. It can be done."

Lawrence laid his hands flat on his desk. "I will have nothing to do with it. And neither will any of my people. Especially Halstead."

Eldridge grinned. "Like I told you, Mr Lawrence, this is our pigeon. I'll see you around."

Lavrenty Beria hummed as his aircraft settled onto the runway outside Astrakhan. He always enjoyed visiting his dacha. Quite apart from being so far removed from the constant intrigue of Moscow, the constant stress of having to cope with Stalin's progressive paranoia, he always enjoyed being with Sonia, and now, with her daughter; the pair of them were so obviously happy together. It warmed the heart. Even if he knew they both hated him. But they were the symbols of what he would one day achieve. Would he? Had he waited so long that his entire plan had dwindled to the status of a dream? He kept telling himself, certainly not. But his plan was so immense it could not be risked by any premature action. He intended to inherit the mastership of Russia, which, now that it too possessed the Atom Bomb, was one of the two most powerful nations on earth. He was well aware that the Americans were experimenting with something new, or so his agents told him, but he took that with a pinch of salt. Anyway, if the Americans did build a more destructive version of the Bomb, his people would simply have to get hold of that secret as well.

It was Russia he wanted. And he had to have it, legitimately, certainly in the eyes of his fellow members of the inner circle. There could be no doubts. All of those men, who like himself were responsible for thousands of deaths, baulked at the idea of murder amongst themselves. Without that mutual trust they

158

could never function. Stalin himself could never have functioned had not Lenin died, virtually before the eyes of the world, as a result of a series of strokes. And Stalin himself had never dared murder his arch-enemy Trotsky for some fifteen years after he had been expelled from Russia. Thus the pattern had been set. But Beria had never envisaged that it could go on this long. Lenin had been only fifty-four when he died. Stalin was now past seventy! It was incredible that a man who had lived such a life, suffered so much stress, was overweight, ate and drank more than was good for him, and had a sexual problem, could have survived so long. Beria still believed that the introduction of a spectre from his past – or even two as he now had two available – might induce the fatal heart attack he so desperately sought. The question was, when. To attempt it and *not* induce a heart attack could be catastrophic. When!

Polkov was agitated. "There is a message for you, Comrade Commissar. To call Captain Gosykinya the moment you arrive." Beria frowned at him. The little witch was presuming, commanding *him* to call *her*. She could have contacted him on the plane by radio. But had she done that, their conversation could have been overheard. He tapped his chin as they drove into the courtyard before the dacha.

"Lavrenty Pavlovich!" Sonia's expression belied the apparent warmth of her greeting. Every time he came here she had to expect it to be the moment she both anticipated and dreaded.

"Sonia!" Beria embraced her, regarded Anna, who gave a little bob. She had filled out very well, but her hair was dead white and the years of suffering, firstly at the hands of the Germans and then the Soviets, remained etched on her face. Beria presumed Sonia had confided in her the truth of their seclusion. But if that were so, then she would at least feel secure in her future, as he had promised Sonia her daughter would survive, and be allowed to leave Russia, provided *she* fulfilled her part of the bargain. "It is good to see you both looking so well," he said. "Now I must make a call."

He went into his office and used his private line. "I understand

Caprtain Gosykinya wishes to speak with me, Maria," he told his secretary.

"She is waiting now, Comrade Commissar."

"Well?" Beria demanded as Tatiana came on the line.

Tatiana's voice was strained. "Comrade Commissar . . . there has been an assault on Gulag Number One."

"What? What did say?" Beria could not believe his ears. No one had ever attacked a gulag. No one outside the KGB and the prison guards even knew where they were. "Are you mad?"

"I have received a call, from the Commandant, Comrade Karpova. She states that an assault force of masked men attempted to force the gates this morning."

"Masked men? That is ridiculous. From where?"

"She does not know. They must have come across the Afghan border."

"You are telling me, Tatiana Andreievna, that one of our prisons has been attacked by Afghans?"

"No, Comrade Commissar. These were not Afghans. They were Caucasians."

"From where?"

"Comrade Karpova does not know. They carried no identification. But she is sure they were westerners."

"You keep using the past tense."

"They are all dead, Comrade Commissar."

There was a relief. "Did any succeed in entering the prison?"

"Yes, Comrade Commissar. But they were all shot down before they could reach their objective."

"Ah! Their objective. What was that?"

"Comrade Karpova thinks they were seeking the Princess; several of them were carrying photographs of her. She only knows her as Number Seven Hundred and Six, but she knows she is very important. That is why she called me."

Beria did some very rapid thinking. "Who else knows about this?"

"Only the people at the gulag."

"It must be hushed up. Tell Karpova to have the bodies buried and forgotten. You are sure none of them survived long enough to be interrogated?"

"Comrade Karpova says they all died instantly."

"Very good. Carry out my instructions."

"And the Princess?"

"What about the Princess?"

"I merely wondered, Comrade Commissar, if you wished her disposed of. After all, if some Western group can be so concerned as to wish to take her out of a gulag . . . out of Gulag Number One . . ."

"They have to be demented," Beria said.

"Yes. But that means someone, somewhere, knows where she is."

"If they were after the Princess, Tatiana Andreievna, I think you need to think very carefully about that. Because only you and I know where she is, am I right?"

"Well . . . are you accusing me of treason, Comrade Commissar?"

Beria chuckled over the phone. "Of course I am not, Tatiana. Of all the people in my employ, I trust you the most. I do not believe they were after the Princess. But if they were, well, perhaps they will try again. And the next time, perhaps Comrade Karpova will remember to take one of them alive, so that we may learn some more about them. Good day to you, Tatiana."

Tatiana slowly replaced the phone. Maria, a brilliant blonde, who, apart from her buck teeth, was a handsome woman, hovered anxiously. "There is nothing wrong?"

"Nothing is ever *wrong*, Maria Feodorovna," Tatiana said. "Some days are just more interesting than others." Beria had not made the point, or had forgotten, that there *was* a third party privy to their secret. She had never supposed that Atya would ever dare betray them. Yet Atya was a woman of secrets. That boyfriend of hers was a secret. Who would ever have supposed that Atya would possess a boyfriend. Which was no doubt why she had kept him a secret. But her investigations had indicated that he had been nothing more than what he claimed, a low-grade civil servant to do with the railways, by name of Romanowski. In any event, the romance appeared to be over; he had not been to see Atya, to her knowledge, for more than a year.

Anyway, Atya, who was not very bright, spoke no language but Russian, and was a devoted Communist, could not possibly have any contacts with the outside world powerful enough to launch an attempt at rescuing the Princess Bolugayevska. Who on earth would want to do that anyway? Priscilla's family was shattered, she had few real friends outside the family . . .

As Beria had said, perhaps whoever it was would try again. And this time . . . she picked up the phone again, and called for the private line to Gulag Number One.

Lawrence had never been so angry in his life. "Do you realise just what you were risking?" he demanded.

Even Eldridge managed to look embarrassed. "Sure. And we've lost eight of our best people."

"And my people? When your agents are made to talk . . ."

"Look," Eldridge said. "None of my agents had ever heard your name or Halstead's, or had the slightest idea where we obtained our information from. They were merely told to go in and get the dame. They failed. We failed. It has nothing to do with you."

"May I ask who they were told to get?" Lawrence inquired, coldly. "Gulag Number One is full of, as you put it, dames."

"They had each been given a photograph to study. Don't worry, none of the photographs had a name to it; just the Princess's number. We don't have milk behind our ears, Mr Lawrence."

"I am glad to hear that," Lawrence said. "Because I have had to consider the necessity of pulling my people out of Russia, thanks to your piece of idiocy."

"They're in no danger," Eldridge insisted. "We are the ones who lost out."

"And when you try again?"

Eldridge hunched his shoulders. "We're not going to try again.

Orders from the top. We know where the Princess is. As far as we're concerned, she can fucking well stay there for the rest of her life."

"I'll say Amen to that," Lawrence agreed.

Chapter Eight

The Conspiracy

There was only a small gathering at the graveside; the Bolugayevskis had always kept very much to themselves. Equally, Joseph Cromb's religious affiliations were somewhat confused, with a Jewish father, a Protestant wife, and a Russian Orthodox background; Alex had chosen a rabbi to conduct the final ceremony. Now, as he escorted Elaine back to the waiting limousine, they encountered Eldridge. "Nice of you to come, Mr Eldridge," Alex said.

"Did you see anyone interesting?" Elaine could not resist the question.

"Maybe," Eldridge said. "What exactly did he die of?"

Alex shrugged. "The doctors say he never fully recovered from that shooting."

"Heck, that was five years ago," Eldridge said.

"So maybe he just died of despair," Elaine said. "At the loss of his wife."

"Yeah," Eldridge said. "Could be. Keep in touch."

"I don't think we will do that, Mr Eldridge," Elaine said, coldly. "Have a nice day."

Josef Stalin glared at the list of names on his desk. "There is a conspiracy," he muttered. "A conspiracy," he repeated. "A conspiracy!" he shouted.

The three men standing before his desk seemed to coagulate.

"Jews!" Stalin shouted, the veins in his neck and temples standing out like ridges. "They are a canker in our hearts. They always have been. Well, enough is enough. Poison one of my marshals, would they? Attempt to poison my ministers, would they? Next thing they will be attempting to poison me! We will deal with this. These doctors, first. Arrest them all. Interrogate them, try them, shoot them. Then use what you learn from them to take the case further. It is a conspiracy. A gigantic conspiracy. It stretches far beyond the doctors. But we will root it out and destroy it. You . . ." he pointed, "will root it out and destroy it." He waved his hand. "Go on. Get out. Destroy these vermin. You wait a moment, Lavrenty Pavlovich."

Beria glanced at Kruschev and Malenkov as they filed out, visibly shaken. Then he looked at his master. Stalin was still trembling with rage. Or was it fear? "Zhdanov," Stalin said. "Andrei Zhdanov. He is behind it."

"Zhdanov? With respect, Josef Vissarionovich, Zhdanov is a Hero of the Soviet Union. He defended Leningrad against the Nazis. He denounced the bourgeois movement in art. He is one of *us*."

"He is a Jew," Stalin said. "If he defended Leningrad so gallantly, as you put it, that was because he is a Jew. All else is lip service. I have no doubt at all that he is behind this conspiracy. It is your business to root it out, Lavrenty Pavlovich."

"Yes, Josef Vissarionovich." Beria looked as if he would have said something more, then changed his mind. "It may take a little time to get to the bottom of such a conspiracy."

"Then take a little time. But only a *little* time, Comrade."

"I shall be as quick as I can."

"I also want you to deal with the other matter." Stalin's voice was unusually soft.

Beria frowned. "What other matter, Josef Vissarionovich?"

"Jennie. You are aware, Lavrenty Pavlovich, that Jennie Ligachevna is a Jew?" Stalin's tone indicated that if his chief of police did not know that, he was in deep trouble.

Beria cleared his throat. "With respect, Josef Vissarionovich, that is not correct." Stalin raised his head to glare at him. "Her mother was the Countess Patricia Bolugayevska," Beria said. "And her father was the American shipping magnate, Duncan Cromb. Who was also her cousin. There was no Jewish blood in the mainstream of the Bolugayevski family, down to the marriage of Prince Alexei with Sonia Cohen."

"You are telling me that Jennie's brother is not a Jew?"

"Well, that is true," Beria conceded. "But he is her half-brother, Patricia Bolugayevska's son by the man Joseph Fine, whom she met when in exile in Siberia at the turn of the century."

"And with whom she was deeply in love," Stalin remarked. "I remember Krupskaya telling me of this. She and Lenin were in exile with them."

"Well, perhaps she was in love, Josef Vissarionovich. It is all a long time ago."

Stalin pointed with his pencil. "If Patricia was in love, with all the romantic fervour of her nature, then she would have imbibed everything her lover, who was also the father of her first-born, had to offer. Especially his views on religion, and on politics." Beria opened his mouth and then closed it again. He had never been exiled to Siberia, as he had still been a boy when the Romanovs had been liquidated, but from what he had learned the exiles to Siberia had had more important things on their minds, most of the time, than lecturing each other on politics, or certainly religion. "Therefore," Stalin went on. "She would have become, to all intents and purposes, a Jew herself. Therefore she would have brought up both her children as Jews. Then there is the fact that she is a Bolugayevska. I had supposed she had turned her back upon all that. Now it is clear to me that she has been hoodwinking us all of these years. First she continues communicating with her sister-in-law. And now she is in communication with her niece-in-law. You knew about this?"

"Of course, Josef Vissarionovich. The woman Bolugayevska-Cromb applied for a visa at our Embassy in Washington. The request was referred, as always, as I require to be informed of anything to do with that family. I turned down the request, of course."

"Why did you do that, Lavrenty Pavlovich?"

166

"Well . . ." Beria smoothed his bald head. "We do not wish any questions asked about the Princess, do we?"

"Questions are obviously *being* asked about the Princess," Stalin went on. "After five years in her grave, she still rises up to haunt me. And questions will go on being asked until we have destroyed this whole family. That includes Jennie. I am sure you agree with me?"

That was not a question Beria was keen on answering. "You wish me to arrest Jennifer Ligachevna? To interrogate her?" Well, he had long looked forward to being in a position to do that. But he had never expected it to happen on the orders of Stalin.

"I consider that to be necessary, yes. In due course. But first of all, issue a visa."

"For Elaine Bolugayevska-Cromb to visit Russia?"

"No, no. For Alexei Bolugayevski. He is the one we want. The very last Bolugayevski. I gave orders for his execution, six years ago. Now we shall make sure of it."

"He will smell a trap, and not come."

"He will come, because he is a Russian prince, a man of honour. And more importantly, because it is his mother about whom he seeks information. He will come. And you will postpone arresting Jennie until you have told her that this nephew will be allowed into Russia, and until she has written to him, welcoming him and promising to assist him in any way possible. Until in fact he is here. Jennifer will never suspect we have her in our sights. Let me know when you are ready to take her into custody. I wish to oversee the questioning."

Another woman, Beria thought, who you have always longed to possess, and never been able to manage it. But he had a more important consideration on his mind. "And Tatiana?"

Stalin leaned back in his chair. "Tatiana," he said thoughtfully. "You are pleased with her progress?"

"I am very pleased, Josef Vissarionovich. She is one of my best people."

"And it is my impression that she and her mother have never really got on," Stalin mused.

"Absolutely," Beria said enthusiastically.

"Then there is no need to involve her, at this stage. But you must watch her carefully, Lavrenty Pavlovich. The first sign of deviation, or resentment, and she must be disposed of."

"I will watch her closely, Josef Vissarionovich," Beria promised. As if he did not already do that, constantly; in the two years since the attempt to rescue Priscilla by that as yet unidentified squad, they had become as intimate as man and wife in the sharing of secrets. But as always, after one of these policy-making chats with Stalin, he felt as if he had been run over by a bus. He stepped outside, to find Malenkov and Kruschev waiting for him.

"Do you believe Kalinski was poisoned?" Malenkov whispered. "I mean, deliberately?" Beria shrugged.

"But you are going to arrest them all," Kruschev remarked.

"That is my duty. If there is a conspiracy, I will unearth it. And I will root out the conspirators, no matter who they may be." He was paving the way for the sensation that would follow Jennie's arrest.

"What you mean is, you will unearth a conspiracy, whether it is there or not," Kruschev said.

The two men glared at each other, and Malenkov hastened to make the peace. "Whether it is there or not, Josef Vissarionovich certainly believes it. It is affecting his health. You can see it." Both Beria and Kruschev turned to look at him, and he flushed. He was not the most observant man on earth. "Well," he said lamely. "One fears that these violent rages of his may . . . well, have a bad effect. Suddenly."

Now they both looked at Beria, who they knew was closer to their master than either of them. "I should keep such thoughts to yourself, Georgi Maximilianovich," Beria said. "Josef Vissarionovich is in the best of health. I have the report of his last medical examination to prove it. Good day to you."

He went to the door, and checked, as Kruschev said softly, "But the examination was carried out by a Jewish doctor, was it not, Lavrenty Pavlovich?"

Beria sat at his desk and smoked a cigarette held in a bakalite holder. If those fools thought he was going to confide any of his plans to them, they needed their heads examined. But the whole business was taking longer than he had anticipated. If only that fool Spiridonov had not determined to try that potion on Kalinski, but had gone straight to the top. Spiridonov had been too aware of the dangers, and the difficulties, principally the fact that Stalin's food was tasted. Therefore whatever was going to be fed to him had to be undetectable, both by taste or smell, or by immediate effect. It had to be experimented with first. Neither he nor Beria had supposed that Stalin would overreact in this way. It was another example of the paranoia that was slowly driving the dictator mad.

But it was also illustrative of the dangers inherent in deviating from one's plan, through impatience – Stalin was simply living too long. Even more was it an illustration of the dangers of going outside one's own people for assistance. Spiridinov would never stand up to interrogation. He pressed the buzzer on his intercom, and Tatiana came in. Over the past year he had promoted her to his first assistant. This was not only so that he could look at her, touch her, have her, whenever he wanted – and he wanted all of those things with considerable regularity. It was also because since the abortive attempt to rescue the Princess Priscilla, Tatiana had become his ultimate creature, a depraved harpy clad in the most beautiful of physical garbs. That knowledge, added to her beauty, added to the understanding that she was entirely his, made her irresistible.

And every time he gave her a mission, as now, he wanted her more. "Two things," he said. "The Premier has decided that action must be taken against those doctors who were on duty the night Marshal Kalinski died. They are to be arrested and prepared for trial." He handed her the list. "You will observe that they are all Jews. It will be our task to implicate as many Jews as possible, and bring them also to trial."

Tatiana had been reading the list. She raised her head. "Andrei Zhdanov?"

"His name is on the list, yes."

Tatiana continued to read. "Michael Spiridonov?"

"Ah. I wish to talk to you about him."

"He is my mother's physician."

Beria raised his eyebrows. "I did not know that." Tatiana was surprised. She had supposed her master knew everything. "That only adds a dimension to what I am telling you to do," Beria said. "We do not wish your mother to be involved in anything unpleasant, do we, Tatiana? Anything treasonable? Before anything else happens, I wish you to visit Dr Spiridonov. Make an appointment in the ordinary way. But when you see him, I wish you to convince him that he is about to be arrested, and that he will be tortured, and that his wife and children will also be tortured, until they all die, slowly. Before him." Tatiana licked her lips. "Then persuade him that the only way out is to take his own life. If he does that, now, and without speaking to a soul, his wife and children will be inviolate. Give him my word on this." He grinned. "Help him to die, happy. Then come back here. I have something I wish to discuss with you."

Michael Spiridonov slowly lowered himself onto the chair in his examination room. He stared at the naked body in front of him. The most perfect naked female body he had ever known. When she had made an appointment, he had been delighted. For all the years he had visited Jennifer Ligachevna, he had never been allowed to do more than look at her daughter; as a member of the KGB Tatiana had her own doctors. Thus today had surely been his lucky day, especially when she had required a most complete examination, inside and out, as it were. He had never spent a more enjoyable half-an-hour.

And then, lying there, she had begun to speak. Now she was sitting up, swinging her legs off the examination table, and descending, lightly, to the floor. "If I refuse?" he asked, hardly able to articulate.

Tatiana delicately pulled on her drawers. "You cannot refuse, Comrade."

"You think so? I can take Beria down with me. And you, Tatiana Andreievna."

"You will do neither of those things, Comrade. If you refuse, I will place you under arrest now. I will gag you and take you to the Lyubyanka. There I will slice you into little pieces before

170

your eyes. But before I do that, I shall slice your wife and your two charming children into pieces, also before your eyes. As they will not be gagged, you will be able to hear them scream, and beg you to put them out of their misery."

He stared at her. "Are you a woman, or a monster?"

Tattie put on her skirt. "I am what I wish to be, Comrade. What I am commanded to be." She went to her tunic, which hung on the hook by the door, felt in a pocket, and brought out a tube. From the tube she poured four tablets into the palm of her hand. "These are relatively painless," she said. "They say that two will kill a man in ten seconds. I suggest you take all four, then perhaps you will die even more quickly." She went to the washbasin, filled a tumbler with water. Then she returned to the man, who was staring at her as if hypnotised. Tatiana sat on his lap. "I wish you to be happy," she said, and lifted his hand, placed the four tablets in it. "It must be done, now."

Still acting like a man in a bad dream, Spiridonov placed the tablets in his mouth. Tatiana placed the tumbler in his hand. He raised it, spilling some water onto her skirt because his hand was trembling. He threw back his head and swallowed. Tatiana took the glass from his hand and placed it on the table. Then she took his hand, and placed it inside her blouse. Spiridonov's fingers closed on her breast, gently, and then suddenly his entire body was convulsed. The fingers tightened.

"Ow!" Tatiana said, at the same time placing her hand across his mouth as he tried to scream, while his eyes rolled and his body heaved beneath her. But she thrust her feet down to anchor herself, and a moment later the tight grip on her breast relaxed. "I did say *relatively* painless," she pointed out. "But you must agree that it was quick."

Carefully she got off him, holding his shoulders to make sure he would remain upright in the chair, pushing his lolling head back so that it would not overbalance him. She buttoned her blouse, looked in the mirror, brushed her hair. Her face was expressionless, yet there were pink spots in her cheeks; watching someone die always had this effect on her. But the receptionist would merely suppose that as a pretty young woman she had been embarrassed by the

171

examination. She opened the door, stepped outside, closed the door behind her. "Dr Spiridinov does not wish to see another patient for a little while," she said. "He has some analysis to complete. He will ring when he was ready."

"Of course, Comrade Gosykinya," the woman agreed. Tatiana left the surgery.

"Hi!" Even over the phone Alex could tell that Elaine was excited. "Listen. Do you remember two years ago I applied for a visa to go to Russia?"

There was a moment's silence, and Elaine could tell, also over the phone, that her husband was raising his eyes to heaven. "Yes," he said. "I remember. And they turned you down flat. As I said they would do. And thank God for that."

"Listen," she said. "I didn't tell you, but when I was refused, I wrote Aunt Jennifer."

"You did *what*?"

"I wrote her and asked her if she could help. And guess what? She's at last written back to say that of course she'll help, if we feel that somehow Mom has got herself into Russia and can't get out again."

"That's what she says, is it? Elaine . . ."

"Listen. And to prove how willing she is to help, she writes that she has arranged a visa for you, and that you can go along to the Russian Embassy and get it, whenever you wish."

There was another silence. Then Alexei said, "Would you mind repeating that?"

"Well, I know I asked for a visa for myself. She's got one for you; she must have got it mixed up. But that's even better, don't you think?"

There was another silence on the end of the line. Then Alex said, "You don't think this may be some kind of a trap?"

"Look, it's your Aunt Jennifer. She was as cut up as any of us when I told her Joe had died. Now she wants to help, if she can. It's your mother we're looking for, Alex."

"This is excellent," Lavrenty Beria said. "Do you know, Tatiana

172

Andreievna, I feel like a man whose house is full of flies, and who has laid a slice of bread, thickly covered with treacle, on his table, and who watches the flies come onto the bread, one after the other. He is a patient man, so he just watches, while each one is trapped in the treacle, until they are all there, and then . . . a single great swat, and they are all dead, and he is troubled no more."

"Is that what you intend for Alexei Bolugayevski, Comrade Commissar?" Tatiana asked, with apparent ingenuousness. Her old comrade-in-arms. But a man who had rejected her, at the end.

"That is what I intend for . . ." Beria hastily changed his mind about what he would have said. He had come so close to this woman that he had nearly told her the truth. "Of course," he said. "But first, we must let him incriminate himself. I am sorry he is your cousin, Tatiana. But the Bolugayevskis are a poisonous brood. You are the only good member of the family. You and your mother, of course."

Tatiana checked a frown; she knew how heartily Beria disliked Jennie. "It is good to hear you say so, Comrade Commissar. But you do understand that Alexei is coming to visit my mother. And me."

"Well, I am quite sure there can be nothing dangerous in him seeing your mother. Of all the people in Russia, I am sure Comrade Ligachevna is the most reliable."

Once again Tatiana checked a frown. He was really laying it on very thickly.

"But I agree, I do not think it would be a good idea for him to meet you again. I am sure it would be embarrassing for you, and it might even be dangerous. Let me see . . ." he checked his desk diary. "He arrives in Russia, by plane, would you believe it, in three days' time. He'll be here for the Premier's birthday."

Tatiana nodded. "Mother intends to meet him. She expects me to accompany her."

"Yes, but you will not be here."

Tatiana raised her eyebrows.

"I have a mission for you," Beria said. "A very secret mission." Tatiana waited. Her heart no longer even pounded when she was about to be sent out into the field. It had lost its glamour for

173

her; she was only disappointed that she was not to be given the opportunity of seeing Alexei again. But, as her master had suggested, it *might* just be dangerous. "You have kept an eye on the Princess Bolugayevska, as instructed? And she is fit and well?"

"As instructed."

"Very good. Now I wish you to remove her from the gulag. Do not worry, I will give you the necessary order. It will have to be a carte blanche, as we do not wish any questions being asked. But you will have it."

"You wish her disposed of?"

Beria smiled. "What a bloodthirsty creature you are, my Tatiana. All in good time. But first, I wish you to take the Princess to my dacha in Astrakhan. I will join you there. You will fly from Moscow to Alma-Ata, go to the gulag from there, then return to Alma-Ata and fly to Astrakhan. Requisition whatever transport you require. But you will of course tell no one, not even your mother, where you are going and the purpose of your mission, and the Princess must be kept incognito at all times."

"I will need some assistance."

"It will have to be somebody absolutely trustworthy."

"Oh, yes," Tatiana said. "I know who it will be. She helped me to deliver the Princess in the first place."

It was Beria's turn to raise his eyebrows. "She *must* be trustworthy. Are you sure it is wise not to have disposed of her?"

"Do you trust me, absolutely, Comrade Commissar?"

"Of course."

"Because I am your creature, your creation. Well, the woman Atya is to me what I am to you. I am all she has in the world."

"Well, then, I wish you joy of her. When you reach Astrakhan, you will hand the Princess over to my man, Polkov, and return here with your assistant. Understood?"

"Of course, Comrade Commissar."

"And as we are going to be separated for a few days, Tatiana, I wish you to come to me, tonight."

Tatiana did not change expression. "Of course, Comrade Commissar."

For the last time, Beria thought, as he watched the door close

174

behind her. It was a great shame. But quite apart from Stalin's requirements, she really was growing too big for her boots. Having her own 'creature'! He tapped on his desk, and Kagan came in. "You heard all that?" Beria asked. "You must wait until after she has collected the Princess. It must be done on the drive back to Alma-Ata from the gulag."

"Will Comrade Gosykinya have a driver?"

"No. She will drive herself. She enjoys driving. But she will have this creature of hers."

"And all three of them are to be disposed of? The Princess as well?"

"Yes."

Kagan sighed. "It will be a pity, to dispose of two such beautiful women at the same time."

"Oh, enjoy them first, if there is time," Beria said. "That will be poetic. Tatiana Gosykinya, the daughter of two traitors, attempts to be a traitor herself by freeing an enemy of the State, and in the course of her escape is set upon, raped, and murdered by Kazakh bandits. Oh, very droll."

"And you will not miss Tatiana, Comrade Commissar?"

"She has served her purpose," Beria told him. And besides, he had the photographs of her locked in his desk beside the spare set of the Princess. There would be no need to forget either of them.

"Listen," Atya said. "I have to go away. On a mission. With Captain Gosykinya." Halstead raised himself on his elbow.

"We are leaving tonight," Atya said. "I do not know where we are going."

"Shit!" Halstead commented.

"I know. But, as we are going together, and for at least a week, I may be able to learn something from her." She giggled. "She is really very fond of me."

Halstead grinned. "Who do you enjoy more, her or me?"

Atya wriggled sensually. "She makes love beautifully."

"I hope there's a but."

"Oh, yes. I love you."

"And not Tatiana Gosykinya?"

"It is not possible to love Tatiana Gosykinya," Atya said, seriously. "She is a creature of the night."

"I would like to meet her, one day," Halstead said, and realised that he too was quite serious; such a meeting would be a culmination of his career, one way or the other. "You go and enjoy yourself, and bring me what I want to know."

"You will wait for me?"

"Not here, darling. People would talk. But I will come to you, a week today."

"Alex! Alex Bolugayevski!" Jennie swept forward, arms outstretched. In her fur coat and fur hat she looked somewhat like a Russian brown bear.

Alex allowed himself to be embraced. "It is very kind of you to meet me, Mrs Ligachevna."

"Aunt Jennie. I am your Aunt Jennie," Jennie insisted, still holding his hand.

"My luggage . . ."

"You, bring that luggage!" Jennie commanded, and the man obediently collected the two suitcases.

Alex stared in amazement. But so did everyone else and the Arrivals Lounge was crowded with people, both Russian and foreign. Jennie paid them no attention, swept her nephew to a waiting car. "I'm afraid it is a long drive to Moscow."

"I'm looking forward to it," Alex said. What memories this all brought back. He and Elaine had been in Moscow, for several months, in 1941, before they had been tricked, as he now knew, into volunteering to serve with the partisans in the Pripet Marshes. By then Moscow had been under constant bombardment, there had been craters in the streets, and half-destroyed and burning buildings. Now the city was spick and span, with high-rise flats sprouting in every direction. But thinking about those days brought back other memories as well. "Is Tatiana well?" he asked.

"Oh, indeed. She so wanted to be able to meet you. But she is out of Moscow at the moment. Something to do with her job."

"Oh." Alex was disappointed; he had been looking forward to seeing his old comrade again. besides, he also felt Tatiana might be more help in obtaining information about his mother than Jennie. "May I ask what her job is?"

"Oh . . ." Jennie made a vague gesture. "She works for the government." She giggled. "She is a civil servant. You'll meet her when she gets back. She will only be gone a week. Now what is all this about Priscilla disappearing."

"It happened some years ago," Alex said. "I thought Elaine had explained it all in her letters."

"Well, she did. And about poor Joe. Oh, poor Joe. He had such a hard life. Still, being married to Priscilla must have made up for some of it. Poor Joe. But Priscilla disappearing . . . And you think she may have returned to Russia? I really can't imagine her doing that. Here we are." The car had stopped before the apartment building.

Alex decided not to carry the conversation further until they were safely inside the apartment. But as the chauffeur opened the door, instead of allowing Jennie out, he stepped aside and his place was taken by another man, who got in.

"What on earth . . ." Jennie demanded.

Alex had turned to his door, which was also being opened to allow a man in. This man sat beside him, as the first man was sitting beside Jennie; two more men got into the front seat, one behind the wheel, and the car moved off. The temptation to resist them all, violently, was immense. But he was Jennie's guest, and had to take his lead from her.

"Will you stop this car instantly," Jennie commanded.

"There are questions that must be answered, Comrade Ligachevna," the man in the front said, turning round to look at them.

"Do you know who I am?" Jennie demanded.

"Of course," the man in the front said. "Or we would not have arrested you."

"And do you know what will happen to you when Premier Stalin learns of this outrage?"

The man smiled. "Your arrest has been ordered by Premier Stalin, Comrade."

Atya thoroughly enjoyed flying with Tatiana, because Tatiana always dined on caviar and champagne when she travelled on official business. The two of them sat alone in the first-class compartment as the Ilyushin turboprop hummed through the air on its way to Alma-Ata. Atya already had a fair idea where they were going; they had made this trip five years ago, with the two prisoners.

That had been a disconcerting journey, because of the Princess's lack of interest in what they were doing to her. She had been a crushed flower, a woman existing in limbo, preparing to die. Well, surely she was dead. Equally disconcerting had been the fact that Tatiana had not let her play with the man. She had not touched him either. Perhaps because he had been too crushed to realise what was happening to him. He had spent the entire journey, his wrists and ankles tied except when his ankles had been released for him to relieve himself, staring at Tatiana. Perhaps the intensity of his gaze had frightened her. But when she had had to touch him, or to feed him, she had reminded Atya of a mother with her babe. She was a strange woman, Atya thought.

Tatiana looked at her watch, and smiled one of her lazy smiles. "Another hour." She turned Atya's face up for a kiss. She was far more exciting than the man Johnny. But Johnny, whatever his machinations and his long absences, was her very own; she knew that to Tatiana she was just a toy. Besides, Johnny held her life in the palm of his hand. But did not Tatiana also? And suddenly Tatiana nipped her on the lip. "Tell me about this man," she said.

Atya pulled her head away. "Man, Comrade Captain?"

Tatiana stroked her cheek, lovingly. "You should never lie to me, Atya. You have been seeing a man. It has been reported to me. A man who is not always here. But when he is here, he sleeps in your apartment. You must be very fond of him."

Atya wished she had not had that last glass of champagne; she needed to think very quickly and very clearly. "He is an old comrade, Comrade Captain," she said.

"How old?"

"We met in the War, Comrade Captain. He is like a brother to me."

Tatiana's hand drooped onto the front of Atya's blouse, caressing the breast, and suddenly squeezing very hard. "Incest is a crime," she whispered.

Atya gasped for breath. "I will not see him again," was all she could think of saying.

Tatiana released her. "A woman should have a man, whatever her other amusements," she remarked. "But you should have told me of him. Tell me of him, now."

"He works for the State, Comrade. He travels for the State. When he is in Moscow, he comes to see me. We met many years ago. During the War."

"So you said. What is his name?"

"Romanowski. Peter Romanowski."

"Peter Romanowski," Tatiana said to herself, and Atya realised that she already knew the name. "When we get back to Moscow, I should like to meet Comrade Romanowski. We have a lot in common." She gave one of her girlish giggles. "You." Then she turned away, abruptly, to stare out of the window. Atya breathed, slowly and carefully. There was a crisis, looming. And yet . . . Tatiana had not seemed to be angry, or even upset. Jealous?

Tatiana brooded out of the window at the darkening sky. Even Atya, she thought, has a man. And I have . . . Atya! Nobody else in the whole, wide world. They had robbed her of Gregory, and she was determined to avenge his death. When the time came. She had always hated Shatrav, who had taken her as his own, entirely against her will, during the early days in the Pripet, before she had become the Group Commander. Oh, yes, she would settle with Shatrav. When it could be done with safety. But that would not bring Gregory back. And in truth, his memory had all but faded. It had been overtaken by Morgan.

Morgan had fallen in love with her, had asked her to flee Russia to be his wife. No one had ever asked her to be his wife, before or since. And she had betrayed him, tortured him, and then consigned him to a living hell. Because she had been unable to believe his love? Because she was too loyal a servant of the Soviet State ever to contemplate any other course of action? She liked to tell herself that was the case. What terrified her was that it might be because she was unable to accept love from any human being, even her own mother. She was too conditioned to hatred and destruction.

But the temptation, as she was coming this way anyway, to drop in at Gulag Number Seventeen, was enormous. It was only a hundred miles away from Number One. To drop in and see him again, reassure herself that he was still alive, touch him, perhaps . . . and be repelled by the half-human creature to which he would have been reduced after four years in that hell. She sighed, looked out of the window as the aircraft began its descent. "We have arrived." Her mouth twisted. "And it is snowing."

One of the most amazing aspects of Tatiana's personality, Atya thought, was the way in which in a moment she could change from being a lazily lecherous creature of the flesh into a highly efficient and concentrated machine. No doubt that was one of her great strengths. By the time they had landed she was again the KGB official. A car was waiting for them, with a driver, but Tatiana dismissed him. "We will be back here tomorrow morning," she told the local commandant, who had met them.

"The aircraft will be waiting, Comrade Gosykinya."

"But the very minimum of people," Tatiana told him.

"As you wish."

Tatiana got behind the wheel, Atya sat beside her, and they drove off. It was very cold, and the snow still drifted down; the sky was like a dark blue marble vault. "We are going to the gulag?" Atya ventured.

"Yes," Tatiana told her. The main road from Alma-Ata led north-east, skirting the western end of the huge reservoir on its way to Taldy-Kurgan. Tatiana took the secondary road, which branched off to the north-west just after they had driven through the town of Kapchaga, the car bringing the children out on to the street in cheering masses. The road swung away the moment it crossed the bridge over the Akchi Kurty, where it flowed into the lake. The road then ran beside the river, as it would do until it reached the town of Pomar, some two hundred miles away, on the banks of Balkash, a lake so enormous as to be almost considered an inland sea. But Atya knew they would not be going that far, as

180

the country grew more and more desolate and uninhabited, even in the darkness a featureless steppe. And indeed, after driving for some fifty miles, they reached a narrow track leading away to the west.

It was utterly dark by now, and they followed their headlights over the hard-packed but thin snow that covered the road, but as they turned the corner Tatiana braked. The track was certainly bad, but Atya had not supposed they would reduce speed that much – she had driven with Tatiana before. Now the car slithered sideways for some yards before Tatiana regained control. "Is there something the matter, Comrade Captain?" Atya asked.

Tatiana increased speed again, and they bumped into the darkness. "Did you not see a gleam of metal back there?"

"No, Comrade Captain."

"I think it was a car," Tatiana said, half to herself. "What would a car be doing, parked beside the road, in this remote place?"

"I cannot think, Comrade Captain."

Tatiana said nothing, and half-an-hour later they were at the gates to the gulag, where Tatiana, the moment she identified herself, was shown into an office, Atya as ever at her side. The room was empty when they arrived, but a few minutes later the commandant arrived, wearing a dressing gown and very obviously nothing else. Atya remembered her from the last time she had been here, a big, bony woman with flowing red hair and huge breasts and thighs. A woman with a voracious appetite, for every aspect of life. And no doubt death as well. "You come at strange hours, Comrade Captain," she remarked, ignoring Atya.

"I am required to do so, Comrade Karpova," Tatiana agreed, and Atya wondered if her boss had ever shared *her* bed. "I wish the woman Seven Hundred and Six."

"Ah," the commandant commented.

Tatiana frowned. "I hope she is in good health, Comrade Karpova. I gave orders that she was not to be harmed, or starved, or worked more than enough to keep her healthy."

"And I have obeyed your orders," Karpova said, having had time to think. "I will send for her."

"Well, hurry," Tatiana said. "I wish to be back in Alma-Ata by dawn."

Karpova left the room, and Tatiana sat down. Atya sat also, but as Tatiana did not speak, she kept quiet as well. It was fifteen minutes before Karpova returned, with two of her female guards, and Priscilla. Tatiana was immediately on her feet. Priscilla was fully dressed, in the prison uniform of pants and blouse, but she moved as if sleepwalking, her eyes half shut. "What have you done to her?" Tatiana snapped.

"It is necessary to keep her under sedation, from time to time. She has attempted suicide several times," Karpova explained.

Tatiana peered at Priscilla. She looked healthy enough, and, as ordered, her hair had not been cut and had indeed been recently washed. But her eyes revealed little awareness of where she was. Or perhaps who she was. "You have kept her under sedation, for five years?"

"No, no," Karpova said. "She has these moods of despair. She is in one, now."

Tatiana put her hand under Priscilla's chin and lifted her head, peered at her. "What are those marks?"

"When she is in a mood, she will not eat. Then it is necessary to force feed her."

Tatiana continued to hold the almost lifeless head. Priscilla might indeed have been dead, but for the slow flutter of her nostrils. "If her brain has been damaged, you will pay for it, Comrade Karpova," Tatiana said.

"When she recovers from this dose she will be as good as new," Karpova said. "But then she may be difficult. We have had a hard time with her, I can tell you, Comrade Gosykinya."

"Well, she will not trouble you again. Has she nothing else?"

"You brought her with nothing else," Karpova pointed out.

Tatiana continued to stare into Priscilla's eyes for some seconds, then she said, "Bring her down to the car. We will need a coat and gloves. And thick stockings."

The guards received a nod from their commandant, who then said, "Will you not stay awhile, Tatiana Andreievna?"

"I am in a hurry," Tatiana told her. "Call me when next you are

182

in Moscow, Valentina Pavlova." Karpova's mouth twisted, but she made no comment. The guards returned with the necessary warm clothing; Priscilla was made to sit down while the socks were pulled over her feet and her flat shoes replaced with furlined boots. Still she showed no emotion. "But I wish a favour of you," Tatiana said.

"Of course." Karpova bristled with anticipation.

"I wish a tommy-gun." Tatiana gave one of her girlish giggles. "I will use it for shooting foxes, on the drive back."

Karpova looked puzzled, but it was not her business to criticise or even argue with a KGB officer. She sent one of her aides to fetch the gun. Atya followed Tatiana and the Princess and her guards down the stairs; Tatiana carried the tommy-gun under her arm. "Do you think the Princess is all right?" Atya asked.

"We shall have to find out. Put her in the back seat," Tatiana told the guards. Priscilla was inserted into the back of the car. "Get in beside her," Tatiana said, "and hold her head up." She laid the tommy-gun on the seat beside her.

They drove out of the compound and the gates swung to behind them. "Is she all right?" Tatiana asked.

"I think so, Comrade Captain."

Already the sky was lightening as they approached the main road. And again without warning, Tatiana braked, the car slithering to and fro on the snow. Taken by suprise, Atya fell forward and bumped her head. Priscilla fell over behind her, on the seat. "Check your weapon," Tatiana said. Atya rubbed her head as she sat up, pulled her automatic pistol from its holster. Tatiana had doused the car lights, and was also checking her pistol as well as the tommy-gun. "That car is still there," Tatiana said. "I do not like it."

"Perhaps it has been abandoned, Comrade Captain."

"I do not think it has been abandoned. I think we will return to the gulag and obtain some additional help." She began what would have to be a five-point turn on the narrow road, but as she did so a shot rang out, followed by several more, which were then smothered in the rattle of automatic fire. They came from the little ridge of high ground to the left of the waiting car.

"Shit!" Tatiana snapped, as her tyres exploded and bullets thudded into the coachwork. "Get out. Take the Princess."

Atya scrabbled at the door on the side away from the firing, thrust it open, seized Priscilla's hand, jerked her out, and together they tumbled into the ditch, which was half full of ice and water. Spluttering, Atya dragged Priscilla's head up, and watched Tatiana rolling away from the car, the tommy-gun in her hand, as a bullet struck the petrol tank and it burst into flames. "They are trying to kill us," Atya gasped, still spitting water.

"Yes," Tatiana said grimly. "Is the Princess all right?"

"I think so," Atya said.

"There are four of them," Tatiana said. "Only four!" Atya gulped. Although she had received training as a KGB operative, she had never engaged in a real shoot-out before; neither had she seen active service during the War. "Make sure the Princess cannot slide into the water," Tatiana said, never taking her eyes off the four figures who were surveying the burning car from the ridge. "My God," she muttered. "One of them is Shatrav. Oh, yes, Shatrav. I have waited for this moment. Atya, prepare to shoot. When I say so."

Atya propped Priscilla against the side of the ditch; she was sitting in freezing water from the waist down, and this seemed to be reviving her – her eyes were open and her breathing more regular. But Atya obeyed orders, drew her pistol, and crouched just beneath the edge of the bank. "They have waited long enough," Tatiana said. "They are coming. Fools."

Because the presence of Shatrav confirmed what she had already deduced; only one man had known where she would be found, on this day and at this hour. Her master, in every sense. Her entire being was filled with fury. But she remained absolutely calm as the four men approached. Each was armed with a tommy-gun. "You must shoot absolutely straight and for the belly," she told Atya. Atya swallowed, and gripped her pistol in both hands.

The men came up to the car, having to approach carefully because it was still burning. But even from some yards away they could see there were no bodies lying about. "Now," Tatiana said, as the first man turned towards them. She rose to her knees, her pistol also held in both hands, and shot him in the heart. As soon as she had squeezed the trigger she was turning the gun to the second man. This shot blew the top of his head away. Beside her Atya had hit the fourth man, on the other side of the car, but although he fell he was not dead. The third man, also on the other side of the car, dropped to the ground and sent a burst of automatic fire in the direction of the women.

Tatiana flattened herself against the parapet as the bullets whistled over her head. "Stay down," she told Atya. But Atya was still peering over the parapet, and before she could respond she gave a shriek and collapsed into the ditch, half in and half out of the water, whimpering as blood welled out of her tunic. From the amount of blood Tatiana did not consider it necessary to go to her help; she was clearly dying.

She was neither concerned about the death of her lover nor alarmed at her own situation. Her intended assassins would not dare leave until they knew *she* was dead. "What is happening?" Priscilla asked.

"Don't move," Tatiana told her. She was listening. The flames had nearly died now, and the only sound was the movement of feet. Coming closer. Tatiana holstered her pistol, picked up the tommy-gun; at close quarters this was the more deadly weapon. Carefully she controlled her breathing, looking up, and a man appeared above her. Shatrav! Tatiana fired upwards, squeezing the trigger to send a cloud of bullets skywards. Shatrav dropped the sub-machine-gun and came tumbling down the embankment beside her, his groin and stomach ripped open by the flying lead. But the wounded man had also reached the parapet. He was staring at her as he brought up the tommy-gun. Tatiana fired at him too, and heard only clicks; that bastard Valentina had given her only a quarter of a magazine! She stared at death, then there was an explosion and the man turned away from her and fell. Tatiana looked at Priscilla, who had fired Atya's gun. "For five years I have wanted to kill someone," Priscilla said.

"I am glad you waited," Tatiana said.

Priscilla turned to look at her, still holding the gun.

"If you kill me, you will die," Tatiana told her. "They will

185

recapture you very quickly, and they will execute you. But I can save your life."

"You?" Priscilla asked. "You tortured me."

Tatiana shrugged. "It was my job to do so."

Priscilla's knuckles were white on the trigger. "And you enjoyed it."

"One should always enjoy one's job, don't you think, Princess? But now we are on the same side. I have been betrayed, as you were betrayed. I will save your life, and we will seek vengeance together. Is that not what you want? Vengeance?"

"Does it matter?" Priscilla asked. "My husband is dead. My son is dead. My family have been destroyed. Vengeance . . ." she shrugged. "Perhaps, before I die."

"Your son is alive," Tatiana said.

Priscilla's head came up, sharply. "You are lying. I was told both Joseph and Alex were dead."

"The people who told you that were lying. Your husband is dead, yes; he never recovered from the wounds he received when you were kidnapped. But Alex is not only alive, he is at this moment in Moscow. He came here, looking for you. He is staying with my mother. We must get him out of Russia. Get you out of Russia." She smiled. "Get us all out of Russia. After I have settled a few scores."

"Can you do this?" Priscilla asked.

"I don't know, but I mean to try."

"Tatiana," Atya moaned. "Tatiana, help me. I am freezing."

She had slipped down so far only her head was out of the water. Tatiana knelt beside her, watched the air mingling with the blood dribbling from her mouth and nostrils. "I cannot help you, Atya," she said. "You are dying."

Atya stared at her. "Then listen," she muttered. "I have betrayed you. Betrayed Russia."

Tatiana frowned as she bent lower.

"My man," Atya whispered. "My Johnny . . . he is an English agent, named Halstead. His code name is Moonlight." It was Tatiana's turn to stare. "He is returning to my apartment, tomorrow," Atya whispered. "For my report on our journey. He . . ."

186

she gasped as the blood choked her, opened her mouth, closed it again . . . and then it sagged open a last time.

"She is dead," Tatiana said. "Moonlight! A man called Halstead! For how long have we searched for that man, and he has been under our very noses, all the time." She looked up. "I will still help you, Princess. If you will help me."

"What do we do first?" Priscilla asked.

"We increase our strength," Tatiana told her.

Part Three

Death of a Tyrant

During his office treason was no crime,
  The sons of Belial had a glorious time.
                                    John Dryden.

Chapter Nine

The Chase

Kagan sat at his desk and stared at the phone. He willed it to ring. But it would not. It was eight o'clock in the morning in his office in Moscow. The time zone scale for central Asia was a mosaic mess, thus, although at eight o'clock in Moscow it was ten o'clock just across the Urals, and twelve o'clock in Central Siberia, the area around Balkash was unique, in that it had its own scale, and it would only be eleven o'clock there. But even so, Shatrav should have reported back to Alma-Ata by now.

What could have gone wrong? Shatrav, one of the most experienced men in his section, and three other hand-picked operatives, sent to eliminate three women, one a debilitated prisoner, one a cripple . . . and Tatiana Gosykinya. Kagan had always considered Tatiana a vastly overrated operative, had always resented the fact that she was so overrated by Commissar Beria himself. Surely there was no way that even Tatiana Gosykinya could have resisted four agents of the KGB headed by Shatrav himself. He began to wish he had gone himself, availed himself of Beria's invitation, enjoyed the Princess . . . and Tatiana Gosykinya as well, before executing them. Now . . . he could wait no longer, picked up the telephone. It took some time to get through, but at last Smorodsky was on the line. "Report!"

"I have nothing to report, Comrade General," Smorodsky said. "Captain Gosykinya arrived here last evening, as scheduled, and left in a car. She told me to have the plane standing by at dawn this morning for her return. But she has not yet returned."

"And Major Shatrav?"

"Major Shatrav arrived here yesterday morning, with his companions, again as scheduled. They also left in a car. I have not heard from him since."

"You do not find this suspicious?" Kagan inquired.

"I am not paid to be suspicious about KGB activities, Comrade General."

God save me from fools and incompetents, Kagan thought. As for what Beria would make of it . . . but Beria could not be allowed to know of it, until it was sorted out. He needed to be in Alma-Ata himself. Yet it would take him more than four hours to get there. That would be mid-afternoon, local time. Shatrav had been supposed to have done the job by sun-up. "Listen," he said. "I am coming to visit you. But before I get there, I wish you to go to Gulag Number One. That is where Captain Gosykinya has gone. I wish you to find out what is keeping her there."

"I will send immediately, Comrade General."

"Smorodsky," Kagan said. "I do not wish you to send, immediately. I wish you to go yourself, immediately."

He could hear Smorodsky gulp on the other end of the line. "Yes, Comrade General."

"Leave now, find out what is the problem with Comrade Gosykinya, and meet me at the airport this afternoon." He replaced the phone, looked at his secretary. "Telephone the airport and tell them to have a plane ready for me. I will be out there in half-an-hour."

"Yes, Comrade General." The woman turned for the door.

"And Anya," Kagan said. "Should anyone inquire after me, *anyone*, I have been called away on urgent personal business, but will be back this evening."

The two women dried themselves and their clothes by the heat from the still burning car before resuming their journey to the north-east. It was necessary to stop in Ayaguz for petrol, by which time they had skirted the eastern end of Lake Balkash, and were heading out

192

into the vast steppes of central Siberia; although the sun was high in the sky, it remained very cold, and the snow-covered road was very poor. They were accompanying the railway line, and soon after eleven a train went blaring past, the passengers leaning out of the window to wave at the automobile, a rare sight in these parts, certainly in winter. They had not spoken much. Tatiana reckoned that Priscilla was still recovering from her drugged state, and was equally trying to understand what had happened and was happening. While Tatiana had a lot on her mind. That she had been betrayed, and condemned, by Beria, was obvious. What she could not understand was how he had dared; she was Stalin's protégée. Therefore something very sinister was happening.

Her immediate instinct, if she was now an enemy of the state, or of the KGB, had been to free Morgan, and enlist him, and perhaps enjoy him, before the axe fell. She did not regret that decision for a moment. But as her sense of anger and outrage began to simmer rather than boil, she was thinking beyond merely freeing Morgan. She had first to figure out who was behind her betrayal. If Beria had acted on orders from Stalin, then her only hope was to get out of Russia. But if Beria was acting on his own, as part of some plot *against* Stalin . . . and this seemed very likely, in view of her instructions. He wanted the Princess, for some reason of his own. He wanted her taken to his own private dacha in Astrakhan. Curiouser and curiouser, she thought as she watched the petrol being poured into the car; she had merely flashed her KGB warrant and been served immediately with everything she wanted.

But if that were so, all she needed to do was regain Moscow, and Stalin's side! And watch Beria crumble into dust. It was a risk worth taking. "Let's eat," she told the Princess.

They lunched in a little bar on the far side of town. "Where are we going?" Priscilla asked.

"To another gulag." Tatiana smiled at the expression that flitted across Priscilla's face. "Don't worry, I am not going to lock you up again. I am going to pick up your friend Morgan." For the first time Priscilla looked down at her clothes, at the same moment putting up her hand to her hair; her prison suit was concealed beneath the coat she had been given, but the coat itself was old and shabby.

"Oh, you are not terribly well groomed." Tatiana said. "But I do not think Morgan will mind. He is in love with me. Or was," she added thoughtfully.

"After the way you treated him?"

"Before," Tatiana acknowledged. "But now I am his only hope of survival. Yours too, Princess," she reminded her, well aware that as Priscilla regained full control of her faculties, she would remember just how she had been treated before she had been sent to the gulag – and by whom.

She paid for the lunch again by the simple method of flashing her KGB identity card, and they got back into the car, Tatiana shooing away the crowd of young people, of both sexes, who had surrounded it. "I wish you would tell me exactly what is happening," Priscilla said as they drove out of the little town, as before heading north-east.

"All you need to know, Comrade Princess, is that I have released you from prison, that I am about to release your accomplice from prison, and that your only hope of surviving, or getting out of Russia, is to obey me in all things."

Priscilla digested this, then said quietly. "Morgan was never my accomplice."

"As you will."

They drove in silence for a while. Then Priscilla asked, "That woman who was killed . . ."

"You remembered her, did you? From the Lyubyanka. That is remarkable, as it was so long ago."

"I shall never forget a moment of the Lyubyanka," Priscilla said.

"I shall never forget Atya," Tatiana said. "She was my aide. But she was also one of my lovers. Have you never had a woman lover, Princess? They are far more reliable than men. And they know how to please, more than men. Most men are simply anxious to please themselves."

Priscilla's cheeks glowed as she stared at the road unfolding in front of them. "And yet you just walked away from her, leaving her lying in the water."

"She was dead," Tatiana pointed out. "There was nothing I could do for her."

"You could have said a prayer." Tatiana turned her head to look at her. "I forgot," Priscilla said. "It's not part of the Communist ethos."

"Would you like to be my lover?" Tatiana asked. "You are still a very beautiful woman, you know. I find you exciting. We could stop the car for half-an-hour."

"Don't you think we have rather a lot to do?" Priscilla asked.

Tatiana grinned. "You are in a hurry to regain your male lover."

"Morgan was never my lover," Priscilla snapped.

"Oh, come now, Princess. You have never had a woman lover, are you now going to claim you have never had a male lover? What a waste of all that beauty."

"I have had three husbands," Priscilla said with dignity.

"And Rotislav?" Tatiana asked, softly. Priscilla's head turned, sharply. "It is on file," Tatiana said. "We keep files on everyone who interests us or may be of use to us. You were Rotislav's mistress for a year."

"I was his prisoner for a year." Priscilla nearly spat the words out. "Thus he abused me as he felt like it. I do not call that having a lover. And I watched him hang."

Tatiana glanced at her. "So you are not just a pretty face. I would like to make love with you, Princess. But I agree it will have to wait because we are nearly there. Now listen to me very carefully. I am your only hope, and Morgan's only hope. Support me in everything. Fail to do so and you will die."

Priscilla swallowed. "Tell me what you intend to do."

"I have told you, just obey me, and I will save your life."

It was mid-afternoon before they arrived at Gulag Number Seventeen. "Just how many of these places are there in Russia?" Priscilla esked.

Tatiana shrugged. "A writer once described them as an archipeligo." She stopped the car. "I am going to handcuff you now. You are wearing prison clothes, and therefore you must be a prisoner, right? Just sit there and keep your mouth shut." She took a pair of handcuffs from the glove compartment, where she had known they would be, pulled Priscilla's arms behind her back, and clipped the wrists together. Then she turned Priscilla round to sit straight in the seat. "Now, remember. Keep your mouth shut."

She drove up to the gate, showed her pass, and it was opened for her. She drove into the compound, and was immediately surrounded by armed guards. She got out. "I have come to remove a prisoner," she said. "Take me to your commandant. And make sure that one does not leave the car." Two men immediately stood beside the car, one on each side. Priscilla didn't like their looks at all. As Tatiana could see. "There is nothing to be afraid of," she told the guards. "She is handcuffed, as you can see. However, she is not to be touched. Understood? Now hurry," she told the man waiting to escort her.

Priscilla stared straight in front of herself. She was still trying to come to terms with her situation, with the great mystery that was unfolding about her. She had been so utterly crushed by the realisation that Joseph and Alexei were dead that the first few weeks of her 'arrest' by the KGB had seemed remote, a nightmare, certainly, but one from which she would soon enough awake, no doubt in death. Certain things stood out in the mind – being photographed, the icecold bath, and perhaps more than anything else, the sight of that so nice young man standing naked before her, like herself, a victim of nightmare.

Perhaps Andrew Morgan had stayed in her mind so firmly because she had been about to enter a world of nothing but women. Then nightmare had become reality. And yet, it had been a limbo rather than a hell. She still remembered the fate with which Tatiana had threatened her, had braced herself for a continual unacceptable ordeal which had surely to result in madness or death . . . and it had been like falling off a high building, knowing that only concrete death lay beneath one, and instead arriving on a rubber mattress, which absorbed the shock and left one gently bouncing up and down. Her guards had enjoyed physically examining her – but they had not, as Tatiana had said they would, cut her hair or shaved her body. Nor had they beaten her. The other inmates had looked at her shimmering hair, her white body, her exceptional beauty, with lip-licking anticipation . . . but she had been placed

196

in a solitary cell, her only human contact the guards who fed her and exercised her. It had occurred to her that these subterranean minds might suppose solitary confinement over a period of years would drive anyone mad, but it had been what she wanted more than anything else. She had sufficient memories on which to live, for the rest of eternity.

Even being raped by the Commandant had been remote, because the Commandant had been a woman of peculiar tastes. Whether she was afraid of her charges, or was afraid of herself getting too close to any of them, or merely was so corrupted by her position and her power that she could not contemplate the least resistance or perhaps, even enthusiastic compliance, with her desires, the fact was that on every occasion she had been summoned to her bed, Priscilla had been injected with a sedative drug which, while leaving her awake in the sense that she would respond to motor impulses, had turned her brain into an uncertain grey awareness, without actually being aware. True awareness came later, when the drug had worn off, but even then, memory was filtered. She *knew* she had been abused, but could find no marks of it on her body; the Commandant had apparently not been into biting. Those incidents had become the punctuations of her imprisonment. The unchangingly dreary food, the unchangingly monotonous exercise round and round the yard, the unchangingly eventless days spent sitting in her cell, had merged one into the other; she had lost all concept of the passage of time. The summons to the Commandant's quarters had been bursts of light, even if they had been immediately muted in her mind. The Commandant had given her vodka to drink, had sometimes even made up her face. She had been played with as a toy. So I am a toy, she had thought. I have experienced every other thing in life; being a toy cannot be worse than Rotislav or Stalin himself. She had been in the Commandant's bed when Tatiana had so suddenly reappeared in her life.

That had most certainly been a flash of lightning cutting across the grey. Drugged as she had been at the time, she had had no immediate understanding of what was happening. Now she was fully awake. But understanding was utterly confusing. She had been forced to accept that Tatiana probably hated her more than anyone else in the world; well, when she remembered that ice-cold bath, and what the girl had said to her, Priscilla felt absolutely mutual about that. But now, she said, she was going to save her life. And that of Andrew Morgan. Something very unexpected and dramatic had happened, and was still happening. And at the moment she could do nothing to influence events. And supposing she found herself in a position *to* influence events, some time in the future? She had to be absolutely rational, as she had forced herself to be rational so often in the past, and survived. She wanted to watch Tatiana Gosykinya hang just as much as she had ever wanted to see Rotislav the Butcher hang. But that pleasure would have to take second place behind escaping this dreadful country. With Morgan? Supposing he was still worth saving.

And there he was, walking across the compound towards the car, with Tatiana. Like the Princess herself, he wore prison clothing, and his steps were halting. He also wore a prison sidecap, but the cropped hair on his temples and neck was grey. He had not been spared. They came up to the car, and the guards. "Remember," Tatiana said, and pushed him into the back seat.

Priscilla dared not turn her head; she had seen that he too was handcuffed. The guards saluted, Tatiana got behind the wheel, and drove out of the compound. Within minutes the gulag was out of sight. "My God, your highness," Morgan said. "To see you again . . ."

Now at last Priscilla could turn in her seat, gaze into the eyes, count the pain wrinkles that creased his face; he had aged ten years in the four since last she had seen him. "What have they done to you?" Suddenly she was afraid.

"Nothing I can't stand," he assured her. "And you?"

"Nothing at all." She glanced at Tatiana who was concentrating on the road. "Will you take off these handcuffs, now?"

"Not now," Tatiana said.

"I thought you were going to help us."

"I am helping you. But I must begin by removing you, and myself, from the reach of the KGB. This can only be done by speed. We are going to Semipalatinsk, where there is an airport. From there we will fly to Moscow."

"Moscow?" Priscilla and Morgan spoke together.

Tatiana grinned. "It is our only hope, believe me. But you must travel as my prisoners. I am not going to betray you."

"Do you expect us to believe *that*?" Morgan's tone was suddenly bitter, as he remembered everything this woman had done to him.

"Yes," Tatiana said, not looking at him. "Simply because you have no choice." She looked at her watch. "Now be quiet. We must reach Semipalatinsk before dark."

It was five o'clock and dark by the time they reached Semipalatinsk, and just starting to snow. The roads leading to the city had been bad, and slippery, but at least they had been largely empty. Now they came into rush-hour traffic as workers poured out of the meat-packing plant – the largest in Russia – and although there were even fewer cars in this part of the country than east of the Urals, there were large numbers of trucks and vans, horse-drawn vehicles and even bicycles, slithering in the snow, blaring horns, ringing bells and shouting. Tatiana sat with her hands tight on the wheel, blowing her horn as loudly as anyone. Morgan and Priscilla sat silently beside and behind her; they both had the feeling they were caught up in some surrealist play.

At last Tatiana was able to swing down the approach road to the airport, to encounter a barrier and two armed guards. She rolled down her window. "The airport is closed, Comrade," said one of the guards.

"Why? Because of a little snow?"

"Because the last flight has just left." He pointed skywards; they could still make out the lights of the airliner as it circled to gain height.

"Oh, my God," Priscilla muttered. If she still could not bring herself to trust Tatiana, the thought of being recaptured and being returned to the mercy of Valentina Karpova, after having killed, or at least overseen, the killing of four KGB agents, was horrifying.

"Is there not a military section of this airport?" Tatiana demanded.

"What is that to you, Comrade?" The guard could not make out her uniform in the darkness.

Tatiana pulled off a glove, reached inside her tunic, and produced her KGB identity wallet. "I wish to go to the military section."

The guard studied the wallet with his flashlight, then returned it and stood to attention. "Of course, Comrade Captain." He signalled his partner, and the barrier was raised.

"Whew!" Morgan said. "But what will the military have to offer us?"

"An aircraft," Tatiana said.

"You mean you can fly a plane?"

"They will supply us with a crew," Tatiana said.

Priscilla turned her head to look at him, and he waggled his eyebrows. More sentries, more showing of identities, then they found themselves stopped before a command building. "Inside," Tatiana commanded.

Priscilla and Morgan filed inside to face several officers and men who had obviously been waiting for them, alerted by the call from the gate. Tatiana chose the one with the highest rank. "Your name, please, Comrade Colonel?"

"I am Colonel Goronski. The sentry on the gate called to say you were on your way, Comrade Captain. He also said something . . ."

Tatiana handed him her wallet. Goronski swallowed. Tatiana reckoned there was not an officer in the Red Army who did not have some secret he would like to keep from the KGB. "What do you require?"

"To speak with you in private." Goronski hesitated, then gestured to his inner office. Tatiana jerked her head, and Priscilla and Morgan followed. One of the other officers would have checked them, but Tatiana glared at him and he let them, and her, past. She closed the door. Goronski had retreated behind his desk, but was looking very anxious. "Now, Comrade Colonel," Tatiana said. "I need an aircraft and a pilot. It must have a range of three thousand kilometres. It must also be fast."

"Ah . . . you are asking for one of our light fighter-bombers, Comrade Captain. I do not think . . ."

"Comrade Colonel, it is essential that I deliver these two prisoners to Commissar Beria by dawn tomorrow morning."

For the first time Colonel Goronski appeared to realise that Priscilla and Morgan were handcuffed. "Have you no aide?" he asked. Another irregularity.

"This is a top secret operation, Comrade Colonel. No one is to know of it. All I wish you to do is give the orders for the aircraft to be placed at my disposal. It will return to you tomorrow morning, with a commendation from Comrade Beria."

The Colonel pulled his ear. "Should I not telephone Comrade Beria for confirmation?"

"Do that, and you will undoubtedly be shot. I am risking my own neck in giving you this much information."

"You will give me the authorisation in writing?"

Tatiana bent over the desk, and the pad of paper he thrust at her. She wrote, 'This requisition is for the loan of a military aircraft from the base at Semipalatinsk for the use of the KGB on vital national security. Tatiana Gosykinya, Captain, KGB.'

Goronski read it. "You have not mentioned the prisoners."

"Nor will you, if you have any sense. Keep that authorisation, until you are told from Moscow to destroy it. That will be tomorrow."

Goronski stared at the paper for the last time. "You realise the weather is closing down, Comrade Captain," he said. "There is a front coming up from the south."

"It is not here yet," Tatiana said. The Colonel sighed, and picked up his phone.

Because of a snowstorm, it was four o'clock before Kagan touched down at Alma-Ata, and already the evening was closing in, the temperature plummeting. Kagan stamped into the control building, slapping his gloved hands together. "Who are you?" he demanded of the man waiting for him.

"Station Commander Boros, Comrade General."

"Where is Comrade Smorodsky?"

"I do not know, Comrade General. He went out this morning, and has not returned."

Kagan went to the plate-glass window and looked out at the snow clouding down. To telephone would be to risk blowing this whole thing wide open. But he had no choice. "Call that number," he told Boros, opening his notebook and indicating a figure.

The Station Commander peered at the figures. "With respect, Comrade General, that number . . ."

"I know what that number is," Kagan snapped. "It cannot be reached without a code. There is the code."

Boros's fingers trembled as he dialled the code. When it rang, Kagan took the receiver from his hand. The number was repeated by a woman. "This is General Kagan," Kagan said. "Let me speak to Commandant Karpova."

Valentina Karpova was on the phone in seconds. "Comrade General," she said. "I am glad you called. Will you please tell me what is going on?"

"I wish you to tell me that," Kagan said. "Have you been visited today?"

"Twice," Valentina said. "Firstly, very early this morning, by Captain Gosykinya and an aide. She brought a command for the release of the prisoner Seven Hundred and Six into her custody."

"You did this?"

"The command was in order, Comrade General."

"Very good. What time did she leave?"

"Just before dawn."

"With the prisoner?"

"Yes, Comrade General."

"Very good. And your second visitor?"

"Colonel Smorodsky, from Alma-Ata. He arrived just after one."

"What did he want?"

"I cannot say, Comrade General. He was in a highly agitated state. He merely ascertained that Captain Gosykinya had been here, and had removed Prisoner Seven Hundred and Six."

"When did he leave?"

"Just after two; he stopped to have something to eat."

Kagan looked at his watch. "That is more than two hours ago," he said.

"I think he has returned now." Boros had been looking out of the window at the car park behind the building, in which there was a sudden blaze of lights.

"Thank you, Comrade Commandant," Kagan said into the phone.

"The order for the release of Prisoner Seven Hundred and Six was signed by yourself, Comrade General," Karpova said, anxiously.

"I know that," Kagan said, and hung up. Smorodsky stamped into the room, brushing snow from his shoulders, slapping his gloved hands together, then peeling off the gloves to hold his fingers close to the stove. "You will get chilblains," Kagan remarked.

"With respect, Comrade General, I would like a glass of vodka. What I have seen . . ."

"Leave us, Comrade Boros," Kagan commanded.

Boros hesitated, glanced at his immediate superior, received a quick nod, and left the room. Kagan himself poured the glass of vodka, then took one for himself. "Speak."

Smorodsky was trembling so much he had to hold the glass in both hands to convey it to his lips. "Shatrav, dead. All his men, dead. Their car a burned out wreck. A woman, dead, frozen in the stream . . ."

"A woman?" Kagan's voice was suddenly sharp. "What did this woman look like?"

"Short, yellow hair . . ." Kagan drew a deep breath. "With a crippled leg," Smorodsky went on.

Kagan released his breath in a deep sigh of relief. But still, Shatrav and his people, all dead . . . he would not have believed it possible. "So what did you do after discovering these bodies?"

"I went on to the gulag, as instructed, Comrade General, to inquire after Captain Gosykinya. She had been there, she had received custody of a prisoner, and she had left again."

"So you had lunch and then returned to the death scene," Kagan said. "What of the other car?"

Smorodsky had drunk, deeply, and had regained some composure. "What other car, Comrade General?"

"There should have been another car, Smorodsky."

203

"I saw no other car, Comrade General."

"Well, then, wheel tracks."

"There were no wheel tracks, Comrade General. There had been a fresh fall of snow."

Kagan stood before the huge wall map of Kazakhstan. "It must be her aim to get out of Russia. She can hardly hope to drive to Afghanistan, in the dead of winter. She needs an international airport. Which is the nearest international airport to Alma-Ata?"

"Semipalatinsk, Comrade General." Smorodsky prodded the map.

"Get them on the phone." Kagan himself called the weather room. "Is it snowing in Semipalatinsk?"

"Semipalatinsk is clear, Comrade General."

"Shit!" Kagan said.

"But the weather is closing in," the man said.

"Keep me informed." Kagan looked at Smorodsky, who was holding the receiver.

"The last flight left half an hour ago."

"Bound where?"

"Kabul."

"Contact our embassy in Kabul. Tell them I wish the plane met, discreetly. I do not wish an international incident. On the aircraft there will be two women, one dark, the other fair, both extremely good-looking. I wish them followed, and a report made to me . . ." he looked through the window at the weather; there was no hope of his regaining Moscow until tomorrow. "Here. I will then give orders for their arrest."

"I will see to it, Comrade Commissar."

"Then find me a bed for the night. And a woman." He needed to relieve his tensions.

Once they were in the aircraft, Tatiana released Priscilla and Morgan. There was no risk in this, as the other two crew members were aft with them. "Just behave yourselves," she told them, speaking English. "Remember we are in this together." She smiled at them, "Till death do us part, eh?" The she changed to Russian. "Keep an eye on them," she told the crew.

"How long is the flight?" Morgan asked.

"Several hours. I would have some rest if I were you." She went forward to sit with the pilots. Soup and vodka were produced as soon as they were airborne. "I wonder if the pilots are having the same dinner," Morgan remarked.

Priscilla looked out of the window into the darkness. At least it had stopped snowing for the time being, but she could see little ice particles forming against the window. She wondered if it was her fate to die in a plane crash; she had experienced almost everything else. "Was it very bad?" Morgan asked. Priscilla glanced at him. He flushed. "I mean, I know . . . well . . ."

"It was not worse than Rotislav," Priscilla said. "But I was a girl, then. Now . . ." she sighed. "And for you?"

"I never knew Rotislav," he said grimly.

"I think it must be worse for men," Priscilla said. "More humiliating. Can you now understand how I felt, wishing to see Rotislav hang?" Her hand slid over his, and he turned his head in surprise. "I wish you to know," she said, "that there is no one I would rather have shared this ordeal with. Should we survive, I would like us to be friends."

For a moment he was too taken aback to respond. Then he raised her hand and kissed the gloved fingers, and looked up to see Tatiana, who had left the flight deck, smiling at him. At them both. "One can hardly say, young love," she remarked. "I did not rescue you to be the Princess's lover."

"Is that all you think of?" Priscilla asked.

"There is not much else worth thinking about," Tatiana pointed out. "However, I have not the time to be jealous. Time enough for that, as you say, Princess, when we have survived."

"Are we going to survive?" Morgan asked.

Tatiana shrugged. "A great deal depends on whether we land in Moscow before anyone can work out where we are."

Kagan slept heavily. Not only was he very tired, but Smorodsky had procured him a Tatar woman, and there was nothing so calculated as to bury a man in a sexual sea as a Tatar; he was a Tatar himself. When he awoke he was drowsy in the extreme, blinked at the light, and at Smorodsky, standing anxiously by the bed. Kagan looked at his watch; it was just after midnight. "Well?" he demanded.

"The Kabul flight landed half an hour ago, Comrade Colonel. Our people are on the line. They say no passengers answering your . . . the descriptions we gave them disembarked." Kagan sat up, looked at the tousled dark hair on the pillow; the woman had sensibly buried her face. "They are awaiting your instructions, Comrade General," Smorodsky said.

"Tell them to forget it." Kagan got out of bed, pulled on his uniform while Smorodsky hurried back to the telephone.

The woman rolled over and opened her eyes. "Am I to go?"

"Stay there," Kagan commanded. He pulled on his boots and stamped down the stairs. Smorodsky and Boros and two male secretaries waited for him, all highly nervous. "What are conditions outside?" Kagan demanded.

"We are snowed in, Comrade General."

"What are conditions in Semipalatinsk?"

"There is a blizzard, Comrade General."

Kagan stood before the map. "There is an airport at Ablaketka. That is only a hundred miles east of Semipalatinsk. They could have gone there instead."

"The Ablaketka airport is a small local field, Comrade General. It does not handle international flights."

"But we now know they did not take an international flight," Kagan said. Yet if they are not attempting to flee the country, he wondered, where can they go? Then he snapped his fingers. He had been thinking from only one point of view. But Tatiana did not know, could not know, either that her mother had been arrested, by Stalin's order, or that Stalin had himself given the order for her execution. Her obvious course was to reach the safety of the dictator's aegis, in which security she had lived all her life. He pointed. "Get Semipalatinsk."

Smorodsky nodded to Boros, who began the process. "You think they left on an earlier flight, Comrade General?" Smorodsky asked. "They would hardly have got there in time."

"I have Semipalatinsk, Comrade General," Boros said.

"Tell them we wish to know if any KGB agent chartered an aircraft yesterday afternoon."

Boros put the question, then shook his head. "No, Comrade General."

"Damn," Kagan said, and stamped to the window to peer out at the white-lined darkness. "I want a list of all flights out of Semipalatinsk yesterday."

Boros got busy. "I would say they missed all the flights, and are still there, waiting for the weather to clear," Smorodsky suggested.

"And we cannot get up there," Kagan growled.

"Can you not order their arrest by phone?"

Kagan ignored him. "When is this weather due to clear?"

"Not before tomorrow morning, Comrade General," said the Met Officer.

"Damn," Kagan said again.

"Here is the list of flights, Comrade General." Boros held out the sheet of paper. "This does not include military movements, of course."

Kagan raised his head from perusing the sheet. "Military movements?"

"There is a military airbase at Semipalatinsk."

Kagan pointed at Smorodsky. "Why was I not told this?"

"I . . ." Smorodsky bit off the obvious retort, that the General had not asked. "They could not leave the country in a military plane, Comrade General."

"An officer in the KGB can do anything, if he, or she, has the will," Kagan said. "Get me the commanding officer of that base."

Five minutes later he was speaking with a sleepy and terrified Goronsky. "She said she was acting on orders from Commissar Beria himself, Comrade General," the Colonel said.

"What time did they leave?" Kagan asked.

"Just after six."

Kagan looked at his watch. It was just one o'clock. "Then they will have landed in Moscow."

"Well, Comrade General, conditions are not good . . ."

207

"But there is an east wind. That will have boosted their speed."

"Do you wish me to contact Moscow, Comrade General?"

"No," Kagan said. "I wish you to forget everything that happened yesterday afternoon. That way you may just save your neck."

Chapter Ten

The Fugitives

Kagan was more worried about his own neck. "I wish a private office," he told Smorodsky.

"Have mine, Comrade General."

Kagan sat behind the desk, waited for Smorodsky to close the door behind him, then dialled, using the access code to reach the appropriate number. "Yes," said the female voice, above the background noise.

Kagan sighed. It was not yet midnight in Moscow, and his chief was having a party. Kagan had only once in his life attended one of Beria's orgies; he had been so obviously disapproving that the invitation had never been renewed. "I wish to speak with the Commissar," he said.

"And you are?" the woman asked.

"Kagan, you stupid slut," Kagan snapped.

The woman put down the phone with a clunk, but she had not cut him off, and he listened to the sounds of revelry in the background for several seconds before Beria spoke. "Where have you been, Kagan? I wished to speak with you this afternoon, and your secretary said you had stepped out."

"I am in Alma-Ata," Kagan explained. "Shatrav has fouled up."

"Where is he?"

"Lying in the snow, dead. Together with all his people. I came out here as soon as I realised something was wrong,"

Kagan explained. "But my movements have been hampered b
the weather."

Beria had got his thoughts together. "Where is Tatiana?"

"I think she is in Moscow, with the Princess. And possibly a
accomplice."

"Moscow?" Kagan could imagine Beria looking over hi
shoulder, as if expecting to see Tatiana standing behind him
gun in hand. "I don't understand."

"Lavrenty Pavlovich," Kagan said, with as much patience a
he could muster. "Shatrav fouled up, as I have said. And Tatian
killed him. And three others. There can be no doubt of that. Tha
means she knows that she is marked for execution, and is nov
on the run. With the Princess. She commandeered an army plan
to bring her to Moscow, and by my reckoning will have lande
perhaps an hour ago."

"But this is terrible," Beria protested. "You have failed me
Kagan."

"There is no necessity to panic, Lavrenty Pavlovich. It is m
estimation that Tatiana is not aware that the Premier himsel
ordered her execution. Thus she is certain to try to reach him
All you have to do is post extra guards and make sure that she
and the Princess, and their accomplice, are arrested should the
attempt to gain access to the Premier. Or better yet, shot on sigh
I will be back just as soon as the weather clears."

"I wish you back, now," Beria snapped, and hung up. H
remained glaring at the phone for a few seconds. In this world
if you wanted something done properly, it could only be done b
oneself. He did not imagine for a moment that he could matc
Tatiana Gosykinya in a shoot-out in the snow, but when hi
people had her trussed up like a chicken . . . the veins on hi
bald head stood out as he contemplated such a pleasant sigh
And the Princess, of course. But there were side issues. Such a
the fact that Stalin presumed the Princess had been dead for fou
years. Beria stroked his chin. Just as Stalin supposed that Soni
Cohen had been dead for more than ten years! Ghosts from th
past. And now, a ghost from the present, come to haunt him
Could it be time at last? There was an easy way to find out. H

210

clapped his hands. "Get out, all of you. Get out." He summoned his current secretary, a leggy blonde, half naked and full of vodka, slapped her face. "Pull yourself together."

She gulped and swallowed, while the other revellers hurried from the room. "Call my car," Beria said. He went to his room to wash his face and straighten his clothing. Half an hour later he was at the Kremlin, stopping at the gate to speak with the captain of the guard. "What is your name?"

The officer stood to attention. "Captain Stagykin, Comrade Commissar."

"Well, Captain, listen to me very carefully. I have unearthed a plot against the Premier. These are desperate people who will probably seek to gain access to the fortress. They are headed by an ex-KGB agent named Tatiana Gosykinya. You cannot mistake her. She is tall, well built, and handsome. She has black hair. And she will use her KGB identity card to gain access. I wish you to place her, and anyone who is with her, under close arrest. Do not underestimate these people, Comrade Captain. They are very dangerous. Truss them up as you would a pig for market. I will have agents remove them to Lyubyanka as soon as they are in custody."

"Yes, Comrade Commissar. Suppose they resist arrest?"

"I wish them alive, Captain."

Beria drove on, along the slippery road leading out of the city, to the little dacha. He was checked at the gate, but allowed through as soon as it was realised who he was. The dacha itself was in darkness, although there was a sentry on the door. He too was not going to refuse entry to the Commissar for Internal Affairs, but inside, once he was past the inner two sentries, it was necessary to encounter Valechka Istomina, the massive woman who 'did' for the Premier, in every possible way now that he was past other pleasures. Beria had no idea whether she and the Premier had ever slept together, but he did not consider it likely; Stalin liked beauty too much and this creature was ugly as sin. On the other hand, there could be no doubting her devotion to her master. "The Premier is not to be disturbed," she said. "He is asleep."

"This is a matter of national importance," Beria told her. "I must insist you wake him, now."

She glared at him, but then retreated into the bedroom. Beria listened to the sounds of Stalin waking up, and a few minutes later the Premier shuffled into the room, wearing a dressing gown over pyjamas, looking more like a bear than ever. "What has happened?"

Beria glanced at Istomina. "Leave us," Stalin said. Another glare at Beria, then she banged the door behind her. "Do you know the time?" Stalin demanded.

"Treachery never sleeps, Josef Vissarionovich."

"Treachery?" Stalin's voice was a growl.

"I have discovered a plot of terrifying proportions, Josef. Sit down." Stalin sat, brows drawn together in a deep frown. "As you required, I issued orders for the elimination of Tatiana Gosykinya. I sent her on a mission to Kazakhstan, to get her well out of Moscow while we arrested her mother. My orders were that she was to be dealt with on that mission. Now it appears that she evaded her executioners, and indeed, slew them all."

Stalin's cheeks were suffused. "Who was in command?"

"Shatrav. He used to be a good man. And he fought with Tatiana in the Great Patriotic War. If he underestimated her, he was a fool."

"Shatrav. Shatrav! Did I not once order his execution?"

"You indicated that might be necessary. I decided to give him another chance to prove his worth. I am sorry to say that I have been proved wrong. However, I accepted that he was no longer of value in the field. I would never have used him for such a mission."

"Who selected him?"

"Kagan."

"Is he trustworthy?"

"I would have said so. I will deal with the matter. However, I felt you should be informed, Josef Vissarionovich, because all our information indicates that Tatiana has returned to Moscow. There can be only one reason for this: she wishes to reach you." Stalin gave a little gasp, and clutched his chest, as if he had just suffered a sharp pain. "What concerns me more," Beria went on, as if he had not noticed his master's discomfort, "is that as far as I can make out, she is accompanied by Priscilla Bolugayevska."

Stalin stared at him in stark horror, his mouth opening and shutting. It was some seconds before he could speak. "The Princess Priscilla is dead," he gasped, and pointed. "I commanded you to execute her!"

"And I issued the orders for her execution – to Tatiana. She assured me they had been carried out. At that time I had no reason to distrust her. But now it turns out that instead of executing her, she secreted her away in Gulag Number One, which is in Kazakhstan, as you know. The Princess was kept there as a number only. No one else knew of her identity. But there were special orders regarding her, that she was not to be ill-treated or harmed in any way."

The veins on Stalin's neck were throbbing. "Who issued these orders?"

"I assume Tatiana, as she was the only one who knew the Princess was alive."

"And how have you found this out?"

"From the description of the woman with Tatiana now, and from a conversation with the Commandant of Gulag Number One, who confirms that Captain Gosykinya delivered to her a special prisoner on the twelfth of September 1947. The date fits. And who also confirms that yesterday Tatiana removed that prisoner again."

"The bitch," Stalin muttered. "The bitch!" he suddenly shrieked. "They are both bitches! You . . ." he pointed again. "You find them, Lavrenty Beria, and you take them to Lyubyanka, and you call me, and together we will watch them die. We will make sure of it. You . . ." he gave a choking gasp and fell back against the settee, his face purple.

"Help!" Beria shouted. He ran to the door, threw it open. "Help! Get a doctor! Help!" Istomina pushed him out of the way as she ran past him into the room, knelt beside her employer. The two guards from the front room also hurried in. "Get a doctor!" Beria shouted again.

The two men stared at him, then at the Premier, who, assisted by

Istomina, was slowly sitting up. Beria also turned to look at Stalin Stalin waved his hand. The guards exchanged glances, then left th room. "You need a doctor, Josef Vissarionovich," Beria said.

Istomina had gone to the sideboard and poured a glass of vodka This Stalin now drank, while his colour slowly returned to normal "Doctors," he growled. "Quacks who are trying to poison me."

"I do think you should be examined," Beria said. Damnation he thought; that had really looked like it. But . . . it was obvi ously close.

"I am all right," Stalin snapped. "Go and carry out my instruc tions. But no one is to know of them. Or this."

"Of course. Your birthday . . ."

"We will celebrate my birthday as usual," Stalin said. "Ther is nothing the matter with me."

Beria looked at Istomina, who waggled her eyebrows. Then h left the room. So near, he thought. So near. But surely one mor push – Stalin's birthday was always an occasion for a great dea of drinking, followed by . . . it was a time to act, once and fo all. "I will leave the Premier in your care, Comrade Istomina, a he seems to prefer you to a doctor." He had no doubt that the tw guards were listening at the door.

"Oh, get out!" Stalin shouted. "Find those women."

Beria drove back to Lyubyanka, disturbed sleepy sentries an clerks; it was now three in the morning. But Maria had prudentl remained on duty, leaving the Commissar's apartment to go to hi office. "You are a good girl, Maria Feodorovna," Beria said.

"Is there trouble, Lavrenty Pavlovich?" she asked. She wa permitted to be familiar when they were alone together.

Beria stroked her hair. "Yes, there is trouble. But nothing wit which I cannot deal. Now, I must go to Astrakhan. Call the airpor and have my plane ready; I will be there in an hour."

Maria looked at her watch. "The weather is bad in the east Lavrenty."

"This is an affair of state," he said sternly. My state, he though Maria picked up the phone. As for Tatiana and Priscilla . . . Beri wondered what they would do. If they attempted to see Stalin the

214

would be arrested and brought to his cells. If they attempted to shoot it out and got themselves killed, his arrangements would have been proved correct. If they got through the guards and reached Stalin . . . they could tell him nothing he did not already know. He might even have another attack. Beria did not think there was anything he need fear from Tatiana and the Princess. They would fall into his hands like overripe apples, the moment Stalin died.

Tatiana handcuffed Priscilla and Andrew once again just before they landed. "This is purely cosmetic," she assured them. "From now on we must trust each other, eh? Without me, you are lost." They had to believe she was telling the truth; there was no other reason for her to have rescued them from the gulags.

The aircraft taxied to the military section of Moscow Airport, where, as the pilot had radioed ahead, they were met by various local KGB officials. Priscilla had feared that they would immediately be rearrested, but apparently no one had as yet any reason to challenge Tatiana's credentials, and a car was immediately provided for their drive into Moscow, while the crew of the aircraft busied themselves with refuelling in order to make the return flight to Semipalatinsk. "We are just that far ahead of them," Tatiana said. "And now they will never find us."

"Then where to now?" Andrew asked. "The Kremlin?"

"It is a matter of reaching Premier Stalin," Tatiana said. "And he prefers to spend his nights at his dacha just outside the city. But that is where they will expect us to go, I think, and I do not know how much time we have."

"They?" Priscilla asked.

"Those who wish to eliminate me," Tatiana explained. "It is better you do not know their names, yet. What we need to do is out-think them. So, in the first instance, I think we will go to my mother. She will be able to gain access to the Premier without anyone suspecting, or at least, being able to stop us." They had no difficulty in gaining the city, Tatiana passing the various checkpoints with a simple flash of her identity wallet. They drove along beside the Moscow River, and took the bridge below the Kremlin, into the Kiti-Gorod, the old market centre.

It was now midnight, and the city was dark except for the street lights, but at almost every one there was a policeman, seeking the identity of the driver of this car so strangely about at such an hour.

As always, Tatiana had no problem with these, and when they were into the Kiti-Gorod she pulled down a side street and stopped. "We get out here," she said. "They will have made a note of the number, and when the alarm is given, they will look for this car; it must not be found near my mother's apartment. Now, I am going to unlock your cuffs. But I must tell you that any sign of treachery and I will shoot you both. Please understand this."

"Treachery, from us?" Andrew asked.

Tatiana smiled. "Times change, Andrew." She released them, and they rubbed their hands together. "Follow me," she said.

It was three in the morning, Priscilla calculated; she had no watch. She walked beside Andrew, and occasionally their hands touched. Then she grasped his fingers, and he squeezed back. How odd it is, how things turn out, she thought. She had loved Josef and would always love his memory. But she had liked this young man from the moment of their first meeting, and if he had never actually touched her body, he yet knew more of her than perhaps even Josef had ever managed; Josef had never watched her being immersed, screaming and struggling, into a freezing bath, and held there to the point of death. Josef had only ever known her on top of the world. This man knew her better. And now they might be going to die together.

They returned across another bridge and now she remembered where they were, although it was several years since she had been in Moscow, and visiting Jennie. The Moscow River ran by on their right, and behind it was the bulk of the Kremlin, always to her mind a sinister building. While in front of them, rising above the average apartment block, was the Government Building. The ground floor of this showpiece contained a restaurant and a cinema. Both were shut at this hour in the morning, but on the first-floor landing there was a concierge, blinking sleepily at the KGB officer and her two companions, then staring in consternation

216

as he recognised Tatiana. "Comrade Captain," he stammered. "Oh, Comrade Captain."

Tatiana frowned. "Is there something the matter, Boris?"

Boris licked his lips and hastily wiped them on the back of his sleeve before they froze. "Comrade Ligachevna . . ." he panted.

"My mother is unwell?" Tatiana's voice was soft. Behind her, Andrew and Priscilla could only wait.

"She . . . Oh, Comrade Captain!"

Tatiana stepped against him, forcing him against the wall. "Speak, man."

"She did not come home, yesterday. She was meeting her American friend, and she did not come home. Instead . . ." he rolled his eyes.

"How many are upstairs?" Tatiana asked.

"There is nobody upstairs, Comrade Captain. The apartment is sealed."

"When are you due to be relieved?" Tatiana asked, drawing her pistol.

The concierge licked his lips in terror. "Istvoltna comes in at eight, Comrade Captain. But I will not tell of your visit. You can trust me, Captain."

"I know you will not speak of it, Boris," Tatiana said, and hit him a savage blow on the side of the head with the butt of her pistol. He subsided down the wall without a sound. "Until eight o'clock, at any rate. Help me."

Andrew hurried forward, and between them they carried the unconscious Boris into his cubbyhole of an office. There they laid him on the floor, and Tatiana efficiently bound and gagged him, using his belt and tie and socks. Priscilla watched them. "What did he mean, about an American friend?"

"Your son," Tattie said. "My old friend Prince Alexei."

"Oh, my God! But . . . you mean Alexei is in Moscow? And has been arrested by the KGB?"

"Along with my mother," Tatiana said. She was angry, but she was also realising that the crisis was far bigger than she had imagined. There was only one person in Russia would have dared order the arrest of Jennie Ligachevna, while Stalin lived. So, either

Stalin was dead, and Beria was concealing that fact, or it was Stalin who had ordered her execution, at the same time as he had ordered the arrest of Jennie. Her Uncle Joe!

And by now the KGB would know that she had returned to Moscow. With two prisoners. They would be in no hurry. They would know she had to fall into their lap, some time. By eight o'clock this morning they would be able to trace her movements, at least this far, "What are you going to do?" Andrew asked; he remembered that this woman's mother was all she really had in the world.

"We have to disappear, until I can find out exactly what is happening," Tatiana said. "And I know the very place. Follow me. Quietly." She went to the stairs.

"You are going to remain here?" Priscilla was aghast.

"It is the one place they will never look for us," Tatiana said. Priscilla and Andrew exchanged glances, then followed her up the stairs. They reached the landing opposite the door to Jennie's flat, and saw the seals. Tatiana jerked her head and they went up another fight, to the floor above. Here she again cautioned them to be quiet, while she took a key from her wallet, inserted it into the latch, and turned it, very carefully. The door swung in, and Tatiana stepped through, beckoning them to follow her. "Stand still," she whispered, and closed the door behind them.

They waited, while their eyes became accustomed to the darkness; but it was still impossible to move without tripping over something, unless one knew the apartment very well. Which Tatiana apparently did. She moved across to the inner door, then again beckoned them to follow her, exactly. Again, very carefully, Tatiana turned the knob, and the door swung in. But this door squeaked, very faintly. Instantly there was movement from the bed, and Tatiana switched on the light.

There were two women in the bed, both now sitting up, the covers pulled to their throats, blinking at the sudden light, and at Tatiana, standing now above them. One of the women was in her late forties, Priscilla estimated; she remembered her very well from her visit to Moscow during the War. The other was a younger edition, clearly her daughter. "Tatiana!" The older woman was incredulous. "Oh, Tatiana!" Her voice rose.

"Sssh," Tatiana said. "You remember the Princess Bolugayevska?" Tatiana said. "Princess, you remember my mother's friend, Galina Schermetska?"

"Yes," Priscilla said.

Galina Schermetska gazed at her in consternation, then looked past her at Andrew "And I am sure you also remember Mr Andrew Morgan," Tatiana explained. "As you can see, both he and the Princess have been guests of the government for the past few years." She smiled at the young woman. "Good morning, Helena."

Helena Schermetska stared at her as a rabbit might look at a snake. "But Tatiana," Galina said. "Your mother . . ."

"I know," Tatiana said. "They are after me, too. And my friends. Thus you must help us."

"Me? But . . . if they come here . . ."

"There is no reason for them to come here, as this is the last place they will look for us," Tatiana said. "We will only stay for a few days . . ."

"A few days?" Galina looked left and right.

"It will be crowded, I know," Tatiana agreed. "But we are all friends." She took off her coat.

"If they find you here we will all be executed," Galina said.

"That is the best of reasons for them not to find us here," Tatiana pointed out. "Listen, we could do with a meal and some hot tea. And then a bath. And I will tell you what we will do."

They ate first, as both Galina and Tatiana knew that for the apartment block to be filled with the sound of running water in what was still the middle of the night might cause questions to be asked. The woman Helena sat in a corner of the lounge while her mother prepared food, staring at them. Both Andrew and Priscilla, exhausted and basically undernourished as they were, could do no more than sit and sip tea, enjoying the warmth, enjoying the fact that they were still alive when they had each supposed the other dead. Galina's hands trembled as she set the table. Only Tatiana was as cheerfully confident as ever. "Are you not afraid?" Galina asked. "Do you not know what they will do to you?"

"What they are already doing to Mother," Tatiana said thoughtfully, as she sipped tea. "And Alex. Well, Alex is hopefully still as tough as when we were fighting the Nazis. Mother now, she has always fallen on her feet. We must hope she does so again."

"You are callous," Galina declared.

"I have been trained to look life in the face," Tatiana said. "But you should remember that I wept for your daughter, when she died in the Pripet."

Galina flushed. She had never discovered the truth of her youngest daughter's death. She only knew that she had gone to that fateful summer camp in 1941 as a protégée of Tatiana the daughter of her best friend, that she had been trapped in the Pripet by the sudden German onslaught, like Tatiana, that she had become a partisan, like Tatiana, and that she had died in those endless marshes . . . unlike Tatiana. "What can you hope to achieve?" she asked, seeking to change the subject.

"I had hoped to achieve three things," Tatiana said. "One is to find out just what is going on at the top, because there is *something* going on. I do not know if I am going to be able to do that, now, but I intend to try. The second is to try to find out why Mother and Prince Alexei were arrested, and what has happened to them."

Galina snorted. In common with most loyal Russians, she knew there were only two certainties in life. One was that those taken into the Lyubyanka never emerged again save for the purpose of being tried and then executed. The second was that everyone taken into the Lyubyanka was by definition, guilty, of whatever the charge. To consider another possibility was not only disloyalty to the regime – it filled the mind with unacceptable thoughts. "The third thing I need to do," Tatiana said, "supposing I cannot find acceptable answers to the first two, is to get out of the country, with Mother and the Princess and Mr Morgan. And Prince Alexei."

Galina snorted again. "From Moscow? With the entire KGB looking for you? That is a dream."

"Perhaps. Perhaps not. But here is where you will help us. There is an address I wish you to visit. There, either today or tomorrow

220

you will find a certain Comrade Peter Romanowski. You will tell him you are from Atya, that she is hurt and is desperate to see him, and you will bring him here."

Galina licked her lips. "Romanowski? Well . . ."

"You will pay this address your first visit today," Tatiana told her.

"Well . . . it would be better if Helena did it."

"Me?" Helena's voice was a squawk.

"Helena will not do it," Tatiana said, "because she is not going out to work today. She had a touch of 'flu. You will telephone her office and tell them this." Galina looked from face to face. Tatiana smiled. "I am a cautious woman, Galina. When you return this evening, with or without Romanowski, I will be waiting for you, with Helena, and if anyone enters that door I do not like I will shoot her in the stomach, in such a way that she will die before your eyes, in great agony." Galina clasped both hands to her throat. So did Helena. "But so long as you do nothing stupid, why, we shall all be one happy family. Won't that be nice?"

There was only sufficient hot water for a single tub, and Tatiana, with a sudden awareness of their respective positions, allowed Priscilla first go. There was no door to the bathroom, only a curtain, and thus privacy was next to impossible, but after her six years in the gulag Priscilla was not bothered by that. Galina had already left. Helena washed up the breakfast dishes at the sink. Tatiana lay on the bed; highly trained as she was to withstand the worst of emotional or physical fatigue, she was more exhausted than she would dare admit to any of them. There was so much to be thought about, but that would have to wait until she had rested.

Andrew prowled the apartment, restlessly. He was only just coming to terms with the complete overturn in his situation, his recall to life from the living death he had experienced for the past five years. But he too was exhausted. "Who's next?" Priscilla asked.

Tatiana drew the curtains. Priscilla gave a little start, but did not attempt to conceal herself in any way. It was slowly dawning on Tatiana that this woman, who, for all of her looks she would

221

have described as old, was perhaps far tougher, and certainly more resilient, than anyone she knew – perhaps even herself. "I will be next," she said. "But all three of you, in here."

Andrew and Helena went into the bathroom, glancing at each other; the woman – he supposed she was perhaps a year or two older than Tatiana – was not at all bad looking; there were pink spots in her cheeks; she was embarrassed by the whole thing. He looked at the Princess, who continued to dry herself with the utmost composure, only half turned away from him. Tatiana placed her pistol on the side of the bath, then undressed, facing them. "Anyone would suppose you do not trust us," Andrew ventured.

"I do not," Tatiana agreed. Naked, she stepped into the bath and slipped beneath the still warm water with a little sigh. "Please remember, darling Andrew, that I can reach the gun long before you."

"Has it occurred to you that if you shoot at any of us, everyone in the building will hear?" Priscilla had finished drying and was picking up her prison uniform.

"Do not wear those filthy, degrading things," Tatiana said. "You are much of a size with Galina. We will find you some clean clothes in a moment. Just stand there. You are nice to look at. As for alarming the building, Princess, if the police come here, I will shoot myself. But you, and Helena, and Andrew, will be returned to your gulags, and this time, Princess, there will be no order preserving you from a daily beating. It would be very unwise for you to be returned to the clutches of Valentina Karpova."

"And you reckon you can keep us all under guard all the time?" Andrew asked. "You have to sleep sometime, Tattie."

"We all have to sleep," Tatiana said equably, stepping out of the bath, and picking up Priscilla's discarded towel with one hand and her gun with the other. "Now you, Andrew." He stripped off his prison garb. Helena turned away but the other two women, who already knew him so well, were not embarrassed, even by the effect their own naked bodies had had on him. "It is nice to see that you are still capable of interest," Tatiana remarked.

Andrew soaped. His brain was ticking as fast as any of theirs, even if he was just as emotionally drained. But no matter how he looked at the situation, Tatiana held all the trumps – at the moment. "This friend of Atya's," he ventured. "You really think he can help us?"

"I think he may have some ideas." She handed him the towel, waited while he dried himself. "Getting some decent clothes for you will be difficult," she said. "Now, we all need to sleep. In there." She pointed at the bedroom with her gun. "I need a washing line," Tatiana told Helena. "A good deal of washing line."

Helena obliged, and Tatiana used a kitchen knife to cut it into strips, while her three prisoners watched her. Priscilla and Andrew stood together, and she gave his hand a quick squeeze. He didn't know whether she was encouraging him to try something or warning him against it. But he had seen too much of Tatiana to risk chancing his arm unless he held a substantial advantage, and at the moment she was the one with the gun. "Now," Tatiana said. "Helena, sit in that straight chair against the wall. I know this is going to be uncomfortable, but it will only be for a few hours. Then we will all be friends again, eh?" Helena glanced at Priscilla and Andrew, then sat down.

Tatiana knelt beside her, placing the gun on the floor. "Please remember not to be stupid," she told Priscilla and Andrew, and very quickly and efficiently bound Helena's ankles to the chair legs, then passed the line under the chair and brought it up the back to secure her wrists, then passed it twice round her chest before making it fast to the chair back. "Just relax," she recommended, "and it will not feel so uncomfortable. Now for you two." She studied them for several seconds, while Andrew found he was holding his breath.

"Andrew on that side," she said. "Lie down on your back." Andrew obeyed. "Arms above the head," Tatiana commanded, and secured his wrists to the iron bedhead. "You look good enough to eat," she said, "and I mean that literally." She pulled his legs together, looped some of the line round his ankles, and secured them to the bottom end of the iron bedstead. "Now," she said. "Lie on top of him, Princess."

Priscilla gazed at her with her mouth open.

"Well," Tatiana explained, "there is really only room for two

223

people lying beside each other on that bed. And I need my sleep as well. I am actually doing you a great favour, Princess, as I am quite sure you have long had it in mind to be intimate with Andrew." Priscilla looked at Andrew. Her face as always was composed, but there were pink spots on her cheeks . . . as there were on his. She drew a deep breath and climbed onto the bed, sitting on Andrew's thighs, one leg to each side.

"Now lie down," Tatiana said. Slowly Priscilla lowered herself on to Andrew's chest, her golden hair flopping on his face. "Extend your arms," Tatiana commanded. Priscilla obeyed, and had her wrists secured to the bedhead between Andrew's. Tatiana then brought her ankles together, and secured them to the bottom of the bed, immediately above Andrew's.

"Now you see, you should both be quite comfortable. But try not to wake me up." She lay down on the bed herself, her thigh brushing Andrew's, pulled the covers over all three of them, and almost immediately, it seemed, fell fast asleep.

Priscilla's left cheek was against Andrew's right, so that his lips were aginst her left ear. He kissed it, to make sure he had her attention, not that he could doubt that he had; he could feel every contour of her body implanted on his. Her lips were against his right ear, and it was some seconds before she responded; she could see Tatiana, where he could not – Tattie's face was in fact only inches from her own – and she was waiting to be sure their captor was asleep. Then she whispered, "Can you breathe?"

"Yes," he whispered back. "You are not very heavy. Your highness . . ."

"Be patient. Try to sleep. We must sleep."

"If I sleep, with you on top of me, your highness . . ."

"If it happens, it happens," she said. "Presumably it will amuse her."

"And you?"

She raised her head, and moved it, so that now her lips were on his. "I believe in God's will, Andrew."

He kissed her mouth. Perhaps he had wanted to do that since he had first seen her. Or even before than, when he had first read of her. And to his surprise and delight she responded. She was, he reminded himself, a woman who made her own rules for life, and had always done so. How he longed for his arms to be free, so that he could hug her against him. But could he possibly hold her closer than she was now, pressed down by her own weight, and held there by the cords binding her wrists and ankles? And now she was after all moving her body on his, her breasts on his, her belly on his, her thighs against his, and her pubes against his. "Princess," he gasped. "Princess." Priscilla sighed.

And Tatiana smiled. "Filthy capitalist beasts," she murmured. "Now perhaps we may get some sleep." They slept, and awoke with a start as they heard the key in the lock. Tatiana was out of bed in an instant, the revolver in her hand, opening the bedroom door and stepping into the lounge as Galina entered the apartment. With her was a man.

Chapter Eleven

The Death of a Tyrant

The weather in Kazakhstan cleared by dawn, and Kagan was able to take off. By then he knew that Tatiana and two companions had landed at Moscow, without hindrance, requisitioned a car, and driven off, presumably into the city. No one at the airport had had any orders to hinder the KGB captain. As Beria was obviously handling things at the Moscow end, Kagan did not enlighten anyone he spoke to. But when he called the Lyubyanka just before taking off at eight o'clock, and asked to be connected with the Commissar, he was simply told that the Commissar was not available. It was, of course, only five o'clock in the morning in Moscow, yet it still seemed to be absurdly confident of Beria to have gone to bed. But there was nothing Kagan could do until he reached Moscow himself, and the flight was something over three thousand kilometers. That was five and a half hours by his private jet, and even going with the sun, it was ten-thirty before he landed. He had his pilot maintain radio silence, apart from routine requirements. He was prepared to be patient.

There was absolutely no indication of any crisis. He presumed that Beria had things entirely under control. But he drove straight to Lyubyanka, marched up the stairs to Beria's outer office, and encountered Maria. "The Commissar is not here," she announced.

"Tell me where I can reach him."

"I am sorry," Maria said primly. "I am not at liberty to do

226

that." Kagan seized her by the shirt-front and half carried her into the inner office. "What are you *doing*?" she shouted. Like most women, she regarded physical contact with Kagan as being scarcely more acceptable than with an ape.

Kagan sat her on Beria's desk, scattering pens and pencils and paperclips. "This is a matter of state security," he said. "If you try to play games with me, my sweet little thing, I am going to twist your knickers into a knot – with you in them."

Maria panted. "I am doing as I was ordered," she said. "As you say, a matter of state security. That is what Comrade Beria told me, before he left. He did not tell *me* where he was going, Comrade Kagan. Simply that he would be back this evening, for the Premier's birthday party. State Security!"

Kagan glared at her, but he knew she was telling the truth. So, either Beria had discovered something about Tatiana's movements he did not yet know, or he was removing himself from the scene of action, so that *he* could not know what was happening, and thus could not be held responsible. The bastard! But this was Kagan he was dealing with. "Very well," he said. "Get out."

He released the shirt-front and Maria straightened her brassiere as she slid off the desk. But she was Beria's creation, not Kagan's. "I cannot leave you alone in the Commissar's office, General Kagan."

"You can and you will, because I am telling you to," Kagan said. "Get out, and stay in the outer office. And do not attempt to listen in to my phone conversations." He grinned at her. "State Security, Comrade."

Maria backed out of the door and closed it. Kagan sat at Beria's desk and used the Commissar's private phone. "Voronski," he said. "Has the Commissar for Internal Affairs used an aircraft today."

"I am not allowed to tell you that," the Airport Commandant protested.

"Voronski," Kagan said earnestly. "This is General Kagan. If you do not wish me to come down there and place you under arrest you had better answer my question."

Voronski could be heard to gulp, even over the phone. If he feared Beria, he feared Kagan more. "The Commissar flew

227

out at eight-fifteen this morning, Comrade General. In his private jet."

"For where?"

"He told me that information was classified, Comrade General."

"Right," Kagan said. "Consider yourself under arrest, Colonel. I am sending a car for you now."

This time the gulp was even more audible. "The Commissar went to Astrakhan, Comrade General. To his dacha. He said he needed a rest."

"Astrakhan," Kagan repeated, slowly. "To his dacha. Thank you, Comrade Colonel. You are no longer under arrest. But you will be, if you repeat a word of this conversation, to anyone." He hung up, and brooded at the desk. Beria had flown out, in the middle of a crisis, on the Premier's birthday, to his dacha in Astrakhan. Needing a rest! But he had told Maria that he would be back for the Premier's birthday party tonight. As it was a flight of several hours to Astrakhan, and several hours back, even if the flying time was not interfered with by the weather, he would scarcely have the time to spend an hour in his villa before he would be on his way back. That was a rest?

No, no, Kagan thought. Beria had gone to Astrakhan for a purpose. To see someone. Or to fetch something. Or someone! Now who could that be? He flicked the pages of Beria's desk diary. So, with a renegade KGB agent running loose round the city, Beria takes off to his personal dacha. But intending to return for the birthday party. Of course, it was always possible that the man had cracked under the strain and gone mad. But then again he might not. And either way . . . Kagan reached the list of Beria's private telephone numbers, and selected one. When the phone was answered, he said, "Let me speak with Comrade Kruschev."

Tatiana swung her legs off the bed and stood up. "Welcome," she said. "Are you Comrade Romanowski, Moonlight, or Mr Halstead? Or perhaps all three?"

Halstead looked her up and down, and then at the two people on the bed. "I seem to be interrupting an orgy."

"Just passing the time," Tatiana said. "Galina, you have done well. Now you may untie these people. Mr Halstead, you and I need to talk."

"Do you mind putting something on?" Halstead asked. "I find it a little hard to concentrate."

"Flatterer!" But she put on one of Galina's dressing gowns and led him back into the lounge. Galina meanwhile was untying Helena.

"Where is Atya?" Halstead asked.

"Atya is dead."

Halstead's eyes narrowed, and he gave another quick glance around the room. "So I have walked into a trap."

"Does it look like it? I believe you need me as much as I need you." Tatiana sat on the settee, throwing one long leg over the other. "How strange it is, that we should meet in these circumstances."

Halstead sat opposite her. "I don't yet know what the circumstances are, although I imagine that were they different they would be uncomfortable for me. Is Atya really dead?"

"I'm afraid she is. You are not showing a great deal of grief."

Helena rubbed her hands together, while her mother began untying Priscilla.

"I hope she died well. She was an old friend. More than ten years."

"Whom you used shamelessly," Tatiana remarked.

"It is my job," Halstead pointed out. "As you have used people shamelessly, no doubt."

Priscilla rolled off Andrew, and sat up, her back to him. Galina began to untie him as well. No one spoke; apart from their emotions, they were listening to the conversation in the other room. "She died with a gun in her hand," Tatiana said. "Which is as well as any of us can hope for."

"And you already knew about me?"

"I knew she had a lover, which was strange, for someone in her condition. It was she who told me who you were, just before she died."

"But you did not execute her."

"No, Mr Halstead. We were on the same side when she died."

Andrew sat up, and like Helena, rubbed his chafed wrists. Still Priscilla did not look at him. But she said, "Tatiana mentioned something about clothes."

"I will see what I can find," Galina said. "We are much the same size."

"So why have you brought me here?" Halstead asked. "If it is not a trap?"

"I wish to do a deal with you, Mr Halstead. As you may have gathered, I no longer work for the KGB. I believe that I have uncovered a plot to murder, or at least remove, Premier Stalin. But he is so unaware of it that he has even turned against me."

"And you wish me to help you save his life?"

"I wish you to get me and my companions out of Russia."

"Tall order."

"Mr Halstead, you must do it all the time."

"One person may go where six would be immediately suspect."

"You only have to do it once. I know it will mean you may never be able to return to Russia, but it would be highly risky for you to do so in any event, as you have no Atya to help you and conceal you. And you will be taking out with you, this last time, information of incalcuble value. You may be sure that whatever happens inside the Kremlin will not be released to the world for a very long time. But you will know, now."

Priscilla tried on Galina's underwear. "What about Mr Morgan?" she asked.

"That will be difficult," Galina said. "He will have to stay with his prison uniform."

"How do I know this is not some even more elaborate trap?" Halstead asked.

"Because there would be no point in it. I knew where you were to be found, Mr Halstead. I also knew who you were. Had I still been a KGB agent, what would have been simpler than for me to have you arrested, and taken down to the Lyubyanka, with all the kudos that would have accumulated to me? Besides, what of the people in the other room? Do you know them?"

"I'm afraid not."

"But you know of them, perhaps. The woman is the Princess Bolugayevska. kidnapped by the Bolsheviks six years ago. The man is Andrew Morgan, a British citizen, arrested by the Bolsheviks at the same time."

"You serious?"

"Then you do know of them?"

Halstead got up and walked to the bedroom door. Andrew was dressing himself in his prison garb. Priscilla was now fully dressed, in Galina's clothes. Both looked at him, inquiringly. "I do assure you that what Tatiana says is true," Priscilla said.

"Atya told me she tortured you," Halstead said.

"Me? Not really, beyond a cold bath. Andrew here had a hard time."

"And you are prepared to trust her?"

"Times change, Mr Halstead," Priscilla said. "I have observed this in the course of my life more than most people. Right now, Tatiana is on a hiding to nothing. She has to escape Russia. She reckons her path, as a defector, will be eased by taking Andrew and me with her. So, we are allies. History has often required strange bed fellows to lie down together, Mr Halstead."

Halstead turned back to Tatiana. Who shrugged. "The ball is in your court, Mr Halstead. But . . ." she produced her pistol from the pocket of her dressing gown. "I will have that gun you are wearing stuffed into your pants."

"I thought we needed to trust each other."

"We do. But I trust people better when I am in control. Just hold the barrel, will you. And if you have any doubts about my ability to kill with a single shot, ask the Princess."

Halstead forced a grin. "To fire a shot would have half the Moscow police in here."

"Absolutely," Tatiana said. "Then we would hang, shoulder to shoulder. I am sure we would both enjoy the experience, but isn't it something we should postpone for as long as possible?" Halstead reached beneath his jacket. "Butt first," Tatiana reminded him.

He gave her the gun. "I can take you out," he said. "We will leave tonight."

231

"No," Tatiana said. "I must first find out what has happened to my mother, and if possible rescue her. There is also an old comrade in the cells of the Lyubyanka."

"My son," Priscilla said. So much had happened in the past twenty-four hours she had actually forgotten her principal duty.

"You have got to be crazy," Halstead protested. "You are a wanted traitor . . ."

"We do not know that, yet," Tatiana said.

"If we are going to get out, every moment is crucial. I don't know if it can be done, anyway. Just how many of you are there, anyway?"

"I do not know, yet. But I am in command," Tatiana said. "We are perfectly safe here, because this building is the last place anyone will think of looking for us. As for my being a proscribed traitor, that is also something we shall have to discover." She smiled at Galina.

As usual, Polkov was waiting when Beria's aircraft touched down. It was hardly less cold in Astrakhan than in Moscow, and there had been a recent snowstorm. "I had not expected you at this time, Comrade Commissar," he admitted.

"Why not?" Beria asked.

"Well . . . is not today Premier Stalin's birthday?"

"Indeed it is. I have come to collect his birthday present."

The car swung into the dacha's grounds, stopped before the steps. "The ladies are walking," Polkov said.

"Have them brought in," Beria said.

He went upstairs, from where he could overlook the gardens and the walks by the shore; the shrubs and trees were covered in the light dusting of snow. And he could make out the two women, wearing fur coats and hats, strolling along one of the paths, two guards walking behind them. Polkov returned to stand beside him. "I have sent for them, Comrade Commissar."

Beria nodded, as he watched another guard hurry up to Sonia; the women immediately turned and walked back to the house. "Now listen to me very carefully, Polkov. I am taking Madame Cohen out of here today, back to Moscow. The daughter will

232

remain here. At some time over the next day or so I will telephone you with a message, a single word, Dispose. At that time you will dispose of the daughter. I do not wish her body ever to be found. But until you get my message, she is to be treated with every courtesy, as she is now. Do you understand me?"

"Yes, Comrade Commissar."

"And should her mother telephone, they are to be allowed to speak."

"I understand, Comrade Commissar."

Beria looked down at the steps beneath him, where the two women were just mounting. "Now leave me."

He went inside, opened a bottle of champagne, and filled three glasses. Then he faced the door as Sonia and Anna came in, pulling off their gloves; they had left their hats and coats downstairs. Over the five years she had spent here with her mother, Anna had filled out and regained much of her strength. Her face remained haggard, but that was because of the treatment she had received, first of all in a Nazi concentration camp, and then in a Russian 'rehabilitation centre', places hardly better than the gulags. But it had become a happy face, as Sonia also radiated happiness. Mother and daughter, reunited after a lifetime of separation and enmity. He had brought Anna here as an added safeguard that Sonia would never let him down, and he would use her as that to the end. But he was pleased that they had had these happy four years together. If he was totally amoral, ethically as well as sexually, he enjoyed dropping crumbs to those who hovered about his table. "Comrade Commissar," Sonia said, and frowned, as he handed her a glass; he was not usually so generous.

But he was giving a glass to Anna, as well. Sonia had a sudden quite painful stab of indigestion. She had now been in this man's custody for eleven years, waiting for him to require her to sacrifice her life. But eleven years is a long time. She was in the position of someone told they have six months to live because of an incurable disease, and yet continuing to live, month after month and year after year, until the realisation that one is a condemned woman ceases to have importance – one is no more condemned than any other human being, however apparently healthy. Even so, the realisation that the moment has finally come can be a considerable shock. "What are we celebrating?" Anna asked. "Is Premier Stalin dead?"

She was a woman who would never be the slightest bit cautious, even when she might be uttering treason. But after four years she no longer feared even Beria. Sonia held her breath as Beria stared at her for several seconds, then he laughed. "Ha ha. Ha ha ha."

"Ha ha ha," the women echoed.

"We are celebrating . . . the end of winter," Beria said. "It will not be long now." Anna looked at her mother. They had never celebrated the coming of spring before. "I am leaving again this afternoon," Beria said. "I wish you to accompany me, Sonia."

Sonia's limbs felt weak. But she could control her voice. "Then I need to pack."

"No," he said. "That is not necessary. There will be a change of clothing for you in Moscow."

"Moscow?" Anna asked. "You are taking us to Moscow?"

"I am taking your mother to Moscow," Beria said. "Just for a day or two. You will remain here."

Anna stared at her mother with her mouth open. Was it possible that Sonia had never told her the truth of why they were both alive? "I'm sure you'll be all right here without me," Sonia said. "For a day or two."

"*Is* she going to be all right?" Sonia asked, as she and Beria sat together in his private jet to fly west. She would not attempt to bargain for her daughter's life, but Beria had no doubt that if he did not guarantee Anna's safety Sonia would reserve her right to act as she thought fit, when she thought fit. She was about the most cold-blooded woman he had ever met, beneath that mask of yielding femininity. Well, in view of the life she had led he supposed that was an inevitable result.

But he could not help wondering if that other softly yielding female, the Princess Priscilla, was similarly ruthless when the chips were down? Her life had hardly been less demanding. But she too was coming to the end of that life: Kagan would undoubtedly have both her and Tatiana under lock and key by now. "Of course she is going to be all right," he told Sonia. "I have told Polkov that, on receipt of a code word from me, he is to see her across the border into Afghanistan. She will be supplied with a passport and sufficient money to reach her family in the States."

"She has no family in the States."

"She is Joseph Cromb's cousin, and the Princess Priscilla's stepchild as well as cousin, is she not? They will certainly look after her."

Sonia couldn't argue with that. Priscilla and Joseph had certainly looked after *her*, when she had fled to them following Trotsky's murder. "Thank you," she said. "I am very grateful."

"Who knows," Beria said jocularly. "If all goes well, you may be accompanying her."

Sonia's head turned, sharply. "I do not understand."

Beria chuckled. "What, did you suppose I intended to introduce you in Stalin's company with a bomb concealed beneath your dress? Or a revolver? Or even . . ." he chuckled again, "an icepick? My dear Sonia, it is essential that Josef dies of natural causes. A heart attack. That is all we need. And then you can be on your way back to Astrakhan, to Anna, Afghanistan, and safety."

"Do you seriously suppose that the sight of me will give Stalin a heart attack?"

"The sight of you, appropriately dressed, and at the appropriate moment, will I think prove sufficient to reduce him to the condition I desire."

They landed in Moscow at six o'clock. It was already dark, and snowing. Before they landed, Beria had Sonia put on a thick veil. His car was waiting for him and they were whisked through the almost empty streets to Lyubyanka. Here Beria, acknowledging the salutes of his people, took Sonia directly upstairs to his office. By the time they reached there she was breathing hard. It was not merely the fact that she was an old woman and the stairs were steep, he knew; she had nothing but unpleasant memories of this office. Maria was waiting for them, frowning at the veiled woman. "General Kagan has been asking for you all day, Comrade Commissar."

"Get hold of him and tell him to come directly to me," Beria said. "And take this lady to my private apartment. Keep her there, Maria, until I come for her."

"I would like to telephone Astrakhan," Sonia said.

Beria grinned. "One would suppose you do not trust me, Sonia. But of course you may telephone Astrakhan. Do it from my apartment; Maria will get it for you." She was behaving exactly as he had anticipated; once she had reassured herself as to Anna's safety she would obey him without question.

Kagan arrived a few minutes later. "May I ask where you have been, Comrade Commissar?"

"I went to Astrakhan to collect my birthday present for the Premier," Beria explained. "Have you arrested Tatiana?"

"I have not, Comrade Commissar. I have no idea where she is."

"That is very serious," Beria remarked. "I had counted on you, Comrade."

"As I had assumed you would deal with the matter yourself, Comrade Commissar," Kagan said equably.

"Well, you get out there and find her," Beria said. "I am going to dress now to attend the Premier's birthday party. When I return to this office tomorrow morning I expect Captain Gosykinya, and her accomplices, to be downstairs in the cells. Do you understand me?"

"Yes, Comrade Commissar. Is it to be a large party? At the Premier's dacha?"

"No," Beria said. "There will just be Comrade Malenkov, Comrade Kruschev, and myself." He grinned. "And presumably Comrade Istomina, as well as the guards."

"Enjoy yourself," Kagan said, and left.

Beria hurried to his apartment, where Sonia and Maria were sitting, chatting, like two old friends. Maria had only become his secretary after the end of the Great Patriotic War, and thus could never have seen Sonia in her life – Sonia had been arrested during the War, and secreted away. But the sight of them together . . . "What are you talking about?" Beria demanded.

"This and that," Sonia said equably.

He glared from one face to the other, but Maria merely looked bewildered. "Leave us, now, Maria Feodorovna," he said. "And do not mention to anyone that you have met this lady. Do you understand me?"

"Of course, Comrade Commissar." Maria was clearly more confused than ever. She had worked with Beria long enough to know that he was a man of the most perverted tastes, but that he should have brought in a woman well over seventy . . . the stranger was well-educated, well spoken, and very refined, but she could hardly be a very exciting sexual companion, in Maria's youthful opinion. She closed the door behind her. "She is devoted to you," Sonia said.

"I pay her well," Beria said. "Now listen very carefully to what you have to do."

Sonia listened. "Is that all?" she asked.

"That is all."

"And afterwards?"

"I will return you to Astrakhan, to join Anna, and you will leave Russia together."

"With the story of what has happened here?"

Beria grinned. "No one will ever believe you, my dear Sonia. And if they do ever decide to do so, by that time I shall be premier, so it will not matter. Have you spoken with Anna?"

She nodded. "Very good. Prepare yourself as I have instructed. You will find all the necessary make-up in the bathroom. I will be back as soon as I have dressed."

He watched her go into the bathroom, then he returned to his office, picked up the phone, dialled his private number in Astrakahan. "Polkov."

"Dispose," Beria said.

It was snowing as Beria's limousine reached the gates of the Premier's dacha, where guards peered at him, seated in the back, and then the veiled woman at his side. "My birthday present, to the Premier," Beria said.

The guard grinned. Beneath the veil, there were no means of

telling how old, or how young, Sonia might be; she had always kept her figure slim. The gates were opened, and they drove in. The two other limousines were already there. "The lady will remain here until she is summoned," Beria told his driver. "You are forbidden to speak with her."

"I understand Comrade Commissar."

Beria squeezed Sonia's gloved hand, and to his surprise, she squeezed back. But she was trembling. Then he went into the house.

Had it been a game, in which he was the referee, Beria did not think it could have gone better. As had to be expected, Stalin wanted to know the situation with Tatiana and the Princess, which meant that Malenkov and Kruschev had to be taken into their confidence, to Malenkov's alarm, certainly. But Beria was able to reassure them that all was in hand, and that the criminals would be in custody by morning. Whatever blame had to be apportioned he laid squarely on Kagan's incompetence. Then, again as he had anticipated, the four of them drank bottle after bottle of wine as they ate, while swapping stories of the old days, as Stalin liked to do. Equally as he had anticipated, Stalin had clearly not fully recovered from his last attack; his eyes were bloodshot before the evening began, and his movements clumsy, his breathing stertorous.

The only one of them who was not his usual cheery self was Nikita Kruschev, who drank less than usual, and spent a good deal of his time staring from face to face. At his face in particular, Beria realised. But Kruschev, in his opinion, was a nonentity. He found an opportunity to take Istomina aside. "Did the Premier see a doctor, as I wished?"

"He would not do so."

"And now he is drinking too heavily."

"Well, Comrade Commissar, if you think that, why do you not tell him to stop."

"Have you no concern for him?"

"I have every concern for him, Comrade. But I know better than to attempt to stop him enjoying himself."

Perhaps there would be no need for Sonia at all. Beria rejoined

238

the party. "Josef Vissarionovich," he said. "It is late, you are not well, and you are drunk. It is time for you to go to bed."

"What?" Stalin shouted. "Me, drunk? Me, unwell?" Malenkov and Kruschev gazed at the throbbing purple veins in dismay. "You . . ." Stalin pointed. "You concern yourself with matters that are not your province, Lavrenty Pavlovich. Ha ha. You . . ." he sat down very suddenly, almost missing the settee, leaning back, head lolling.

"He has passed out," Malenkov said.

"He has had a stroke, you mean," Beria said. "He had one only yesterday. I begged him to see a doctor, but he would not. Now . . ."

Istomina pushed her way past them. "He has had too much to drink," she said. "That is all. Help me take him to bed, comrades." The four of them carried the inert dictator into his bedroom, laid him on the bed.

"We should send for the doctor," Beria reiterated.

"That will not be necessary, unless Comrade Stalin wishes it," Istomina said. "Do not fret, Comrade, soon he will wake up and call for a cup of tea. Then he will sleep peacefully."

"Well," Kruschev said. "Then we had best leave him."

Beria followed them into the night, bade them goodnight, watched their limousines drive away. Then he went to his own car. "It is time."

Sonia got out. Beria led her back into the dacha, where the guards came to attention. "For the Premier," Beria said.

The guards allowed Sonia through. "Should they not have searched me?" she whispered.

"They should," Beria agreed. "They will undoubtedly be punished. But Istomina will certainly search you.'"

"What's this?" Istomina emerged from the kitchen. "I thought you had gone home, Comrade Commissar."

"I could not mention it in front of the others," Beria explained. "But Josef Vissarionovich expressly requested a woman tonight." Istomina gazed at him in astonishment. She knew, probably better than anyone, just how incapable her master was of having sex. Beria grinned. "He just wishes to look, and touch. Do not worry, she understands this."

"The Premier is asleep, as you know, Comrade Commissar."

"But he will wake up, as you yourself have said," Beria pointed out. "I would like his present to be waiting for him when he does. If he no longer wishes her, he has merely to send her away."

Istomina hesitated, then shrugged. "I must search her."

"Do so."

Istomina stepped up to Sonia, ran her hands up and down her body. "Scrawny," she commented. "Raise the dress."

Sonia glanced at Beria, who nodded. She lifted her dress and allowed Istomina to check between her legs. Obviously Istomina would realise that she was not a young woman, but Sonia was amazingly well preserved. When Istomina made to lift the veil, Beria checked her. "The lady's identity is to be known only to the Premier and myself," he said.

Istomina raised her eyebrows, but shrugged. "Well, sit down, comrade," she suggested. "Make yourself comfortable. We will know when he wakes up, because he will ring his bell."

"Then I will bid you goodnight, again," Beria said. "Make him happy, Comrade," he told Sonia.

The door closed behind him. "Would you like a cup of tea?" Istomina asked. Sonia shook her head. "Can you not speak?" Again Sonia shook her head.

Istomina snorted, and went into the kitchen. She made herself a cup of tea. Sonia sat absolutely still. The heavy make-up was beginning to itch. But she dared not scratch, and now her heart, which had been pounding wildly when she had entered the dacha, was slowing. This was far better, far simpler, than she had ever expected. And if Beria's plan did not work, and Stalin merely awoke and savaged her, and then, having recognised her, handed her over to his guards, well, what had she lost? What a life she had led, beginning with her arrest in St Petersburg in 1893, through her exile to Siberia, her escape, with Lenin and Krupskaya and Patricia and Joseph Fine – poor Joseph had been the only one of them not to make it; then, she and Priscilla smiling at each other as they had prostituted themselves to live until they could regain

Bolugayen. Prince Alexei, lifting her emaciated, tortured body to bed, and then wooing her. The happy years! The catastrophe of Stolypin's murder. The War and her rearrest by the Okrana. Rasputin, who had used her as a servant. The Tsarina and the Grand Duchesses, who had used her as a friend. Trotsky! Always Trotsky. And now the man who had ordered Trotsky's death. No, she thought, if Beria's plan does not work, I will strangle Stalin with my bare hands and die happy.

She was alerted by a snore. Istomina had finished her tea and had nodded off – as Beria had said she would. It was time. Sonia got up, tiptoed to the inner door, her boots soft on the carpet. She pushed it in, closed it behind her, stood above the bed. A light burned on the far side of the room, and Stalin slept half on his back, mouth open. He was not a pretty sight, but his breathing was shallow and quick. Sonia took off her veil, and sat beside him. Gently she shook his shoulder. "Josef," she said. "It is I."

He had stirred when she depressed the mattress. Now he stirred some more, moving his legs as he rolled entirely on to his back. "Josef," she said. "Won't you wake up? I have come to kill you. Trotsky has sent me. Trotsky, Josef, the man you thought you had murdered."

Stalin exhaled, loudly, and one eye opened, then the other. He looked at her, frowned, and stared at her. She wondered what he had seen first? The caked white make-up, of course, which made her look like a long-dead corpse. But then he had identified the features, the glowing eyes, the haughty curl of the lip. He opened his mouth, but no words came. The veins in his neck throbbed, as did those at his temples and in his forehead. "You . . ." he gasped, with an enormous effort. "You are dead."

"I am here, Josef. I have come to take you, to see Trotsky, to talk with Trotsky, your old companion. Will we not have much to talk about?"

Stalin made an enormous effort to sit up, gasped again, and fell back, rolling on his side. Sonia rested two fingers on his neck; there was a pulse there, but it was enormous, a huge throb, as if his heart was about to burst. She realised she had done all she could, and it was time to think of herself. She stepped into the bathroom, washed the make-up from her face. Behind her there was no sound. Then she heard the door open. She stared at her face. Almost every trace of the make-up was gone. Certainly, no one was going to notice the odd vestige around her ears. She opened the bathroom door. "You!" Istomina whispered. "What are you doing in here?"

"The Premier called. You were asleep, so I came in." Istomina was staring at the bed. "He was restless," Sonia said. "He wanted to touch me. Then he went back to sleep. I will go now. I do not think he will awake again."

Istomina continued to stare at the bed. There was no sound in the room above that of breathing. Their breathing. Sonia held her arm and half pushed her from the room. "Let him sleep," she said. "Will you tell the guards to let me through?"

"You have no transport."

"I will walk," Sonia said. "I always feel like walking, after sex."

Istomina glanced at her. But the woman was clearly confused, uncertain what to do. She herself escorted Sonia into the outer room. "This woman is to go home now." For the first time she peered into Sonia's face. "You are an old woman," she said. "What did he want with an old woman?"

"We are old friends," Sonia pointed out. "He wanted to talk about old times. And touch, old things."

Istomina watched her leave the house, then she went back into the lounge, made herself some more tea. It was past four, and she knew she would not sleep again. She drank her tea, sat still for a few minutes, then got up again and went to the bedroom door. This had been the oddest night that she could recall. Who *was* that woman? But she had been a friend of Beria's, which was reassuring. Supposing Lavrenty Pavlovich *had* any friends.

She stood at the door for several seconds, then returned to her chair. But she continued to be restless. The Premier had been awakened by an old friend, a woman he had wanted to touch. Therefore he had wanted to have sex with her, but had been unable to do so. That was normal. What was not normal was that, sexually aroused and unable to harden, or even ejaculate –

s she knew was his problem – he would simply turn over and go back to sleep. Normally he would be fretful and bad-tempered for hours, difficult to approach . . . but he had simply rolled over and gone back to sleep. To a very deep sleep.

Istomina finished another cup of tea, got up again, stood at the door again. It was now five. He often awoke at five. Cautiously she opened the door. The room was heavy . . . and silent. Istomina held her own breath, and heard nothing. Her heart gave a great lurch as she moved to the bed. She stood above the inert figure; he had not apparently moved a muscle for the past hour.

Istomina found that she was panting. Obviously she had anticipated such a moment as this for over a year now; she knew better than anyone how dangerous had been the Premier's lifestyle. But one can anticipate disaster without ever actually visualising what it might be like. What the consequences might be like. She rested two fingers on the dictator's neck, and gasped again. Then her nerve cracked, and she ran for the door. "Awake!" she shouted. "Awake!" she screamed. "Premier Stalin is dead!"

Chapter Twelve

The End of an Era

Sonia rubbed her gloved hands together. She was very cold, firstl
from having had to stand on the roadside waiting for the the ca
to pick her up, and partly at the realisation of what had happened
What she had done!

No one would ever know, of course. No one could ever know
But then . . . she frowned as a terrible truth dawned on her. N
one *could* ever know. Therefore, despite Beria's assurances, ther
was no way she could be allowed to accompany Anna into exile
To attempt to escape might be to condemn Anna to death. But i
she was going to die anyway, then Anna would also; Beria woul
not wish a single trace of his diabolical, and successful, plot t
remain. Anna's best, Anna's only, hope of survival lay in th
survival of her mother. Beria would not dare kill the daughte
while *she* remained alive.

She saw the lights of a car in the distance, made an instar
decision, slid down the embankment beside the road, waded acros
a shallow stream, the ice crackling beneath her boots, and plunge
into the woods beyond. The men in the car would have in the fir
instance to suppose she had not yet completed her task, and woul
therefore wait. By the time they realised she must have alread
been and gone, she would be beyond their reach.

In the first instance. But where could she seek shelter? She ha
no money, no clothes save what she was wearing, no friends. Ther
was only one person in all Moscow she even knew, outside of th

Lyubyanka – and Jennie was a close friend of Stalin himself. But Jennie might give her shelter, in exchange for a revelation of what was happening. If she told a convincing enough story.

The man twisted his hat nervously between his hands. He had never seen his master in pyjamas, a huge white hulk, looking somehow more menacing than when in uniform. He glanced from Beria to the woman. She also wore pyjamas, an evocative sight. Perhaps she took dictation all night. "What do you mean?" Beria asked.

The man licked his lips, more nervous than ever. "The woman was not there when we arrived, Comrade Commissar. So we waited. As we were instructed to do. We waited for half an hour. Then we realised something was wrong, that she might not be coming at all. So we considered it best to return here, and report."

Beria's brain spun round in circles. The man suspected nothing of the truth, of course; his orders had merely been to pick up a woman from the side of the road, a mile away from the Premier's dacha. But what could have gone wrong? Had Sonia betrayed him? Or had Istomina been less stupid than he had supposed, and had her arrested? What to do? The telephone was jangling. All three of them looked at it together. "Take it," Beria told Maria. "But . . . I am not here. I have left the city on state business." He simply had to have time to think.

Maria licked her lips, picked up the phone. "Yes? . . . Who? The Commissar has left the city on security business. What did you say?" She looked at Beria with enormous eyes. "Would you repeat that, please? The Premier has had a heart attack? He is dead? My God!" So far had she forgotten that she was living in Soviet Russia.

She was still staring at Beria. "Ask who was present," he mouthed.

Maria gulped. "Was anyone with the Premier when he died? No one? I see." Beria made a quick gesture with his hand, drawing it through the air in a chopping motion. "Yes," Maria said. "I will see if I can contact him. Yes. Do nothing until you hear from the Commissar." Slowly she replaced the phone. "The Premier . . ."

"I heard," Beria said. "Well, I begged him to see a doctor, an
he refused, time and again. You . . ." he pointed at the agent. "D
not mention this to a soul, until I tell you."

The man swallowed. "Yes, Comrade Commissar."

"Remember," Beria said. "Now go home to bed."

The man hurried from the room. "Do you think he will kee
his mouth shut?" Maria asked.

"Long enough."

"But I do not understand. Should you not go out there immed
ately, Lavrenty Pavlovich?"

"Let others handle it."

"But . . . if the Premier is dead, you . . ."

"I must be chosen," Beria said. "Let others begin the choosing.
Go out there, and perhaps come face to face with Sonia? He had t
find her, before he could do anything. It had just never occurred t
him that she would betray him, or even attempt to escape him. Nc
while he held her daughter. The bitch! The cold-hearted savag
animal. He had always known her for that, and yet had suppose
he could command her, through a mother's love. "Get me Kagan,
he said.

By the time Kagan reached the Lyubyanka it was nearly ligh
Beria was fully dressed and in his office, Maria hovering. "Clos
the door," Beria said. "Something terrible has happened. Th
Premier is dead."

Kagan frowned at him. "When did he die?"

"A few hours ago."

"Then should you not be out there?"

"What am I supposed to do? I am neither a doctor nor a
undertaker. I will be going out there in a little while. Mear
while, there is a mystery which we have to resolve. The Premie
asked for a woman, last night. I was against it, in view of hi
health. But it was his birthday, and he is a difficult man t
argue with."

"You provided the woman?"

"Yes, I did. She is a very respected whore. Not in the first flus
of youth, but someone who, I was quite sure, could be trusted, bot

246

to please the Premier, and to keep her mouth shut afterwards if he . . . well, failed to perform."

"And you think this woman did so well she induced a heart attack?"

"I think that is extremely likely. It is even more likely because she has disappeared."

Kagan rubbed his nose. "She did not leave with you?"

"Well, of course she did not, Kagan. I took her there, and left her there. The Premier wanted sex with her, not me."

"Did Comrades Malenkov and Kruschev know of this?"

"No, they did not," Beria said. "It was a private matter between the Premier and me."

"And you think this woman may still be out there?"

"No. I think she left. I do not know whether she knows the Premier is dead or not, whether he died in her arms or after she left. But she must be found, Kagan. And very quickly. Have you arrested Tatiana Gosykinya yet?"

Kagan shook his head. "She seems to have vanished off the face of the earth. But I know she is in Moscow. I have men watching every possible exit, be it road, or train, or plane. She will surface some time, and we will get her then."

"I hope you do. But this woman is more important."

Kagan got up. "I will find her. And when I do?"

"I think it would be for the good of the state if she were to disappear, Comrade General. Whether she actually brought about the Premier's death or not, she now will know too much about him. So, no interrogations. Immediate disposal."

Kagan nodded. "Very good." He left the office, paused for a moment in the outer office to look at Maria. Who seemed to curl in her seat. She was terrified. Kagan gave her a pleasant smile, and went out.

Maria went into the inner office. "He knows," she said.

Beria looked up. "Knows what, Maria Feodorovna?"

"About that woman, Lavrenty Pavlovich."

Beria leaned back in his seat. "What woman, Maria Feodorovna?"

Maria licked her lips. "The one you brought in from Astrakhan."

"Did I bring in a woman from Astrakhan, Maria?" Maria stared at him with her mouth open. "If I did," Beria went on, "you are the only person in this building who knows of it."

Maria panted. "I . . . I would never betray you, Lavrenty Pavlovich."

"I have no doubt of that," Beria said. "Because you know that with the Premier dead, there is only one possible successor. And that is me. You are in a very fortunate position, Maria Feodorovna, in being so close to the new head of state. Do you not think so?" Maria's head jerked up and down like a puppet on a string. "So now, tell me, what makes you think that Kagan knows anything of this woman?"

"Just the way he looks at me, his expressions."

"You are setting up to be a psychiatrist, Maria. But it is better to deal in realities. Like you, Kagan knows who is his master. He will not fail that master."

"And the woman?"

"The woman," Beria said, "is history." An apt summing up, he thought.

It was well light by the time Sonia reached the Government Building. It had been a long walk for someone of her age, and she had had to stop and rest several times, while whenever she saw a patrolling policeman it had been necessary to make a deviation to avoid questions. She was exhausted. The concierge eyed her without interest. "Which apartment, Comrade?"

"The apartment belonging to Comrade Ligachevna, Comrade."

The concierge did not even raise his eyebrows, although his heart pounded. One of *them*! Sooner than he could have hoped. But he had his orders, from General Kagan himself. "Fifth floor, Comrade."

"Thank you." Sonia peered at the bandage on his head. "Are you hurt, Comrade?"

"I fell over," the concierge said.

"I hope it is nothing serious," Sonia said, and went to the stairs. The concierge watched her disappear at the first landing, then picked up his telephone.

* * *

Sonia went up the stairs, slowly; she felt that every bone in her body was creaking, and she had to pause for breath several times before she reached the fifth floor. Then she peered at the door to Jennie's flat, and frowned. She had lived in the heart of the police state that was Soviet Russia long enough, as Trotsky's companion, to recognise a door that had been sealed by the police. Jennie's door?

But if something had happened to Jennie, she was lost; the concierge had let her in without question, thus the police would already be on their way. She might as well go to the nearest window and jump out. But she could not do that. Not only was it not in her nature, but she had to stay alive for as long as possible, for Anna's sake. Then what was she to do? She bit her lip as she tried to think, and remembered that Jennie had had a friend, who lived in the apartment above. It was the faintest of hopes, but it was all the hope she had. The friend would at least know what had happened to Jennie.

She climbed the next flight of steps, slowly and painfully, knocked on the door. It was not immediately answered, but she could hear movement within. Then the door swung in, so suddenly she was taken by surprise. The woman facing her was as breathless as her, but this was the breathlessness of fear.

Sonia licked her lips. The woman was in her forties, and therefore fitted the age bracket. Anyway, there could be no turning back now. "I am a friend of Comrade Ligachevna," she said. "I have come to see her, but her apartment is . . . empty. Can you tell me where she is?"

The woman looked her up and down, then half turned her head, and clearly received an instruction from inside the room. She jerked her head, at the same time grasping Sonia's sleeve and almost pulling her through the doorway. Then the door was closed and locked. Sonia looked left and right at the people. She had not expected this. But . . . "Priscilla?" she whispered.

She could not believe her eyes. But it was Priscilla, although she wore no make-up and borrowed clothes which did not fit her very well. And her face had changed. Sonia had always known that behind the mask of beautiful innocence there had been a very tough mind; she had shared the trauma of their imprisonment by the marauding soldiers in 1917, and she knew she would not have survived but for Priscilla's cool determination that they should both do so. But to see her here . . . the last time she had seen the Princess had been the day she had been arrested, in 1942. She had thought then that Priscilla had also been arrested, but Beria had refused to discuss the matter. Priscilla was equally astonished. "Sonia?" she asked. "But . . . we were told you were dead!"

"Explain," said one of the other women.

Sonia had never met Tatiana, but she knew she was looking at a Bolugayevska, even if a brunette one. And a Bolugayevska who was wearing the uniform of an officer in the KGB! "This is Sonia Bolugayevska," Priscilla said. "My first husband's first wife."

"Trotsky's woman," Tatiana said.

"And you are Jennie's child," Sonia said, the penny dropping.

"You were executed, in 1942," Tatiana said.

"Then I am a ghost."

Tatiana was frowning. "You have been a prisoner, all this time? You have been in a gulag?"

"I have been a guest of your boss," Sonia said. "Lavrenty Beria. A very secret guest." She watched the people in the room exchange glances, and realised they knew things she did not. Just as they were an incongrous lot. The very sight of Priscilla was incredible. Of the others, she presumed from the facial resemblance that the other young woman was Galina's daughter. But the men . . . she would have sworn neither was Russian. One was almost nondescript in appearance, but had piercing eyes. The other was big and handsome, dressed in prison clothing. "May I ask what is happening? Are these people under arrest? Where is Jennie?"

"You came to see Jennie?" Tatiana asked. "Why?"

"That is my business," Sonia said. She certainly could not take these people into her confidence until she found out just who and what they were. But Priscilla's presence was reassuring.

"But you came here," Tatiana said, "openly . . . how did you know where to come? How did you know which was my mother's apartment?"

"I knew it was in the Government Building," Sonia said. "As to which it was, I asked the concierge."

"And he let you in? Shit! We have been betrayed, by this stupid woman. We must get out of here. Now."

The others stared at her.

"Coats. Guns," Tatiana told them.

"But where can we go?" Priscilla asked.

"Anywhere. Otherwise . . ." she checked as noise seeped up through the building. She moved to the window, looked down. "Too late. The building is surrounded."

"Well, then . . ." Halstead picked up his pistol.

Priscilla looked at Andrew. How long ago seemed that immense moment they had shared. Galina burst into tears; Helena threw an arm round her shoulders. "I don't understand," Sonia said.

"My mother has been arrested by the KGB," Tatiana spat at her. "Your coming here and asking for her has killed us all; the concierge has reported to the police."

Sonia bit her lip. They still hadn't told her what they were all doing in this tiny apartment; they were clearly conspiring. But if Jennie had been arrested, presumably her daughter was also seeking shelter – despite the uniform. "Wait a moment," Andrew said. "If the concierge has reported the arrival of Madame Bolugayevska, looking for your mother, Tattie, then the police have come to arrest *her*. They still don't know we are here."

"Don't you think she will tell them?" Tatiana demanded.

Sonia drew a deep breath. "Perhaps I can help you. Those people, are they city police, or KGB?"

"They will be KGB," Tatiana said.

Sonia's brain was racing. If only she knew more about the set-up within that most terrible of organisations. But she did know that her survival, and her assignment, had been kept the closest of secrets by Beria. He wanted Russia. He had not dared share that ambition, with anyone. There were feet on the stairs, moving stealthily, but still audible. "We are lost," Tatiana said. She looked at the Princess. "It seems that I must break my word, your highness. But I think we have one final chance. An appeal to the Premier."

"Supposing you are allowed to get there," Halstead pointed out.

"The alternative is to shoot ourselves, now," Tatiana said. "I am not going to allow Beria to put an electrode between my legs."

"I can save all of your lives," Sonia said. Every head turned towards her. "Put down your weapons," she said. Halstead and Tatiana exchanged glances. "I wish to live, myself," Sonia said simply.

Tatiana placed her revolver on the table. Halstead did likewise. Priscilla instinctively moved towards Andrew, and held his hand. Helena and Galina were already holding hands. The door burst open, torn right off its hinges, and they faced several men, each carrying a sub-machine-gun. Tatiana raised her hands, and the others followed her example.

Then there was another man, short and thick-set, and armed only with a pistol, which he had not even drawn from its holster. His men made way for him as he came into the room. "What a clutch," Kagan remarked. "Tatiana! I have been looking everywhere for you. Princess! What a pleasure it is to see you alive and well, after having been dead for so long." He looked at Galina and Helena, and then at Morgan and Halstead, clearly not placing any of them. Nor did he place Sonia.

But the concierge was at his elbow. "That is the woman, Comrade General," he said.

Kagan looked at Sonia. "You will have to explain to me why you were asking after Comrade Ligachevna," he said. "Would you like to do it now, or in our cells at the Lyubyanka. That is where you are going, Tatiana, together with your friends. Commissar Beria wishes to interrogate you, personally."

Tatiana looked at Sonia.

"There is no necessity for that," Sonia said. Kagan looked at her in astonishment, taken aback by her calm confidence. "What I have to tell you is far more important than anything Tatiana may have to say," Sonia said.

"Then say it."

"In front of your people? Are you sure you wish that?"

"Do you think I am going to lock myself up alone with you lot?" Kagan said contemptuously.

"Very well," Sonia said. "I think you should know that Premier Stalin is dead."

Again every head turned towards her. Even Kagan frowned. "How do you know this?"

"Because I was the last person to see him alive," Sonia said.

"You!" Kagan cried. "The woman! Beria said you were a whore." Anyone could see that Sonia Bolugayevska was not a whore.

"It was his plan that I should appear so. I am Sonia Bolugayevska."

Kagan's frown deepened, as he reached back into memory. "Trotsky's woman?" He was incredulous. "And before that, the Princess of Bolugayen?" Now he looked at Priscilla.

"What she says is perfectly true," Priscilla told him.

"Sonia Bolugayevska is dead!"

"Premier Stalin condemned me to death, Comrade General," Sonia said. "But Comrade Beria thought it best to keep me alive, for use at a later date. As a spirit risen from the dead. This I have done, successfully."

Kagan looked at his two men, and at the concierge. Then he looked at the people in the room. "You will admit this, openly? You will state this, to the Politburo? Even if it may cause your execution?"

"I will say it if you will guarantee the safety of my daughter, who is presently being held by Beria in Astrakhan. That is where I have been held since the end of the War."

"Astrakhan," Kagan breathed. A great many marbles were clearly dropping into place.

Tatiana decided it was time for her to intervene. "Aunt Sonia will only confess to the truth of this matter if her life too, is guaranteed. She has done nothing more than obey orders, and she did not actually kill the Premier."

"It is a matter to be considered," Kagan said.

"Then consider it now, and quickly. Because you may be sure that Beria is at this moment planning to take over the State. But Aunt Sonia will also refuse to say a word against him unless our safety is also guaranteed."

"*Your* safety?" Kagan snorted. "You killed four of my men."

"Who Beria sent to kill me. Did you know that, Comrade General?"

Kagan considered her for some seconds; she did not know of his involvement – yet. Then he asked, "Who are these people?"

"The Princess and and Mr Morgan you know. The Schermetskas have nothing to do with any plot. I happened to use them as a refuge."

"And him?" Kagan pointed at Halstead.

Halstead held his breath. His life, sacrificed, would also be a bargaining counter. "Comrade Romanowski is Atya Shulenskaya's betrothed," Tatiana said. Halstead slowly allowed his breath to escape. "Beria's people killed Atya," Tatiana said. "Comrade Romanowski seeks his revenge, like me. Then we wish to leave Russia."

"Once Comrade Beria has been brought down," Kagan said. "and that is not going to be a simple matter. Comrade Beria is seen by most of the Party as Stalin's natural successor. He also has a formidable weapon at his disposal, as you and I know, Tatiana: the KGB. He must be proved to have plotted the death of the Premier before he can take steps to eliminate those who would give evidence against him."

Sonia and Tatiana looked at each other; that included both of them. "If Madam Bolugayevska were to make a nationwide address on television and radio," Priscilla suggested.

"Princess," Kagan said, "this is Russia, not the United States. She would not survive as far as the studio. In any event, whatever is proved, it must be sufficient to sway a majority of the Politburo. Nothing else, including the opinion of the country as a whole, matters."

"Then we're done," Halstead said.

"Not necessarily. I happen already to be in contact with a prominent member of the Politburo. All I have had to offer him so far are suppositions; now I have facts. But as I have said, it will take time."

"During which you will protect us?" Priscilla asked.

"I cannot do that without arousing Beria's suspicions." Everyone in the room stiffened. "You will have to trust me," Kagan said. "Madam Bolugayevska I will take into my own custody. The rest of you I am going to place under arrest, and take down to the Lyubyanka."

"Are you crazy?!" Tatiana demanded. "Do you know what he will do to us? To me, anyway."

"I said, trust me. I guarantee you your lives. All of your lives."

"But nothing else."

"I will do what I can for you," Kagan said. "I will save your lives. And I will bring Beria down, as quickly as I can. You must trust me." He gave a brief grin, and gestured at his men's guns. "In any event, you have no choice."

Tatiana gazed at him, as did everyone else. "Will you also promise me his execution?" Tatiana asked at last. "At my hands?"

"I guarantee that you will be his appointed executioner," Kagan said. "I cannot guarantee that he will not commit suicide when he is confronted with the facts."

"Well, then," Tatiana said, "should he do so, you will have to give me his dead body." She held out her wrists for the handcuffs.

Lavrenty Beria leaned back in his chair and smiled a great, happy grin. "All of them? Downstairs in the cells?"

"That is correct, Comrade Commissar."

"List them."

"Tatiana Gosykinya. The Princess Bolugayevska. The man Morgan, who was the third in Tatiana's party; apparently, after taking the Princess from Gulag Number One, she took Morgan from Number Seventeen. Obviously this was all part of her conspiracy. Then there is a man named Romanowski, who was apparently the lover of the woman Shulenskaya. I am not sure yet what part he played, or was to play, in the conspiracy, but I will find out. And then there is Galina Shermetska, and her daughter, who were giving shelter to the conspirators."

"And who were thus conspirators themselves," Beria said.

"Oh, undoubtedly," Kagan agreed. "They will all make full confessions, I promise you."

255

"It must be done as quickly as possible," Beria said. "And they must be executed, as quickly as possible."

"Of course. Do you wish to interrogate any of them yourself?"

"Yes," Beria said. "Oh, yes. But what about the woman? The one who was with the Premier when he died?"

"I am sure there is a mistake there, Comrade Commissar. Istomina says there was no one with the Premier when he died."

"Well, before he died. Istomina cannot deny there was a woman. I want her found, Kagan. This is a most important matter."

"We are searching for her, Comrade Commissar. But at the moment she appears to have disappeared into thin air. This is the trouble with whores. They can do this."

"She is not a whore!" Beria shouted, and then bit his lip.

"But you said . . ." Kagan began.

"I described her as a whore. Yes. But she does not stand on street corners. She is a courtesan. That is what she is. She is an old courtesan. And she has nowhere to hide, in Moscow. She comes from out of town."

"From Astrakhan," Kagan suggested.

Beria glanced at him. "Yes," he said. "She is from Astrakhan. Find her, Kagan."

"And when I do?"

"I have told you what to do. I have no doubt at all that she is responsible for the Premier's death. Execute her on the spot. I give you carte blanche. No questions. Just a bullet in the brain. Do you understand me?"

"Of course, Comrade Commissar. A bullet in the brain."

Kagan saluted and left the office, pausing to smile at Maria. The moment he was gone she scuttled into Beria's office. "He knows."

Beria looked up at her. "Knows what, now, Maria Feodorovna?"

"Ah . . ." she licked her lips.

"Maria Feodorovna," Beria said. "You are becoming an hysteric, and that I will not have. Pull yourself together."

"Yes, Comrade Commissar." Anxiously she held her notebook in front of her. "There is to be a meeting of the Politburo to discuss the crisis this evening at six."

Beria raised his eyebrows. "Indeed? Who ordered this?"

"Vice-Premier Malenkov. Do you wish me to cancel it?"

Beria shook his head. "No, no. There *is* a crisis. And Malenkov is Vice-Premier, so obviously he is temporarily in charge. However, there are certain steps we need to take." He wrote out a series of orders, for the dispositioning of KGB troops in and around the capital, and more importantly, in and around the Kremlin. "We will, of course, proceed with the utmost legality," he said. "But there is no harm in taking precautions, just in case others are prepared to act *illegally*, eh? Type those up, distribute them to the appropriate commanders, and then . . . how would you like to be amused for a couple of hours?"

"If . . . if that is what you wish me to do, Comrade Commissar."

"Well, just type up those orders." She left the room, and Beria leaned back in his chair, taking off his pince-nez to polish it. Never had a man had such a plum fall into his lap. He felt like shouting for joy. But that would be undignified. Well, then, he felt like drinking a magnum of champagne. But he still needed a clear head. Malenkov was entirely doing his duty by calling a meeting of the Politburo. Vacuums were always dangerous and political vacuums were more dangerous than any other. Russia needed a head of state.

Of course Malenkov would be dreaming of succeeding to that position himself; he had been Stalin's deputy for some time now. But he had never been allowed to exercise any power, nor had he revealed any suggestion of the ability *to* exercise power. Kruschev, now, he was a different proposition. And Beria was well aware that Kruschev did not like him. But Kruschev had no broad power base, certainly in Moscow. He was a party boss, nothing more. He could not snap his fingers and summon a hundred thousand dedicated men and women to his support. Above all, neither Kruschev nor Malenkov had a Kagan. Kagan might be boorish and uncouth, but he was the ideal man to have standing at one's shoulder when there were great issues at stake. So, time to do all the things he had wanted to do, for so long, and been prevented. "Are you ready?" he asked Maria.

"The orders are here, Comrade Commissar." She was breathless. She also understood she was in the midst of great events.

"See that they are distributed to the regimental commanders," he said. "Then you may join me in the interrogation block." He took his private elevator into the underground section. "Take me to the prisoners General Kagan has just brought in," he commanded the duty guard.

The gaoler scuttled in front of him along the dank corridors. "Number Seventy-One," he said. "The man Morgan and the man Romanowski."

Beria frowned. "Why are they together?"

"We are very crowded, Comrade Commissar. General Kagan said it would be all right, as these people would not be with us long."

"Hm." Beria snapped his fingers, and the gaoler opened the window. Beria looked in, at the two men, who sat side by side on the floor, their backs to the door. Their heads jerked at the sound of the window, but they did not turn. Beria snorted. Their naked bodies were unmarked; they must have surrendered without any attempt at resistance. But they did not interest him. "Next," he commanded.

The gaoler shut the window, proceeded along the corridor. "Number Sevety-Seven. The woman Schermetska and the woman Bolugayevska."

Beria's frown returned. "Shermetska?"

"She lives in the apartment above that of the Criminal Ligachevna," the gaoler explained.

"Schermetska," Beria said thoughtfuly, entries in his most secret files drifting through his memory. Another snap of the fingers, and he peered in at the women. His breathing quickened slightly as he saw the Princess, as beautiful as ever. She was a promise of what the future held. But the woman . . . "That is not the woman Schermetska," he said. "The woman Schermetska is at least fifty That woman is not yet thirty."

"Ah," said the gaoler. "You are thinking of the older Schermetska Comrade Commissar. This is the daughter."

"Then where is the older Schermetska?"

258

"In Number Eighty-One, Comrade Commissar. With the woman Gosykinya." Once he had been Tatiana's comrade.

Beria gave a shout of laughter. "Is that amusing, Comrade Commissar?" the gaoler asked.

"That is very amusing," Beria told him. "Bring them out." Vladimir unlocked the door. Helena started to her feet in terror; Priscilla merely turned her head. "Get up, Princess," Beria said. She stared at him. She had, of course, never seen him before in her life. But she could guess who he was. "Come along," he said. "It is time for you and me to have a little chat."

She licked her lips. "Am I to be executed?"

"Perhaps. But not until I am ready. Come along. You too, Helena Schermetska. I have a treat for you." The two women stepped into the corridor. Helena went first, after a push from Vladimir. Beria walked behind the Princess, twined his fingers in her hair. Her head jerked, and her breathing quickened, but she would not look round, even when Beria's hand slipped down her back to squeeze her buttocks. "That is something I have wanted to do for a very long time," he confided. "But there are other parts of you I am looking forward to squeezing even more." Still she would not turn her head. "Show me Number Eighty-one," Beria commanded.

They walked the few steps further, and the gaoler opened the window. Beria looked through, and licked his lips. There was nothing attractive about Galina, overweight and sagging. But Tatiana . . . he had enjoyed everything Tatiana had to offer, save the one thing he wanted most – to watch her writhe in agony and scream in despair. But that now was going to be his pleasure. "Open up," he commanded.

The gaoler licked his lips. "Comrade Commissar, the woman Tatiana Gosykinya is very dangerous."

Beria drew his revolver. "Open the door, Vladimir."

Cautiously Vladimir turned the key, pulled the door to. The women both turned, on their knees, and looked into the muzzle of Beria's revolver, held at a safe distance as he was still in the corridor. Priscilla and Helena stood beside him, but their feeling of helplessness was increased by their nudity, and Helena

259

would do nothing that might harm her mother. "Lie down," Beria commanded. "On your faces!"

Tatiana glanced at Galina, and gave a quick nod. They lay down on the stone floor, on their bellies. "Vladimir is going to handcuff you," Beria said. "Please understand that at the slightest sign of resistance I will shoot you both."

Tatiana and Galina lay still, while Vladimir knelt beside them, pulled their wrists behind their backs, and handcuffed them in turn. "That was good thinking," Beria said. "Now, get up."

The two women rose to their knees, and then their feet. Tatiana looked at Priscilla, breathing very slowly and evenly. Galina looked at Helena, in sheer relief at seeing her as yet unharmed. "I have a treat for you," Beria said. He jerked his head, and Vladimir pushed them into the corridor. "Number Ninety-Seven," Beria said.

Vladimir chuckled, confident now that the dreaded Gosykinya was helpless. He walked in front of them to the cell door, opened it at a nod from Beria. Alexei stood against the wall, gazing at them.

"There is no need to handcuff *him*," Beria said. "He is an American." His tone was redolent of contempt.

"Tattie?" Alex asked. He had clearly been beaten but there was no lack of spirit in either his voice or his eyes.

Tatiana returned his gaze, silently.

"She would prefer not to speak," Beria said. "She is too humiliated by the catastrophe that has overtaken her. What about this woman? Do you not know her?"

Alex looked at Galina, frowning. "Yes," he said, slowly. "Mrs Schermetska. We met in Moscow, in 1942. You lived above Aunt Jennie."

"But that was before you served under Comrade Gosykinya in the Pripet," Beria said, jocularly. "Come along. I have a surprise for you."

Alex stepped into the corridor, and checked. "Mom? Mom!" he shouted, and embraced Priscilla. "Oh, my God. I knew you were alive. Joe always said you were alive, before . . ."

"I know he is dead," Priscilla said, quietly. "It is good to see you again, my darling boy."

"But . . . what is happening to us?"

"You will have to ask this gentleman," Priscilla said.

"Nuumber One Hundred and Seven, is it not?" Beria asked Vladimir. Vladimir chuckled some more, hurried ahead of them to unlock the door. Jennie sat in a corner, shrouded in her red-grey hair. She scarcely stirred as the door opened. "You look distraught," Beria commented. "I have brought Tatiana to see you."

Jennie's head moved, then she stood up. "Tattie?" she whispered. "Oh, you dear girl."

"What a family reunion," Beria said. "Come along." He marched them to the interrogation room. Jennie tried to get beside Tatiana, but she was pushed ahead. Beria had made the usual arrangements, and there were four men in the room, as well as the doctor and the secretary. "Well, now," he said, as Vladimir closed the door. "You have spent so many happy hours in here, Tatiana. Now you will spend a last happy hour, but I will be the one laughing. Do you know why?"

The prisoners stared at him, each possessed by his or her thoughts, his or her own terrors. Tatiana's face was, as always, composed. Jennie kept looking from one to the other; her body still showed the signs of the beatings she had undergone, and she trembled. Alex was trying to be as composed as Tatiana, but he too was trembling. Galina and Helena were holding hands. Only Priscilla matched Tatiana in her composure, but she never took her eyes from her son.

"One great happy family," Beria said, sitting down and throwing one leg across the other. "Jennie, and her best friend, Galina. Where else would Tattie seek refuge, but in the apartment of her mother's best friend. Who was the mother of her own best friend. You have always trusted in the friendship of Tatiana and her mother, haven't you, Galina Petrovna?"

Galina licked her lips. "We are friends, yes," she said in a low voice.

"You have been friends for years," Beria said. "Since your chidren were children together. Were you not happy to allow your daughter Sophie to go off to summer camp, in 1941, under Tatiana's care?"

For the first time Tatiana's face changed. "You bastard," she said.

"You will call me more than that before today is out," Beria said. "What happened to poor Sophie, Galina? Did you ever find out?"

It was Alex's turn to catch his breath, and Beria smiled some more. "My Sophie died fighting the Germans," Galina said. "This is well known."

"This what was reported for public consumption," Beria pointed out. "It is not what happened. You!" He swung, pointing at Alex. "Tell us what happened to Sophie Schermetska?"

Alex licked his lips. "Comrade Schermetska died before I ever reached the Pripet."

"Oh, indeed. But how she died was fairly common knowledge, amongst the partisans. And therefore you knew of it."

"I know nothing of it," Alex said stubbornly.

"Do you think you can play games with me, American?" Beria asked, quietly. "Him first," he told his people. Two men hurried forward, and strapped Alex to the bars, facing them. Beria himself attached the electrodes. "This will only hurt a little," he promised you. "We will hurt you seriously, just now."

Helena began to cry. While Priscilla continued to watch her son, her face as cold as ice, Beria noticed. "Don't worry, Princess," he said. "I will soon get around to you. *That* is something I have been waiting to do for years. They will hear you screaming in America. But first, this bastard." He moved to the control box, and Alex inhaled so deep a breath it seemed his lungs would burst.

"Very well, Lavrenty Pavlovich," Tatiana said, as Beria moved to the control box. "If you will have it so. I will tell Galina the truth about Sophie."

Beria still depressed the button, but only briefly. Alex gave a shout of pain as the electricity coursed through his chest, his entire body arcing away from the frame before it subsided in shuddering gasps. "Then I suggest you do so," Beria recommended. "This Sophie, this innocent young girl, placed in your care by her loving mother, captured beside you by the Germans, who lay beside you while you were both raped, and killed beside you to escape to the marshes, and who then fought beside you . . . what did you do with her, Tatiana Andreievna?"

Tartiana sighed. "I drowned her."

Every head in the room turned towards her, even Alex's, still gasping. "You drowned my Sophie?" Galina asked, incredulously. "You?"

"She disobeyed an order when in action with the enemy," Tatiana said. "I had previously made it clear that any insubordination was punishable by death. I had no choice. I led those people, those wolves, by example, by making them afraid of me, and by dispensing equal justice. I could not show mercy, even to my friend, and still hope to lead." She looked at Beria. "I suppose it was Shatrav told you of this. Shatrav was the one who actually held Sophie under the water."

"But you gave the order," Beria said.

"Yes," Tatiana said. "I gave the order. I was the commander."

"You bitch!" Galina said.

"Oh, Tattie," Jennie moaned.

"So, now," Beria said. "I am giving you your chance for revenge, Galina." He snapped his fingers, and Alex was unstrapped. Left to himself, his knees gave way and he sank to the floor; Priscilla knelt beside him to cradle him in her arms. Tatiana was put in his place, the belts drawn tight. Beria himself applied the clips, between her legs, smiling at her as he did so. "I have looked forward to this for a long time," he told her. "Now, Galina. Punish her. Oh, do not be afraid of her dying. She is going to die. But if I may make a recommendation, use only a little at first. Make her scream. Even Tatiana Gosykinya will scream, eventually, you know. Then, when she is screaming, you can slowly apply more and more, until she dies. But make sure she knows what is happening to her."

He gestured at the box, and Galina slowly moved forward. "And afterwards?" she asked in a low voice.

"Afterwards, why, I do not think there will be any charges against either you or your daughter, Galina Petrovna. In fact, I am sure of it."

"Galina," Jennie said. "You cannot do this. You are my friend."

"As my daughter was *her* friend," Galina said, her words dripping venom.

"I did what was necessary," Tatiana said, her voice clear.

"Make her scream," Beria said. "Make her scream, Galina. I am sure poor Sophie screamed, as they were pushing her beneath the surface of that swamp. Make her scream."

Galina touched the button, tentatively, but enough to send Tatiana's body arching away from the frame, every muscle standing out like a cord. But she did not scream. "You will have to do better than that," Beria suggested, and turned, as the door opened. "What the devil . . ."

It was Maria, breathless as ever, her hair drifting down from its tight bun. "Ha," Beria commented. "You are late."

"Comrade Commissar," Maria panted, and Beria saw that there were men behind her.

He frowned. Kagan? "What are you doing here? Comrade Kruschev?" Then he looked past them as well, at the woman who stood with the guards armed with tommy-guns; of his own four people only two were armed, besides himself, and they carried only pistols. They already had their hands in the air.

"We found her, you see, Comrade Commissar" Kagan explained.

"Then what . . ." Beria's head swung to look at Kruschev.

"General Kagan thought it would be a good idea for Madam Bolugayevska to speak with me before you, Comrade Commissar," Kruschev said, his normally jovial face grim. Now he pointed. "You are an assassin. You are under arrest."

Beria stared at him, then at Kagan, then looked left and right at the other people in the room. But if he expected any of them to come to his rescue he was clearly mistaken; even Maria was standing as still as a stone. Then he acted with surprising suddenness, picking up Galina, who was still standing beside him, and hurling her into the ranks of the men opposite, at the same time drawing his revolver and blasting shots into the corridor. Men fell each way, Sonia tumbled to the ground, and Beria was over them. But as he ran for the corridor, Alex suddenly came out of his pain-trance and threw both arms round his knees. Beria gave a grunt and fell forwards. But now he was like a wild animal, and

264

he still held his gun. He struck down once, twice, as hard as he could, and Alex fell to the floor in a pool of blood.

Now at last Priscilla spoke. "Alex!" she screamed, again seeking to cradle him in her arms.

Beria was back on his feet and running along the corridor. Kagan was first to recover, and drew his own pistol as Beria reached the corner. "No," Kruschev snapped. "He must be brought to trial." Kagan lowered his gun. "Where can he go?" Kruschev asked.

Kagan looked at Maria. Beria had disappeared. She licked her lips. "He will take his private elevator to his apartment, and from there use his radio to take control of the city. He has already made his dispositions."

Kagan glared at Kruschev. "You should have let me shoot him."

"Can he not still be stopped?" Kruschev demanded.

"He has the ability to seal himself in his apartment," Maria said.

"And I cannot tell how many of the people in this building will support him," Kagan said; of his four men, two had been hit and were being tended by their comrades.

"Then we must get out of here as rapidly as possible," Kruschev said.

"The dispositions cover the apartments of every member of the Politburo," Maria said. "As well as the Kremlin."

"Then we are finished." Kruschev's normal chubby ebullience had quite disappeared.

"Free me," Tatiana said. "I can get into his apartment," she said. "Even if it is sealed. I have the combination to his private entrance. I will arrest him."

Kruschev snorted. But Kagan was nodding. "Release her," he told the guards, and they did so.

Tatiana rubbed her hands together to restore the circulation. "The first thing you must do is secure this floor."

"Of course." Kagan snapped his fingers, and his own people followed the corridor to the stairs and the general elevator.

"Will they assault us?" Kruschev asked.

"Not until he is sure of all his other dispositions," Tatiana said. "Now, there are certain things I want."

"There is no time for that."

"There is time, Comrade General."

"By the time you get to him, he will have issued his orders, and we shall all be dead men."

"It cannot happen that quickly, Comrade General. I shall persuade Comrade Beria to rescind his orders. If you will guarantee, before these witnesses, that I shall be restored as a member of the KGB, and promoted colonel." Kagan nodded. "I also wish your guarantee that the people who were arrested with me are allowed to leave Russia, freely and without hindrance."

Kagan looked at Galina, who was just sitting up, her head cradled in Helena's arms. "Including her?"

"Not including her. I should not think she would wish to leave."

"And your mother?"

"Mother stays with me. I am speaking of the Princess, Prince Alexei – she glanced at Alexei; Priscilla had staunched the flow of blood from his head, but he was still unconscious – and the two men, Romanowski and Morgan."

"Romanowski is a Russian. Isn't he?"

"Of course," Tatiana said. "But he wishes to emigrate. Time is passing, Comrade General."

"Give her what she wants," Kruschev said; he was clearly in a very frightened state.

"Very well, Tatiana," Kagan said. "Your friends will be deported, *after* you have arrested Comrade Beria. In fact, it seems to me that you may need some help in carrying out the arrest. You will take Morgan and Romanowski with you. I am sure you would rather trust them than any of my people. Let them prove that they are on our side one last time, eh?"

Tatiana knew what he was anticipating, and even hoping. She tossed her head. "I agree with you. I will need her, as well." She pointed at Maria.

"Me?" Maria cried.

"You Maria Feodorovna. You should consider that if you do not prove yourself to be *against* Beria, you may well find yourself standing against a wall . . . beside him. I will also need

266

guns," Tatiana said. "For myself, Romanowski, and Morgan. And clothes."

"Where am I supposed to find clothes?"

"There is a storeroom where prisoners' clothes are kept, just along that corridor. There is also an armoury." She smiled. "The clothes do not have to fit."

Kagan nodded, and signalled three of his guards to fetch the gear. "Tommy guns," Tatiana called after them.

"You do understand, Tatiana Andreievna," Kagan said, "that if you try to betray me, us, you and your companions will all be executed."

"I have no intention of betraying you, Comrade General."

"Wait a moment," Sonia said. "I have a stake in this."

"You are needed to address the Supreme Soviet, Comrade," Kruschev said. "We cannot risk anything happening to you. No matter how much you may personally hold against Beria."

"I will go," Priscilla said.

"You, Princess?" Kagan asked.

Gently Priscilla laid Alex on the floor. "I have as big a score to settle as anyone. That man murdered my husband, and now has all but murdered my son."

"I commanded the American operation. You were my prisoner."

Priscilla's lips twitched in a cold smile. "You were the messenger boy, General Kagan. Were you not?"

They gazed at each other, and Tatiana remembered the look Priscilla had given her, the day she was leaving the Lyubyanka for the gulag. She wondered if Kagan felt the same as she had done? Now he shrugged. "You have my permission."

"Will you find out about my daughter?" Sonia asked.

"Of course."

"Then let us make haste." Tatiana was already dressing herself. Now Priscilla too was given a KGB uniform, and a moment later they were face to face with Andrew and Halstead, who had also been dressed and armed.

"What the hell is going on?" Halstead demanded.

"Come." Tatiana ushered them into the private elevator, and

they went up. "We have been given the task of arresting Comrade Beria," Tatiana said.

"Us?" Andrew asked. "When Kagan has the whole KGB at his disposal?"

"That is the one thing Kagan does not have," Tatiana explained. "He cannot be sure who, if any, of the KGB will back him against Beria. The facts of Stalin's death are not yet known. The fact *of* his death is not widely known, if it is known at all. Besides . . ." she smiled. "There is another point, much in Kagan's mind. He knows Beria will not surrender easily. Some of us may be killed. He has promised you all safe conduct out of Russia, and he has promised me reinstatement in the KGB. He will not break his word. But it would be a great relief to him if some of us, me in particular, were to stop a bullet." Maria turned to look at her, face ashen. "I am sure he will not shoot *you*, Maria," Tatiana said, reasssuringly.

"I do not understand why you need me at all," Maria complained. "I know nothing about guns and killing."

"We need you, Maria Feodorovna," Tatiana said, "because I lied to Kagan when I told him I could get into the apartment by the private entrance. Beria did give me the combination, once, but I have forgotten it. But you know it, don't you." Maria swallowed, and the car came to a stop. "We are in your hands, Maria Feodorovna," Tatiana said. "But should you try to betray us, be sure I will kill you."

Maria licked her lips, and led them into an empty corridor. "The Commissar's apartment is on the next floor," she whispered. "There is a private staircase. But it is always guarded by people who are absolutely loyal to him."

"And in the apartment itself?"

"There are no guards. But they can be summoned at the touch of a button."

"But if, as you say, the apartment will have been sealed save for this private entrance, that is the only way any reinforcements can get in," Tatiana suggested.

"Until and unless Beria manages to unlock the main doors," Maria said.

Tatiana nodded, and looked over their faces. "Then this has got to be an all out assault. There is just one thing to remember: Beria must be taken alive."

"Even if he is busy killing us?" Andrew demanded.

"I am afraid so, Andrew. If he is killed, what do they say in America, Princess?"

"All bets are off."

"Exactly. For the sake of the country, he must be tried, convicted, and executed. Remember this, because your lives depend upon it. Check your weapons."

They did so.

"Lead us, Maria Feodrovna."

Maria swallowed again, and, incongruously, made the sign of the cross. Then she took a deep breath, and opened the combination lock on the door. They waited, but there was no response from within. Maria opened the door and led them along the corridor and round the corner.

"Maria Feodorovna," remarked a voice. "The Commissar has said . . ." the man checked as Tatiana appeared at Maria's shoulder. "Captain Gosykinya? You are under . . ."

Tatiana levelled her tommy-gun and shot him, then sent a burst of fire at his companion, who had just been getting up. The man crashed over backwards, blood spurting. "Up!" Tatiana yelled, and ran at the stairs, Maria at her shoulder, the other three behind her. The stairs had a reverse bend, and they ran round this to gain the next floor, found themselves facing three men. "Shit!" Tatiana yelled, falling onto her face as she opened fire. But the men were also firing, and Maria gave a shriek, her white shirt front dissolving into red as she tumbled back down the stairs. Andrew also stopped a bullet and fell, although from his language he clearly hadn't been killed. But Halstead and Priscilla were both firing, Priscilla with all the pent-up fury of a woman who had spent the past five years in intolerable conditions, and Tatiana had never taken her finger from the trigger. The men fell to each side.

"Are you all right?" Priscilla knelt beside Andrew.

"I'll survive," he said. "Finish the job."

Halstead was stooping over Maria. "She's dead."

"The stupid bitch said there'd be no more guards," Tatiana said. "Come on."

She ran up the stairs, Halstead at her shoulder, opened the door leading in, was checked by a shot which struck the wall beside her head. Once again she hit the floor, and Halstead did likewise. Again she was firing, although carefully avoiding the figure standing behind the desk. But the hail of bullets was sufficient to send Beria diving for shelter, and before he could recover his nerve Halstead was upon him, kicking the pistol from his hand, levelling his own gun at Beria's chest. Beria dragged himself across the floor to sit against the wall; his pince-nez had come off, and he blinked at them. "You are mad," he said. "I control this building. I control this city. I control this country! The orders have all been given. You are all dead."

"Not if you rescind those orders, Comrade Commissar," Tatiana said.

"What makes you think I will do that?" Beria demanded. "You think killing me will save your skins? My orders will be carried out."

"Of course they will, Lavrenty Pavlovich," Tatiana said. "Therefore you must change them. If you do not, I am not going to kill you. But I am going to shoot you in the balls. I am going to castrate you, Lavrenty Pavlovich, with a bullet. All your orgies will be a memory. But then, so will your ambitions. The Russian people would never accept a eunuch as their leader. So . . ." She levelled her pistol.

Beria pulled up his legs. He was panting. "You would not dare."

"Come now," she said. "You know me better than that, Comrade Commissar." Her finger was white on the trigger.

"If . . . if I rescind the orders . . ."

"You will be arrested, and put on trial. You will have ample opportunity to defend yourself." She smiled. "They are not even going to torture you, Lavrenty Pavlovich. They have the testimony of Sonia Bolugayevska."

"It will be her word against mine. She was a whore I took to the Premier, at his request."

"Then you have nothing to fear," Tatiana said. "Now sit at your radio, and I will tell you what to say."

When Beria had told his men to obey the commands of General Kagan and Commissar Kruschev, Tatiana handcuffed him. By then Priscilla had joined them. "Andrew needs a doctor," she said. "I have checked the external bleeding, but the bullets are still in there. I think there are two." Her hands and her borrowed uniform were bloody.

"We have no time for that, now," Tatiana said. "We must get Beria downstairs and free Kagan and Kruschev. And Mother," she added as an afterthought.

"We must help Andrew, first," Priscilla said.

Tatiana snorted; with success in her grasp, reinstatement and promotion a certainty, she no longer regarded Andrew as more than an incident in her life – especially since he had transferred his affections to the Princess. "He is of no value to anybody, Princess. You have had your fun with him. Now he is nothing. Now kiss him goodbye." She pushed Beria, who had, like Halstead, been looking from face to face, towards the stairs. This brought her level with Priscilla, who suddenly released Andrew and stood up. Tatiana had slung her tommy-gun and drawn her pistol, which she kept pressed into Beria's back. But Priscilla also had a pistol, and the muzzle of this was now thrust into Tatiana's waistband.

"Are you mad?" Tatiana asked.

"I think perhaps I am the only sane person in this madhouse, Tatiana," Priscilla said. "But I am as Russian as any of you. I have a long memory. I can remember that it was your Bolsheviks who killed my husband, destroyed my family and my home. I can remember it is your Bolsheviks who locked up my husband for twelve years and then tried to have him assassinated. I can remember that your great Premier held me his prisoner for over a year. I can remember that it was your Bolsheviks that finally did murder my husband and tried to murder my only son. I can remember that it was you, Tatiana, and this creature here, who

271

had me immersed in an ice-cold bath, and then locked me away for six years."

"That is in the past," Tatiana snapped. "I saved your life. That is what matters now. The future."

"The future for me is Andrew Morgan," Priscilla said. "Tell your boss to call for medical aid now, or I will shoot you both."

"You haven't the guts, aristocrat," Tatiana sneered. "Beria!" she shouted.

Beria turned, in order to free her hand, but instead of turning towards Priscilla as she had intended, he threw himself across the room. Tatiana turned herself, striking down with her left hand as she did so, but Priscilla had anticipated that, stepped back, and squeezed the trigger. The noise was very loud in the enclosed space, and a look of incredulous disbelief spread across Tatiana's face as she slumped to her knees. She raised her pistol, and Priscilla shot her again, this time in the very centre of her chest. Blood exploded from the wound as Tatiana reeled back against the wall. She was already dead, but Priscilla shot her a third time, in the head.

Then she turned the pistol on Beria, who was cowering against the wall, hands held up protectively. "No," Halstead snapped. Priscilla glanced at him.

"They want him alive, downstairs," Halstead said. "I think we need to go along with that." Priscilla drew a deep breath, then slowly lowered the pistol. "May I say, your highness, that you are quite a dame," Halstead remarked.

"What about Andrew?"

"Get up," Halstead told Beria. "You heard what the Princess wants. Get help up here."

"You bastard," Sonia told Beria. "You promised my Anna her life." Beria preferred to say nothing; he was still looking somewhat shell-shocked. "I am going to watch you die," Sonia said.

"It is your testimony that will condemn him," Kagan assured her. "But afterward, I think it would be best if you left the country For ever, Madame Bolugayevska."

*   *   *

Jennie knelt beside Tatiana's body.

"I did what was necessary," Priscilla told her. "She was a murderess, a hundred times over."

"Like her father," Jennie said. "But she was my only child."

Priscilla rested her hand on her sister-in-law's shoulder. "Come with me, back to the States," she said.

Jennie lifted her head, her eyes dark with grief and anger. "I never want to see or hear of you again," she said. "Go away. Leave me alone."

"Your plane leaves this evening," Kagan told Priscilla. "We have been in touch with both the British and American embassies. You will travel incognito. You will fly first of all to London, and there a plane will be waiting to take Prince Alexei and yourself on to the United States. I trust this is satisfactory."

"What about the others?" Priscilla asked.

"Well, Madame Sonia Bolugayevska will be free to join you when she has given evidence to the Politburo. Incidentally, I should mention that this evidence will be in camera, and that her existence, and the part she played in Premier Stalin's death, will never be acknowledged."

"I understand. And Jennie?"

"Madame Ligachevna will presumably pick up the threads of her life as best she can."

"In her old apartment?"

"Of course."

"Beneath the Schermetskas?"

Kagan shrugged. "Life sometimes turns out unfortunately."

Priscilla saw Alexei to a seat; his head was bandaged but he was conscious. They squeezed hands, then she oversaw the lifting of Andrew's stretcher on board the aircraft. He was heavily sedated, and obviously in great pain, but he managed a smile. "Only a few hours, now," she said. "And then we'll be home."

"As far as I can gather, he has no next of kin," Halstead said. "But we will do what we can for him."

"It has nothing to do with you, Mr Halstead," Priscilla said.

Halstead raised his eyebrows. "Mr Morgan is not getting off in London," she said. "I am taking him back to New York."

Halstead looked more mystified than ever. "What as?"

It was Priscilla's turn to raise her eyebrows. Then she smiled. "Shall we say, the companion of my declining years, Mr Halstead."

"Won't that be, well . . . frowned upon by polite society."

"I am a Russian princess, Mr Halstead. I make of society whatever I wish. Besides, it is what my grandmother would have done. I have based my entire life on that of Anna Bolugayevska. I am not going to change now."

Andrew had fallen asleep. Priscilla went forward to sit with Alex. "Now," she said. "Tell me about this granddaughter of mine. The last Bolugayevska. The very last."

Lavrenty Beria was shot on 23 December 1953, having been found guilty of treason. By then, Georgi Malenkov had been installed as Premier.

Epilogue

"I imagine you'll find it pretty dull," Lawrence remarked. "Tied to a desk. But we'll get you a gong. For years of devoted service. There will be no need to specify what services."

"I'll look forward to that," Halstead agreed.

"So, sum up," Lawrence suggested.

"Well, I met two of the most remarkable women that can ever have existed."

"I meant, the political scene. With Stalin dead . . ."

"There'll never be another Stalin," Halstead said. "Certainly Malenkov isn't in that mould, and neither is any other present member of the KGB."

"So what does that mean for us?"

Halstead considered. "Do you remember what Winston said after Alamein? This is not the end. It is not even the beginning of the end. But it is the end of the beginning. I believe Soviet Russia is mortally wounded. It may take a generation, or even forty years, to lie down. There is still a KGB, and there are still men like Kagan running it. But we could just live to see the actual end."

"And according to you, we have to thank the Bolugayevskis for opening up this crack of daylight," Lawrence said.

"It was my privilege to watch them do it," Halstead said.